Second Nature

A Novel

Mark Canter

Second Nature

ISBN 978-1481145466

Acknowledgments

This novel owes its existence to prophetic ideas encountered in the non-fiction books of three engineers: *Engines of Creation*, by Eric Drexler; *The Age of Spiritual Machines*, by Ray Kurzweil; and *Robot: Mere Machine to Transcendent Mind*, by Hans Moravec. Drexler, who coined the term "nanotechnology," is president of Foresight Institute, a nonprofit think tank that concerns itself with future technologies. Kurzweil and Moravec both teach robotics, at MIT and Carnegie-Mellon University, respectively.

Nobel laureate Francis Crick's book, *Life Itself: Its Origin and Nature*, explains in detail the theory of Directed Panspermia, which plays a central role in this story. Additionally, ideas found in anthropologist Jeremy Narby's *The Cosmic Serpent: DNA and the Origins of Knowledge* are woven into the tale.

Redstone Military Laboratories, White Sands, New Mexico

The girl's blood cells floated across the video screen like shimmering blobs of gel. No matter how much Richard Osden finessed the microscope's fine tuning, he could not bring the inner architecture of the cells into sharp clarity.

He'd never before had trouble focusing the instrument. He frowned and blinked behind the hard plastic faceplate of his biohazard suit, wishing he could wipe the beads of sweat that itched his balding scalp. After another moment fussing with the controls, he slumped back in his chair feeling suddenly groggy.

Fuzzy halos surrounded the ceiling lights. The gene sequencer, protein assembler, and other equipment at the workstation blurred as if he peered at them through an oil-smeared lens. Hell, it wasn't the microscope's video field that was out of focus, but his own eyesight.

He felt a vicious hangover coming on; odd, because he rarely suffered hangovers. Sometimes too much red wine mule-kicked him in the skull the next morning, but never expensive Scotch, and he'd not had more than a couple glasses last night.

He shook his head inside the helmet, sending sweat droplets trickling down. The faceplate fogged slightly. He'd gained weight over the holidays, and his double-layered biohazard suit—already the bulkiest in the lab to accommodate his bulges—squeezed his chest now like a sausage casing, making it hard to breathe.

He checked the suit's air flow, supplied by a yellow hose dangling from the ceiling. Air pressure kept the suit stiffly inflated so that any accidental puncture would leak air outward, not suck outside air in. The air hose was functioning normally. Full pressure. But he was getting

1

woozier by the minute. Gray spots swam in his vision. He began to pant.

To hell with this, something's wrong with me. He stood and unplugged from the air hose at the workstation and shuffled in his blue spacesuit toward the inner air lock door. Three steps and the pain hit him like a sledgehammer, smashing through his left arm and shooting up his neck into his jaw.

He clicked on his helmet mike with his chin, barely squeezed out the words through gritted teeth: "Security...emergency. Osden...exiting BL-4." He gasped for air. "I'm...having...a heart attack."

"Ah, roger that, Dr. Osden," said a security guard over the helmet com. "I see you at Airlock One. I'll scramble a medical team to meet you in the staging room."

Osden jabbed the switch on the wall beside the airlock door. With a noisy gush of wind, the door unfurled like the iris of a camera. He stumbled inside and slumped against a curved wall. The door's polished steel petals spiraled shut. Osden's knees wobbled during the minute-long wait while vents sucked out the interior air, whistling through sterilizing filters. Then the far door unfurled with a *pop!* of positive pressure and a hiss of clean air.

He stumbled out of Airlock One into the decontamination suite. A wading trough filled with liquid disinfectant ran along the center of the floor leading to the shower room, where dozens of showerheads poked from the walls and ceiling. The edges of Osden's vision darkened and shrank inward, tunnel-like. He groaned and sagged to the floor, scrabbling on hands and knees, splashing through the green disinfectant fluid toward the second airlock.

From the decon suite, Airlock Two opened into the Staging Room. Here, long-sleeved surgical scrubs and hoods, followed by the blue plastic spacesuits, were donned and removed under a bank of sterilizing ultraviolet lamps. Beyond the Staging Room, a third airlock opened directly to the main laboratory.

A bright red trefoil—the international biohazard warning—emblazoned the door of Airlock Two. Before entering this airlock, biohazard protocol required taking a five-minute shower in a high-pressure blast of germ-killing phenolic toxins.

Osden's tunnel vision turned reddish-black, like congealed blood. He crawled past the shower, heading straight for the keypad on Airlock Two.

"Ozzie? What are you doing? You got a red light." The new voice belonged to Col. Jack Eberhard, project director. "You can't skip the shower."

"No...time," Osden wheezed, struggling to his feet. "I need...help...fast."

"I can't let you leave the decon suite until you proceed through the shower."

"Eberhard, you bastard..." he puffed, "the pain...Let me out."

"You cannot enter that airlock, mister. Return to the shower. That's a direct order."

"I'm...not...one of your soldiers...I'm coming through."

Osden reached toward the airlock keypad. His hand shook inside its thick rubber glove as he fumbled to tap keys. Tears of pain mixed with perspiration and ran into his straining mouth. His sweat stank of fear.

"Warning," said a computer's calm feminine voice. "Protocol violation. Decontamination shower required before exiting this area."

Shut up, bitch, Osden thought. *I wrote your program, and I know the override code.*

"Warning," said the computer and repeated its message. In spite of pain bells clanging in his skull, he managed to complete the dozen digits of the override code.

"Warning. Protocol vio—"

The light on the panel changed to green. Airlock Two opened with a hissing blast of wind. He staggered inside. The door closed behind.

The uprushing air sighed loudly and so did Richard Osden. The crushing pain was starting to lift; the three-hundred-pound boa constrictor was uncoiling from his chest. His head felt more clear. The dimmer switch on his vision was returning to full lighting.

Christ on roller-skates, he thought, maybe I'm going to make it. Plenty of others have survived heart attacks. His own father had outlived one by some thirty years.

He turned around in the airlock to face the door he'd just entered. Now that he could breathe again, he really should go back and take the shower. Hell, he'd help write the safety protocol himself.

While Osden hesitated, trying to decide, Eberhard's voice boomed in his helmet.

"Sorry, Ozzie," he said, "you leave me no choice."

At the same instant the meaning of the words dawned in Osden's mind, a massive burst of x-radiation bombarded his body. He wanted to yell, "Wait!" but the word caught fire in his vocal cords as his cells began to cook.

In the flash of his final seconds, he thought of the girl who lived inside the Biohazard Level Four Isolation Unit; the creature Project Second Nature had created. Not created intentionally, no; but she had been born as a result of Osden's tinkering with her mother's genes. He thought of the girl's extraordinary abilities and felt something akin to affection.

Would she remember him, her creator? Was that what it meant to live on in one's children? Was this mysterious

4

sentiment the "love" that others spoke of, the emotion that had eluded him always? So strange to have such thoughts in the last heartbeat of life.

X-rays are invisible, so Osden was surprised to see a mandala of lightning bolts flaring through space, even with his eyes closed. The scientist in Osden raced to get a grip on this final wonder, as his eyes cooked hard like eggs, and the animal in him soundlessly screamed.

1

Gen sat at a kitchen table reading a book of love poems in Bengali. She smiled at the mouth-feel of the words, tender and sweet, like the fruits in the salad she had made for breakfast.

Gen experienced each of the languages she spoke as having its own personality. She visited different languages like other teen-age girls might spend time yakking on the phone or Facebook with different friends. She had favorites: Portuguese, for melody; Bantu, for sheer fun making the tongue clicks; Romanian, for when she pretended she was a gypsy.

Reading the book of poems now, Gen decided that Bengali felt to her like a grandmotherly version of Hindi. She pictured the Hindi language as a white-haired sage, wise but sternly ascetic; Bengali was his kindly old wife, pudgy and overly fond of honey. It would be terrific to chat with a native Bengali speaker, but she had learned the language from tapes and no one else at the lab spoke it. She had to be content reading Ramprasad Sen's verses—which were good, she wasn't complaining. Last night, she had read a bicycle repair manual in Tagalog. It was the best she could do to break the monotony of her days and nights.

Gen looked up from the book at the tall glass walls of her apartment—three layers of thick glass plates. A second vault enclosed the one that confined her, and on the wall of the outer vault a series of airlocks led into the main laboratory room. Beyond the lab building existed "the real world"—which to Gen was a mythical realm she visited only in daydreams.

She surveyed the 20-foot-square glass box: her permanent quarters, her world. Stainless steel furniture—a small kitchen table, a desk, a bookshelf, a bed—occupied a stainless steel floor made of a single, seamless plate. Computers controlled the room's lighting. Video cameras mounted in the ceiling recorded her every move from various angles. A curtain on an overhead track concealed an area containing a stainless steel toilet and a shower stall. After many tearful complaints, Gen had persuaded a committee of scientists to add the curtain as a token to her privacy; the cameras still recorded her actions from above.

She spooned up a plump strawberry and let it roll around in her mouth, feeling the tiny bumps and whiskers with her tongue. She bit into the fruit and closed her eyes at the splash of flavor. She imagined a Bengali-speaking friend—better, Ramprasad himself—sitting at the kitchen table with her. Of course, she had to imagine a chair for the poet to sit on, because the isolation chamber that served as her apartment contained only one chair. Biohazard Level Four did not permit visitors, so there was no point in providing extra furniture. More than anything else in her environment, the single chair had become for Gen a symbol of her loneliness. Sometimes, lying on her bed, she would glance around her bleak room and her eyes would fix on the solo chair; then the ache of solitude wrung her heart until she felt the muscles would fray.

But this morning Ramprasad was telling her about his life as a boy in Bengal in the 1700s. He described in gritty detail the cottage factory where his family made incense. In a wooden press, they squeezed oils from sandalwood blossoms and mixed it with a combustible paste of rice powder, then rolled the paste onto slender stalks of grass. Gen smiled. She could feel the heat and taste the dust, and the smells were overwhelming: sandalwood paste drying, cow dung burning for fuel, and on every sultry breeze, the fragrance of cinnamon trees blooming.

You and I have some things in common, she told Ramprasad. We both love to write poetry, though I could

7

never hope to be as wonderful a poet as you. That made him laugh, and his laugh sounded musical, like his words. See what I mean? she said. You even laugh like a poet.

Ramprasad Sen was unreasonably handsome. He wore a saffron-colored sarong and a simple white muslin shirt. White teeth flashed in his dark face and his black eyes shone like polished obsidian.

Gen wore a shapeless orange nylon jumpsuit. She had dozens more exactly like it, neatly folded and stored on stainless steel shelves; for the laboratory staff did not wash her clothes, they vaporized them in a high-temperature hazardous waste incinerator.

Like you, I have never spoken on a telephone, she told Ramprasad, and then giggled at the confused look on his face. She did her best to explain a telephone and how it worked, converting sound waves into transmittable electromagnetic pulses. She went on to explain radio, television and computers. Not that I've ever used these things, she said, but I've learned about them from books. They let me read books here. And some of the researchers talk science stuff with me.

Know what I would love to have? she said. Tears sprang to her eyes and she blinked them away. It makes me want to cry to think about it, so usually I don't...but I would adore a little pet. A kitten or a puppy. We could play together. She laughed at the feelings the images brought to her. That would be heaven.

She looked around the glass vault. Trouble is, she told him, I think I'd feel guilty. Sorry for the little thing. Because it could never get to go outside. Never see the sun. Roll in the grass. Chase a butterfly.

Her voice caught and she wiped at a tear that started down her cheek. Anyway...what do you think, would it be too selfish for me to have a pet?

Ramprasad had stopped listening to her ramblings. He was gazing intently into her eyes. You are the one with the musical laughter, he told her.

Gen felt herself blushing. His baritone voice was as rich as the fragrance of sandalwood.

Your laughter rings like anklet bells on the feet of a temple dancer, he said. And our Mother Tara, Creatrix of all the worlds, has made your eyes as violet as amethyst gems.

She sighed and turned away from his fiery black stare.

Someone tapped the outer glass wall. It took Gen a couple seconds to realize that this new sound was real. Her imaginary companion vanished and she found herself alone in a cage of glass. Sorrow spread through her chest like a cold and heavy wave.

Outside the vault, a figure in a blue biohazard suit shouted to be heard through his plastic helmet and the heavy glass. "*Ohayo gozaimasu,*" he said. Good morning, in Japanese.

Ah, Toshi. She felt better. Dr. Toshi Yamato was her only friend on the research team at Redstone Military Laboratories. He could have used his helmet mike to broadcast over the room's loudspeakers. But Toshi was polite; he always gave her the opportunity to invite him into her personal space. Privacy virtually did not exist in her life, so the gesture meant a lot to her.

She clipped a dime-sized microphone to the collar of her orange jumpsuit, then crossed to the thick glass wall. "*Ohayo,* Toshi." She bowed deeply. "*Ogenki desu ka?*— How are you?" She mimed for him to turn on his mike.

He clicked on the mike with his chin. "*Hai, genki desu,*" he said. "*Okagesama de*—I'm healthy, thank you." Now his voice came through speakers on her side of the glass apartment. The dome of his helmet gave his voice a hollow ring. She often wondered how her voice sounded to him, if her mike picked up the room's faint echoes.

Toshi grabbed a yellow air hose that dangled from the ceiling of the outer vault and plugged the brass nozzle into a coupling at the base of his helmet. Then he thrust an arm through one of a dozen segmented steel sleeves that lined the glass wall. He extended a heavy rubber glove and shook her small hand. She bowed again. He withdrew his arm from the mechanical sleeve and managed a semblance of a bow in the rigidly inflated Chemturion suit.

"*Onaka ga sukimashita ka?*—Are you hungry?" she asked, and waved a hand toward the bowl of fruit salad on her table. Proper etiquette if she were a Japanese hostess, and a standing joke between them. Six-inch tri-plate glass separated Toshi from the offered meal. If he made an unauthorized entrance into Gen's chamber through the airlock, a billion-roentgen burst of x-rays would shower them both, killing—sterilizing—every cell in their bodies.

He grinned. "Happy birthday!"

Gen gasped and put a hand to her chest. She had forgotten, but Toshi had remembered. "You're so good to me," she said, and bowed again.

"Here, I brought something to show you." He opened a stainless steel specimen container marked with a red trefoil, and took out a photo. He pressed the photo against the thick glass so Gen could study it: a miniature Japanese red-leaf maple, growing in a rectangular Ming porcelain pot. "This tree has belonged to my family for six generations."

"Oh, how lovely!" Her heart strained with longing as she touched fingertips to the cool glass. "Toshi, tell me how it feels against your fingers."

Gen had been isolated since birth at Biohazard Level Four, the ultimate level of biological quarantine. She had never looked upon another person who was not sealed in a biohazard suit; never heard a voice not broadcast from a

10

speaker; never been touched except through thick rubber gloves at the ends of hermetically sealed sleeves. Through such gloves up to a couple dozen scientists would examine her today, as they had examined her yesterday and would do so again tomorrow: measuring the healing rates of her wounds, drawing blood, cutting out small plugs of living tissue for biopsies.

Gen often asked Toshi how things felt when touched.

"The bark feels rough," he said, "like...uh..."

"Canvas?"

"Like canvas. But rougher—little ridges under your fingertips. And the leaves are silky."

She knitted her eyebrows. "I don't know silk."

"Silk feels...smooth. Maybe something like the material you're wearing."

Gen stared at the photo of the tiny tree. Her fingertips lightly stroked the glass over the photo while her other fingers touched the sleeve of her nylon jumpsuit.

"Does it have a fragrance?"

He smiled. "The soil contains volcanic ash from Mt. Aso, so it smells like my boyhood home near Kumamoto Castle. The leaves smell to me like my grandfather—he was a bonsai gardener."

Gen returned his smile, though she suddenly felt like crying. "Could you bring it here, Toshi? The actual tree?" It hurt to hope for things, and she usually managed to hold her desires to a trickle, but this yearning had burst forth before she had time to halt the flood.

"Ha. Get serious, I—"

"Oh, please, Toshi." Her heart beat faster. What would she do if he said no? How could she shove this longing back inside her chest? "I'd love so much to see it."

"Impossible. Never get it past security."

Her big eyes filled with tears, but she continued to smile. "I'll let you share my breakfast with me every morning."

He laughed and returned the photo to the hot-box, screwed the lid down tight, resealed it with yellow-and-black striped bio-static tape. "I'll try. But no promises."

The flesh on her new legs still looked pink, but Gen managed to bow low to the floor, fingertips touching, like a geisha. "*Domo arigato gozaimasu!*" Then she straightened and rewarded him with a little dance of joy.

"Okay, okay," he said. "Remember—no promises."

"Of course," she said, then whispered, "I can't wait to see it!"

The airlock door hissed open behind Toshi. Gen instantly recognized the scientist in the biohazard suit because of his slouching gait: Dr. J. Anandamurti. His Sanskrit surname meant *image of bliss*, which was a joke, because the geneticist was always crabby. She secretly called him Dukhamurti, *image of dissatisfaction*, but she liked him. He'd taught her to speak Hindi and with much cajoling, she could get him to tell her stories from the Ramayana.

Toshi gave a slight bow to his colleague and Anandamurti returned a barely perceptible nod. Gen placed her hands together in the attitude of prayer and bowed. "*Namaste, Maharaji.* Good morning." She addressed him as "Great King" to coax a smile out of him.

His mouth turned down. "Good morning? I had not noticed." He spoke with a strong Indian accent, *D*'s formed with the tongue-tip far back on the palate.

Without another word, Gen rolled up a sleeve of her jumpsuit and hopped into a chair next to a pair of manipulators called "waldoes" that extended from the outer to the inner vault.

Anandamurti stuck his arms through the manipulator sleeves and opened a drawer near her chair to take out a tourniquet, needle, Vacu-tainer, and two blood collection tubes with red and purple stoppers.

While the geneticist drew her blood, she and Toshi chatted in Japanese about the history and culture of bonsai trees. Gen was excited about the possibility of getting to see the actual bonsai red maple. The air lock in the outer vault opened with a *pop!* followed by loud hiss that petered out in a breezy sigh. Negative air pressure in the vault ensured that air always flowed inward, never outward, so airborne particles could not escape through the airlocks. Compressed air tanks pumped fresh air in, sterilizing filter systems sucked stale air out.

Col. Jack Eberhard entered the outer vault's workspace. Toshi stiffened and Gen switched to English in mid-sentence; she and the others were allowed to speak foreign languages only when alone—Eberhard's orders.

All biohazard suits bore a name stenciled in red letters across the chest, but no label was necessary to identify Eberhard. He was much taller than the rest of the research staff. Toshi, who was only an inch taller than Gen, came up to the colonel's collar bones. Biohazard suits are bulky, and most workers shuffled. But even in a stiffly inflated spacesuit, Eberhard strode.

"Why are you here, Yamato?"

"Uh, just leaving, sir."

"Fraternizing is counterproductive to this project," Eberhard said. "I want these little social visits to stop. You're to report here only when you have scheduled work to perform."

"Yes, sir. Understood." Toshi hurried toward the airlock. He refused to meet her eyes as the airlock door closed.

13

Her heart sank. Toshi's visits had been the highlight of each day. Now that the first phase of the project was complete, the biophysicist would have few legitimate reasons to see her. Why did Eberhard do everything in his power to make her life so miserable?

The colonel just stood there, hands grasped behind his back, staring at her. He made her feel like a specimen in an aquarium, his prize goldfish.

Gen's stomach knotted. Eberhard's early-morning arrival meant one thing: another test. He had designed the current series to simulate combat injuries.

Last week ago, the forty-third trial in the series involved a Chinese-built land mine. The explosion disintegrated her left leg and stripped all flesh off the other, leaving the bare, white tibia jutting down from her right knee like a peg-leg. The clean-up crew had found her right foot lying like a tossed-off shoe near sandbags stacked against the far wall. The orphaned foot had gone into the incinerator along with equipment used to mop up the mess.

By controlling the signaling in her nervous system, Gen had shut down most of the pain, but even so, the amount that first blared through to her brain had been bad enough to tear a scream from her lungs. It took nearly a half-hour to fully neutralize the hurt, make it fade to nothing. In a dozen more hours of bed rest, the missing bones, muscles and other tissue had completely regenerated. By the next day, she was getting around with a slight limp.

Eberhard's tests had started four years ago. Minor wounds at first: scaldings, punctures, finger amputations. But over time, Eberhard kept increasing the harm he inflicted, trying to push her limits—or find out if she had any. So far, no amount of damage had overwhelmed her ability to heal. In fact, her body had learned to repair itself more and more rapidly and efficiently, and she intuitively

14

knew her powers had leaped ahead since the landmine blast.

Even so, she dreaded another test. Although Eberhard had often told her that she was the most important experiment in the history of military science, his latest tests seemed bent on getting as close as possible to killing his precious subject.

What was he going to do to her today? She rubbed at the stone in her belly, feeling like she might vomit or get diarrhea; it had happened before when he'd made her wait too long, worrying. She glanced nervously toward the curtained area in the glass apartment that hid the shower, sink and toilet; but she managed to fight down the rising bile.

Come on, come on. She jiggled her knees below the table. The best thing was to get it over with, quickly.

She got up and carried the tubes of blood to a workstation that spanned most of one wall. State-of-the-art medical lab equipment outfitted the tabletops: a DNA micro-array, gene sequencer and synthesizer, cell culture hoods, high-speed centrifuges, laser spectrograph, stereo optical microscopes, scanning x-ray microscope, and side-tunneling electron microscope. Other tools would be at home in an advanced physics lab: low-energy collimated particle beam, precision-guided lasers, and microwaldoes for manipulating molecules. In one corner of her room stood the white hulk of a CAT-scan machine.

Anandamurti seated himself next to a portion of the workstation on the opposite side of the glass wall, next to several sets of sleeves. The geneticist busied himself examining the daily blood specimen under the electron microscope. The magnified images appeared on a high-resolution video screen. The machine gave off heat and a slight whiff of ozone, but of course, only Gen could detect that, on the inside of the glass boundaries.

15

The blood analysis was routine, but Gen knew Anandamurti would concentrate totally this morning and not glance up from his work. He hated to witness the tests. None of the scientists *liked* to watch. Except Eberhard. The colonel clearly got a kick out of it.

He was still gawking at her. A band of overhead lights reflecting in his faceplate hid his eyes. Just as well. Eberhard's expression revealed nothing. Either he was adept at concealing emotion, or he simply held no emotions to conceal.

The only motive she could read in him was curiosity. Eberhard was a scientist, proud that his rational mind— given the scientific method and enough time—could figure out anything...*everything*.

But he couldn't figure out one teen-aged girl. How her special clock ticked. And that frustration festered in his intellect like a boil.

Gen returned to the breakfast table, plopped into the chair and shifted so her back was to him. Fresh fruit was her favorite food, and in her enclosed world of limited variety, she usually took the time to revel in the sensual textures, colors, flavors, and aromas. Now, she only nibbled at a sliced peach, a coin of banana. She took a bite of rye toast, but her mouth was too dry to eat it; she spit the dough into her hand. She could barely swallow a sip of orange juice past the painful lump in her throat.

She glanced up at a video monitor and saw Eberhard's lips moving, making notes using a voice recorder in his helmet. Then he reached through a pair of sleeves into her room and keyed in a code to unlock the weapon cabinet.

His helmet mike switched on with a faint buzz. "You know the routine. Go stand in front of the shield." He sounded bored.

She hung her head, staring at the blob of bread she'd spit out. What would happen if she refused to obey?

16

"Play coy with me, and I'll take away your books again," he said, as if reading her mind. "Or maybe your music, this time."

When he had finally returned her library, she had memorized each book, word for word. But her music collection was still vulnerable to his threats. All right. Starting today she would record every song in her mind, note for note.

Gen stood and slowly turned toward him, swept a long coil of dark hair from her face with her fingers. Eberhard's arms through the mechanical sleeves held a flame-thrower, pointed at her chest. From early on, she had resolved never to reveal her fear, but now in spite of herself, she shuddered and gulped. As an expert on the pain of every type of injury, she knew firsthand that burns were the most agonizing.

He tracked her as she stepped over to a concave steel backdrop. Steel plating protected the floor in front of the blast shield. Gen held her head high and faced her enemy, arms hugging her chest.

"Uh, for this test," Eberhard said, "The cameras need you to be naked."

She clamped her arms tighter.

"It'll burn the clothes off you anyway. Come on. Use your head."

She stared at her feet.

"You know," he said, "I can get those Mandarin language cassettes you asked for. The Stephen Hawking book? I just want a little cooperation."

She frowned and blew out her breath. Then she unzipped her orange jumpsuit, peeled it off her shoulders, tugged off the pant legs.

"And underwear," he said, too casually.

She imagined Eberhard smirking behind his faceplate. Being treated as a lab test animal was a daily routine, but

17

Eberhard could still make her feel humiliated, and that made her angry at herself. *Don't let him get to you!* She stepped out of white cotton panties. A stir of cool air brushed her bare thighs and made her shiver. She wanted to hide, to flee. But in a glass cage, hiding fled from her.

She stared down the gaping muzzle of the flame-thrower, feeling more angry now than afraid. Good. The pain would be horrible, but she doubted it would last longer than the first scream.

"Okay. Here we go," Eberhard said. "Video rolling." He glanced at a heads-up display inside his helmet. "Time is 0915 hours. Subject awake and alert. Test Series: Combat Injuries, Trial forty-four: Burn Wounds. Flame-thrower...ah, Soviet LPO-50, with 3.3 liter canister...ah, delivering a three-second burst of Napalm-B. From three meters." He flipped a switch on the shotgun-shaped weapon. "Battery on. Igniter on. Timer running...*now*..."

Gen shut her eyes.

"...five, four, three, two, one." He squeezed the trigger.

With a roar like a raging dragon, the weapon vomited a river of fire. Jellied gasoline spewed onto her, slamming her backward against the steel barrier. She bounced forward onto her knees, coated in flames from head to toe. In three seconds, the napalm canister was empty and Gen's whole body had turned into a furiously blazing candle. Heat waves rebounded off the glass wall, making it shudder.

She crumpled onto her side enshrouded in billowing orange flames. Skin cracked and blistered off her face. White bone blackened. Greasy smoke poured from her body, and ventilators sucked the thick haze out of the room.

Gen had shrieked at the first blast of searing heat, then instantly her pain receptors had shut down. As she fell onto her side, a healing force was already spreading from within

18

her cells outward, blanketing her sizzling skin and smoldering scalp in a wet, iridescent fog.

The fog was composed of her protectors; each one of them infinitesimally small, but together forming a force so vast and powerful she called it the Abundance.

The Abundance worked speedily and expertly, obeying the same genetic instructions that had guided the original fabrication of her body from a single embryonic cell. Now, her nervous system came selectively back online and her whole body tingled intensely as trillions of microscopic helpers began the regeneration of ruined tissue: atom by molecule by protein by cell.

Charred muscles changed into red, glistening bands of meat. They bulged as Gen rose shakily, like a dissected cadaver coming back to life. She stumbled, fell onto hands and knees, pitched forward onto her face.

Eberhard gasped. "Hell *no!*" Gen heard the panic in his voice and let him go on fearing that he had finally overdone it and killed her.

Heat had warped the shield behind her body. The tang of hot steel and pungent stink of charred flesh hung in the scorched air. On the floor nearby, her nylon jumpsuit and cotton underwear had burned into a shiny smear and a patch of soot.

Gen rested, facedown against the steel floor plating, metal still hot. Her ears roared like seashells from the furious internal labor of healing.

Skin began to form over exposed muscles. It grew back smooth, flawless, unscathed. Again, she tried to stand. This time, she grasped the edge of the shield and pulled herself upright; then rested her weight against the backdrop, forcing air into her lungs in sharp pants.

Dark hair, renewed in the same pattern of tight ringlets, grew from her scalp and flowed down her back like a slow-motion spill of glossy ink, until it hung to her waist.

"Three minutes, eighteen seconds," Eberhard said, his voice unsteady. "That's incredibly faster than you've ever healed before. It's exponential."

Gen turned her back on him and walked barefoot through a puddle of sputtering fire. She didn't even limp; her regeneration was total.

"What's going on?" he said. "What does it mean?"

She sat down naked at the kitchen table and made herself eat casually.

"Tell me what's happening," he said.

Peaches. Bananas.

"There's something you know that you're not telling me."

Apples. Strawberries.

"Dammit, what is it you know that I don't know?"

Gen felt him glaring at her, heard his ragged breath through the speakers. The colonel was afraid. The striding warrior with his terrible arsenal was badly frightened by her! She half-smiled at the irony of it, but then her heart sank further, and she sighed.

Col. Eberhard studied the multitude of unique organisms that lived inside her. He hoped to learn more about them by repeatedly testing their ability to repair whatever damage he could inflict. But Gen kept a secret from Eberhard, from all of them; even her one friend, Toshi.

She knew the Abundance was more than an army of healers. The microscopic organisms possessed some level of mind, of sentience. A whole civilization within her body. Eberhard and the others suspected the organisms were intelligent, but the researchers couldn't begin to guess what Gen had come to understand: her trillions of servants had their own purpose; she was *their* instrument. This knowledge led to her biggest secret—she was scared, too.

Eberhard had told her she was the vector of an unstoppable epidemic; more lethal than a rain of nuclear warheads. What she contained within her could infect every living thing—break down the planet's biosphere.

Tears wet her face.

She had never held an ungloved hand. Or touched a leaf. A flower. A sea shell. She felt a bodily longing to meet—to touch—all the things she cherished from within her lonely chamber. To be a part of the family of the earth.

Engineers had vigilantly designed the entire lab to prevent her breakout; the escape of any particle of her. But how could Eberhard or any of the researchers think she *wanted* to escape? Did they really believe she wished to bring a scourge upon the earth? Couldn't they see how much she loved the world—if only from a glass-walled distance?

She thought of Toshi, and suddenly wondered if he was afraid of her, too. It broke her heart. She'd read of the Marianna Trench, deepest spot on Earth—but surely, that ocean canyon can't be deeper than this loneliness. The biohazard isolation unit quarantined not only her body, but her soul.

She sniffled, brushed a teardrop from her chin.

If only Toshi and the others could help her understand what was going on. How to control the changes she felt building inside her, like a thunderstorm. How to contact and communicate with the Abundance.

For now, the legions served her. Like an enormous flock of tiny guardian angels, they saved her repeatedly.

But what was their ultimate aim? Their mission?

The Abundance did not *feel* deadly. It produced a steady hum of energy in her body, and each day the electric buzz in her cells surged more powerfully. It sounded in her

21

brain like static, like a stream of chatter among countless radio channels. Perhaps someday she and the Abundance would link minds and communicate directly.

Meanwhile, she could only wait. With intense dread and hope, she waited for the moment she and the society of beings inside her might join minds. Then at last she would *know* the Abundance was harmless—or *know* she was a walking plague of death.

Either way, she would no longer feel lonely. For she would no longer be one isolated self. She would be trillions of selves. She would *be* the Abundance.

Dr. Anandamurti looked up from his analysis of her blood. She watched his reflection on the far glass wall, startled black eyes behind the clear plastic faceplate.

"Col. Eberhard," the geneticist said, in a shaky voice. "Sir, ah, you had better come take a look at this."

Her tormentor didn't budge; he continued to glare at her immaculate nude form.

"Hurry, sir," Anandamurti said. "There's been a change. You need to see this."

Gen felt a stab of fear; a ray of hope. The purring in her cells rose in a crescendo until her whole body trembled.

She closed her eyes and listened to rushing rivers of blood.

Within her sang a choir of a trillion angels.

Or demons.

2

Marine sentries escorted President Jane Campion and two aides down the halls of the Pentagon and into an elevator that opened three stories below the ground. Nobody spoke. Jane Campion's stomach sizzled with a presidential ulcer. It had revealed itself the morning she took the oath of office and had made her wince that same night as her husband zipped up her silver-sequined white Versace gown for the Inauguration Ball. She had come to regard the ulcer as a badge of power: first woman to be President of the United States.

A few hours ago, she had taken a phone call in the Oval Office—on the *red* phone, no less—informing her the National Emergency Council had gathered to deal with a crisis that involved "imminent danger to the planet." That's how Gen. Cunningham, Military Chief of Staff, had put it. Now Marines in gleaming black shoes were sweeping her briskly down tiled halls and she knew very little about what the hell was going on, and the dread was burning a hole through her gut.

As the President's entourage swept through double doors, a waiting assembly of men and women in military uniforms and business suits rose to stand at attention. The sentries locked the doors behind her and took their post in the hall.

Jane Campion arrived at her station at the head of a mammoth mahogany table. The smell of wood polish saturated the oak-paneled chamber. With a curt nod, she acknowledged directors and staff from the National Security Agency, Defense Intelligence Agency and senior military advisors from the Department of Defense. The tension in the room felt like a static charge; tiny hairs stood on the back of her neck.

"Ladies and gentlemen," she said, "please be seated." The President took her seat in a high-backed leather chair. "I can tell by your worried looks that we are in deep trouble, so let's dispense with formalities and get straight to the bad news. This morning I was yanked away from a quiet breakfast with my granddaughter, and informed that our armed forces are standing at Defense Condition One. I know next to nothing about what's going on, and I am more than a little angry about that."

She drummed the polished table top with manicured nails and scowled at the faces around the room. It gave her some relief to indulge in wrath; the only other emotion she had available at the moment was fear. "Would anyone care to explain to me why the President of the United States has been left in the dark on this situation?"

After a pause, a tall man in an Army dress uniform cleared his throat. "Madam President, for security—"

"Your name? Your position?" she interrupted.

"Sorry. Colonel Jack Eberhard. United States Army Chemical and Biological Weapons Response Team, Redstone Military Labs, White Sands, New Mexico."

Colonel Bullet-head. His looks alone made her bristle. Or was it his lordly body language? Eberhard was the kind of man people reacted to when they wondered, Wouldn't it be better if women ran the world? Jane glanced about the table, surrounded by two dozen such men. Precisely the types of leaders who had helped her to get elected on the simple platform that she was *not* one of them. The only other woman of power in the room was Air Force Major-General Paige Paine, who had fought her way up the glory-ladder by kicking and slugging as if she had bigger balls than her competitors; and judging by her flat-chested, square-jawed, sharp-boned looks, maybe that really *was* her secret. The half-dozen other women in the room were mere assistants, secretaries, coffee-fetchers.

24

She nodded. "Proceed, Colonel."

"Ma'am, for security reasons, Project Second Nature from its inception has been ultra-secret. A small, select team has conducted the research and the information has been strictly monitored and controlled."

"What you call a need-to-know basis?"

"Exactly, ma'am."

She felt her face grow hot. "And you're saying, Col. Eberhard, that your Commander-in-Chief did not need to know?" Her dark eyes flashed. "According to a quaint old document called the Constitution, I am the *final* authority over all military and intelligence matters in this nation."

They locked eyes. His gaze was hard and cool, gray eyes the tint of granite. His mouth tightened, but he did not look away. The only way to confront men like him was to show equal grit, which is why so many women who rose to power became stone-hearted bitches. She hoped she had not become one.

"The next obvious question is, Why am I being told now?" She made her fingers stop drumming. "I'm almost afraid to find out."

Eberhard shifted in his chair. "Ma'am, we need your presidential authorization for the underground detonation of a thermonuclear device."

Chrissake, things are that bad? She blew out a loud sigh. "All right. We'll deal with this secrecy issue later. And I promise you, it will *not* be forgotten."

A male aide poured for her a cup of coffee. She sipped it black while glancing around the table at the nation's top defense and security advisors. They all looked scared, and she wondered if her fear showed, too.

"For now, priorities," she said. "So far, all I've been told is that a bio-warfare project has gotten out of control and become critically dangerous. But the tension in this room…it feels like we're huddling in a trailer park, waiting for a tornado."

She turned to a man seated on her right, wearing a gray suit, white shirt, and black bow tie. His white, wooly hair and white beard contrasted sharply with his dark brown skin.

"What can you tell me, Doug?"

Dr. Douglas Freeman, the White House Chief Science Advisor, licked dry lips. "I can tell you…" he sighed, "I can tell you that I'm terrified. I believe all life on Earth is threatened."

Behind eyeglasses, his brown eyes met hers with a grim look. Her heart sounded to her like it was pounding from the bottom of a deep well. She wondered if others could hear the booms. She took a breath to calm herself.

"Start at the beginning."

Dr. Freeman shook his head. "I've just been briefed about this mess myself, an hour ago. Let me assure you, if I had known about the project, I would have argued vehemently for shutting it down long before this." He looked accusingly at the Army colonel seated across the table. "Col. Eberhard is the project's director. Let him tell you."

The President's eyes settled on Eberhard again. Back to you, Bullet-head. He rubbed a big hand through salt-and-pepper hair buzzed in a severe crewcut, then folded his hands on the table. "Madam President, how much do you know about nanotechnology?"

She squinted. "I've heard of it. Small things. Little machines. That's about the extent of my knowledge."

"Yes, ma'am," he said. "Nanotechnology means engineering machines on the scale of nanometers."

The President turned back to her science advisor. "Help me out."

"One-billionth of a meter," he said. "Microscopic."

26

She tried to imagine the scale. "Microscopic *machines?*"

Eberhard nodded. "Yes, ma'am. We call them nanobots—robots the size of proteins. Millions of them can fit into a single human cell."

She shook her head. "But…machines that tiny can actually perform work?"

"Nature's been using them for billions of years," Eberhard said.

She turned to Dr. Freeman. "Doug?"

"He's right. The machinery of nature already operates on the microscopic scale. That's where life is busiest," Dr. Freeman said. "Think about the activities within your cells—the oxidation of foods, defense against germs, tissue repair and so forth. Molecular machines do all that work. We call them white blood cells and hormones and such, but one could regard them as tiny…well, as he said: robots. Nanobots. Each cell has factories to build an amazing variety of these machines—one molecule at a time, you see—according to instructions provided by the genes."

She nodded slowly. "Hard to think so small."

Dr. Freeman shook his head. "Think big. Think blue whales and sequoia trees. The construction work goes on at the molecular level, but the final product…" He raised his palms.

"I see your point." She looked back at Eberhard. "Continue, Colonel."

"Ma'am, Project Second Nature was designed to explore a defensive application of nanotechnology."

She didn't like the sound of that. "Explain."

"Well, imagine a battlefield soldier with trillions of nanobots flowing through his bloodstream, each programmed to break down a chemical warfare agent such as sarin. The soldier could wade through a cloud of poison gas and the nanobots would turn the stuff into water inside him before it did any harm," he said. "Or imagine trillions of nanobots, all programmed to repair damaged cells. A severely wounded combatant could heal in a matter of minutes, maybe even seconds, without leaving a scar."

"Hold on," the President said, raising a hand. "I'm not following you. Each of these machines is extremely tiny—microscopic. Right?"

Eberhard nodded.

She took the last sip of coffee and tilted the empty cup toward him. "So it would take an army of—what? Millions of them—just to scrub out the bottom of this cup."

"Certainly," he said. "If not billions."

"Well, hell—wouldn't it take forever to manufacture trillions of nanobots? Trillions for each soldier? How could you manage that?"

Eberhard smiled, though the strain in his gray eyes did not relax. "You program the nanobots to replicate, just as living cells do. Each one makes many copies of itself. Starting with one of each type, you end up with swarms," he said. "In a matter of hours, in fact."

The President almost blurted *Oh shit*. "These things can *replicate*?"

"That is precisely why nanobots are so dangerous," Dr. Freeman said.

"It is controlled, of course," Eberhard said, and frowned at the science advisor. "You simply program exactly how many copies each nanobot can make of itself before its ability to replicate switches off."

Dr. Freeman slapped the table and the President nearly jumped out of her wool skirt.

"There it is!" he said. "The hubris, the arrogance of science." He glared at the colonel and the man returned his stare. "You act like you've got nature under control—like you've never heard of Murphy's Law."

28

The President closed her eyes, then opened them again. She regretted drinking the coffee. Her mouth tasted sour. Beneath the table she put a hand on her belly and wondered if her ulcer had finally perforated her stomach lining. "Project Second Nature, Colonel. You were getting to the bad news."

He nodded. "Until a few years ago, building nanobots seemed to be a good thirty, forty years beyond our know-how, for a number of reasons. How to provide a power supply that small, how to build a motor and propulsion unit that small, how to program the things. Then the late Dr. Richard Osden, of Lawrence Livermore Laboratories, wrote a paper with a brilliant idea. Why reinvent the wheel? Why not use the cellular machinery the body already contains? His idea was to convert mitochondria into nanobots. That led to the creation of Project Second Nature."

"Back up." The President knit her brows. "Mito—?"

"Mitochondria," Dr. Freeman said. "Tiny, sausage-shaped structures inside the cells. The powerplants of the cells. They convert sugar to energy. The point here is, they were once separate organisms," he said, "bacterial parasites. Then, about two billion years ago they got smart and realized it was better to live inside your host than to kill your host and yourself in the process. So they became symbiotic—um, that means they cooperated—with the primitive cells they invaded."

"And those primitive cells evolved into us," Eberhard added.

"That's right," Dr. Freeman said. "Now all plants and animals contain mitochondria. They're like batteries, they generate energy. So the more active the cell, the more mitochondria it keeps inside. Brain and muscle cells, for example, contain tens of thousands."

"I see," the President said.

29

"Thing is, they still have their own, separate DNA," Eberhard said. "The only place in the body you can find DNA outside of cell nuclei is inside the mitochondria. And they replicate, too; not just when the whole cell divides, but on their own—at their own pace. Do you follow me? They were once independent bacteria and they still act somewhat like distinct animals living inside us."

The President nodded. "I get the picture. Tiny powerplants that make copies of themselves. It was a natural design to work from."

"Like a prototype. Exactly," Eberhard said. "And it gets better. Encoded in the genes of mitochondria are instructions to build parts to enable them to swim about—as they once did. Our team mapped the genome and switched on the genes to return them to the body-plan of free swimmers."

President Campion rubbed her gut, feeling queasy. She imagined countless micro-tadpoles paddling through her bloodstream.

"We called them mitobots," he said. "To begin with, we engineered them to invade and break down cells that produce a high level of waste heat. Since cancer cells have higher metabolisms and produce more waste heat than normal cells, the mitobots singled out and destroyed tumors."

"You tested it?"

He nodded. "Rats, rabbits, pigeons. Cats and dogs. A dozen monkeys. Worked perfectly. The mitobots replicated a prescribed, limited number of times. After they finished their job, we flushed them out of the animal's system."

"How?" the President said.

"A simple diuretic. They flush out in the urine."

"And at that point they're inactive?"

Eberhard nodded. "As in dead. They don't live long after they stop dividing."

30

"I see." Sort of.

"Next, we tested the mitobots on a human subject with an advanced, terminal stage of liver cancer."

"Oh, god. You didn't." The President winced.

"A young woman, a dance major from the University of New Mexico," he said. "We explained the risks. She gave us complete authorization. The test went perfectly. Within minutes, her cancer was gone."

"But now tell us about your little problem," Dr. Freeman said.

Here it comes. The President twisted her lower lip and bit it, bracing for the bad news.

Eberhard studied his folded hands. "The woman became pregnant."

The President wondered if she had missed something. The woman's cancer was cured. Now she was pregnant. "That's bad?"

Eberhard looked up. "She was housed at the laboratory in a Biohazard Level Four Isolation Unit. Level *Four*, the strictest level. No one touched her."

The President shrugged. "She was already pregnant when she came to the lab."

He shook his head. "I'm afraid not. She had never had sexual intercourse. Strict Roman Catholic—she was a virgin."

"But...I don't understand."

"We didn't either, at first. Eventually, we realized that one of the mitobots had deposited its DNA into one of her egg cells. Somehow, it had modified its genes to do the job. Incredible, really. As soon as the egg cell had the full complement of genes, it began dividing, turning into a fetus."

It took a few seconds for the President to close her jaw. Surely the others could hear her booming heart now. "One of the mitobots fertilized an egg, made her pregnant?"

31

"Yes, ma'am."

"Come on! That's not possible." She worked to steady her breathing. "Look, I think I've proven here that I'm no biology expert," she said. "But two species—a woman and a...a...*germ*—two species can't mix, can't mate."

"We... um, don't understand it," Eberhard said quietly. "But the fact is, mitochondria lived inside our ancestral cells and co-evolved with us for a couple billion years... and... " He shrugged.

"And an ancient, symbiotic life-form came up with its own little surprise," Dr. Freeman said.

"So you aborted the fetus," the President said. It was not a question.

Eberhard shook his head. "No ma'am. By the time we realized she was pregnant, she had reached full term and gone into labor."

"For chrissake, your medical staff couldn't spot a pregnancy for nine months?"

Granite-gray eyes fixed on hers. "The entire pregnancy lasted less than two hours."

She gasped. "Oh my god." Others around the table broke into loud murmurs. Her hand rubbing her belly began to tremble. "How could that not kill her?"

He held up his palms. "Apparently, the fetus sent out streams of nanobots that rebuilt her body. She gave birth without pain."

The President swallowed hard. She felt a drop of sweat run down between her breasts. She could smell cologne, perfume, and deodorant, which meant everyone else was sweating, too, despite the room's chilly air-conditioning.

"The baby..." She took a breath to calm the quaver in her voice. "What was it...a freak? A monster?"

He shook his head. "The baby looked perfectly normal. A girl. Almost a clone of its mother, who was...well, she was quite beautiful."

"*Was* beautiful? What happened? Where is the mother now?"

Eberhard's eyes shifted back to his folded hands. "The pregnancy did not harm her physically. But emotionally, the experience...well...she had a psychotic break. Believed the baby was the devil, tried to kill it. We took the infant from her. She, um...managed to kill herself."

This time, a groan came from the U.S. Attorney General at the end of the left-hand row. The President figured he was imagining nightmarish lawsuits if this news left the room. She wondered about the girl's family, her loved ones—what lies had they been told? A sudden sadness mixed with her horror.

"And the baby?" the President prompted.

"Actually, it stayed an infant for less than a week," Eberhard said. "Then—as if it had suddenly made up its mind—it grew up in a few hours to have the size and features of a young girl. Say, nine, ten years old."

The President grasped the edge of the desk and held on for stability. Too much, too much.

"Over the past five years she has appeared to age normally," he said. "She's grown from a ten-year-old to a fifteen-year-old."

"Five years."

"Yes, ma'am."

President Campion had been in office less than a year. "Did my predecessor know about this project?"

"No ma'am, he did not."

Two presidents kept in the dark. Bastards!

"Colonel, you felt safe enough to study this girl for five years. You and your secret club. Why is she a threat now?"

"We surrounded her isolation chamber with banks of high-intensity x-ray generators," he said. "Mitobots are living cells—vulnerable to high radiation. If she tried to escape, or if a breach in the chamber triggered the

33

electronic alarms, a massive burst of x-radiation would kill her, sterilize everything in her body."

"*But*," she said. "Something changed."

He nodded. "She's starting to experiment, try things. She's discovering her abilities. We've studied her intensively and learned a lot, but frankly, we don't know what those abilities might be. Since her birth, she's been producing new series of mitobots in her bloodstream. It's anybody's guess what they're built to do."

Dr. Freeman moaned and slumped his head into his hands, which did nothing to boost the President's good cheer.

She frowned. "Again, I'm no biology whiz, but...where are the genetic instructions coming from? You know, to build these new forms? I thought it takes genes to tell the cell factories how to build stuff. Isn't that what you said earlier, Doug?"

Dr. Freeman lifted his head and managed a wan smile. "Yes, Madam President, you're a quick student, and that is just what I said. But we're dealing with something unfamiliar, here. Ask the colonel how his girl keeps producing new types of mitobots in her system."

She looked at Eberhard and raised her eyebrows.

"Frankly, ma'am..."

"You don't know," she finished his sentence.

"Apparently there are deeper genetic codes, hidden somehow, encrypted *within* the genome of the mitochondria—codes we never mapped."

"Apparently, nature is a bit more profound than you assumed, Colonel," Dr. Freeman said. Eberhard shot him a killing look, but let the comment slide.

"Go on with your report, Colonel," the President said. O Eleanor Roosevelt—or whoever is the Protectress of First Female Presidents—please help me out, here. Tell me what to do.

"A week ago, two major changes occurred," he said. "I'll begin with the second change: the girl, uh...*morphed* again—for lack of a better word." He raked a hand through his crewcut. "She quit being a teen-ager and developed to the height and appearance of a young woman; she now looks to be in her early twenties. And her ability to morph has made a leap, an acceleration: The entire transformation took less than ten minutes."

He pressed a button on a remote control console in the table top. High-definition television screens tilted upward and switched on in front of each seat. The screens glowed blue against dark mahogany. "Ladies and gentlemen, you're about to see the relevant segment from last week's video record. The event occurred late at night, when the lab was empty. The footage has been edited from several cameras."

Each set of eyes stared at the screen before it. Eberhard pressed PLAY.

Abruptly, the teen-aged girl appeared.

The President found herself transfixed, gawking at the slender figure. Images moved on the screen without sound.

The girl stood inside what looked to be a glass-and-steel vault that nested like a Chinese box inside a larger vault. The room held simple steel furniture: a bed, a desk and chair, a kitchen table, bookshelves, a three-quarter-sized refrigerator, and some equipment and features the President didn't recognize. A knobby mound of fruits and vegetables covered the small kitchen table, as if the girl had dumped all the produce from the refrigerator into a pile.

The focus remained tight on the girl. The President gazed at her smooth, dark skin and tried to name its color: caramel, raw honey, café au lait? Long black locks fell in tight, rippling waves to the girl's hips. Exotic, the President thought. Exquisite. The girl reminded her of three stunning daughters in a family of Ethiopian Jews she had met while living in Israel as the U.S. ambassador. That post had been

35

years ago, but the gorgeous sisters remained one of her strongest impressions from the Middle East.

The girl appearing in the television screen outclassed those girls in natural beauty. When the subject gazed up at the video camera, the viewers around the table took a collective breath.

Those eyes!

The President's father had been an ophthalmologist and had joked that he entered the specialty because of a boyhood crush on Elizabeth Taylor—he loved her eyes. He had said the purple hue of Liz's irises was so rare as to be unheard of: the shade belonged to Liz alone; trademark of her beauty. For her father's sixtieth birthday, Jane had given him a gold ring, set with a round-cut amethyst, so he could wear the color of his boyhood fantasies. He adored the ring; she buried him with it.

The clear violet eyes gazing from the television screen matched the tint of that gemstone.

The girl tugged off her clothes: an orange nylon jumpsuit and white cotton underwear. She stood relaxed, feet apart, arms held out from her sides, eyes closed. She placed one hand on the kitchen table. The contours of her body began to blur softly.

The President bent toward the television screen, squinting. An abrupt edit to a close-up view revealed a thin layer of mist flowing over the girl's skin and hair. The mist caused the blurring, fuzzy outline.

Then a wide camera angle showed the whole body again and the President noticed the same foggy coating smudging the table's sharp edges and flowing over the mound of food. The fog thickened and turned iridescent, a shimmering play of colored light. Rainbows wrapped the girl's flesh and the table in a translucent, glittering veil. The President realized she was watching a labor force of trillions of nanobots.

36

Beneath the fog, the girl's body softened like warm wax and began to change and grow. The cloud of microscopic workers scavenged organic materials from the fruits and vegetables to build the girl's new tissue. As she grew, the mound of food shrank to nothing; then even the stainless steel table withered to a skeleton of itself.

The girl's legs and torso lengthened, chest and hips filled out with feminine curves, face molded into a new, more womanly harmony of beautiful features.

President Campion thought of a line from a James Wright poem, "If I could step outside my body, I would burst into bloom." Before her eyes, the teen-ager was flowering, sculpted from within and without into a young woman.

The cocoon of fog began to dissipate, reabsorbed through the skin. The nude figure was no longer undeveloped and girlish but lusciously sexually mature. Some viewers at the table shuffled uncomfortably and a few men stole sideways glances at each other.

The video camera had recorded the images in real-time, not time-elapsed sequences. The President checked the moving numbers on a digital clock at the bottom right corner of the screen. Less than ten minutes had passed, but equal to five or more years of normal growth.

The young woman opened her eyes.

The television viewers reacted again with an in-drawn breath.

Her eyes had darkened from pale violet to deep violet; no longer amethysts, but sapphires.

The transformation was complete. The changes had made her, if possible, even more lovely.

The screens went blank. A long silence overtook the room.

"Wow. And I thought my teen-ager grew fast," someone quipped at last, to a trickle of nervous laughter.

"Did you see that table dissolving?" someone else muttered. "Jesus."

It took President Campion another moment to find her voice. "Col. Eberhard, you said two big changes occurred in the past week. We saw the girl change into a woman. What else happened?"

He nodded. "The other change is the critical one. It occurred first. A routine daily blood sample found that the girl has built a new series of mitobots, and, uh…these latest ones…might be actual machines."

A low buzz of murmurs swept back and forth across the table.

The President wondered about surgery for her ulcer. "What do you mean—actual machines?"

"The mitobots began as re-engineered living organisms, like bacteria, built from proteins, and dependent on water and sugar and oxygen—like the rest of the body's living cells," he said. "But this new series is made out of diamond fibers."

She shook her head. "How is that possible?"

"Diamonds are a crystalline arrangement of carbon," Eberhard said. "Our bodies are full of carbon. The mitobots must have assembled the diamond threads, atom by atom." He coughed into his fist. "The point is, these new ones, they really are like tiny machines, at least in their material construction. We're not even sure if they are alive in the normal sense. We don't know what's powering them. It's doubtful x-rays would have any effect on them."

Paige Paine, the Air Force Major-General, spoke up in a Texas twang. "Colonel, you're saying she can't be hurt? Can't be stopped?"

"Ma'am, I'm saying that we don't have that information."

"Does she have the capability—you mentioned it before—to heal combat wounds, all that?"

38

"Yes, ma'am."

The Director of the Defense Intelligence Agency leaned forward and bellowed into his microphone, "Why in hell would you teach her something like that?" His jowls shook and the mike squealed with feedback.

"Well, um, actually, sir, it's already encoded in her genes," Eberhard said. "She didn't need to learn how, no more than you need to know how to form a scab over a cut. We performed a series of tests on her ability to repair major tissue damage. She can do it. With ease."

"You *wounded* her?" the President said. "You injured that little girl just to find out if she can heal herself?" It was getting ever easier to hate this man.

"Ma'am, you should not think of her as a girl," Eberhard said. "She only *looks* human."

"Then what is she, Colonel?" a Marine Brigadier-General said. "You make her sound like a creature from another world."

"Well, sir, she *is* a new kind of life-form," he said. "Dr. Freeman has explained that mitochondria have lived inside us for eons, beginning as parasitic invaders of our ancestral cells, then evolving to cooperate with their hosts." He dragged a hand through his crewcut. "But..."

"What?" the President said.

"But...it seems now, the mitochondria may have had their own agenda all along."

"Christ in a cowboy hat!" Major-General Paine said in her Texas drawl, "you got me pissin' in my dress blues. What are you saying? These little buggers are intelligent? An army of smart lil' ants?"

"General, we don't understand it, but...yes, apparently they do possess intelligence...though, uh, I wouldn't say like ants."

"What *would* you say?"

39

"I don't know…" Eberhard shook his head. "More like us."

General Paine made a spitting sound. "Hogwash. How can some teensy, itty-bitty cells be as smart as us? I mean, what the hell size brain could something that small possess?"

"I know it sounds far-fetched, General, but a member of my staff suggested that the cells are acting as biological computers, using sections of their own genes as switches to record and process information. MIT has done some basic research along those lines using *E. coli* bacteria. The germs managed to compute elementary math. Primitive stuff—one plus one—but it worked; the principle is sound."

"My bet is that it goes well beyond using genes as switches," Dr. Freeman said. Every head swiveled to face him. "I don't claim to understand the physics behind it, but I've read about the possibility of processing information at the sub-atomic level, using fluctuations of energy states as computer switches. The nanobots may be operating as quantum computers," he said. "If so…" He shook his head.

"Go on," said the President. Complete this nightmare.

"Well. Figure, we've got nearly seven billion people on the planet. The girl has *trillions* of beings inside her of extremely high intelligence. That means she has—or the mitobots have… not sure where one stops and the other begins—they have far more brain power than everyone on Earth put together."

"Damnation!" Major-General Paine growled. "That…that so-called *girl*…should be treated like an alien invader!" Her lips tightened to a thin pale strip. "Or, to use a quaint lil' term from the neck-o'-the-woods where I was brought up, she's kinda *devil*."

Dr. Freeman held his head again, mumbling something into his hands.

40

"What if this... *organism* gets a hankering to break out of the lab—go to the mall, grab a cheeseburger?" the Major-General said. "What *could* stop her? Not sarin—you've already told us that. Not acid. And if you blew her legs off, she'd simply grow new ones."

"Actually, it would be most imprudent to wound her." Dr. Freeman's hands over his face muffled his voice. He lifted his head, cleared his throat. "That would hasten the spread of the nanobots. They'd float on the breeze like deadly pollen—making copies of themselves."

He locked eyes with the president, gripped her arm. "Madam President, this young woman—what's inside her—makes Typhoid Mary seem like a housewife with a mild cold." He squeezed her arm painfully. "Imagine a fucking *intelligent* plague!"

The President blanched. Douglas Freeman, M.D., Ph.D., the White House's Chief Science Advisor, smartest man she'd ever known, had just used the f-word. In thirty years of friendship, she had never heard him curse. Not even when his wife had been killed by a drunk driver. Of everything she'd heard this morning, that scared her most.

"Nanobots could make or disassemble *anything*," Freeman said. "Build artifacts bigger than Manhattan. Or break down the whole biosphere—turn trees and birds and people into organic sludge."

Her heartbeat accelerated from trotting to galloping. Faces around the table wore expressions of horror, and the President tried her best not to look as panicked as she felt. Just breathe. Breathe.

"There's more to it," he said. "The properties of any object are a function of the pattern of that object's atoms and molecules. If she could learn to control the elemental patterns, she could control *every* attribute of matter. It blurs the line between science and magic; it's hard to imagine anything she could *not* do."

41

She gulped. "Good God!"

He nodded gravely. "Yes. I think we *are* talking about a new species of god."

Everyone began talking, shouting, at once.

"Ladies and Gentlemen. Order!" the President said. "Order."

The room grew quiet. "Thank you." She took a deep breath. "All right. The purpose of this emergency session is to decide how to deal with this problem. So let's decide. Quickly. I'm open to suggestions."

People began shouting again. "Order!" the President said, and for lack of a gavel, she slammed down her coffee cup on the tabletop so hard it shattered. That shut them up. "We're going to maintain order now, understand? One at a time."

Colonel Eberhard jumped in: "Clearly, the need has arisen to terminate the experiment," he said. "A thermonuclear explosion will vaporize the subject. Diamonds and all. That's a fact I do know."

"You are some piece of work, Colonel," the President said. "You want me to—what?—authorize you to take this young woman out to the middle of the desert and *nuke* her?"

He held her in a rock-hard gaze. "There is no other choice."

She wondered if the colonel was trembling with anger or fear. She looked hard at Dr. Freeman. His judgment she trusted completely. "Doug. What do you say?"

He took off his eyeglasses and rubbed a hand over his face. "I'm afraid I can see no alternative, Jane." He called her by name and spoke softly, as if they were the only two people in the room. "Microscopic, self-replicating, intelligent machines. As a formula for doomsday, I'd say that's close to perfection. If we don't annihilate this threat, it could bring the end of civilization, of life itself." He

42

placed his palms flat on the polished tabletop and took a deep breath. "Therefore, I believe it is your terrible responsibility to authorize the bomb."

The President nodded slowly. She thought of her own twin daughters, both of them married now, with kids of their own. She loved kids. She was the woman president, the one who was supposed to protect life, because she was a giver of life.

"Ladies and gentlemen," she said, "I want each of you to make a brief comment—I emphasize *brief*—followed by your recommendation; starting with General Cunningham on my left, going clockwise around the table. Please begin."

She folded her hands as if in prayer, tapped them on her chin while she listened. She remembered giving birth to her twins, Casey and Suzette. Nursing them. Such pretty babies. Such splendid women. She thought of her eight-year-old granddaughter, Brooke, who wanted to be an astronaut when she grew up.

The commentary took a half-hour. As she had expected, the assembly showed unanimous support for nuclear extermination. Some of the military staff seemed anxious to nuke the woman themselves.

The President stared at her reflection in the dark gleaming surface of the table. Jane Campion: Commander-in-Chief. Why couldn't I have gotten hit with something easy, she thought, like the Cuban Missile Crisis?

"All right. I'll authorize the nuclear explosion," she said quietly. "I just hope our ambassadors can put the proper spin on this. This stands the nuclear test ban treaty on its ear. We'll never hear the end of it from the world press."

Even beneath his uniform, she could see tension melt from Colonel Eberhard's shoulders. "Tell them the truth," he said, suddenly animated. "Part of it, anyway. Tell them

43

we're eliminating biological warfare material that has become too hazardous to store. Explain that the only way to safely destroy it is with a nuclear blast."

"Col. Eberhard, I want you to know, I'm ordering a congressional investigation into this project," the President said.

The Attorney General spoke up. "Madam President, I don't believe that's a good idea," he said. "So far, Col. Eberhard and his team have managed to keep this whole thing ultra-secret. Hell, even most of us here didn't know about it until this meeting. And I think it must remain that way. The press would have a feeding frenzy over this. It would certainly become an international crisis, a worse predicament than it already is."

The President bristled, but realized he was right. "Okay. You've got a point. We'll keep the lid screwed tight. But I want Project Second Nature shut down—hear me, Colonel? Shut it down. I'm going to assign an independent group of overseers to make sure of that."

"Yes, ma'am," Eberhard said. "We are planning to close up shop as soon as the subject is terminated."

The President thought of her granddaughter, Ella, just turned nineteen. Ella had announced at breakfast three hours ago—a week ago?—that she had been invited to become a member of the New York Ballet Theater.

The beautiful creature in the lab, who was *she*? Even if she was not a human girl, she was innocent. And her mother, the dancer who had killed herself—what had been her crime? She had merely been brave or desperate enough to undergo an experimental treatment for cancer.

"Does your *subject* have a name?" the President said.

He looked confused.

"The young woman, dammit. Does the woman have a name?"

"Gen," Eberhard said. "Short for Genesis. The lab techs named her."

"And what was her mother's name?"

"Arista Monteverde."

President Campion had promised herself, when she chose public office, that she would never allow herself to cry in public. Politicians who shed tears are rejected as weak. Tears had helped to sink Geraldine Ferraro.

Jane Campion had promised, but a tear sneaked down her cheek before she could blink it back.

"Well, tonight," she whispered hoarsely, "I am going to say a prayer for Gen and Arista. And believe me, I'm going to ask God's forgiveness for my role in this tragedy."

3

Gen jolted awake to a noise like a dragon's angry hiss. She knew the sound: The first airlock door had opened in the outer vault. She sat up in bed.

Ceiling lights in her isolation chamber glowed dimly like distant moons. Wall-mounted video cameras monitored the room in infrared mode. A digital wall clock read 23:50 hours; military time for ten minutes to midnight.

An electronic keypad chimed in the access panel of the isolation vault's air lock. An indicator light on the inside door turned from red to green. Someone was coming through the off-limits air lock directly into her quarters!

Gen swallowed hard. Only Eberhard had authority to enter the innermost isolation unit itself. But why did he arrive now, without switching on lights? Had he scheduled a test for the middle of the night?

She hopped into fresh clothes from a shelf stacked with identical orange nylon jumpsuits. As she zipped up the suit's front, the airlock door seal popped open with a loud *hissshhhh*!

A figure too small to be Eberhard stepped through into her quarters, silhouetted by the green glow of the airlock console light. Gen gasped and covered her mouth. The man was not wearing a biohazard suit.

"Gen!" he whispered.

"Toshi?" Her heart made a squirrelly leap inside her ribcage. *Toshi was inside her room*—dressed only in black denim jeans and a black T-shirt. "Toshi, are you *crazy*? Where's your suit?"

He crossed to her, eyes shining wildly in the dim light.

"Where's your suit?" she demanded.

"Shhhh." He glanced up at a security camera. "I'm going to take you out of here."

"*What?*"

"You heard me. You've got to leave this place. I'm here to help you escape."

His words hit her like an earthquake, with her heart as epicenter. The air itself seemed to echo with the shock of what he'd said.

"Escape?" She whispered the next word as if it were a holy name, forbidden to be spoken, "*Outside?*"

"Yes. Come on." He eyed the security cameras again. "I drugged everybody and his brother, we don't have much time."

"But…" Gen's heart pounded. "I can't. You know that. I could destroy the world. A plague. That's what everyone says."

"I don't believe that." He reached out quickly and grabbed her hand in both of his.

She yanked away in horror and stepped back. "No! My God! What are you doing?" The warmth of his hands had shocked like electricity. Skin to skin! She clenched her fingers where their hands had met. She had always longed to be touched, yet it had been the most frightening thing that ever happened to her.

"What were you thinking?" she said. "I can kill you with one touch."

He nodded. "Maybe. But I don't believe so." He inhaled deeply. "If your mitobots are floating loose in the air I'm already infected anyway."

Tears ran down her cheeks. "Why are you doing this to me? I thought you were my friend."

His eyes shone. "I am. More than you know. Look, I don't have time to explain. It's a scientific hunch. I don't think the mitobots inside you are set to destroy life. That's the real reason I smuggled the bonsai tree in here. It was an experiment."

47

Gen thought of the red-leaf maple. Toshi had hidden the tiny tree in a sealed food bin and passed it through the airlock. She had handled the tree secretly, while unpacking groceries from the bin. Such a beautiful living creature! Touching it had been the greatest sensual delight. But it had sickened her to think that Toshi would have to incinerate the tree later for safety's sake. She had not meant for Toshi to let her *touch* the bonsai, only to see it through the glass; she'd actually been upset with him over the best experience of her life.

"I didn't burn the tree," he said. "Instead, I examined it closely. Not a trace of mitobots remained in the tissues, but they had definitely spread there earlier."

"Oh, God."

He shook his head. "No, no, they didn't harm it. Quite the opposite. When I smuggled in the tree, I had just pruned a branch—remember that dime-sized wound on the trunk? Blight had infected the branch and I was actually quite worried about the tree's health. Then you returned it and I almost didn't believe my eyes—the branch had regenerated! It was whole and perfect."

"Really?"

He nodded. "I believe the mitobots inside you only *protect* living tissue. They're not killers, they're healers."

Her heart pounded with a thrill of hope. "But…they say I'm deadly, a plague. Col. Eberhard—"

"He's terrified of anything so far beyond his understanding or control. And he's trying to keep you from wanting to escape. See? He knows you'll willingly remain his prisoner, rather than endanger the world."

Toshi's words filled Gen's head like pure oxygen; dizzying and enlivening. "If that's true…oh, Toshi!" Just the possibility that she was not a threat to the world made tears of joy leap from her eyes. "That would be so wonderful!"

48

"I need to make one more test," he said. "Do you trust me?"

She stared at her one true friend. His face looked older than she had pictured, but more handsome. Streaks of white marked his dark hair like chalk lines on a blackboard. To her surprise, he wore his hair long; it hung past his shoulders in a thick ponytail. Now his gaze held hers with a warmth that penetrated to her soul, and laugh-lines rippled at the corners of his eyes, as if someone had dropped pebbles into two deep pools.

"Toshi, you're the only person I do trust."

He took a scalpel out of his tunic pocket. "You know the old cowboy movies? Where someone cuts into a snake bite and sucks out the venom?"

She drew back. "What are you going to do?"

"I need to get a sample of your blood into my body, quickly. Cowboy or vampire, whatever—I need to drink a bit of your blood."

She grimaced and took another step backward. "No!"

"I've got to see what your mitobots do to me. Inside me."

She shook her head. "I can't let you be a guinea pig. What if—"

"Gen, listen to me. The colonel is planning to kill you."

Her jaw dropped open.

"Tomorrow," he said. "Just a few hours from now."

She tried, but couldn't catch her breath.

"His team is planning to freeze you with liquid nitrogen, then truck you to a remote desert site and detonate an H-bomb, blow you to smithereens."

Her emotions derailed like a runaway train. She staggered backward and plopped into a chair. Her stomach knotted until it seemed the size of a fist. "W-why?"

Toshi knelt on the steel floor in front of her. "I've told you, Eberhard is terrified. The diamond structure of your latest mitobots—they're practically invulnerable. With that kind of power, Eberhard can't let you live. The important thing is, we've got to get you out of here tonight."

He reached for her arm. "Let me do this test. I've got to be sure Eberhard is as paranoid as I think he is."

She twisted away. "If I am a threat to the world…" The thought made her hate herself violently. "I *should* be destroyed." A storm rumbled deep in her chest and sobs poured out like a cloudburst. She hung her head and tears rained down in her lap.

"What if you're not a threat?" Toshi said. "Gen. Look up. Gen…" Toshi was crying softly now. "I won't let them kill you."

The full implication of her friend's sacrifice hit her. Toshi was betting his life on his belief in her; willing to risk death to prove it was safe to set her free.

"Toshi, no. What if—?"

"Then I'll be dead, and you won't get anywhere without the air lock code I hacked from the Colonel's computer." He held her gaze. "And you'll know, Gen. You'll finally *know*."

Gen sniffed and wiped at her tears. Then she slowly extended her left arm. "You are a dear, brave man."

He gripped her arm firmly and sliced a deep gash across the wrist. The radial artery squirted a fountain of blood and he bent and clamped his mouth over it and sucked the stream down his throat, swallowing deeply. Within seconds, her wound closed and healed over, without a scar.

"It's done." He stood, wiping scarlet gore from his lips and chin. "The mitobots from your bloodstream are definitely inside me now. We'll wait a few minutes. If I

50

start to melt into a blob, we'll know I'm wrong, and Eberhard is just an asshole, not a paranoid asshole."

She didn't laugh at his gallows humor. "Toshi. No. Please don't say that." She jumped up and threw her arms around him. His body was warm, soft on the surface and harder just underneath; pliant, living. Real. Not a photograph. She burst into fresh sobs. It was the first time in her life she'd ever felt the exquisite joy of a human embrace. It felt unbelievably nice. Better than she had imagined—and she'd imagined it uncountable times.

The two clung to each other for a timeless moment. Toshi's heat enveloped Gen like rays from the sun she had never known. The fragrance of his skin and hair reached down into the valley of her heart, where a deep river of affection flowed.

Finally, Toshi pulled away. Tears streaked his face. "See? I'm still here." He checked his watch. "Six minutes. By now your mitobots, if they were going to, would have chewed holes through me like Swiss cheese."

"How can you be sure they still won't?"

He shrugged. "I doubt they'll even stay in my system. They invaded the bonsai tree, right? But they didn't stay. You're their home, Gen, their mother ship. They thrive only inside you, where they belong."

She sighed. "I just pray you're right."

He grinned. "Trust me, I'm Japanese—we make very smart scientists."

She started to protest, but he turned toward the airlock. "Put on your shoes," he said over his shoulder. "Our getaway dirt bike is waiting."

"A motorcycle?" She hurriedly tugged canvas sneakers onto bare feet.

"I cut a slot in the fence," he said. "We're heading through the desert."

"You know how to drive a motorcycle?"

He turned back and winked. "You're looking at the 1980 High-School All-Japan Motocross Champion."

Her eyes flashed like violet flares. "Dr. Yamato, I never realized you were so much fun."

4

Col. Jack Eberhard could never sleep before an important military operation. He sat alone in the living room of his officer's quarters, a one-bedroom adobe bungalow inside the secured perimeter of the Redstone Military Laboratories compound, one of a cluster of top-secret installations within the White Sands Missile Range. His digital watch read 03:19. In another hour, technicians in blue spacesuits would swarm through the isolation lab preparing the subject for transportation to the detonation site.

First, the subject would be hard-frozen in a Lucite-walled tank of liquid nitrogen, sealed inside a stainless steel container, then loaded into a specially-fitted Heavy Humvee. By dawn, the Humvee would be rumbling down a utility road deep inside the White Sands Test Range. The restricted zone covered more than 3,000 square miles of white gypsum sands, black lava flows, sunburnt grasslands, rugged hills and sandstone canyons—an area bigger than Rhode Island and Delaware combined. Across this habitat of jackrabbits and mule deer, sidewinders and Gila monsters, the Humvee would transport its frozen cargo to ground zero.

As team leader, Eberhard would be riding shotgun, circling high above the desert in an E-3 Sentry Airborne Warning and Control Systems jet aircraft. In case of a major screw-up, he would remote-detonate a W80 nuclear warhead mounted inside the Humvee.

If the nuke failed to explode, a B-2 Stealth bomber, patrolling from an even higher orbit, would launch a W80-tipped cruise missile from its weapons bay.

And as final failsafe, a trailer-launched Pershing II guided missile with a 400-kiloton kick would be stationed near the foot of Salinas Peak, keeping a wary radar-eye locked on the slow-moving Humvee.

At 06:00, the cargo would arrive at Omega Test Site, a place marked by sand heat-fused into jagged lakes of glass. The Humvee would descend by elevator to a concrete vault at the base of a six-story deep, steel-reinforced shaft. Helicopters would then evacuate all on-site crew. Checklists would proceed to countdown.

At 07:00, a hydrogen bomb would detonate with the violence of 50 million tons of TNT, and Eberhard's worries would vaporize. When the rumbling earth settled, all that would remain of Gen would be a chunk of radioactive glass buried deep below the dunes.

Eberhard sipped Seagram's Scotch on the rocks from a ceramic beer stein printed with the words, "Class of '68," above the logo of the U.S. Military Academy at West Point. Two Mission-style oak chairs with matching lamp tables were the living room's only furniture. A fire of cedar logs in the hearth washed the room in an undulating, ruddy glow.

Eberhard enjoyed gazing at fires; it reminded him of his teen-age years as an Eagle Scout, and he found it a meditative way to relax. Nights in the desert were cool enough that he could indulge in a small blaze in the fireplace even now, at the start of summer. A work crew delivered wood to the backyard of his bungalow weekly, but Eberhard chopped and split the logs himself. The Redstone complex did not have a gym, and swinging an axe and sledge kept him in shape.

A burning log shifted and dropped in a cascade of golden sparks. Eberhard swallowed ice-cold Scotch and smiled. He liked this house, built in traditional hacienda style, with open ceiling beams of cedar logs that projected through the outside walls. In the 1940s, a number of famous figures from the Manhattan Project at nearby Los

Alamos had used these quarters as a place to relax. Rumor had it that Oppenheimer, Fermi and the gang had partied in this very room. *EINSTEIN SCHLAFTE HIER*—German for "Einstein slept here," was carved in neat block letters into the bed's headboard, but that had been somebody's gag; maybe Richard Feynman, the practical jokester among the physicists who built the atomic bomb.

On the room's left wall hung a display case with a Jicarilla Apache eagle feather headdress; the right wall held a framed collection of several dozen arrowheads and spear points. A 95-year-old Navaho rug, woven in the black-and-gray "eyedazzler" pattern, covered the red oak flooring in front of the fieldstone fireplace. Over the mantle hung a large framed display of military medals, stark against a backdrop of black velvet.

The collection spanned four generations of Eberhard males, starting with Civil War medals from his great-grandfather, who had served as a captain in the Confederate Army cavalry; his grandfather, a West Point graduate and Army infantry colonel in World War One; his uncle, an Annapolis graduate and Marine major in World War Two and Korea; and his father, another West Pointer and Army Airborne colonel in Korea.

At the apex of the display, a Medal of Honor spread its spangled blue silk ribbons like wings of victory. Congress had awarded the medal to his father, Robert E. Lee Eberhard, for combat heroism at Cho Sen Reservoir, Korea, 1957. Ike had pinned the medal on his father at the White House, but his father insisted the medal had been awarded posthumously. That's because, condemned to a wheelchair by shrapnel wounds, he had considered himself already dead. For the next few years the old man had withered away in bitterness until he finally took his Army-issue Colt .45 and blew an exit door from his misery, through the roof of his mouth and out the top of his skull.

Jack Eberhard had shed no tears at his father's funeral. Before his wheelchair days, the brute had beat him regularly. The paralysis had actually bought a stay of execution, for the boy had been planning to put a bullet through the old man's skull himself. His father committed suicide on December 23, 1961—the best Christmas surprise Jack ever got. Old soldiers never die, they just blow themselves away.

Jack Douglas Eberhard went on to graduate valedictorian from the Citadel, then third in his class, and *summa cum laude*, from West Point. He'd earned a mechanical engineering degree with a minor in physics, and had pursued a research career in smart weapons systems.

Eberhard had been one of the principle designers in the development of the Star Wars missile defense system. When the project turned into a political boondoggle and the funding evaporated, he had felt betrayed; he'd wasted a decade of his best research work. To add insult to injury, a stink of professional discredit had clung to him afterward— as if his weapon designs and not the political climate had caused the project's failure. The image that struck him at the time was that he had become a *ronin*, a wandering samurai with no liege lord to serve.

Then in the early 90s, he'd chanced across an editorial and scientific papers in *Physics Review* that alerted him to the emerging field of nanotechnology.

Nanotech. Manipulating molecules. Building from the bottom up, instead of from the top down. The epiphany had jolted him like an electric shock: *To think big, one had to think small.* All at once, his former work in "bulk engineering"—whittling materials down to the desired size and shape, then assembling a thousand parts with ten thousand connectors—had seemed obsolete, even primitive. Nanotech was the future of weapons design; it was the future of *all* engineering design.

56

What was it that old fart, Freeman, had told the president? Control the atoms and molecules, and you can control every attribute of matter. He'd said, "It blurs the line between science and magic." Quite true.

Someday, molecular engineers would be able to *grow* a weapon—a tank, an aircraft, a submarine—from a tiny seed, and the craft would be incredibly lightweight and strong, without screws, bolts or rivets, plates or seams.

Conversely, engineers could create offensive weapons the size of germs, designed to waft into enemy territory on a breeze, programmed to infect soldiers and turn their bones to jelly; enter tanks and planes and corrode them to sludge.

After his epiphany, thirty years ago, Eberhard had completely redirected his professional life; he'd devoted himself to the development of nano weapons. He had lied to the President: Project Second Nature had not been a study of defenses against biological and chemical warfare. The secret project's goal had been to build the first programmable, microscopic assault weapons.

At least that had been the goal nine years earlier, when research had gotten underway. But five years ago, they had suddenly ended up with something far surpassing expectations—and well beyond anyone's understanding.

Gen.

The birth of the girl had changed everything. The research shifted toward finding out what the hell she was, exactly, and how she had been created. To duplicate her healing abilities held mind-boggling potential for a battlefield soldier—or better yet, for a born leader, like himself. For in the past year, Gen had inflamed in Eberhard a private purpose, a secret goal.

He laughed and shook his drink and the ice cubes clinkled. He recalled his early ambition, to reach the rank of general. None of his male relatives had risen higher than full colonel, and Jack Eberhard had been determined to climb to the top. But the Pentagon had valued his research on laser weapons too highly to allow him to serve in Kuwait, and without the crucible of combat it was next to impossible for even ambitious officers to be promoted beyond colonel. He had reached that plateau rapidly and it had frustrated him a long while.

But the good Dr. Freeman had said it: Gen was a new species of god. However inadvertently, Eberhard had helped to create a god. Now, attaining the power of an Army general seemed like a puny aspiration. He had a much more exalted ambition. In Gen, he had witnessed the true potential of personal power. Now he wanted to become, like her, a living god.

Yes. He smiled and took a long swig of Scotch and it burned icily as it ran down his throat. That was his destiny; his Rome that all roads led to. With all he had learned from Gen, he could become invincible—hell, possibly immortal. He shuddered with a physical thrill that was almost erotic.

Whoa, cowboy. Enough booze. Better lay off. On duty in an hour.

He got up to brush his teeth. The original cedar plank walls in the bathroom still gave off a woodsy fragrance; a clump of purple sage in a ceramic pot on the back of the toilet added a sweet topnote to the perfume. Reaching for his toothbrush, he noticed his hand trembling slightly. An overload of stress these past few days, but he was getting back his nerve. He felt disgraced that he'd had to go begging the president to authorize a nuke to destroy Gen. Being forced to reveal some of the project's secrets infuriated him. But he had to admit he'd found it easier to breathe from the instant the president had given her go-ahead.

He'd been lucky. He prided himself on staying in control, and things had nearly leapt out of his grip.

Gen had kept evolving. Like some kind of intelligent weapons system, the nanobots seemed able to learn, to adapt to everything he could throw at her. That was unanticipated, and it had impressed him—and in order to impress Jack Eberhard, something had to scare the shit out of him.

Diamond fibers. Her latest surprise. That, and morphing into an adult. What the hell was she up to? Who really knew what she was capable of? What would stop her from growing a layer of diamond fibers over her skin—an exoskeleton as flexible as silk—and escape from the lab, immune to the killing x-rays?

Of course, the girl did not want to escape. He had drummed into her head that the nanobots within her would invade and disassemble anything she touched. She believed she was death to the world.

Eberhard had once believed it himself. In the third year after Gen's birth, he'd been forced to destroy Dr. Richard Osden because the fool was about to exit the outer airlock without first passing through the sterilizing showers. Ozzie should have stayed put; let others come to his aid, but he'd panicked. That had not been the project's best day—killing the team's chief scientist in order to maintain safety protocol.

But lately, Eberhard had become convinced that the trillions of microscopic machines inside Gen bore some kind of benign intelligence, as if they *knew* not to harm living tissue. It seemed uncanny, incredible. But he'd arrived at that conclusion, based on his own series of secret tests with her blood in various bacterial and tissue cultures. The mitobots healed any injured cells with which they came in contact. He had not found a single case of them damaging or disassembling tissue.

He intensely hoped he was right. He yearned to become a deity. And who wants to be a god if all your

59

subjects dissolve at your touch? That would be worse than the curse of King Midas. He spat into the sink a pink blob of toothpaste and blood, and was reminded that he scrubbed his teeth too hard and fast when he felt impatient.

Eberhard would acquire Gen's godlike powers. And he understood himself well enough to know he would be a jealous god; he could tolerate no other gods before him. It had become paramount to annihilate Gen. Not because she threatened the world, but because she threatened his plans.

He rinsed his mouth with a handful of water, then patted his lips with a towel. He practiced a divine smile. Beneficent, but harsh on those who disobeyed him. A strict but just patriarch, commander of his own private armed forces.

"You showed the way, Gen," he said aloud. "I've learned from my mistakes. Next time, things will go differently."

Eberhard's team had begun to dismantle Project Second Nature at Redstone Labs. All research had been terminated. Officially, anyway. The president did not need to know the project would be re-established underground—literally—at a five-acre subterranean bioweapons complex at the Nevada Test Site in the Amargosa Desert.

Soon, frozen cultures of Gen's blood would be transported in cryogenic containers to the secret desert facility, just sixty miles northwest of Las Vegas. Financing for the project had actually increased, flowing from a covert fund established by the National Security Agency for important work whose nature is too sensitive to reveal to the fickle and changing administrations in the White House. The key figures on the research team were eager to continue the experiment; all except Toshi Yamato, who had quit in protest over the plans to destroy Gen. What a sentimental ass Yamato had turned out to be.

Unfortunately, Dr. Yamato was also a terrific biophysicist; he'd be hard to replace.

On the positive side, the late Dr. Osden, whose breakthrough was to convert the body's own mitochondria into nanobots, had left behind neatly organized and beautifully handwritten research notes. The whole set of notes displayed a precision and thoroughness that only someone of Ozzie's obsessive-compulsive genius could produce. Ozzie had been exploring new ideas about genetically programming the mitochondria, maintaining tighter control over the next experiment.

Tighter control, Eberhard thought. No more surprises. One must tread carefully on the path to godhood.

He entered the bedroom to select an Army dress shirt from a closet full of dry-cleaned and starched uniforms. His beeper buzzed and he jerked, snapping out of his reverie.

Man, you *are* spooked. Take it easy.

He unclipped the pager from his belt, reached for a cell phone, and dialed.

"Col. Eberhard here."

"Sir, switchboard at Hollomon Air Base. Got an urgent call for you from Capt. George Hughes."

Eberhard glanced at his watch. Oh, christ, what now? Capt. Hughes was security chief for the White Sands Missile Range.

He took a breath. "Patch him through."

5

Capt. Hughes came on the line and got right to the point. A night patrol had picked up a van-load of Mexicans, illegal aliens, in the desert's military restricted area.

"Sometimes runners try to smuggle in wetbacks by sneaking along utility roads through the missile range," Hughes said. "It's a big place. Often there's not a soul around. But this time, a chopper spotted them."

In the living room of the bungalow, Eberhard began pacing. "Where?"

"Broken down southeast of the San Andres. A banged-up old Econoline van with eight adults inside, a few kids, including an infant. Stranded four days. They siphoned water out of the radiator and drank it."

"Four days. Did they see any prep activity at Omega?"

"No sir. They were a good fifty, sixty miles away, with the mountains between them and the site."

Eberhard sighed with relief. "So everything's under control now?"

"Well, sir, you said to report to you anything unusual. This runner and the wetbacks with him, they claim they saw a miracle. Virgin Mary, or something. A young woman with purple eyes. Supposedly, she healed the baby."

Eberhard stopped pacing abruptly, as if the living room floorboards had sheered off from under his toes, dropping into a bottomless pit. He teetered on its brink. "Repeat that, captain?"

"The Virgin Mary, sir. I speak a bit of Spanish, but the Mexicans are pretty much babbling, not making a lot of sense."

"Purple eyes, you said purple eyes."

"Yes, sir. Well, violet—'*los ojos violetos*'—that's what they keep mumbling."

Eberhard felt suddenly dizzy, afraid of heights. Don't look down.

"They're are all badly sunburned, sir. Must've been hallucinating," Hughes said. "Anyway, I decided to contact you because...well, it *is* unusual."

Hysterical peasants, Eberhard hoped. Stoned out of their gourds with heatstroke, seeing visions. But he didn't believe his hope, his fear was too convincing.

He ran.

He burst through the front door of his quarters, cell phone in hand, hurtling toward the main lab building. "Captain," he said, huffing, "I need you to stay on this line and not hang up. I've got to check the security status at the lab. *Don't hang up!*"

"Wilco."

Eberhard was tall and heavyset, built like a fullback, not a sprinter. But he dashed the whole quarter mile to the lab. He found the guard in the security room slumped low in his chair, chin on chest. A string of drool from his bottom lip formed a pancake-sized blotch on his shirt. On the console in front of the guard, blinking red lights warned that a couple dozen videotape recorders were not recording.

"Fuck!" Eberhard shoved the unconscious man's shoulder and he spilled out of the chair onto the floor like warm taffy. Eberhard sat down and his fingers flew over the console. The dark screens of a bank of TV monitors winked on in full color, fed by video cameras in the air locks and isolation chamber. He scanned the empty screens and his guts froze.

No movement.

No sounds.

Nobody home.

Eberhard flipped the intercom switch to All-Stations and shouted into the microphone. "All stations, red alert.

The dragon is out of its cage. This is not a drill. Repeat: This is not a drill. Red alert. The dragon is out of its cage."

He stabbed a button. Klaxons began whooping all over the perimeter of the compound, while dozens of steel doors throughout the lab complex locked electronically. Eberhard hurried out of the security room with a handheld infrared key that unbolted doors before him as he ran.

He shouted into the cell phone, "Captain?"

"Right here, sir. What's happening?"

"Where are the Mexicans now?"

"On the base. In holding cells. I'm going to contact Border Patrol in Cristo Rey in the morning and have them transported back to Ciudad Juarez."

"No! That's a negative."

"Sir?"

"Send them here to me, ASAP."

"Redstone? But...you don't have the facilities."

"Let me worry about that. Just get them here."

"There are a couple kids, Colonel. The baby, too. Sure you want this mess dumped in your lap?"

"Captain, you were right to call. Don't fuck up your Brownie points now. I'll take over responsibility the instant you get those people here."

"Right, sir. A van could get them over to you in an hour."

"Negative. I want them as fast as you can fly them here."

"Uh, in that case, we can load them right back into the Blackhawk that brought them in. ETA in, uh, twelve minutes."

"Do it. My security team will meet you at the helipad. Now move it!"

"I'm gone." The connection clicked off.

Eberhard burst outdoors, sprinting toward the communications center. Squads of security personnel ran past him carrying M-4 automatic rifles. He nearly laughed at the absurdity—as if such beanshooters could stop Gen. He gritted his teeth against the sickening fear that things were absolutely *not* in his control.

His boots crunched on the gravel and crushed shell roadway. A geodesic dome housed the communications center, surrounded by a triangular array of three 40-foot satellite dishes. A zit-faced corporal saluted as Eberhard dashed inside the dimly-lit room.

"We've picked up her signal, Colonel," the corporal said, pointing to a blip that pulsed on a wall-sized green-glass monitor.

It had been Eberhard's idea to imbed a tiny transponder in the ulna bone of Gen's right forearm. The device, no bigger than a watch battery, transmitted a steady pulse to a military satellite system that now pinpointed her location to within half a meter. The blip tracked slowly across the large, flat screen.

"Sir, velocity and altitude indicate the target is airborne."

"No shit, soldier." Why do they recruit kids? This boy looked too young to shave. "What's the closest TAC base to their present position?"

"Colorado Springs, sir. I've already called. They have a radar lock on the aircraft. They think it's a small business jet."

"Toshi," Eberhard said, with disgust.

"Sir?"

Toshi Yamato was a pilot; multi-engine, jet-rated. Who else could it be? The guy had been the weak sister on the team, and he'd become emotionally attached to Gen. Why had Eberhard failed to see this coming?

Thanks to Toshi's top-level clearance, he'd somehow managed to break Gen out of the lab and the compound and make it to a nearby business airpark; Alamogorda had one in the east, Las Cruces to the west. They were in a jet now, cruising at 22,000 feet over Arkansas, heading east, at 560 miles per hour. Eberhard figured they had a two or three-hour lead, depending on how long it had taken them to get to the airfield.

Two or three hours! Inexcusable. The guards from the security room and the front gate were going to pay for this shit with all their rank, and immediate transfer to a NORAD listening post, well above the Arctic Circle.

The blip that betrayed Gen's whereabouts blinked steadily on the screen. But where were they going? Why eastward bound? Eberhard would have predicted that Toshi would fly west, to California; from there to try to leave the country, get to Japan.

Well, of course that was it, wasn't it? Toshi had wanted to do the opposite of what Eberhard expected. Too bad about the transponder, pal.

"Redial Colorado Springs."

A voice answered at the Tactical Air Command wing and Eberhard snatched the phone from the corporal, identified himself, and asked to speak to the base commander, Priority One. Minutes later, a pair of F-16 Falcon supersonic fighters scrambled into the sky to intercept the jet carrying Toshi and Gen. Their orders were not to fire upon the aircraft, but to make their presence known and keep the target in sight until it landed.

Eberhard slammed down the handset in its cradle. Gen, you can run from me, but you can't hide.

He unsnapped a walkie-talkie from his belt as he stalked out of the com-center. By the time he had gathered a security team to meet the Blackhawk arriving from Holloman, the thrumming drone of the helicopter's rotors could be heard over the eastern horizon.

6

The van driver's name was Gilberto Timican. He was mestizo, part Mexican, part Mescalero Apache. Gilberto sat on the only chair inside the Level Four Isolation Unit. Eberhard stood, wearing special biohazard suit coated with conductive film; a powerful electrostatic current surged over the suit's exterior as a barrier against microscopic invaders.

The illegal immigrants huddled on the floor of the glass apartment, wearing masks of confusion and worry: four men, three women, two small boys and a babe in arms.

Gilberto's tobacco-brown face twitched in a nervous dance between a frown and a grin. He spoke in heavily accented English: "We hear this motorcycle, you know? Then we see him coming toward us over the dunes. We start to yelling, 'Help!" and we jumping up and down, waving shirts."

The man held a stained cowboy hat in cracked and grimy hands. Tremors in his body made the hat's brim shake.

"They was a man and a girl. A Chinese man, I think."

Right! Eberhard's big fist slammed the top of the refrigerator and electric-blue sparks spit and popped from his suit. A stainless steel cup hopped off and clattered on the steel floor. Toshi Yamato, you misguided bastard. I knew it.

Gilberto drew back with a grimace. Tears of fright shone in his bloodshot eyes, reflecting overhead banks of florescent lighting.

"Japanese," Eberhard said, nodding, "He's Japanese. Go on, go on. What happened next?"

Gilberto fidgeted, turning his filthy cowboy hat in circles. "The girl, she was so beautiful, with long, wavy hair and violet eyes. They was in a real big hurry. But to us they gave their canteens of water. They was about to leave, and Consuela—that's her, there..." He nodded toward an Indian woman in a faded flannel dress, an infant asleep in her ample lap. "She beg of them to take her baby, because the little one, he was doing real bad from the much sunburn. He was almost, like, dead."

His worried smile looked more like a sneer.

"Go on." Eberhard said.

"The girl, she ask to hold the baby. She just hold it in her arms, no? But then, it was like a...*niebla*—you know this word?"

"A fog."

"*Sí*, a fog—a fog come out of the girl. I swear I don't lie to you, señor. I look around and everybody, they seeing it, too. The baby was coated in this, like, wet, shiny fog. *Dios mío!* When the fog goes back into the girl, the baby— he is perfect! No blisters, no sunburn, no nothing. Perfect. Just look at him."

Eberhard glared at the infant and Consuela tucked the baby closer to her.

Gilberto glanced around at the others in the room. They looked back at him with terrified, dark eyes, not grasping a word of the English. One woman shook as if she had palsy; she rocked in ceaseless, tearful *Ave Marias*.

"We was all scared real bad. Watching the girl, thinking maybe she is the Virgin, you know? So I'm crossing myself like this and wondering what am I supposed do about it. We all just staring, crying, not saying nothing. Not even thank you, we don't say. She gets back on the motorcycle, and they go." Gilberto's black eyes cast downward. "I wish that we had maybe said, 'Thank you.'"

Eberhard couldn't catch his breath. He actually checked for a kink in his yellow air hose before realizing the air supply was not the problem. An iron fist clamped his

68

chest, seeming to squeeze his pounding heart up into his throat. Finally, with real physical effort, he sucked air into his lungs.

He nodded encouragement to Gilberto. "*Te oigo, amigo*. I'm listening."

"That's all I know to say, señor. That beautiful girl, she healed the baby." He crossed himself and a tear traced its way down the dark creases of his face. "A miracle, no?"

A miracle, yes. Everything was miraculously fucked-up. Toshi possessed the highest level of security clearance. Only someone of his status could have pulled off such treason.

Sweat soaked Eberhard's cotton surgical scrubs inside the biohazard suit; droplets snaked down his ribs. His mouth tasted like whiskey and sour stomach.

He looked down at the other squalid peasants. He could manage conversational Spanish, but he no longer cared to interview the rest of the wetbacks. What was the point? The unthinkable had happened; that was all he needed to know from them, verbally.

More critical information was forthcoming shortly. A group of suited-up lab workers in the outer vault worked at microscopes examining blood and tissue samples from the immigrants. The exams would reveal what Eberhard really wanted to discover: Had nanobots infected the Mexicans and the security personnel at Holloman? If so, he had better be right that the mitobots were harmless. He fought back rising bile. God, this was too damn scary. Had the plague already begun? Could this be the end of the whole fucking world?

Gilberto turned his hat around and around in his hands. "Señor, what was, you know, what did we catch out there in the desert? Germs? Is all this about germ warfare?"

Eberhard shook his head. "Not germs."

"But…you wear that suit. They took our blood."

"Just need to check on something."

"We are going to die?" His bloodshot, panicked eyes stood out wide in his weather-beaten face.

Eberhard detested this stupid serf—his dull, cloddish looks, his poverty and bad luck, his idiotic superstitions. "Go sit with the others, and shut up."

Gilberto nodded anxiously and forced an apologetic smile. He got up and went to join the others gathered on the floor. Consuela unbuttoned the top of her dress and began nursing her black-haired baby.

Eberhard glanced at a wall clock over the area where he'd tested Gen's recuperative powers. The minute hand crept ahead as slowly as an hour hand. Time *was* relative; Einstein got that right. Finally, he sat in Gen's chair to wait.

The whole mess was incredibly sticky. Gen's very existence was supposed to be ultra-secret, so no local or federal law enforcement teams could be notified to help apprehend her. The jet fighters would force Toshi and Gen to land at a base where a military police force would be waiting. But Eberhard wasn't at all sure how a squad of MPs was going to corral Gen until a capture team could arrive with the proper equipment. It would take a steady blast of liquid nitrogen to freeze her in her tracks. She was virtually immune to any weapon less than a goddam Stinger missile—and besides, to attack her risked spreading the nanobots from her body, with possibly disastrous consequences.

Eberhard strongly believed Gen's nanobots were benign, but he wasn't ready to gamble all life on Earth against his conviction.

A voice came over the room's loudspeakers. "Colonel? We've finished running the tests."

Eberhard spun toward the lab worker in the outer vault. Take your punishment standing; his dad had told him that many times before a beating. The colonel stood up, squeezed his eyes shut and nodded. "Go ahead."

"Test results are negative."

Eberhard gasped, opened his eyes. "Negative?"

"Yes sir. No mitobots in their blood. Everything's normal."

"The baby?"

"Normal. Blood is clean."

Eberhard sank into the chair. No plague! Gen's mitobots had not infected the other Mexicans. Even the baby must have passed any traces out of its body. His conclusions had been correct; the encounter in the desert confirmed his own, private lab trials: the mitobots were harmless.

The god he had helped to create could safely walk among men! At least, it seemed that way. But the quicker he seized Gen, the better he'd feel.

Eberhard dismissed the lab workers. They exited through the air lock.

Gilberto stood, hesitantly. "No germs?"

The colonel smiled paternally at the van's driver. "No germs." He popped the vacuum seal on his helmet and tugged it off. "See?" The odor of unwashed bodies smothered him like a serape tossed over his head.

The Mexican crossed himself. "*Gracias a Dios!*"

The others immigrants picked up the sense of the happy news and laughed and hugged each other.

"Gilberto, thank you for reporting what you witnessed. Capt. Hughes thought you were *loco*—"

"No, señor, I swear to you—"

"Shhh." Eberhard held up a hand. "I believe you."

Gilberto's brows knitted. "You believe this thing I see?"

"I know what you saw. It was not the Virgin, my friend." He glanced around conspiratorially and drew

71

closer. "It was one of *them*. You understand what I'm saying?"

"One of them?"

"Roswell," he whispered. "Area 51."

The Mexicans eyes grew wide and his jaw dropped. "*Ah, sí! Los extraterrestres. Ay yai yai!*"

"How many people have you told about this?"

"Just you and Capt. Hughes. Not nobody else."

"What about the helicopter crew that rescued you from the desert?"

"No señor. I was, you know…I forgot all my English to hell. I talk only with the others, in Spanish."

"Good," Eberhard said. "Listen, I'm going to bring back workers to set up portable bunks for everyone, so you all can sleep in here for the night."

Gilberto smiled with broken teeth. "That is much kindness of you. We all want to sleep."

Eberhard opened the airlock door and a whoosh of air gushed out of it into the glass vault. He stepped inside the airlock, helmet in hand.

"What happen now to us, señor?" Gilberto said to his back. "We going to be took back to Mexico?"

Eberhard turned. "You don't have to worry about that, my friend. Because of what you saw, the President of the United States herself is going to make all of you American citizens."

"Is *true*?" Gilberto broke into a huge grin. "*Muchas gracias!*" He pressed forward, as if to shake the colonel's hand, but the airlock door was already spiraling shut.

Eberhard laughed. In a moment, the far door spiraled open and he stepped out into the outer vault and entered Air Lock One. On the far side of Air Lock One, he underwent a five-minute decontamination shower, for show, if nothing else. Then he passed through Air Lock Two. It sucked open with a *pop!* onto the Staging Room, where he scooted out

72

of his bio-hazard suit and scrubs and donned his Army uniform.

Finally, he entered the main, lead-shielded lab room. He immediately crossed to a wall-mounted switch. The round, steel plate resembled the switches that activated the lab's emergency showers for washing off harmful chemicals; but the skull-and-crossbones emblem and the single word, X-RAYS, identified this switch as a killer, not a savior.

Eberhard punched the switch with the flat of his palm. A klaxon started yelping like a frightened dog. Banks of capacitors under the aluminum floor of the isolation chamber discharged, firing a magnetized ball of superheated plasma up through a conducting column in the room's center to smash against a shield of depleted uranium at the ceiling, triggering a deadly monsoon of intense radiation.

The men, women, and children hugging and congratulating each other in Gen's old quarters never saw the fire that baked them, for it made no flames. In the middle of a hearty laugh, a grateful cry, blood evaporated in the veins like water on a red-hot skillet. Cells coagulated. Flesh mummified.

Three-inch thick lead plates muffled the chorus of screams that reached Eberhard in the main laboratory. Within seconds, the shrieking stopped.

Eberhard ordered a crew to enter the isolation unit and dispose of the leathery remains in the lab's biowaste incinerator. He did not stay to oversee the clean-up, but hurried out of the lab into the paling desert night.

By dawn, the colonel and his select team were aboard a C-141 Starlifter, chasing at close to the speed of sound an escaped god.

7

"Cessna N1007, this is flight leader, United States Air Force Capt. Gifford Mitchum in the F-16 off your port wingtip."

Gen could make out the fighter pilot's name stenciled on the white fuselage under the bubble canopy of the sleek jet. Capt. Mitchum waved a black gloved hand. He wore a brilliant yellow helmet, streaked with blue lightning bolts, and an Air-Force-blue pressure suit. A shiny black visor and rubber oxygen mask hid his face.

"My wingman, Lt. Dan Morrow, is sliding into position off your starboard wing."

Another F-16 slipped into formation on the right, so close to the Cessna Citation X business jet that the two aircrafts' wingtips overlapped. Lt. Morrow saluted at Gen and Toshi. Both fighters' sweptback wings bristled with air-to-air missiles.

"Sir, be advised that you are now under military escort by myself and Lt. Morrow under authority of the United States Air Force Tactical Air Command. Please acknowledge."

Gen's heart sank into her lap. She looked at Toshi in the pilot's seat; he shook his head in stunned disbelief. How had Eberhard found them so easily? The Citation's flight plan, filed at the Alamogordo Air Park, claimed the rented business jet was headed west to San Diego. Instead, they'd flown toward the rising sun; their actual destination: Grand Bahama Island. They had just crossed Mobile Bay and the gulf shores of Alabama. Now the distant, squiggly coastline of Florida's panhandle, studded with tiny islands and pocked with bays, spread along the northeastern horizon, while the Gulf of Mexico stretched ahead southward like a bolt of unfurling blue silk. Gen and Toshi had begun to relax and enjoy their adventure, believing they were going to make it.

"Cessna N1007, you are being hailed by a military escort. Respond now if you copy my transmission."

Toshi depressed the com-button on the Citation's control yoke and spoke into his chin mike, his voice thick with anger. "Yeah, yeah. I read you."

"Very good, sir. Pay attention, please. About 70 miles north-northeast of our present location, is Pensacola Naval Air Station. That is your destination. You are ordered to turn your aircraft to a new heading of 48 degrees north-northeast. Repeat: 48 degrees north-northeast. We will begin a 35-degree left bank on my command. Over."

Toshi sighed. "Roger."

"Banking to the left after three…three, two, one, bank."

The three jets lifted their starboard wings and turned in a smooth formation until their noses pointed toward the white curve of the Florida Panhandle.

"Well done, very nice," said the deep male voice in Gen's headphones. "Now tune your radio to 09166 and obey the landing instructions of Pensacola Naval Air Station Air Traffic Control. Repeat: dial 09166 and do not deviate from the guidance of Air Traffic Control. In about, ah, twenty-six minutes, you will land your bird at the Naval Air Station. Meanwhile, Lt. Morrow and I will stick to you like Super-Glue. Acknowledge."

Toshi gave a dispirited nod.

"Sir, I need to hear an acknowledgement."

"Roger," Toshi said.

Gen sat in the co-pilot's seat, watching everything with big eyes. A couple hours earlier, the sun had crested the curved horizon, fading the stars like evaporating dew drops. Then the clouds caught fire, glowing pink and gold, while the sky turned azure. In spite of the tension of fleeing, the beauty had overcome her. And to think the sun came up every day! Tomorrow and tomorrow, another light show.

The Citation had flown over painted deserts, snow-capped mountains, and patchwork quilts of farms and ranches, and in the last hour, emerald green forests, coastal marshes and the Mississippi Delta.

Gen had gazed upon splendors, touched a new world, and tasted freedom. And now they were going to steal it all from her. They may as well snuff out her soul. It made the threat of the H-bomb less terrible. She would rather be vaporized then spend one more day as a test subject caged in glass.

Toshi hammered his fist into the armrest of the pilot's seat. "How did they find us?" he said. "There are thousands of planes crisscrossing the sky. How could they track down one anonymous jet, know we were aboard?"

Gen stared at her hands in her lap; the long fingers tapered like graceful candles. She had hoped to give her hands a lifetime of touching and exploring the beautiful artworks of nature.

"They couldn't have," he said. "That's the plain answer. There's no way they could have done it...unless..." His black eyes bored into hers.

"What?"

He continued to stare, thinking.

"*What*?"

"You've been bugged."

She shook her head.

"Yes. You've got a radio transmitter on you—no, no, it's *in* you. Of course. That's it. That's how Eberhard's mind works. You've got a transponder implanted inside you."

The idea made Gen sick to her stomach. "Where?"

"I don't know."

She ran her hands over her body, patting herself down like a policeman searching for contraband.

"You're not going to find it like that. It's inside you, Gen. Probably embedded in bone. They've been tracking us by radio signal."

She tried to remember.

"Did the colonel ever have the opportunity—?"

"I'm thinking." Eberhard's earliest experiments had involved breaking or crushing her bones. He had entered the vault and attacked her with a sledgehammer. Bones had jutted from torn flesh like splintered stakes. At first, it took her all day long to heal. Had Eberhard managed to implant a signaling device inside a shattered bone?

"He had the chance," she said, "several times. But that doesn't tell us *where*."

Gen closed her eyes to concentrate. She did not know how to communicate with the microscopic machines inside her, but she knew they were intelligent. Without any better plan, she simply asked them, thinking the words: Locate the foreign device implanted in me.

"Fuck you, Eberhard," Toshi said. "We're not going back."

She waved him to be quiet. The Abundance was talking to her. Not *talking*, not with words. But responding; informing her with a sudden hunch. The idea arrived in her mind as a surprising flavor. The experience felt bizarre; she could now *taste* the foreign object buried in the ulna bone of her right forearm.

"It's in my right arm, near the wrist," she said, rubbing the spot. "What should we do?"

Toshi got a crazy look in his eyes. She'd never seen it before. "I have an idea," he said. "It will make you free of that bastard forever. He's not going to win."

Gen was not sure she wanted to revive her hope of escaping. It had felt so painful to crash from that height.

77

"The plan is simple," Toshi said. "But you're not going to like it."

"Try me."

"First of all, you've got to realize those fighter jocks are not here to shoot us down."

"They're not?" She eyed the Sidewinder missiles slung under the wings.

He shook his head. "My guess is, they've got express orders *not* to shoot us down, no matter what. They certainly don't want to spread your nanobots all over creation."

"So why——?"

"To keep an eye on us. So we can't hide. The Colonel and his goons will be waiting for us on the ground when we land. They're going to freeze you, Gen. Nuke you. Me, they'll kill, too—with a lot less effort."

"What's your plan?"

"First, you cut the transmitter out of your arm."

"I can do that," she said without hesitation.

He nodded. "See those clouds?" He pointed with his chin out the windshield on her side. An anvil-shaped thunderhead of altocumulus clouds rose from the Florida coastline up to 28,000 feet. The gilded thunderhead resembled a mighty cathedral, complete with flying buttresses and spires.

"In a moment, I'm flying straight into that morass," he said. "When we enter the clouds, we'll be visually hidden from the fighters. They'll still have us on radar, and the transmitter will be signaling, but their eyes won't see anything but white."

"Okay."

"The turbulence in that weather system is going to toss us around. The fighters will have to spread out to keep from colliding with us and each other. It'll be a very bumpy ride, but I want you to make your way back to the door and open it."

Gen thought she grasped his plan. "You want me to toss the transmitter out the door?"

He shook his head. "Won't do any good. They've got us on radar. They're not about to lose this airplane. They'll be on us again as soon as we exit the cloud."

She knitted her brow. "What, then?"

"You," he said. "*You're* going out the door."

She gasped.

"They'll never see you leave the plane. And your transmitter will stay in the cockpit with me."

Gen took a second to recover her breath. "Toshi! Are you nuts?"

"No, but I *am* a physicist. I know you can survive the fall. There's something called terminal velocity, which I don't have time to explain—"

"When wind resistance equals acceleration due to gravity."

"Right. Sorry." His smile held real affection, and sadness. "Never underestimate someone who learned Japanese in a couple hours."

"It won't work."

"Yes, it will. You can't fall faster than terminal velocity—which means you'll hit the ground at about 125 miles an hour. Gen, you can survive that. I promise."

"It won't work."

"I am absolutely certain that you'll survive. The impact will burst your organs, break every bone. But you'll survive, Gen. You'll heal without a scratch."

"It won't work, Toshi, because I'm not going to leave you."

He laughed. "I can't very well leap out with you."

"Right. So I'm staying here, too."

"That's suicide."

She wrapped her arms tight across her chest. "You're my one, true friend. And now we're in this together. All my life I've been kept apart from everybody, from everything." Tears brimmed in her violet eyes. "I…I don't want to lose you. I can't bear that."

Toshi studied her. "What's worse? Surviving on your own, or getting obliterated by an H-bomb?"

She didn't answer for a moment. "I'd rather be dead than to feel so lonely again," she said quietly.

He sighed. "All right. Forget it. We'll go with your idea. We enter the clouds, you open the door and toss out the transmitter."

She smiled at him with relief. He dug in his jacket pocket and came up with a Swiss Army Knife. "Here, I think they make one blade specifically for digging transponders out of bone."

She opened several blades and selected a short, sharp one. She didn't know how The Abundance managed it, but she was not surprised when the incision caused no pain. She gouged into the bone to extract a device the size of a watch battery. Only a smattering of blood appeared, and her tissue healed in seconds with no scarring.

"Here it is," she said, holding up a blood-smeared silver disk.

"Let me see it." Toshi took it from her and stuffed it deep into his pants pocket. "Girl, we are cloud bound." He steeply banked the Citation, turning to a new heading of 132 degrees southeast. The F-16s dodged the Citation's wingtips, but clung to their quarry like fox hounds.

"Cessna, you have veered off course. Resume the correct heading immediately."

"See those clouds, Captain? That's my new course. I'm flying straight into them." He pushed the throttle handle forward as far as it would go. The twin Rolls-Royce turbofan engines whistled louder as the Citation accelerated to its top speed of Mach .92, just under the speed of sound.

"Sir, we have you on radar—airborne and ground-based," Capt. Mitchum said. "Flying into a thunderhead is a very dangerous move. And it's not going to accomplish a thing. You can't get away."

"Maybe not. But I'm flying into those clouds, just the same."

"I'm afraid we can't let you, sir. Our orders are to shoot your aircraft down if you attempt to evade this escort."

"Understood, Captain. You and your wingman are going to have to do just that to stop me."

Toshi glanced at Gen and she read the tension in his eyes. Sweat droplets clung to his forehead. She hoped the fighter pilots did not have the authority to call his bluff. She watched the flight leader speaking into his throat mike, conferring with his superiors on the ground at Pensacola Naval Air Station. Maybe talking with Eberhard himself. She shuddered.

The F-16s peeled away from the Citation. The business jet's radar showed the fighters reform in a loose formation, three miles behind.

"They've been ordered to let us go," Gen said.

Toshi didn't take his eyes off the radar screen. "Either that, or they're lining up a proper firing angle for an air-to-air missile."

The clouds loomed ahead, dwarfing the jet like a mountain dwarfs a mountaineer. Gen had heard clouds described as "soft as cotton candy," but the wall of white in front of the jet rose up as solid-looking as snow-shrouded Everest.

The Citation punched through the first wisps of vapor, then plunged headlong into unbroken white. Immediately, the plane began to buck and shudder, pitch and yaw. The winds inside the thunderhead roared with mad fury. The artificial horizon and roll indicator swung crazily.

Toshi gripped the control yoke with one hand and dug into his pocket. "Here, take it." He dropped the transmitter into the pocket of her jumpsuit. "Go back, open the door and get rid of it."

Gen unclipped her shoulder harness and lurched out of the cockpit and down the aisle, grabbing seatbacks to steady herself as the plane buffeted wildly. She made her way back to the door in the fuselage in front of the port wing.

A lever mechanism locked the door. The printed instructions were simple: pull up on the handle to unlock the lever, then swing the lever clockwise, and push the door outward. Gen unlocked the lever, grasped it tightly, and swung it around to the DOOR OPEN position. The door seal popped with a sound like a gunshot. The cabin depressurized with hurricane force, instantly sucking Gen out of the plane.

Her heart leapt into her throat from the sensation of falling, falling. Icy wind yanked her long hair into a whipping streamer, tore at her clothing and forced her to keep her eyelids squeezed shut.

Toshi had tricked her. Whatever he'd dropped in her pocket was not the transmitter.

From 28,000 feet, Gen plummeted like a broken sparrow.

Toshi wasn't going to survive. He had betrayed her, to save her life.

Falling. Falling.

Terminal velocity. No more acceleration. No more sensation of falling.

Floating.

Or, perhaps she was flying.

It took a long time to reach the ground.

*   *   *

Toshi snugged his lapbelt and shoulder harness tighter as Gen got up from the co-pilot's seat and struggled back toward the door. His tears began to flow freely.

He wished he could say good-bye. Tell her he was sorry for the ways he had contributed to causing her pain. On the other hand, he didn't feel regret for having played a role in bringing about her birth, her existence. She was a wonderful being, greater than human. He felt proud of her. He loved her.

This was the only way to save her. He just worried that she would suddenly realize his deception before she opened the door. She had devoured the physics textbooks he had given her, and if she stopped to analyze the situation, she would surely realize that opening the door of a fast-moving, pressurized aircraft at 28,000 feet was an insane idea.

But Eberhard had never allowed Gen to watch television or movies. In so many ways, she was naïve. Unworldly. A true innocent. He hoped the anxiety of the moment would distract her from applying the abstract information stored in her head.

He heard a metallic click as the door's lever unlatched. Good! He tensed and braced for violent decompression. The loud pop of the door seal was the last noise he heard before his eardrums burst.

Oxygen masks dropped down in front of the pilot and co-pilot's seats. Toshi fastened the oxygen mask over his nose and mouth. His brain felt on fire.

Vibrations in his headphones told him Capt. Mitchum—or maybe Eberhard himself—repeatedly hailed him.

Toshi smiled. He had won. He felt heroic. The perfect antidote to years with Project Second Nature, when he'd known himself to be a coward. All in all, redemption was every bit as good as it was cracked up to be.

He did not hear himself as he spoke aloud a Shinto prayer.

After another ten minutes of jolting and bouncing, the Citation zoomed out of the white void of clouds into pure blue sky over the Atlantic. The F-16s emerged to his north, about four miles away. The fighters cautiously closed in until they were a hundred feet from his wingtips.

Toshi saluted. Capt. Mitchum or somebody was still jabbering away. Toshi couldn't make out a word. He gingerly removed his headphones and a rivulet of blood ran down his neck from each ear. The pain made stars sparkle in front of his open eyes.

Toshi wondered what he could make the Cessna Citation do. The sweet-handling business jet boasted a high-performance design with 37-degree swept back wings, as radical as the F-16s. How far could he push the aircraft before it crumpled?

He kicked hard rudder and snap-rolled the Citation to the left. Dust and air charts tumbled in the cockpit like laundry in a dryer. Toshi felt the Citation's wings shudder and groan, but the aircraft rolled out in one piece. Not bad!

The fuselage door had banged shut in the slipstream, but the roll had sucked it open, causing the jet to veer sharply to port before the wind slammed the door shut again. The F-16s had withdrawn to a safe distance from the lunatic in the business jet.

Toshi the Test Pilot! He grinned.

How about a loop?

He pushed the yoke forward into a steep dive to pick up airspeed, then he pulled the yoke all the way back to his gut. The big bird nosed up and up and over. The fuselage vibrated only slightly as he pulled out of the dive into level flight.

Impressive. Still one piece.

Now for an *outside* loop.

Toshi shoved the yoke forward and held it there, firmly. The aircraft nosed straight down and began an inverted loop. Heavy rattling increased to severe jolting and the port wing suddenly twisted upward and snapped loose.

The maimed aircraft spun downward toward the water like a twirling cherry blossom. Toshi knew the aviation fuel would explode on impact and splatter fires on the sea. It would look like the burning paper boats the Shinto priests floated out on the tide, in honor of the past year's departed souls.

Toshi had planned to remember his ancestors in the last seconds of his life: his mother, who had died before he was eight; the father he'd never met, killed defending Okinawa; his grandfather, who had raised Toshi and taught him bonsai gardening.

But strangely, the beings that flashed most vividly through his mind were the miniature trees themselves. The peaceful hours he had spent tending the bonsai were compressed into a single instant of joy. The noble little trees had outlived many gardeners. Including this one.

A Shinto sect claims that a soul reincarnates as whatever creature one holds in mind at the moment of one's death. If so, Toshi wished to be reborn as a red-leaf maple.

He relaxed and closed the leaves of his eyelids as the spinning blue surface of the Gulf rushed up.

8

The woman awoke on her back. Wet, gritty sand beneath. A massive thunderhead roiling above. White dunes all around.

A humid breeze softly caressed, trembling downy hairs on her arms. The air smelled salty, pungent, rich. She sat up and sucked in her breath at the watery expanse before her.

What is this place? How had she gotten here?

Falling. She remembered the sensation of falling, falling, falling.

Now she found herself in an impact crater in the sand; its rim reached to her waist. Orange nylon cloth clung to her body in bloody tatters. Am I hurt? She carefully moved her limbs. Not the slightest pain.

A shimmering mist flowed over her body, head to toe. Even in the dim light, it glittered like diamond dust.

The woman peered up into the sky. Murky clouds flashed with deep, interior light. Haze filled her head; but like the storm clouds, flashes of light swept through her brain, building in energy.

She stood up. Shreds of nylon slid to the sand. Sea oats nodded in the freshening wind. Lightning cast a golden net across the gloom.

It all seemed alive. The world pulsed like a heart and breathed like lungs; its rhythms not heard, but felt. Waves unfurled and broke upon the shore. Palm trees swayed and rustled. Dusky seagulls rose and dipped, crying: *Kee-reeee! Kee-reeee!*

And when the woman identified her own strong heartbeat among the blended layers of rhythms, a most basic question occurred to her: Who am I?

Thunder boomed. A thud ran through the sand and through the girl's bare feet.

What's my name?

She did not feel afraid. This had happened before, she knew. Many times. She would remember soon.

Her skin reabsorbed the sparkling fog. Electric signals traced a web throughout her brain. All her parts were linking up, coming back online.

Then abruptly, Gen remembered everything.

"Oh no, no, no." She clutched a hand to her bosom. "Toshi!"

Her rescuer had kept the transmitter with him in the Citation and led Eberhard's fighter jets away from her. He had saved her life. But at what cost?

Toshi. She began to sob. She had wanted to stay with him, but he'd tricked her. How could she have been so dumb? Of course, the high air pressure in the Citation's cabin and low pressure outside had vacuumed her right out the door. She would have foreseen that outcome if she'd stopped to think.

Suddenly, the vivid image of Toshi's grinning face shone through her sadness, and Gen couldn't help but smile. Thank you, my friend. She wiped tears from her cheeks. You set me free. You gave me the world.

Gen's heart felt full to bursting with sadness and joy as the first fat drops of rain splatted down.

Rain! She turned up her face to greet it. It smacked upon her skin. Cold. Fresh. She caught the raindrops on her tongue. Delicious.

Bless you, Toshi. She recited a Shinto prayer for her friend's *kami* to be happy in its new, spiritual home.

Butterflies flitted past, chasing each other through the downpour. She recognized the species from a guidebook she had studied: Eastern Tiger Swallowtail. She laughed. The photo in the guidebook had lied. Colored ink on paper cannot capture butterflies. No more than words can capture rain—its sound and smell and taste. Its *touch*.

Brown pelicans soared across lacy crests of waves, wingtips nearly brushing the rain-dimpled sea. Black-and-white sandpipers sped along on comical stick-legs, outpacing each gushing sheet of foam. Ants in single file braved deep canyons and flash floods in the wet sand at her feet.

Tears of awe streamed down Gen's face. All the photos and names she had memorized: illusions. She could speak many languages; but the sum of all their words was unequal to this moment.

The living world was a paradise beyond learning. Naked to the sky, baptized in the rain, Gen touched everything; everything touched her.

But after another moment's ecstasy, Gen's smile twisted into a grimace. Eberhard had told her repeatedly that she was a deadly plague in human disguise. What if it were true? What if she really was lethal to this whole beautiful world?

Toshi himself had once feared it, dubbing it "the gray goo problem"—nanobots replicating exponentially, breaking down molecules, reducing the seas and continents to a gray goo. And the planetwide spread of death would be complete, not in years, or even months, but in weeks.

But when he came to her quarters last night, Toshi convinced her he no longer believed she was a danger. Her nanobots had restored the bonsai tree, Toshi said. "They're not killers, they're healers."

Lightning branched across the leaden sky in rivulets of molten gold. Thunderclaps overhead mixed with the rumble of shorebreak. Gen hugged herself tighter and shivered. Her long hair hung plastered against her shoulders and breasts.

She desperately wanted to know beyond a doubt she was no threat to life. She tried to reassure herself. After all, the Abundance had healed the baby in the desert. She had simply held the infant, and a flock of tiny guardian angels swarmed over it, knowing exactly what to do.

But Gen couldn't shake her feelings of dread. She openly breathed the salty air; she might be spreading disease with each exhalation.

What if just by being here, breathing on this beach, I can destroy the world? "Then, I'll hurry back to Eberhard," she vowed, "to the H-bomb." But what if it's already too late? The plague might already have infected everything around me.

Fear paralyzed her. She covered her mouth, froze her breaths to tiny sips of air.

A high-pitched whine made her glance down. A mosquito perched on her forearm, sucking blood. Was the Abundance invading the mosquito as she watched? Would dissemblers break down the insect into a gray goo?

If the mosquito starts to melt, I'm going to scream...I'll...I'll...

But what *could* she do to save the world? It did not even seem possible to kill herself. And if she did manage somehow to destroy her body, a swarm of replicating entities would still be set loose upon a defenseless environment.

Too late. Too late to stop the scourge. Too late to save the world. The mosquito's belly distended like a tiny red bead. She lifted a hand to swat it. Kill a mosquito, save a planet?

Gen's heart turned to ice. What was the use? Too late, too late! The mosquito staggered into the air, so blood-laden it could hardly fly.

She wished she had stayed in the isolation unit. She wished she had never been born. God, why had she listened to Toshi? Pure selfishness.

Rain pelted down. The last tatter of clothing washed to her feet. She hung her head, clad in nothing but misery.

Then the constant electric hum in her cells surged powerfully, as if her body had cranked up a rheostat. Within the buzzing chatter, Gen "heard" the Abundance more clearly than before.

She closed her eyes.

The entities did not speak to her in words. Instead, their message...

She knit her brows in concentration.

Taste...she could taste the message. Flavors of meaning. They communicated in a chemical language of infinitely subtle variety.

Gen tasted trillions of sentient cells exchanging an unbelievably rich pool of information at incredible speeds. She could not analyze the data. Far too fast. Far too much volume at once.

But...the Abundance meant no harm. That was the overriding flavor. She tasted their benevolence.

no harm

Understanding the message was like recognizing a well-known face in a bustling crowd, or hearing a familiar voice in a roomful of bubbling conversation. Within the flood of chemically transmitted data, good will was the spice that permeated the recipe.

no harm

The multitude of conscious cells had its own plan, a program to fulfill, but the plan did not require spreading throughout the environment, or hurting any of the beings of the world. The glass vault of the isolation lab had never been necessary.

But why did the Abundance need Gen? Why did they use her as their vehicle?

no harm

Could she trust the Abundance?

no harm

Again, she thought of the bonsai tree and the Mexican baby. Unscathed. Indeed, she suddenly knew the entities had repaired a birth defect—a tiny hole in the baby's heart—though how she knew this was a mystery, for she had not experienced it directly. *They* had experienced it. She tasted their memories.

no harm

What other choice did she have but to trust them?

A twig snapped behind her. She spun around to find a wild mare and its colt standing in the downpour, nibbling poke salad at the edge of a saltmarsh, not a hundred feet away. Gen gave a little cry of astonishment. The sable mare jerked up its big head, sniffing; a long blonde mane spilled over in a wet, shaggy forelock. The mare suddenly turned and bolted with her colt into the woods; they disappeared into the shadows of loblolly pines.

Gen shook her head in wonder. How did people go about their lives in this world without feeling intoxicated by its raw beauty? To belong to the Earth was, itself, heaven. She wanted to roam this new land, this Eden; to meet everything. Touch everything.

no harm

"No harm," Gen repeated and smiled and allowed herself to relax. As she let go, a ray of happiness spread from her heart throughout her body. Gradually, the swelling emotion grew into bliss, until the potency of the feeling overwhelmed her sense of self. She sank to her knees in the sand. In that instant, she felt her molecular structures shift like melting wax. Her nervous system switched off and she lost all tactile sensation.

Gen recalled what she'd read about the metamorphosis of a caterpillar into a butterfly: Inside the chrysalis, the flesh of the caterpillar liquefies; then genes direct the rebuilding of the cellular jell into a radically new form.

Gen was liquefying, her form coming unglued and transforming at the protein level. A rush of fear seized her mind.

Twice before, while in the lab, she had chosen to transform in this way: first, from an infant into a girl; and later, from a girl into a young woman. But those transformations had been under *her* control. This time, the Abundance itself was choosing a new form for her, without her consent. She did not even know into what new form she was morphing.

Stop! *Her mind screamed.* Stop!

The melting sensation slowed. For a long, disorienting moment, Gen found herself in a terrifying limbo between forms, her flesh more gelatinous than solid. Finally, the changes began to reverse themselves.

In another minute, she was Gen, again. Bones, organs, muscles. A woman kneeling in the sand.

For now, the Abundance had heeded her will. She had fought the metamorphosis, and gradually, the change had reversed itself. Still, the power of the Abundance horrified her. Trillions of sentient cells in her body had been reconstructing her, transforming her—into *what*? Would the Abundance take over her mind, her life, to accomplish its mission?

What *was* its mission?

no harm

Okay. No harm. But what do microscopic cells understand? What is their reality? Did they recognize her existence—her identity as a human being, living in a macro-world? Could they perceive the vast universe *outside* her body? Or did they only relate to the tiniest details of matter—repairing damaged tissue, protein by protein and cell by cell?

In the laboratory, Gen had waited for years, with a heart-clenching mix of hope and fear, for the advent of real communication with the sentient cells inside her. Now, at last, a mind-connection had begun. But it was not yet anything she could call a dialogue. A powerful race dwelled inside her body, and Gen had no clue what it was up to.

Her relationship with the Abundance, so far, had been symbiotic; she had served as their vehicle and they had repaired her injuries. Now the Abundance seemed bent on taking charge. Gen hated becoming a puppet, to do the bidding of masters whose purpose remained unknown.

no harm

"Oh, shut-up, already," Gen said. "What do you know about what *I* want? And how do I turn you guys off?"

The rainfall lightened to sprinkles. Gen stood. Wind-rippled dunes surrounded her. Sea oats tossed in the offshore breeze. She peered out from around the dunes that hid her nakedness. The sugar-white beach seemed deserted. Carefully, she looked up and down the shoreline.

Nobody.

The sea beckoned. She ran toward the waves. As soon as her feet splashed into the water, a multi-chorded music of countless flavors flooded her senses. So much life! It hit with a shockwave of pleasure, an unthinkable richness. Right through her skin, she sensed—*tasted*—hundreds of species of plankton alone, as the ocean swirled around her ankles. And each living thing she touched imparted to her its essence.

The bonsai tree, the baby in the desert, the mosquito—even Toshi—she could taste their essences, too.

Gen suddenly grasped what was going on. The Abundance was recording genetic blueprints. It had been busy sampling DNA from everything she touched; even from the pollen, spores and bacteria in the air she breathed.

Already, she stored in her bloodstream a library of genetic codes of myriad life-forms. And the Abundance could now replicate each complete organism, from diatom to Japanese scientist.

She did not know why. So many questions. Fears she did not want to deal with.

Gen dug her toes into the squishy sand and the outrushing water sucked around them. Within seconds, she had captured the gene sets of a hermit crab, moon jellyfish, sand flea and several species of seaweed.

She distinctly tasted the precise molecular architecture of each life-form. Most of the organisms were constructed from the same twenty amino acids that composed the proteins of her own human body; each protein configured according to a unique blueprint encoded within the same double-helix molecules.

Life was everywhere for the tasting. Open maps of evolution poured through her mind. The torrent of information left Gen feeling drunken and giddy. She staggered in the shorebreak and a large wave bowled her over backward. The undertow dragged her into deeper water.

Genetic knowledge continued flowing into her as strong as the currents under the sea. The Abundance was hungrily sampling thousands of sets of DNA and the flavors were utterly intimate, delicious, gratifying.

Gen did not surface for air. After another moment, gills in her neck made it easy to breathe underwater. A dim part of her mind balked as she swam into the colder, blue depths.

What…? What am I doing? It's happening again. The Abundance is taking over. She struggled against the deeply sensual delight of surrendering to the Abundance.

I'm a woman; I am human. Let me control the changes. I've got to remain human.

*so many living ones to *touch* *taste* *be*

But I want to choose. I'm supposed to remain human.

94

*so many living ones to *touch* *taste* *be*

Am I supposed to remain human?

Am I human?

A pod of bottle-nosed dolphins sped by like gray torpedoes, then swerved in formation and came back to Gen, staring with curious, intelligent black eyes. Gen felt them pinging her with staccato bursts of clicking sounds, trying to understand what kind of sea creature she was. She did not know. Long hair billowed around her torso in the water, and human arms reached toward the dolphins, but silvery scales covered her limbs and flowery pink gills opened and closed in her neck.

Am I a mermaid?

Several dolphins darted close enough for Gen to touch their slick, spotted skin.

In the next moment, Gen exchanged her gills and scales for a pair of lungs and a powerful, streamlined body.

She swam ahead with the pod, clicking and chattering with giddy excitement. *Family!* she whistled. *Friends!*

On her bottle-nosed face, she wore a dolphin's smile.

9

Col. Eberhard was an Army man, not Navy. He hated the sea. Hated the oily smell of fish. Hated endlessly bobbing on endless swells. Hated puking, which he'd already done three times this morning. The sea was chaos, forever beyond the control of man; and Eberhard hated not being in control.

If he were forced to join the Navy—say, at the point of a cutlass—he'd want to be assigned to submarines. Submarines don't spend a lot of time tossing about on the ocean's confused and disordered surface. It's much smoother sailing deep below. And the first thing Eberhard would do as a submariner would be to sink the U.S.S. Harrelson, over whose starboard railing he now hunched, dry heaving. He would enjoy watching this deep-sea salvage vessel flip stern high and plunge to the bottom, with all hands aboard. He was the only person on the ship who was seasick. It made him look weak, and that he despised most of all.

The search and recovery operation so far had consumed five days. One day to pinpoint the location of the Citation's wreckage. Four days now of hauling twisted debris to the surface, and sifting through it, nut by bolt, hunting for evidence of what happened to Gen.

Eberhard would have believed that Gen had the capability to survive the impact of the air crash. He thought of the massive injuries he'd inflicted on her in the combat series of lab tests. Hell, he'd gotten trigger-happy toward the end, at times nearly disintegrating her body. She'd recovered from such appalling wounds at an ever-accelerating rate of healing.

So why did her transponder now send its plaintive beeps from the floor of the Atlantic? Could it really be true? Had she simply drowned? Jesus. Was it that easy to kill her after all?

He wiped a string of foul-tasting drool from his mouth. "So much for invincibility."

What about the mitobots inside her? First, they had lived like free-swimming bacteria, relying on Gen's bloodstream to supply them with simple sugar for fuel. Gradually, they had evolved to something more machine-like, less "alive" in the ordinary sense, but they still needed a fuel source, right? So they must be dead, too. They had perished with the drowning death of their host.

Eberhard felt bitterly disappointed. Gen had turned out to be a goddess with clay feet. Or lungs. She was down there now among the fragments of the aircraft, bloated like any other week-old, drowned corpse: dark blue lips in a face as swollen as the white belly of a puffer fish. Who needed an H-bomb? Fill her lungs with water and it's all over. But, like a fool, Eberhard had spilled his guts to the president, pleading for a big nuke. Fuck, he could have drowned Gen at the lab by stuffing her head into her toilet bowl.

"Pardon the pun, Gen," he said to the ugly water, "but this puts a dampener on my little enterprise."

Eberhard consoled himself with the fact that he did know how to swim, quite well. He had been a West Point 500-meter medley champion, and an alternate on the U.S. Olympic Swim Team in 1968. Drowning would not be *his* Achilles heel. Even so, the emotional letdown was hard to take. He had believed that Gen's mitobots injected into his bloodstream would transform him into a virtually invulnerable human.

But would it really be just as easy to kill him as it had been to kill Gen? What was the chink in his armor? What fatal flaw was he failing to see?

A lieutenant hurried to meet him at the rail. "Col. Eberhard, sir, we've found it."

Eberhard jerked up his head and a sardine oil of nausea splashed through his brain. He lurched back over the rail and his stomach heaved but nothing came up.

"Uh, sir? Are you okay?" The lieutenant stood by, uncertainly at attention.

"Just give me your report, sailor," Eberhard whispered hoarsely.

"We've found the transponder, sir."

"*What*?"

"The transponder. We brought it up in the last haul."

Eberhard shook his head to clear it. Bad idea. When he'd recovered from another grip of gut spasms, he stammered, "What do you mean? The device was implanted in her right forearm. You found her forearm?"

"No, sir. But we recovered one of Dr. Yamato's forearms," he said helpfully.

Eberhard's face grew hot. "If you find his asshole, you can shove his arm up it. I'm only concerned with the *woman*, lieutenant. What about *her* body parts?"

The lieutenant shook his head. "All the human tissue we've found has been genetically identified as belonging to Dr. Yamato. But the last dive team did bring up the transponder, sir. Just the device. By itself."

"Christ, it was imbedded in bone. No bone fragments? No tissue at all?"

"No, sir. In fact, the transponder was wrapped in a scrap of cloth we've determined to be part of Dr. Yamato's pants pocket."

The news struck Eberhard like a backhanded slap. "Wild goose chase!" he growled, and shook the deck railing so hard it rattled. "She knew about the transponder. She cut it out of her arm. She jumped. And Toshi led the jets away on a wild goose chase."

98

The lieutenant's brow furrowed. "Sir?"

Eberhard's eyes scanned the wide, empty horizon. "She's not down there. She's gone. She escaped."

The Navy man knew nothing about Gen's mitobots and stared at him as if he were crazy. "But...how, sir? By parachute?"

"Never mind how," Eberhard said. "Tell Capt. Reevers I'm calling off the search."

"Colonel, the divers have covered only about a third of the grid of the wreckage field. There's a lot more junk strewn around down there."

"They won't find anything important, lieutenant. The operation is officially closed. Please go inform your captain."

"Aye, sir." The lieutenant saluted and spun to go back to the bridge.

"Lt. Raye?"

He stopped and turned around. "Sir?"

"Tell Capt. Reevers to thank the entire crew for me. Excellent job, sailor. The operation was a success. I've learned what I needed to know."

The lieutenant smiled. "Aye, sir."

"And I, uh, I'd appreciate it if we could get underway, back to port, as soon as the captain can make it so."

"Aye, Colonel." The lieutenant turned and hurried away.

Eberhard was surprised to discover a smile had formed on his own lips. Shouldn't he be upset? Gen's escape from the lab had made him look incompetent.

His smile broadened to a teeth-baring grin.

Gen had survived; that was good news. She *was* difficult to kill, and he'd not been a fool to request the H-bomb, after all. Now he seemed less incapable and she seemed more menacing.

Eberhard's favorite sport was hunting. Since boyhood, he'd hunted ducks, geese, boar, deer, elk, bighorn sheep, bear—even lions, once, on safari. His father and both his uncles had been avid hunters. Hunting was in his blood. He prided himself on being born to it, a natural predator.

Gen was still alive, at large. Now she made it necessary for him to do the thing he most loved to do: track a quarry on the run; chase it down until it grew exhausted; trail it to its place of hiding.

And kill it.

10

Cade Seaborne glanced up at a tattered gray blanket of scud riding in fast on a freshening onshore breeze. The chop was still small, one to two feet, and the tagging work was going smoothly, but they would need to head back within the hour, because he could see and smell a squall brewing on the horizon. Not a threat, but no use trying to net and tag dolphins while bouncing around in heavy swells.

"Wind's picking up," he said.

Jimi MacGregor nodded, prescription sunglasses pushed back atop his head, one eye glued to the view through a digital camera. He videotaped an Atlantic spotted dolphin lying on a foam rubber mat on the deck of Cade's 30-foot Hatteras dive boat. "I'm listening."

"We need to call it quits soon. Head in"

"No problem." Jimi looked up and his auburn pony tail, sun-bleached to orange in strands, brushed the middle of his back. He squinted at the darkening clouds in the west and flipped down his sunglasses. "Yeah, looks nasty. We're almost done here." He plugged the digital camera into a laptop computer and uploaded the dolphin video.

In spite of the afternoon heat, Jimi wore a long-sleeved white T-shirt and pajama-like pants to protect his fair skin from the sun's burning rays. Between videotapings, he shaded his face with a long-billed fisherman's cap, but the sun had still managed to microwave his nose to a tender-looking pink.

By contrast, Cade was shirtless over faded denim cut-offs and weather-beaten boat shoes. The sun had deepened his café au lait skin tone to a rich chocolate that accentuated bright green eyes. Long dreadlocks spilled over his bulging shoulders like thick ropes of dark brown wool, sun-streaked with golden highlights.

Jimi read aloud the white numbers on the blue plastic tag stapled to the dolphin's dorsal fin. "Three-twenty-eight."

Haven, Cade's nine-year-old daughter checked the tag against numbers listed in a notebook alongside descriptions of dolphins. "It's Sawtooth," she said. "See the cuts in her dorsal fin?"

"Yeah. Thought so." Jimi stooped and drew a syringe of blood from Sawtooth's pectoral fin. "Look at her nipples. She's got a new calf."

"Awww..." Haven jumped up and leaned over the gunwale. "Where?"

"Close by, for sure," he said.

Haven stared at the blue water of Coolahatchee Bay, watching for a dorsal fin. "There, I see it." She pointed with her ballpoint pen. "Oh, how cute! So little."

"Cade, can you get me closer?" Jimi said. "This'll be the last tag, we'll head in."

Cade started the Volvo Marine inboard diesel, spun the wheel, and nudged the throttle ahead slow. He didn't bother to haul in the sea anchor, but let it drag slowly along the sandy bottom.

When they neared the place where the baby dolphin had breached, Jimi hoisted onto his shoulder a fat tube that looked like a miniature bazooka. As the baby breached again, he quickly aimed and pulled the trigger. With a loud pop, a CO_2 cartridge shot a net from the tube in a squiggly ball that spread open in flight like a spider web. The weighted net draped over the dolphin calf and instantly sank.

Cade quickly tugged the seine net alongside the boat, then bent down and with Jimi's help, hauled the baby dolphin aboard. They laid the speckled dolphin on a foam rubber pad and Haven sponged it with saltwater. She made cooing sounds to it, and petted its slippery smooth skin.

"It's adorable."

Jimi flipped the dolphin on its side and with a fingertip gently palpated the outer edge of the genital slit. "Male." He drew a syringe full of blood; placed the blood specimen in a rack inside an ice chest.

"Your mommy's all right, little guy," Haven said. "We're gonna let you both go in a second, Zooper."

Jimi laughed "Zooper?"

"Yeah," she said. "He just looks like a Zooper."

"Okay. Write it in the notebook. Zooper gets tagged with—" He lifted a tag from a box. "—Number 401." With a tool that looked like a large metal stapler, he clipped a red plastic number tag onto the dolphin's dorsal fin.

Cade Seaborne had been assisting Jimi in the dolphin tagging operation five summers in a row. It didn't pay as well as taking out a dozen scuba divers to dive the local wrecks, but dive tours were mostly winter work, when the snowbirds flocked south. Besides, tagging work was much more interesting, and Cade had gotten close to Jimi as a friend.

In principle, the work was simple: locate a pod, net a dolphin, take tissue samples, tag the dolphin, and release it. One radio tag per pod, all others dolphins received a numbered plastic tag. Then Dr. Jimi MacGregor of the FSU Marine Biology Laboratory would type in key data on his laptop: date, time, latitude and longitude, water temperature, number of dolphins in pod.

From the first summer, Haven had begged her father to come along. This year, Cade had decided she was old enough to join them.

Now he watched her, jotting in the notebook, pleased with how much help she'd turned out to be. Haven's skin was the color of cinnamon and her thick hair formed a golden nimbus over her head and shoulders. She was beginning to look more and more like his sister, her Aunt Lana.

"All set, Cade," Jimi said. "Let's get them back in the water."

Together, they lifted the mother dolphin and dropped her overboard with a splash. Next, Cade scooped up the baby dolphin, rubber mat and all, and carefully slipped it over the side into the gulf waters. The pair of dolphins immediately raced toward the bottom and disappeared.

"Great work, guys," Jimi said. "Let's go home."

Cade pulled up the anchor. He stepped to the wheel and turned the ignition key. The Volvo Marine started on the first crank and settled into a smooth bass hum.

"Holy Moses!" Jimi said. "Look at that one's eyes!"

Cade followed Jimi's pointing finger. A dolphin, apparently a straggler, hovered in the water with its head poked high in the air like a trained dolphin waiting to catch a tossed mackerel. Even from a dozen yards away, the dolphin's clear eyes shone. Cade had been born and raised on the shores of Coolahatchee Bay and had spent a good deal of his life on the gulf waters. Like most sailors, he had a natural affection for dolphins and over the years, he'd watched them, snorkeled with them, photographed them underwater, and—for the past five summers—tagged them.

But before today, he'd never seen a dolphin with violet eyes.

*   *   *

Gen swam with dolphins, spoke dolphin language, thought dolphin thoughts and knew herself to be a dolphin; but in another compartment of her awareness, she knew she was Gen. Weird—like having multiple personalities— except that her two selves didn't take turns; both minds, human and dolphin, appeared simultaneously. Gen worried about how long she should remain in the sea-mammal form, or even if it was safe to have changed into a dolphin in the first place.

Her former sense of time had slipped away. Time had expanded, partly because dolphins never sleep; they only rest, when needed, in a relaxed trance; but also because dolphins are not planners; they live in the present, give their full attention to the hunt, the game, the race, the experience of the moment. Gen's human mind noticed the rising and setting of the sun; the change in the activity of sea life from the blue-black realm of night to the blue-green realm of day. She remembered one high-spirited feast of spawning jellyfish; the larvae had glowed beneath a full moon like ten-thousand edible lanterns. The full moon had now returned, so Gen figured she had lived with the pod at least a month. All that while, the pod had been swimming a slow back-and-forth pattern in a favorite warm-water spawning area, for several of the dolphins were pregnant.

Fascinating new flavors filled the sea world. Delicious, not just to her dolphin's tongue, but in their inmost essence. With every new thing Gen ate, or simply touched, she tasted the DNA of another species, and fed her deeper hunger to record the life essence of all beings.

Her drives confused her. The hunger to touch, to taste, to record, was insatiable, a craving born in her soul. She felt a growing sense of urgency, of a mission that must move steadily forward before time runs out. Yet she had no clear knowledge of what that mission was, or exactly why time was critical.

At least, she had regained some sense of control; she had discovered something about the power of the Abundance. Its way was not to command, but to beguile. She had not been forced to become a dolphin; she had been seduced. The temptation to experience the dolphin's beauty had been irresistible. Gen sensed she could change back to human form any time she willed it, but for now, it felt so good to be a daughter of the sea.

Dolphin minds are amazingly quick. She could whistle-talk with one dolphin and click sound-pictures to another—two conversations at the same time. They had wonderful names. They told stories and legends, made poetry and songs. They knew their history, as far back as when their ancestors walked on land.

Best of all, her new friends welcomed her, calling her Eyes-of-Sunrise. For the first time in her life Gen felt part of a family. A pod. The emotion of bonding swelled her heart. Gen belonged to her fellow dolphins; not like a piece of property—such as Eberhard's test subject—she belonged through ties of love and cooperative society. To thrive, the dolphins needed each other, and because they recognized that need, the members of the pod were fiercely loyal.

Gen realized that when dolphins appear to be playing, laughing, dancing, it's because they *are* playing, laughing, dancing. Now she and the juvenile dolphin shot forward in a game of tag, spiraling around each other, streaming ribbons of air bubbles. The water gushed around Gen's slick, sleek body as she pumped her flukes, shot to the surface and rocketed into the air—up, up, arching back into a back flip—*kerplooshhhh!* The juvenile male timed his leap to tumble on top of Gen. His rubbery body bounced off hers and he zoomed away, cackling. Now Gen was "It."

He was fast and tricky. Gen couldn't catch the little squirt, whose dolphin name meant, basically, "Little Squirt." She lunged downward to nip his flukes, but he dodged and Gen almost drove her beak into the bottom. Little Squirt chuckled, forcing bubbles out of his blow hole. Gen saw the shiny black eyes and gray-flecked bodies of the other pod-members as she sped past them, but mostly she relied on a new sense organ deep in her forebrain,

106

where sonar echoes took shape as three-dimensional objects. So detailed were the sound-images, she could tell the difference between a scallop and a snail, even buried under the sand. Clicking in the distance now, she clearly pictured Little Squirt zig-zagging through the sea.

Suddenly, the pod leader whistled a loud, low-frequency alarm that cut through the chatter and alerted everyone to danger. Little Squirt instantly reversed his course and hurried back to the protection of the pod.

Ahead in the distance, commotion and rapid pinging. Gen's own clicks echoed back to reveal members of a different pod circling frantically. She arrived on the scene and heard the other dolphins calling to their mate who had been captured and hauled out of the water onto a boat. The abducted dolphin was a nursing mother. Its baby swam in frightened orbits, pinging helplessly. Suddenly, when the baby breached to gasp air, a net fell over it and sank on all sides, drawing together like a string purse. The netted baby was also lifted out of the water into the boat.

The human and dolphin parts of Gen's dual-mind cried out together. What were they doing to the dolphins? How could she save them? She poked her head high above the water to see. Two men and a girl were on the boat. The dolphins looked unharmed, lying on pads on the deck. The girl kept the dolphins wet with a sponge bath.

One man drew blood from the baby dolphin. Gen cringed with a physical memory of endless blood lettings from her life in the laboratory. Her heart lurched against her ribs when one man raised a silver gun. The fear stirred the Abundance inside her, and Gen felt the beginnings of the melting wax sensation that preceded morphing to a new form. But then she saw that the silver object was not a gun, but some kind of tool. She heard a snapping sound, and saw the man had affixed a red plastic tag to the dolphin's dorsal fin. Similar red plastic disks tagged several members of her own pod.

In another moment, the men dropped the mother dolphin back into the water. The mother's darting eyes strained toward the boat, while she whistled to her pod that she had not been hurt. Gen's pings detected the mother's heart pounding like a drum, afraid for her baby. But in the next moment, a big man gently lowered the little dolphin into the water.

Gen was moved by the careful way he had handled the baby dolphin. She liked the smile on his face as he watched the little dolphin rejoin its mother.

The released dolphins and their pod dove deep and raced off, hugging the sandy sea floor. Gen's own pod retreated swiftly, calling her to follow. But Gen hovered in place, fascinated by the people aboard the boat.

The big man was beautiful. She watched as he hauled up the anchor, his thick, corded arms like twin branches of rain-darkened oak.

Little Squirt rushed back to Gen, circled around her, agitated, nudging her with his beak and flukes, "Eyes-of-Sunrise!" He whistled for her to follow him. Finally, the smaller dolphin gave up and darted away in the direction of his pod.

Gen bobbed in the water, still watching, when one of the men spotted her.

*　　　*　　　*

"Hurry!" Jimi said. "Those eyes! We gotta net it." He quickly stuffed the net into the tube of the net launcher, checked the CO_2 cartridge, and hefted the rig to his shoulder. Cade inched the boat toward the violet-eyed dolphin.

108

Thook! The net whistled out over the water and splashed down around the animal. Jimi set down the net launcher and grabbed for the draw line. He gave one tug, but as he reached ahead for the next pull, the startled creature bucked backward with surprising strength and tore the line from his grip.

"Oh-oh! Shit!" Jimi said. "The net!"

Cade cut the engine and rushed over to the rail. "What happened?"

Jimi whipped off his hat and T-shirt. "I lost the damn line. Dolphin's wrapped in the net. It'll drown." He yanked off one shoe.

"No, stay with the boat," Cade said. He kicked off his deck shoes, snatched the knife from his belt, stuck the blade flat between his teeth, and dove over the side.

Underwater, the dolphin's purple eyes, huge with fright, locked on his. He tried to pull the net away, but it had entangled the dolphin's fins. The weighted net sank toward the bottom, dragging the dolphin down, and its panicked struggles only trapped it further. The nylon net slashed into the dorsal fin and flukes. Clouds of blood billowed, looking dark green in the sunlit water.

Cade's heart beat in his temples. He clung to the net, following it down into the gloom, sawing the bindings in two with the knife.

In a couple seconds, the flukes came free. Cade guessed he was forty feet down, still sinking. The deepest free dive he'd ever made was to sixty-five feet. He figured he had about four more seconds to free the dolphin before he himself wouldn't make it back to the surface to breathe.

He held tight, gliding down fast. The water turned darker and colder. He could barely see. He felt with his hands, and realized he had no choice but to hack with the sharp blade through both net *and* fin. At last, the upper half of the dolphin's fin parted and the dolphin swam free.

Cade looked up and kicked toward the surface as the dolphin sped away. He dropped the knife, his best fishing knife, to get rid of the extra weight, and kicked harder, afraid now for his own life. He saw the white hull of the boat, the yellow anchor line, the shimmer of sunlight through the swells. His chest burned, squeezed into a knot, holding back his lungs from the reflex of gulping for air.

Thirty more feet. He chased a column of exhaled bubbles upward toward the sunlit realm, where all the air he could ever want waited below the blue sky for his taking. Nine more feet. Too damn far. He wasn't going to make it. His head buzzed with dizzying pain. The edges of his vision formed a tunnel of darkness, closing in. He involuntarily made a straining noise in his throat as it spasmed. In another few seconds, he would know how it felt to drown.

Suddenly he saw the rescued dolphin shooting up toward him at ramming speed. He knew dolphins killed sharks by bashing them in the gut with their hard beaks, but he was on the brink of blacking out, much too weak to evade the attack.

As his vision went dark, he saw the dolphin turning into a woman.

*   *   *

Nylon mesh trapped Gen as lead weights along the bottom edges of the net dragged it down. She shoved backward, thrashing mightily, but only became further entangled.

She heard a splash above and looked up to see a man swimming down toward her with swift, powerful strokes of his arms. His clenched a knife between his teeth like a marauding pirate. Gen could only stare helplessly, not knowing if he planned to save her or slash her.

110

He caught up to the sinking net and hung on with one hand, grabbed his knife in the other. To Gen's relief, he began hacking at the squares of netting. In a couple seconds, several strands popped loose, freeing her flukes. The man sank deeper with her while he groped at her dorsal fin and found it hopelessly ensnared in the net. Then the knife slashed through the fin's upper half. It stung for an instant, but it set her free.

The man immediately kicked upward toward the surface. Gen could see he was already in trouble. The man had risked his life to rescue her from the net; now he was close to drowning.

With a rapid pumping of her flukes, Gen shot forward through the sea like a slick torpedo. As she swam, long hair streamed across her eyes and she swept it away with a free hand. I'm changing back into a woman! Arms and hands had sprung from her body without conscious bidding. She grabbed the man as he sagged in the water and bolstered him to the surface in one continuous motion.

*   *   *

Cade felt himself boosted from below to the surface. He gasped and filled his burning lungs with cool air. The boat bobbed a dozen feet away.

"You okay?" Jimi shouted.

Cade spun around in the water to look for the dolphin. He thought he'd seen it transform into a woman. He thought he'd felt strong hands grab his waist. He treaded water, turning in a complete circle. She was gone.

"Daddy, you all right?"

Cade waved to them, still peering into the blue depths. He blinked, refusing to believe what he'd just experienced.

"Daddy, come on. Let's go home." Haven's voice broke and Cade knew she'd been crying.

"Everything's okay," he said. "I'm fine." He swam around to the stern of the boat.

"You scared the shit out of us, man," Jimi said, as he bent to help Cade up the dive ladder. "You were down there *forever*."

"Please don't do that again," Haven said and hugged his waist.

"Did you see that?" Cade said. "Did you see her? What *was* that?"

"What are you talking about?" Jimi said.

Cade's knees felt wobbly. "I gotta sit down."

"Here, Daddy, sit here." Haven moved a tool box off a built-in bench. She picked up a Navy gray wool blanket and wrapped it around her father's broad shoulders.

"The dolphin, it was...so weird." He wiped a hand through soggy dreadlocks, swept them back off his forehead. "I cut through the net and I was on my way up, but I wasn't going to make it. Then the dolphin came zooming up at me. Fast. Thought it was going to ram me, you know?"

Cade hesitated and looked at both of them with an embarrassed smile.

"For chrissakes, what happened?" Jimi said.

Cade shrugged. "I saw the dolphin turn into a woman."

"You mean you hallucinated," Jimi said.

Cade shook his head. "A woman," he said. "Long hair streaming in the water. She came up from below me and boosted me to the surface. I felt her hands on me, on my waist."

Haven's face wore a mask of astonishment. "A mermaid! You saw a mermaid?"

"Get real, you two," Jimi said. "Don't go Disney on me."

Haven ran to the side of the boat and looked out over the water. "What did she look like?"

112

"Her hair was waving around like strands of kelp. It hid her face."

"Your brain was oxygen-starved," Jimi said. "It triggered a hallucination."

Cade touched his waist where a pair of hands had squeezed. "What about her hands? I felt fingers grip my sides."

"You were blacking out," Jimi said. "The brain does strange things."

Cade shook his head slowly, remembering the woman in the water. "It felt so real."

"I'm sure it did, but c'mon, man. A mermaid?"

"I never said mermaid."

"Okay, a woman. So how could she be out here, seven miles from shore? Look around. No other boats. Where'd she come from? Where'd she go?" He swept the bare sea with his arm.

Cade nodded slowly. "Guess I am pretty shook up." He closed his eyes and sighed. The wool blanket smelled of mildew. "Can you take us in, Jimi? Feel like I could sleep a day and a half."

"Sure, man." Jimi stepped to the wheel and started up the outboard. "You know, Cade, I think I know what really *did* happen out there—and it's wonderful. You saved a dolphin from drowning and it returned the favor. That is so cool. That's going into my next research paper as a sidebar. Definitely."

Cade wrapped the blanket tighter, shivering in the warmth. In his mind's eye a dolphin charged through the sea with powerful whips of its flukes. Then a long-haired woman reached out to him with slender, muscular arms.

He smiled. The perfect sea yarn to tell his grandkids someday.

*   *   *

113

Little Squirt banged hard into Gen's ribs, whistling furiously. The little dolphin's black eyes blinked in confusion as he stared into hers.

She had rejoined her pod, but she wasn't in a playful mood. Her heart ached with a confusing mix of longing and fear. She felt torn between remaining with her dolphin family in the realm below the sea, or rejoining the society of her own kind in the realm below the sky.

Her own kind. What did it mean? She yearned to touch another human again. Like she and Toshi had touched. Or maybe it was the acute hunger to record new sets of genes from the world up above. Was her very soul the source of her yearnings, or was The Abundance in charge?

Who were her kind? Gen's love went out to Little Squirt and she realized that her heart was now of both kinds. But she worried that if she lived any longer among dolphins, her human mind would fade into background noise, like the pinging of a foreign pod heard in the distant depths.

She thought of the heroic man with the beautiful face and gentle ways. She thought of Toshi, and his sacrifice for her.

Gen made her decision. She drew alongside Little Squirt and whistled a sad good-bye. Then, louder, she whistled farewell to all the members of the pod. The dolphins drew around her like spokes around a hub while Gen rose to the surface and exhaled from her blowhole; her last breath as a dolphin. Then she transformed.

Now, in the center of two dozen dolphins, a naked woman paddled gracefully in the water. Long, dark hair swirled around her shoulders like spilled ink. Her eyes were as violet as dawn over the sea.

Her dolphin family escorted Gen back to the boat.

114

Jimi cranked the wheel and pointed the bow toward shore, pushed the throttle ahead one quarter. The boat rode up the backs of the shore-blown swells and surfed down the fronts.

"There! I see her!" Haven shouted. "The mermaid! Look!"

Cade jumped to his feet, shrugging off the blanket. "Cut the engine." He stared off the starboard bow where Haven pointed excitedly. A woman in the water waved her arm above her head. Dolphin fins rose and dipped in the sea all around her.

"Hang on, we're coming for you," Cade yelled. He quickly strung a yellow nylon cord through the belt loops of his denim cut-offs. He grinned at Jimi. "My hallucination is back."

Jimi gawked at the woman. "Impossible," he said. "How'd she get out here?"

"Beats me. But sure looks like she needs a lift back to shore. Here, grab this end." Cade dove overboard and swam briskly to the woman at the center of a garland of dolphins.

*   *   *

As the man drew closer, his brawn intimidated Gen and she suddenly felt afraid, torn again between remaining with her pod in the sea, or returning to the society of people. She remembered the agonies Eberhard had caused her. But she also remembered the kindness of Toshi. Then some impulse—perhaps it was the caring way the big man offered his hand, or maybe it was her hunger to taste, to collect, more genetic essences—made her take his hand at

115

last. His grip was strong. He smiled. Her heart beat quickened with hope and fear. Too late to turn back.

The dolphin escort swam beside Gen all the way to the boat. When she had climbed aboard and stood on deck, wrapped in a sun-heated blanket, the members of her pod leapt high out of the water in twos and threes, then all dove deep, where humans cannot follow.

11

Cade wrapped the wool blanket
young woman's muscular body. Coils
her waist, dripping. Her hair could be ca..
but that adjective wasn't strong enough to describ...
eyes: intensely violet-blue, like radiant sapphires; the most
beautiful eyes—*jewels*—he had ever seen. Her smooth skin
shone with a rich cinnamon tone that facial cream models
would envy.

Yet in spite of those lovely features, she was
shockingly ugly. The poor woman's face was horrifically
deformed. A birth defect, Cade guessed. When he'd first
seen her up close in the water, his impulse had been to
avert his eyes, but he had made himself look into her face
calmly and smile. Now he did the same.

"My name is Cade," he said, offering his hand. "Cade
Seaborne." Her slender hand was strong and unusually
warm. "This is Dr. Jimi MacGregor," he said, "and this is
my daughter, Haven."

She nodded at each introduction and gave a ghastly
smile. Her mouth was too wide, her lips thin lines, her teeth
oddly shaped, almost conical.

Jimi seemed to be overly focused on steering the boat,
perhaps to keep himself from gawking. Haven looked
crestfallen; she sat on a bench near the stern, studying the
molded fiberglass deck at her feet. No doubt, she had
expected the woman to be as pretty as Ariel, the Little
Mermaid. And to have a tail fin covered with glittery
scales.

Cade felt a knot of pity ball up in his gut, but he kept
up his smile. "What's your name?"

When she didn't answer, he wondered if she had
internal deformities as well.

seen people who might be called "horse-faced," . didn't begin to describe the malformed shape of the .an's skull. Her forehead and jaw pushed forward in an .ong curve like a football. Her mouth sliced through the ower part of the curve, but on the upper half, where a nose would normally poke out, flat slits marked her nostrils.

"Can you talk, Miss?"

She worked her jaw, and a garbled sound escaped her throat. One hand reached up to her face and explored its shape. Her brow knitted in confusion, her eyes flashed fear.

"It's okay, its all right." Cade said soothingly, as he would talk to one of the island's wild horses. "We're not going to hurt you."

*   *   *

Gen didn't need to look at herself in a mirror to understand what had happened, what she'd become. She had remained a dolphin too long. Intent on preserving both her identities—woman and dolphin—The Abundance had compromised when it restored her to human form.

Gen had hesitated to give up her dolphin identity and The Abundance had responded by building a brain—the locus of identity—that blended both sets of genes. To accommodate the hybrid brain, her skull and face also became a mix of human and dolphin features.

She sensed she had the power to transform further, to become wholly human, by concentrating exclusively on her human mind, her human identity. The Abundance would rebuild her accordingly. But how could she do that now? Three people had already seen her in this grotesque, in-between shape. If she changed into a woman, she would reveal her secret. First, she must get away from them; then she could change the rest of the way into a woman.

118

One part of her felt horrified at what had happened; touching her face with her fingertips, she could tell she looked gruesome. On the other hand, maybe it was a good thing—for now, anyway. Such a radically new appearance offered disguise. The way she figured, Eberhard was already searching for her.

Knowing Toshi, she felt certain he hadn't allowed himself to be captured by a man as ruthless as Eberhard. Toshi would have crashed the Cessna jet into the sea. And knowing Eberhard, she did not doubt that he had already searched the aircraft's wreckage. Had he found the transponder? Did he know she had survived?

Yes. The probability seemed high that Eberhard had discovered Toshi's trick. Which meant Eberhard was hunting for her; and, if nothing else, the colonel was relentless.

Therefore, her freakish appearance was a good thing. Right? So why did she feel so sad?

*   *   *

Cade watched the woman close her eyes in concentration. When she finally spoke, her voice came out squeaky and high. "Gen," she said. "My name is Gen."

"Gen…and your last name?"

She shrugged. "Just Gen."

"Are you all right, Gen?"

She nodded.

"How'd you get out here?" He glanced toward the pale, thin shoreline. "What happened to your boat?"

"I don't know," she said slowly. "I…I don't seem to be able to remember much of anything."

"You sure you're okay?"

"Yes. But I'm very hungry. I need to eat."

119

"Sure, you bet. Let's get some food into you." He opened a storage bin and lifted out a cooler, handed her a wrapped sandwich. "My sister made it. Ham and cheese, on homemade bread."

"Thank you," she said, and bit into it voraciously, her over-wide mouth devouring the sandwich in a few bites. While she ate, she kept her eyes turned down, staring at her bare feet. Cade couldn't help noticing, with a pang of irony, that her feet were very pretty. At one point she glanced up at him with bright, purple eyes, then quickly lowered them again.

Cruel fate, Cade thought, to fix those rich gems in that poor setting. The contrast had surely made the woman's disfigurement more difficult to bear. Overweight women grew sick of hearing, "But you've got such a lovely face." He could not imagine how tough it must be for Gen to have enthralling eyes, an irresistible figure, too; mismatched with the distorted face of a carnival freak.

"Gen, what's the last thing you do remember?"

She looked up. Her eyes pleaded with him not to pry, but damn it, how in the world did she survive out here without a lifejacket, a raft, clothes?

"Your boat sank?" he said. "How long have you been in the water?"

She shook her head. "I can't remember."

"Where did you put out from?"

"I don't know...tall white dunes, pine woods." She shrugged. "That's all I recall."

"Anyone with you? Any other survivors?"

"I was alone. There's no one else."

"Are people worried about you? Anybody we should notify? The boat's got a radio phone, we can call from here."

She shook her head.

120

"When we get back, then. Relatives, friends—who should we contact?"

"There's no one." She looked stricken by the thought. "Just me. I'm alone."

"She's probably suffered a concussion," Jimi said, from behind them at the wheel. "She's got some degree of amnesia, temporarily at least."

Jimi was talking about her in third-person as if she were not present, and for some reason, that bugged Cade. Since boyhood, he had felt compassion for the underdog: the fat kid, the weird kid, the shy kid. Probably he had learned such empathy from his sister, Lana. When their parents had died, she had raised him to have a heart and to use it.

As early as elementary school, kids who were picked on soon learned they had a defender, and bullies found out equally fast that they couldn't shove around an easy victim without dueling with the little kid's big friend, Cade.

Now Jimi was committing the classic sin against those perceived in that awful category called *different*; he was talking about her as an object. Already, she was "other"— not one of *us*.

"What I'd like to know is, how did she come to be swimming with the dolphins?" Jimi said.

Then why not just ask her, damn it.

"That was fascinating, they way they stuck by her," Jimi said. "I've read some anecdotes from shipwrecked sailors about dolphins protecting them from sharks, or even pushing them to shore. But until today, I'd never observed it firsthand. I wish to hell I'd videotaped it."

"The dolphins stayed close to you," Cade said to Gen. "They seemed to relate to you."

"Yes, they kept me company, helped me to survive."

"I'd love to hear more about that," Jimi said. "I'd like to get a full report from you."

"I'm really tired," she said.

"Just one thing more," Cade said. "Before, when you helped me to the surface…how did you come up from below me like that? For a second, I thought you *were* a dolphin."

"Please, I need to sleep."

"Of course. Sorry. Here, you can lay down on the deck. Less wind down low. Put your head on this sweatshirt." He wadded up a sweatshirt and stuffed it under her head like a pillow, pulled the wool blanket up to her chin.

"My sister owns the Cool Bay Inn. Coolahatchee Bay? That's where we're from. About an hour, we'll get you to the island. Get you some clothes. You're going to be all right. My sister, Lana, is the nicest person in the world. Really. She'll love to have you to take care of."

"Thank you," Gen said, and gave another ghastly smile. She closed her eyes.

Pity was Cade's knee-jerk reaction to looking at the young woman's deformed face. He didn't like the feeling. He sat down beside her and made a point of gazing at her face as she fell asleep, seeing her as a fellow human being with her own unique identity. He knew it would take all the awareness he could muster to treat her, not with pity, but dignity.

In that moment, he chose to be her friend. And the first step would be to stop calling her in his mind, "poor thing."

Her name was Gen.

*   *   *

Gen closed her eyes. Cade put a big hand on her shoulder, gave a tender squeeze, then sat nearby, protectively. The roughness of the wool blanket against her nipples made them suddenly hard. Or was it Cade's touch?

Back in her isolation chamber in the lab, Gen had not been permitted to watch television or movies, but she had read endlessly. Books of every kind, but especially romantic adventures, were her favorite modes of escape from her sterile cell and unrealized life. But even more vivid were the dramas that played in her head, peopled with characters drawn from fiction, and from the scientists, technicians and soldiers at the lab, and from her own imagination. Toshi, in various versions, had starred in some of those fantasies, but the lead male role most often went to a hero she'd invented, named Max Logan.

Max Logan. His musical, baritone laugh echoed his calypso heritage. Max possessed strength, courage, virtue, wit, passion, and mercy. And, of course, great masculine beauty, like a champion stallion. Max could rip her bodice anytime, if she had a bodice to be ripped.

Now, a handsome brown man had rescued her from the dolphin net and brought her onto his boat. Sopping dreadlocks framed his chiseled face. Genuine caring glowed in his green eyes. He shook seawater from his hair and droplets rained down on slabs of chest muscle.

Cade *was* Max Logan. No, Cade was much better, because Max was wispy as a thought. Cade was here in-the-flesh, and every time he smiled at her, it felt to Gen like someone laid a warm hand over her heart.

The instant she had touched him in the water, the Abundance had captured Cade's genes. Gen wondered how a society of microscopic sentient beings related to his genetic code. Were they thinking, Ooh, nice DNA? Because she was thinking something like that, herself.

She opened her sleepy eyes just a moment to peek. Afternoon sunlight burnished his heroic torso and lent copper highlights to his riotous dreadlocks. Cade Seaborne had saved Gen from drowning only to let her swim, dangerously out of her depth, in his jade green eyes.

She closed her eyes again, trying to sort through her feelings to understand her strong reaction to Cade. It was for his sake she wished she didn't look repulsive. Cade had done his best to smile and be nice, acting oblivious to her bizarre appearance. The emotions that now flooded her body were powerful and new, and she was not sure why it mattered so much, but she deeply wanted—down in her cells she could feel the wanting—for Cade to find her beautiful.

What bad timing to have been reborn a monster.

*   *   *

Cade didn't have dry pants to change into, so he kept on his clammy denim cut-offs. He managed to find a windbreaker in the storage chest; it reeked of oil fumes, but kept off the chill. He took a seat next to Haven on a built-in bench near the bow of the boat. Gen, wrapped in a blanket, dozed near the stern.

"What's wrong with her?" Haven said in whisper.

"Probably some kind of birth defect, honey."

"She looks *gross*."

"She does look very strange," he said, "but remember when we talked about the Golden Rule?"

" 'Treat others as you would like to be treated.'"

"Always. Do you believe that's a good way to live?"

"Yeah."

"You sure?"

She nodded. "But she's so ugly it scares me."

He smiled. "Thought that was it. You're way too nice to turn your back on someone just because she looks odd to you. I figured you must be scared of her."

"Guess so."

"But, Haven, put yourself in her position," he said. "What if, through no fault of your own, you were born with a terrible deformity? Or, even if it was your own fault—say you were doing something stupid, like smoking a cigarette

124

while repairing a gas engine, and it blew up in your face. Now you look frightful, like a monster. But would you really *be* a monster inside, because you look scary on the outside?"

She shook her head. "I'd still be me."

"What about your feelings? Would you feel the same about the people and things you love?"

"Sure."

"But you wouldn't need your friends anymore. You wouldn't care about me."

She shot him a glance. "I'd need you more than ever. It would feel so lonely to be different. Like her."

He looked at Haven and let her own words sink in. Her mouth turned up into a quiet smile. "She could use a friend."

He nodded. "No doubt."

Haven looked back at the woman sleeping on the deck at the stern of the boat. A wadded sweatshirt propped up her weird head.

"She was swimming with the dolphins," Haven said. "That was so cool."

"Definitely."

"She's the ugliest person I've ever seen."

"Could be."

"Really. She is. But she's mysterious."

"That's for sure."

"I like mysteries," she said, "and I love dolphins."

Cade watched Haven studying the sleeping figure. The bow smacked through a swell and a chilly spray of white foam sprinkled them both.

"I'm going to be her friend," Haven said. "Golden Rule. I'll try."

"Good girl." Cade hugged her shoulder and drew her to his side; she snuggled an arm around his waist. "You make me proud of you."

125

12

The red sun turned the gulf waters into rippling lava; clouds ignited above the western sea like sculptures on fire. Even the white sands reflected a ruddy glow along the shoreline of Coolahatchee Bay. Cade took the helm from Jimi and eased the throttle back until the engine burbled. The dive boat cruised slowly past a rugged wall of coquina that formed the bay's wide mouth. Riding high on the surge tide, the boat cleared the reef at the bay's entrance by a dozen feet. Cade looked down through clear water at jumbled slabs of coquina as big as Cadillacs sliding under the keel.

On the northern arm of the bay's nine-mile crescent of shoreline, a forest of masts bobbed lightly at Coolahatchee Bay Yacht Club, and Cade heard mast lines jingling against hollow aluminum. Willingham Marina, located mid-point in the crescent, catered to middle-class recreational boaters. And at the bay's southern end, rust-stained shrimp trawlers and grubby fishing boats docked at Taylor's Wharf while their crews unloaded catches.

Several travel writers had pointed out that from north to south, the three tiny beach communities along Coolahatchee Bay slid from rich to middle-class to poor as neatly as a line graph in a sociology textbook. At the northern end, called The Palms, fancy vacation homes on stilts and a twelve-story condominium of flamingo-pink stucco (Cade thought it looked like a giant Jackie Kennedy pillbox hat) crowded the shore near the yacht club. By contrast, the trailers and clapboard cabins sprawled around Taylor's Wharf were architectural classics of the Southern poverty school. And between these two extremes, the houses in the Marina neighborhood were modest cinderblock shoeboxes.

Nearly all the residents at The Palms—the lawyers, golf pros, surgeons, bankers, and CEOs—were white, and nearly all the folks at Taylor's Wharf—the shrimpers, oyster harvesters and grouper fishermen—were black or Hispanic. Any one of the floating castle motor yachts of the moneyed class cost more than the entire fishing fleet anchored off Taylor's.

Cade's mother, Elaine Fairchild, had been wealthy and white, a daughter of The Palms; his father, Samson Seaborne, poor and black, a son of Taylor's Wharf. They met on the bay when her parents' 160-foot motor yacht ran aground at low tide on the reef at the bay's entrance. Samson Seaborne owned a marine salvage business and had managed to stabilize and rescue the luxury vessel after the reef tore a four-foot gash through the hull. Eight months later, the interracial lovers defied both sets of parents by getting married—the scandal of the times. Their further act of defiance was to stay on the bay instead of fleeing the battle, although the couple did settle in Marina, the town in between the war zones.

Cade sighed. He wished he had gotten the chance to know his parents as an adult. They were still his heroes. Always would be.

Peering beyond the crescent beach, Cade could just make out the Victorian wedding cake architecture of Cool Bay Inn crowning a hill above the town of Marina. His sister, Lana, owned and operated the inn, converted from a turn-of-the-century mansion called Stanton House.

The mansion had been built in 1901, when the sprawling Fairchild plantation had dominated the north end of the bay and former slave shacks still dotted the south end. In the unpopulated midland, the railroad tycoon, George Stanton, had ordered his workmen to build Stanton Hill to set a summer home upon, so that guests could overlook the bay from its wide porch. The tons of dirt excavated to make the hill created Stanton Pond, a popular local swimming hole a quarter-mile behind the house.

The house had been George's wedding gift for Lady Francis, his 18-year-old English bride. The Stantons had hosted Parisian-style soirées and elegant dinner parties with European string quartets as entertainment. Henry Ford and Thomas Edison had been among their regular guests. Throughout the 1930s, rich Yankees considered Stanton House an oasis of culture on the Florida Gulf Coast. But after the death of her husband in 1939, followed by the start of the Second World War, Lady Francis had given up on humanity and withdrawn into solitude. The mansion, deprived of its life force, had fallen into decline like the childless widow herself.

While in high school, Lana had become the old curmudgeon's caregiver, and over time, her intimate friend. Lady Francis died at home on her ninety-seventh birthday, bequeathing Stanton House to the teen-age girl who had restored her faith in people.

At age nineteen, armed with How-To books and videotapes and a crew of hired workers, Lana had turned Stanton House into *Cool Bay Inn* and injected the new bed & breakfast with her soul. The major travel guides to inns in the U.S. ranked Cool Bay Inn among the best. With its name painted on its dark, shingled roof in large white letters, the landmark welcomed home sailors as they returned from sea.

It welcomed Cade now. He glanced back at the mystery woman he was bringing home to his sister. He smiled. Lana the Earth Momma would know what to do with such a tragic creature. Hmm, edit that thought—she'd know how to greet Gen.

* * *

The sun had turned into a molten crimson ball rolling down the edge of the world. Gen marveled at the colors of sea and sky. She had enjoyed works of abstract impressionism in coffee table art books, but the scale of this canvas was the dome of heaven, and the art was beyond the scope of human hand and brush.

A feeling of awe returned that she'd encountered many times since awaking on the beach. Again, she wondered if others felt the same thrill she experienced at the beauty of nature. Maybe they gloried in it quietly, even as she was bowing now in her heart.

Did Cade treasure the sunset? Did he feel tears of joy welling up? She looked at his broad back, muscles rolling under light brown skin with the relaxed strength of a tiger. Cade himself was a work of art. Did he appreciate that?

As if in answer to her thoughts, Gen heard, "Gorgeous sunset." She looked as the girl, Haven, plopped down beside her. "I've never seen one prettier," Haven said, "and I watch them all."

Sun-streaks shot through Haven's wavy brunette hair like lightning bolts. Her skin was rich, smooth caramel, and her lips were puffy slices of plum. Gen thought she looked adorable.

"Cade's my daddy."

Gen smiled. "Yes, I know."

"My Aunt Lana says all the women in Cool Bay think he's pretty hot."

Gen's stomach gave a little twist. "I'll bet they do."

"See the Cool Bay Inn?"

"Yes."

"Aunt Lana owns it, and we all live there. Well, Jimi doesn't stay in the big house; he has his own separate cabin in the back that used to belong to servants."

"It looks lovely."

"Yeah, and I bet my aunt asks you to stay with us for a while. She's always taking in wounded things." The girl's face froze. "I mean…"

"It's okay." Gen's heart sank. "I know what you mean."

"Sorry. I didn't mean to hurt your feelings," Haven said. "I'll even be your friend if you want."

Gen smiled tightly, self-conscious of her over wide mouth. "I'd like that." She reached out and touched Haven's cheek. With one brush of her fingertips, Gen gathered Haven's genetic blueprint. The Abundance thirsted for such essential information, instructions on how to build starfish and dolphins and a gorgeous man and his little girl. It wanted Gen to collect more and more genomes. It urged her to touch every new thing she encountered in the whole living world.

13

On the inner wall of the Level Four Biohazard Isolation Suite, the airlock door unsealed with a sharp *pop!* like a burst balloon. Within its aquarium-like cage, a Florida White rabbit glanced up nervously from its feeding tray. It stopped chewing, stood on its haunches and twitched its pink nose, sniffing. It smelled only dried rabbit chow, water in a drip bottle, a bedding of cedar shavings. But the rabbit sensed danger. Instinct whispered, Death is coming. When the man's shadow passed over the cage, the rabbit had already retreated to cringe against the far glass wall.

Wearing a blue plastic spacesuit, Col. Jack Eberhard busied himself with a digital lock on a liquid nitrogen freezer that stored Gen's tissue specimens. The lock opened to his typed-in code. From the upper rack, he removed one of the stainless steel vials that held 10 cc's of Gen's frozen blood. He checked the date to be sure it was a recent sample containing the latest stage of her evolving mitobots.

He set the vial in a warming bath and waited a few minutes for its contents to thaw and rise to room temperature. Then he drew a syringe full of Gen's blood, moved to the rabbit cage, and shoved his gloved hands through flexible sleeves that reached inside the glass. The rabbit's pink eyes bulged with fright, its long ears flattened along its back. The animal kicked up a confetti storm of cedar shavings while trying to squeeze more tightly into the corner.

"Don't be scared," Eberhard said. "I'm not gonna hurt you. Come to Papa." He shot out his hand and grabbed up his test subject by its soft neck fur. He injected Gen's blood into a fold of loose skin and when the syringe was empty, he let the rabbit scurry back to its corner. There it huddled, shaking so hard the cedar shavings vibrated around it.

Eberhard checked his watch: 0200:12. The lab was vacant except for the two guards of the indoor security crew, one roving and one in the video monitor room. Their presence did not worry Eberhard. After all, he was Project Second Nature's director, and with all his browbeating about security measures and safety drills, he had placed himself above suspicion. Besides, he was a notorious workaholic; so as far as the guards were concerned, he was just busy with more wee-hour lab work.

None would guess the purpose of his private research: He needed to learn how the mitobots functioned in someone other than Gen, so that he might one day inject himself with her miraculous blood. Eberhard wanted to be the new god on the block. Then he would find Gen and exterminate her, and he would remain the *only* god on the block.

But the alchemy to change himself into a god might prove deadly. All merits aside, he knew he was, biologically, an ordinary man, created in the ordinary way. Gen was from the very beginning a unique kind of human being. She had been created, not from sperm and ovum, but from a mitochondrion and ovum. Instead of a human sex cell, the free-swimming mitochondrion in her mother's bloodstream had fused its DNA with an egg cell. The embryo had developed in her mother's womb and Gen had been born—all in a rush of two hours.

Gen's mitobots had demonstrated the ability to read her body's genetic code and repair or renew damaged tissue. He could see no reason that same power would not also work in his body. The mitobots would simply access *his* genetic code and do their job, reassembling his injured structures from scratch, protein by protein, cell by cell, tissue by tissue—and in a matter of minutes.

Eberhard believed this hypothesis. But for all he really knew, the mitobots would disassemble his body and he would end up a gooey crimson puddle on the lab's floor. So, like any good scientist, he needed to experiment on an animal first. What was the Latin phrase? *Fiat experimentum in corpore vili*—Let experiment be made on a worthless body.

The albino rabbit remained huddled in the corner of its cage, but it appeared less panicked. It ears pricked up and its pink nose wriggled. As Eberhard watched and waited, it even seemed to grow drowsy, blinking its eyes. He checked his watch again. Forty-six minutes. At the rate the mitobots replicated, he figured they should be saturating the rabbit's tissues by now.

How long would it take mitobots to become active at full strength in a human body? Gen's ability to heal kept accelerating, but obviously, the mitobots required an incubation period in a new body—look at Toshi's fate. Gen's mitobots had infected him, and the son of a bitch had ended up as chunks of bait on the ocean floor. Eberhard estimated Toshi had been infected seven hours. Probably that was enough build-up time to enable the mitobots to repair broken bones and such, but slamming into the ocean from the clouds? Must've been a real sudden stop, pal.

Eberhard thrust his arms through the flexible sleeves and opened a shoe-box sized compartment inside the rabbit's cage. He drew out a surgeon's electric bone saw. A bulge at the base of its stainless steel handle held a battery pack; the other end of the instrument was equipped with a fine-toothed circular blade the size of a drink coaster.

He flicked the toggle at the base to LOW. The saw whined like a metallic mosquito. He switched to HIGH and the spinning blade gave a shrill scream.

"Okay, little bunny," Eberhard said. "*Now* be scared. Papa's gonna hurt you."

14

Wrapped in her blanket, Gen followed Haven and the others off the boat and down a long dock from the berth at Willingham Marina. The group crossed the beach to the base of Stanton Hill and made their way up wooden stairs that switched back twice along the steep ascent to Cool Bay Inn.

At last, a boardwalk led to the wide wrap-around porch on the bay side of the mansion. Gen counted eight gables jutting from the second story, and a three-story tower topped by an enclosed widow's walk large enough to serve a half-dozen widows. The building's paint scheme reminded Gen of photos she'd seen of classy antique homes in San Francisco. The dominant color was dove gray, but every detail of the trim was painted in a coordinated hue— coral, plum, scarlet and white. The festive colors made even such a large building look cute.

Floor-to-ceiling windows gave every room on the bay side a wide-angle view of the water. Under each ground floor window a box planter sprouted with an assortment of riotously colorful flowers. A vegetable garden stood to one side of the inn, with a smaller herb garden as its sidekick. A jungle of hibiscus, azaleas, and Japanese maples completed the landscaping, with a few gigantic magnolia trees showing off blossoms the size of dinner plates. A mix of floral fragrances perfumed the air.

"Like it?" Haven said.

Gen nodded, smiling. "It's enchanting."

"Wait till you see inside."

A golden retriever pushed out through French doors with ornate iron screens. It scrambled down the porch steps to greet them. Gen noticed the dog had only three legs.

"Tripod!" Haven knelt and gave the dog a hug. Tripod whimpered with joy, licking the girl's face. Gen laughed and scratched the pooch behind the ears, making it shiver with pleasure. Gen trembled, too. She'd read about dogs, but had never met one. Tripod seemed to be a big, furry bundle of love. Plus it felt exquisite—bodily satisfying, like quenching a thirst—whenever she captured a genetic code. And the gratification was more intense when the DNA pattern belonged to a new species she had not yet recorded. Now she added canine genes to her growing library.

Gen looked up as Lana appeared at the top of the porch stairs, wiping her hands on an apron. She was a handsome woman, the feminine mold of her brother, statuesque and strong, with a boldly sculpted face and thick, black hair tumbling over her shoulders like storm clouds.

"What happened?" Lana said, eyeing Gen with concern. "Are you all right, honey?"

In contrast to her athletic looks, Lana's gait seemed hobbled as she held on to the railing and stepped stiffly down the wooden steps. She reached out and put an arm around Gen's shoulders, drew her in for a hug. Her body felt warm even through the wool blanket. Lana's arm brushed Gen's cheek and Gen sighed as she registered the woman's genetic code.

"We found her in the water," Cade said. "Her name's Gen. She's got partial amnesia, I think."

"Gen, what a pretty name," Lana said, "Are you sure you're okay? Have you eaten? Come in, come in."

"I gave her one of your sandwiches," he said. "She devoured it."

Lana smiled. "Well, there's plenty where that came from. Follow me." Lana started up the stairs. Again, her steps seemed awkward compared to the almost regal grace with which she carried herself above the waist. Then Gen saw a flash of metal beneath the hem of the dress and realized Lana wore artificial legs.

"I'll run you a hot bath," Lana said as she walked Gen toward the front door. "You can soak in there while I put on soup and coffee and a hot meal."

"Thank you," Gen said. "Thanks so much."

"How in the world did you end up in the gulf, dear? Did your boat sink?"

"I...uh...I'm not sure."

"Aunt Lana, she was swimming with dolphins! They followed her everywhere, like she was a mermaid."

"Really?" Lana said. "That's so wonderful. I've always loved dolphins. I'd like to hear all about it. But let's get you warmed up and into some clothes. I think I can find something that will fit you."

"That would be great. Thanks."

"And after you've eaten, you can sleep as long as you like. We're closed each July, so we've got plenty of beds— five empty rooms, in fact."

"That's so kind of you," Gen said.

Haven caught Gen's eye and gave an I-told-you-so wink; then she dashed off to play with Tripod.

The others entered the inn and passed through its large foyer. It seemed that every available surface held a vase with a flower arrangement. Honey-colored wood paneled the downstairs walls, and the air smelled like flowers and lemony wood polish. The mahogany banister leading up the stairs was especially lovely, carved in a serpentine pattern of grape vines and leaves.

Lana led Gen through a downstairs guest room into the room's bathroom. An antique porcelain-and-iron tub crouched on four lion paws atop red oak floorboards.

"There's plenty of hot water," Lana said. "The snowbirds have flown the coop. Take a long shower or a hot bath. Towels are under there. I'll lay out some clothes on the bed."

The idea of a long, hot soak sounded to Gen like a blessing from the spa of heaven. "This is so great," she said. "I really appreciate all you're doing for me."

Lana's smiled brightly. "No trouble, sugar. You've been through a lot. Make yourself at home."

"Your brother told me you're the nicest person in the world," Gen said. "I see what he means."

"Cade said that? What a sweetie." Her eyes registered delight. "Well, it takes one to know one."

*   *   *

"So what do you think happened out there?" Jimi said.

"I haven't a clue," Cade said.

"More coffee?" Lana got up to refill her cup.

"No thanks," Cade said. "Now that I've finally warmed up, I'd like to have a beer."

"Me, too," Jimi said. "A couple Buds, please." He stood. "Want some help?"

"Sit down. I'll be right back."

The trio gathered around a circular wrought-iron table outside the kitchen on the porch overlooking the bay. Lana brought back two beers in green glass bottles. She wore a chromium-yellow summer dress with spaghetti straps and Cade noticed the way Jimi's eyes followed her breasts as she bent slightly to hand him his beer. Sweat trickled down the cold glass.

"Remember that plane crash?" she said. "Business jet. Went down in the bay. Maybe Gen's a survivor."

Cade shook his head. "I doubt it. That crash, what? A month and a half ago? You think she's been floating out there all that time?"

137

"Wait," Jimi said, "say she had a life raft. Right up to before we found her."

"But a plane crash?" Cade said. "She's not even scratched."

"Maybe it ditched, hit the bay flat. She had time to get out in a life raft."

Cade scratched stubble on his square chin with a thumbnail. "Then she'd have to have supplies to survive five, six weeks. And she's not even sunburned."

"Well, if her boat sank, someone's boat is going to turn up missing sooner or later," Lana said.

"I called Taylor's, Willingham's and The Palms," Jimi said. "It wasn't any boat from here."

Lana smiled. "Good detective work."

"Comes from reading Nancy Drew."

Cade chuckled. "Hey, I used to read those, too."

"Nancy Drew, the Girl Detective?"

"Yeah. I read Lana's old ones. She must've had the whole Nancy Drew library."

"Not quite," she said, "but probably a few dozen."

"That's funny, I read *my* sisters' copies," Jimi said. "Kept it secret, because I thought boys weren't supposed to read Nancy Drew."

"Same here," Cade said, and looked at Lana. "I don't even think you knew."

She smiled. "I knew."

"Wonder how many boys around the country grew up as closet Nancy Drew freaks?" Jimi said.

"Hundreds," Cade said. "Thousands."

"Another double standard," Lana said.

"What?" Jimi said.

"It was okay for girls to read The Hardy Boys," she said. "But not for boys to read Nancy Drew."

"Oh. True," Jimi said. "But I kind of got off on her cardigan sweater sets, white gloves and heels. Cade, what was your favorite outfit Nancy wore?"

Cade laughed and eyed his sister. "Why'd you keep those old Nancy Drews? You kept them for years after you'd read them."

"Oh, I was thirteen or fourteen when I outgrew them, and you were still a tyke, but I figured you'd enjoy them when you got older. And you did, right?"

His mouth fell open. "You're saying you planted them on me?"

She winked. "At last, the truth can be told."

Jimi studied Lana with admiration. She caught his gaze and looked away, sipped her coffee.

A thudding boom made the three swivel their heads toward a construction site a half mile away at the north end of the bay. Bulldozers were clearing pine forest as part of the development of a world-class golf and tennis resort. It made Cade almost physically ill to watch them tear up wildlife habitats to build condos for jet-setters. But there wasn't a damn thing he could do.

The three sat quietly for a while, unhappily reminded of the encroaching development. After a moment, Lana said, "What's wrong with Gen? Her face?"

"My guess, a birth defect," Cade said. "Damn cruel one. Did you see how pretty the rest of her is?"

"Yeah. And I figured you'd noticed."

He shrugged. "She was naked, couldn't help it."

"She's built like a dancer," Jimi said. "Slender, and all muscle."

"You couldn't help it either, huh?" Lana said.

Jimi opened his mouth to say something, then glanced down.

Lana laughed. "Good grief, I was only teasing."

139

Jimi looked up at her. "I'm not looking for a perfect body. I don't need that."

Lana blushed and turned away. Her complexion was darker than Cade's, but he noticed the patch of color that appeared over each cheekbone when blood rushed to her face. He wondered if Jimi could tell she was blushing. Then she casually lifted the hem of her dress and undid the prosthesis on her right leg so she could rub the stump below the knee.

She refastened the artificial limb and stood up. "I'm going to go upstairs and lie down for awhile, guys. I feel funny. Kinda woozy."

"You all right?" Jimi said.

She nodded. "I'm fine. But my head's buzzing like I've had a couple glasses of wine."

"I could rub your temples or something. Be glad to."

She patted his arm. "Thanks. I just need a nap." She left the breakfast nook.

After she walked away, Jimi turned to Cade with a helpless expression and sighed.

"Give it time," Cade said. "She likes you a lot."

"But..."

"Trust me. I know my sister. If she didn't like you, she wouldn't be so self-conscious about her legs." He nodded toward the empty chair. "That little move she pulled just now? That was to remind you she has stumps—hold them right under your nose."

"Like I'm going to forget. It doesn't matter to me."

"It matters to her," Cade said. He swigged the cold beer, gazed out over the bay. He looked at Jimi for a moment and frowned slightly, took another swig. "Did I ever tell you Lana was Homecoming Queen at our high school?"

"No. But I don't doubt it."

140

"That, despite the fact that most folks thought of our parents' marriage as some kind of crime."

"Must've been tough on you guys."

"Tougher on her than me. I didn't come along for another ten years. Things had started to change for the better. But she was born in 1961. Hell, the South was still segregated."

"Man, I can imagine." Jimi shook his head. "No, I probably can't, really."

"Anyway, she was so beautiful that nobody could pretend she wasn't the prettiest girl on campus without claiming it was a school for the blind. So they voted her to be Homecoming Queen and her photo ran in a local rag. Next thing you know, some rich lady at The Palms, sees the photo and says, 'Wow!' Turns out she owns a modeling agency in New York. She offered Lana a contract."

"Really. A model."

"She was seventeen, had a full scholarship to FSU for gymnastics. My parents insisted she not sign with the modeling agency until she finished college. But they did let Richard Avedon shoot some preliminary photos."

"Avedon!"

"Yep. Great stuff."

"Holy shit. Avedon. I'd love to see those shots."

"She burned them."

"Nawww. Come on...*damn*."

Cade sipped beer and stared at the pale pink wash the sun painted over the water, still lighting the western horizon from below. A trawler sat just beyond the mouth of the bay, boom nets silhouetted in the twilight like outspread wings. "Her junior year in college, she had a serious boyfriend, Mike Garcia. A more upbeat and hard-working guy was never born. He and Lana weren't engaged, but everyone figured it was just a matter of time. The day she told him she didn't like cigarette smoke, he quit his pack-a-

141

day habit; the day she mentioned she loved roses, he planted American Beauties outside her bedroom window." He took another sip of beer. "Mike had become a partner in our dad's salvage business and the two of them had just struck it rich."

"They'd found the ship?"

Cade nodded. "The *San Pedro*. I was ten." He remembered how thrilled his dad and Mike had been when they'd begun bringing up Mexican opals and emeralds from the wreck of the small freighter. "They'd brought up maybe half of her cargo when they drowned."

Jimi shook his head. "God, that had to be so hard on you and Lana. And your mother, of course."

Cade nodded. "That was just before her senior year. Lana actually stayed in school. And she still had her modeling contract waiting." He tilted the bottle to his lips and caught the last cold drops. "It was only a few months later that she and my mom had *their* accident. What a year...what a goddam year."

"Lana never talks about it," Jimi said. "You don't either, for that matter."

Cade held the empty bottle to one eye like a telescope and squinted through the green glass. The whole world turned sickening green. He shuddered and set down the bottle on the wrought-iron table.

"They were on their way to Tallahassee," he said. "A cement truck crossed the median and rammed their van head-on. Ford Econoline—you know, flat front-end—impact threw my mom through the windshield, seatbelt, seat, and all. She died instantly, they say. As if they know such things. Lana's legs...no hope."

Cade swallowed past a lump in his throat. "So she never finished college. And needless to say, they didn't want her at the modeling agency." He frowned and stared hard into the deepening gloom over the bay. "She came home from the hospital in a wheelchair. Started taking care of me. And I was an ungrateful shit to her. When I wasn't hiding somewhere, crying, I was so pissed off I wanted to murder the world."

Cade looked at Jimi. "Bro', I'm telling you all this for a reason. So you'll understand my sister."

"Sure. I'm with you, go on."

"She went through rehab, learned to walk again on fake legs. Must've been five, six years before she got up the courage to get romantically involved with someone. And the guy turned out to be a real bastard—Franklin Hauser, asshole still lives over in The Palms."

"Isn't that the jerk with the cigarette boat, *Miss Behavin'*?"

"That's our guy, Frankie. Bad news. He took advantage of her generosity, borrowed money he never paid back, and ended up dumping her. Then she found out he'd been using her loans for coke parties where he hired call girls from Miami for him and his pals."

"Every time I see his boat go blasting by in the No Wake zone, I wish I had a rocket launcher."

"You and me both. Anyway. One night, I hear crying. I knock on her door, see her looking at her portfolio photos by the fireplace. I think she burned them that night."

Jimi shook his head sadly. "God. But she's still beautiful. And she's got heart and soul and—"

"Jimi, you're a fine man. I'd be proud to call you my brother-in-law. But Lana...she hasn't dated since she burned those pictures. That tells you something about her self-esteem when it comes to...to intimacy...you know."

Jimi nodded. "I hear you."

"So my advice is, stick around, be her good friend and be patient. I see her struggling with her feelings for you. That's a positive sign. Like I said, I know she likes you. A lot."

"She said that?"

"Doesn't have to say it. I know my sister."

"Can you talk you to her for me?"

"I could, I suppose. Not that it'll do any good. These things take their own time."

"I guess so. But between my shyness and her holding back...we're both gonna turn gray," he said. "Hey, you think our age difference worries her? You could tell her I'm not hung up on that."

Cade laughed softly.

"Well, she's six years older. Some women would balk at that."

"Man, if you can accept the fact that she's fuckin' missing both legs, I doubt she's gonna worry she's too old for you."

"Right."

They sat without speaking for a long while. In the shoreless void above the bay, the Milky Way sparkled like diamond dust strewn on a jeweler's black velvet cloth. The trawler's running lights winked red and green in the dark. Cade thought he could smell the boat's deisel engine fumes, even at a mile away. Gulls cried to each other over the gush and retreat of breakers.

Finally, Jimi broke the silence. "So, man, what's happening with *you* and the ladies?" he said. "From what I've seen this summer, you've become a celibate monk."

Cade shrugged. "More or less."

"My first seasons here, you were chasing everything that wore a skirt. I was scared to take you to the Scottish festival in Killearn—all those men in kilts."

"Yeah. Well, that gets stale, too."

"Having sex with men in kilts?"

"Being a player."

"Ouch. Don't tell me these things. I keep wishing I could be more like you."

"No, man. Really. It's not satisfying," Cade glanced down at his crotch. "Mister Willy is on recuperative rest while I decide what I truly want out of a relationship."

Jimi looked down at his own crotch. "I'm worried Señor has been on sabbatical too long. He's forgotten how to tango."

"Nah," Cade said. "Just like riding a bike."

"Easy for you to say. You've been a test rider for every major manufacturer. I've ridden just two bikes in my whole life," Jimi said, then laughed. "If you don't count the ol' unicycle."

"Yeah, but Jimi, you're…" Cade hesitated.

"I'm what?"

"I don't know. Wise. Mature. Smarter than me."

"Lonely. Lovesick. Scrawnier than you."

"I want what my mother and father felt for each other. They defied everyone because they trusted their hearts. And they were happy. That's my fondest memory of my folks, their happiness together."

"Woo. Sounds to me like you're going through that change," Jimi said. "What do they call it? *Adulthood*?"

"About time," Cade said. "I'll be thirty next month."

"So will you talk to Lana? Tell her I love her."

"She knows, Jimi. She knows."

The phone rang in the kitchen. Cade carried the empty beer bottles into the house and stacked them in a recycle bin in a kitchen closet. He jumped across the room and grabbed the phone on the fourth ring, just before the message machine switched on.

"Cool Bay Inn, Cade speaking, may I help you?"

"This is Weston Fairchild."

Hearing that voice stunned Cade speechless.

*　　　*　　　*

145

Lana reclined on her antique brass bed while Haven sat at her head, massaging her aching temples. "Oh, pumpkin, you are so good at that."

"It's kind of fun. I like giving massages."

"I know you do, I'm so lucky."

Jimi had offered earlier to rub her head, but Lana had not wanted to invite his intimate touch. Not that she didn't like Jimi MacGregor. Quite the contrary. He was a great guy; brilliant, funny and kind. Over the years, she'd fantasized often about being with him romantically, but she hid those feelings from everyone, especially Jimi. It was not about him; she just wasn't ready to be sexually involved with anyone. She wasn't sure if she could ever let her heart be that vulnerable again.

"So what do you think of Gen?" Haven said.

"She's very...unusual."

"I think she's incredibly ugly, but I can't help but like her. Wish I had her eyes."

"The instant I saw her, it made me think of Ganesha," Lana said. "Have you ever heard that story?"

"Nope. Tell me. I like your stories."

"This one's a Hindu tale," Lana said. "The goddess Shakti gave birth to a boy, Ganesha, while his father, Lord Shiva, was away on a journey. One day, Shakti asked her son to guard the entrance to the bathhouse while she went inside to bathe. Ganesha dutifully stood post at the door.

"At that moment, his father returned home to find an unknown boy who refused to let him into the bathhouse to see his wife. The brave boy did not budge in the face of Shiva's angry threats. Well, Lord Shiva, The Destroyer, was not known for his gentleness, and he finally hoisted his jewel-encrusted, ritual club and swung it with all his might, shattering the boy's head to smithereens."

"Oooh, gross."

"When he went inside and told his wife about the insolent boy, she screamed that he had just beheaded their own son."

"Yuck."

"Shiva raced around in a panic, seeking a new head for Ganesha. He came upon a royal elephant and ripped off its head to fuse upon the bloody stump of Ganesha's neck."

"Freaky," Haven said. "But... wait. The boy wouldn't have the same brain—he wouldn't be the same person, Shiva's son."

"Well, Hindu's believe the real person is the immortal soul and not the body. The soul only dwells *within* the body—in the heart, not the brain."

"Oh, so even with an elephant's head...?"

"Same soul, Shiva's son," Lana said. "Ganesha grew up to have the body of a man and the head of an elephant. He's called The Remover of Obstacles, and he's one of the most beloved gods of the Hindus."

"Weird. Cool story," Haven said. "I think I've seen a picture of him, maybe, in an art book at the library. I remember, like, a fat-bellied guy with an elephant's head and trunk, holding different stuff in his hands, like flowers and things."

"That's him."

"And I think he had four arms, maybe."

"Yep. That's Ganesha."

Haven's warm hands moved down to Lana's shoulders and kneaded the muscles with surprising strength. The massage felt wonderful, but Lana still had a headache and an odd buzzing sensation in her body.

"Now I see why Gen made you think of that story," Haven said. "How does a person get born so deformed? I mean, just her head and not the rest of her body?"

"I don't know. But maybe we can think of her as a kindred spirit to Ganesha. A magical person in our house."

"She *is* magical, Lana. You should have seen her with the dolphins. It's like she was one of them."

"Funny thing about that," Lana said. "If you put Gen into the story, you know, in Ganesha's role, and had to guess what head Shiva snatched up to replace her original head, what would you guess?"

"I'd say… That's right—a dolphin!"

"Exactly. What I would say, too."

*   *   *

Cade stood in the kitchen clutching the phone while an unpleasant shock passed through him as if he'd stepped on a sea skate. The voice on the other end of the line belonged to his grandfather, Weston Fairchild.

Years before Cade was born, Weston had disowned his only child, Elaine—Cade and Lana's mother—for the crime of loving a man of the wrong skin color. The old tycoon wanted nothing to do with his grandchildren, and Cade had never once spoken to his grandfather before now. This could only be about their land. Weston coveted the Stanton Hill acreage for his new golf resort. Several times in the past two years, always via a third-party, he had offered bigger and bigger truckloads of cash to buy it, but Cade and Lana had refused. Now he was speaking in person. He didn't give up easily.

"I would like you and Lana to join me for supper tomorrow night."

Right. Fuckhead. "Look, this is obviously about the land," Cade said. "Our answer hasn't changed, and a new offer is not going to sway us. We don't want to sell, not for any amount of money."

"You're mistaken. This is *not* about a new offer for your land," he said. "I have some very important

148

information to tell you. I could have my lawyer deliver a letter, but I think you'll both want to hear this in person."

Jesus. What the hell was he talking about? Cade had no idea, but coming from Old Man Fairchild, himself, on the phone, it worried him.

"Which shall it be?" Weston said.

The thought of sitting down to supper with his estranged grandfather didn't exactly pique Cade's appetite. "Look, you don't need to wine and dine me just to tell me your news. How about if I pop over after breakfast tomorrow?"

"As you wish. And Lana?"

"Lana prefers to stay close to home. Unless you want to come here to us, it will just be me."

"Fine. I'll expect you mid-morning." Weston hung up without another word.

Cade replaced the phone in the cradle and blew out a long sigh. Nothing about this felt right.

He decided to keep it to himself for now. No use getting Lana upset until he found out what Weston was up to.

15

Gen awoke in an antique poster bed, her body indenting a cloud-soft feather mattress. The bedroom was quiet except for a lone cricket who played his solo mating song from the clothes closet. Through a tall window overlooking the shore, she watched dawn light glinting like pink gold on the bay's glassy surface. She dimly heard the sighs and whispers of tiny breakers washing the sand. Seagulls cried, and somewhere to the south several dogs barked a sermon; one calling, the others responding.

Gen slipped out of bed and padded barefoot across the honey oak floor to the window for a better view. She wore a men's extra-large denim work shirt that draped below her knees. The faded blue fabric had been washed so often it felt softer than linen. When Gen buttoned it up last night, after the world's most gratifying hot shower, she had guessed the shirt was Cade's and the mere thought gave her goose bumps, imagining the soft denim to be Cade's arms wrapping her torso. Her belly grew taut with sudden desire.

She swallowed down the emotion and let out a trembly breath. The feelings were new and strange and overwhelming. She had loved Toshi, but she had never felt lust. Good grief. That's what it was: lust. She was warm and slick between her legs.

This is crazy, she told herself. You don't even know him. And it's hopeless anyway; you're so ugly he thinks you're deformed. She touched her elongated face. She could understand that Cade found her hideous.

Morning glories in the box planter under the window sill unfurled like purple flags to salute the morning sun, rising from behind the inn. Dawn was dazzling, but a heaviness squeezed her chest. She pressed her hand to her heart. Was it beating okay? It ached as if it were too full of blood. She didn't know she was crying until a tear splashed her hand.

Sniffling, she wiped at her eyes. Here I am, trapped again in loneliness. Toshi gave up his life to help me escape from Redstone Laboratories. But I'm isolated still. Set apart by my strangeness. Must I always feel cut off from people?

Swimming with the dolphins had been the happiest days of her life. When she thought of Little Squirt the dam in her chest burst and the tears gushed down. God, she missed Little Squirt. She tried to say his name in dolphin language, but the clicks hurt her throat.

Why hadn't she stayed with her true friends?

Cade. His beautiful face, his masculine aura, had beguiled Gen as surely as the first sight of Prince Eric had captivated Ariel, the Little Mermaid.

A fairy tale, but the story had changed drastically. The Little Mermaid had been beautiful when she washed ashore as the speechless young woman. Gen could hardly be more gruesome. Oh, but then, that was another fairy tale, wasn't it? A new twist on Beauty and the Beast.

I can't go on with this face, she thought. I've got to become fully human, or go back to living among the dolphins.

But she couldn't return her face to its normal shape without exposing her identity to Cade and the others. They would find out who she *really* was. Different is bad; profoundly different is terrifying. She remembered how the lab technicians and soldiers worked around her with constant nervous glances, as if they feared she might suddenly dissolve the glass walls of her prison and suck out their brains through their nostrils.

The Beast. That's me. Even when I look completely human. The idea of Cade fearing her made her sad in all four chambers of her heart. She rubbed her chest again. Her

151

heart still thumped, but the poor muscle definitely felt close to breaking.

She wondered if there was any possibility of leaving, returning her face to its human form, and then coming back to Cade. Yeah, right. As if he wouldn't recognize me by my eyes. Everybody talked about her eyes; even the men who were scared of her. Toshi once read her the romantic poetry of a Japanese swordmaster named Tesshu. He told Gen that Tesshu had searched all his life for the perfection of beauty, and would have considered his quest complete if he had gazed just once upon her violet eyes.

As deeply as Gen cared about Cade's reaction to discovering the truth about her, she admitted there was a far more serious problem. Eberhard. She remembered the two fighter jets tracking her through the sky like hunting hounds locked on a scent. Eberhard would not give up the chase, and he had the support of the U.S. military to help him track and corner his prey.

"I have to leave here," she told herself, "for their sake." To protect Cade and the others from the danger that would trail her wherever she fled.

"I *have* to leave," she repeated, more forcefully. But the idea of leaving made her feel unbearably empty and lost. She loved her dolphin pod, but she wished more than anything to stay with Cade. And with Haven and Lana, and Jimi, too. To be human among human friends.

She wanted to stay.

She had to leave.

"I hate fairy tales!" she whispered harshly.

While her insides churned with conflict and despair, light continued to wash over the world. A thick grove of bamboo, which in the dark had looked like a hunch-backed giant, now reflected green and gold. The sea and sky lent their colors to each other generously. The Earth looked new and resplendent. Which made Gen recall the other reason

152

she had chosen to leave the dolphin pod and go ashore with Cade. She felt compelled to connect with *these* living things, in the realm of sun and rain and soil.

It took a moment to realize that the bird statue in the corner of her view, standing motionless at the edge of an ornamental water garden, was alive. She recognized the bird as a great blue heron. Its color exactly matched the slate-blue of the pond's liner. It poised, stone-still, on ridiculously tall legs, its snake-like neck curved in an *S* against its powerful breast. In a blur, its neck shot out like a whip and its long, thin beak snatched a small frog from the pond. The heron threw back its head, gulped and swallowed. Gen saw the lump of frog travel down what looked like three feet of soft tubing.

Gen leapt toward the bedroom door before she even realized what she was going to do. She needed to touch the bird. She ran through the hallway into the foyer, yanked open the front door, and was outside, bounding down the porch steps.

The heron spread broad wings, beating the air, *whuff-whuff-whuff*, and took off. It pumped hard to climb over a stand of palms, then banked and swam through the air with long, graceful strokes, neck tucked tight and yellow legs held straight out behind like yardsticks.

The intensity of Gen's emotions surprised her. As she watched the bird disappear, a desperate sense of loss clutched her chest; then, when she searched the ground at the pond's edge and spotted a large slate-blue feather, she sighed loudly with relief.

She picked up the feather and immediately drank into her cells the heron's essence. The pleasure made her gasp. But the satisfaction lasted only a moment.

Hunger. That's what drove her. Not hunger of the belly, but a deeply interior need to record the essence of life forms. It was not fulfilling simply to gaze upon the

153

beautiful creatures of the world. The animals and plants that appeared to her eyes were mere vessels for the genes, the inner code. Individual creatures served to transport and transmit genes, while the genes themselves stored the vast memory of entire species. A simple touch enabled Gen to access the ancient archives at the core of each living thing.

Her desire to touch seemed insatiable, yet it was not like the craving of an addict for a drug. It resembled more the longing one feels when separated from a lover; the soul-felt appetite for the loved one to *come home*. Gen felt as if her cells were crying out to her missing sisters and brothers—all the creatures of the world—and she must gather the essence of every living thing to become, herself, complete.

Gen waded into the pond and knelt in cold, slippery mud on the bottom. She held out her arms and swished her spread fingertips through the fishy water. Myriad lifeforms swarmed everywhere she touched. A thrill communicated through her cells. Molecular conversations sparkled in her bloodstream and when she closed her eyes, a blizzard of colored lights danced behind her eyelids.

Instead of hands, I wish I had millions of tentacles.

The water fizzed around her hands, which softened like molten plastic and reformed, branching into dozens of tentacles that further branched into hundreds more, then into thousands, until her countless new "fingertips" had become invisibly fine threads. She harvested the genetic essence of frogs and fishes, lilies and lotuses, grasses, water beetles, dragonfly larvae, snails, algae and countless bacteria. Gen breathed into the bottom of her lungs, savoring the delicious connections at the root of life.

The electric hum in her cells became a musical white-noise; a blend of wind chimes, flutes, bees, harps and waterfalls. She shivered in quiet ecstasy.

154

The Abundance was trying again to communicate with her brain, chattering away in a chemical language of flavors that changed too rapidly to follow. The microscopic beings were explaining their mission. Gen understood little of it, but *no harm* was the now-familiar message she tasted most strongly. Whatever their ultimate purpose, gathering genetic codes was only the first stage.

She learned something else. The sentient cells were not all of one kind. A variety of specialized beings had evolved: genetic code reader/writers, messenger/transporters, assembler/dissemblers, scout/mappers, and translator/ambassadors. The ambassadors had linked with her neurons and were firing a thousand flavors each second.

A girl called to Gen. It took Gen a second to realize it was not happening inside her head. She turned to find Haven darting down the porch steps of the inn. Tripod, the golden retriever, ran by her side, barking with joy. The sun hugged Haven with radiant arms and the sea breeze combed its fingers through her soft hair. The girl's beauty made Gen suddenly self-conscious. With a shudder, she realized she now owned not just the face, but the *hands* of a monster. She shoved her tentacles beneath the mud just as Haven arrived.

Haven stared. "What are you doing in the pond?"

It took a moment for Gen to find her voice. "I was...I wanted to cool off."

"Huh?" The girl gave her a puzzled frown. Gen couldn't think of more to say. The dog whimpered and shuffled its feet with eagerness to join her in the pond.

"Tripod, no!" Haven said; then to Gen: "This pond's for *fish*. We've got a great swimming hole, with a diving board and raft and...hey, what's wrong?"

Gen was breathing hard, straining to make her hands return to normal. She kept the tentacles buried in the mud, willing them to change, but the melting sensation did not come. The Ambassadors were still excitedly signaling her brain.

Listen to me! she told them in her mind. Change these tentacles back into hands!

"Come on out," Haven said. "My aunt's going to make us pancakes for breakfast. You'll have to take a shower, the pond's yucky. You got green scum in your hair."

Hands. I need hands. Gen tasted a fresh barrage of flavors. Apparently, the Ambassadors had just learned to interpret the information processed by Gen's visual cortex, so in effect, they could now "see" through her eyes. It was a tremendous breakthrough for their society. It enabled them to begin to relate to and comprehend the external, macro-world.

That's great. I'm happy for you fellas. Now please change these tentacles back into hands. Hurry.

No fizzing. No melting.

"Uh, Haven, can you bring me a towel?" Gen hoped to get rid of the girl for a minute. "Or a bathrobe? All I'm wearing is this shirt."

"That's all right. Nobody cares. Aunt Lana even let's us go skinny dipping in the swimming hole all summer, as long as there's nobody around who isn't family."

"Good for you guys." Gen thought hard: What did I do to change my hands into tentacles in the first place? She had simply *wished* for tentacles, she remembered. But not from her head. The wish had come on the crest of a wave of emotion that surged from her longing to touch more than two hands could manage. So emotion was the key to controlling The Abundance. They probably responded to neurotransmitters or hormones that strong emotions squirted into her nervous system.

She tried to emote, to create a zeal for hands.

156

"Gen, you all right? You look sick. Should I run and get my mom?"

"No, no, I'm fine...uh...just a moment. I'm getting out."

Cade. He was the one she really wanted to touch, to knead, to stroke; not with tentacles but with a woman's loving hands. She wanted long, slender, tapered fingers to trace the velvety river of black curls that started at his deeply muscled chest and disappeared below the waistline of his cut-offs. Ooh. Yes. God, yes. Let there be hands!

Tripod barked. On the bottom of the pond, the wet mud boiled.

16

Cade watched his sister at work in Cool Bay Inn's large kitchen. He watched Jimi watching his sister. Lana wore a sleeveless white T-shirt over navy blue drawstring pants and white sneakers. She crisscrossed the kitchen from stove to table, making pancakes and homemade pear-applesauce to smear on top.

Jimi's love for Lana may as well have been painted on his face in Day-Glo colors. Cade really felt for his friend. The guy had it bad. He'd gotten to know Jimi well over the course of five summers, assisting with the dolphin research. Jimi was a brilliant marine biologist, he made good money as an FSU research professor and nature writer, and he had a big, kind heart. He'd make a great brother-in-law; if only Lana would look up from her cooking and feed that hungry look on his face with kisses.

Jimi and Lana were a study in physical contrasts. Jimi's Scottish ancestors must have dwelt in misty highlands without direct sunlight; the man's freckled skin was as pale as fresh cream. He blistered if he stayed in the sun for a half-hour. Lana's smooth skin was light brown like milk chocolate; and after a summer of swimming and gardening, she tanned without burning to a rich, dark chocolate tone.

Jimi was skinny—"wiry," if you wanted to be generous. Lana displayed an Amazonian build, muscular and athletic; even her face was chiseled and angular. Cade had once seen a photo in a coffee-table art book of a classic Greek statue of Athena; it was his sister's portrait, without the wooly braids. If Jimi stood at rigid attention, Lana could pick him up like a javelin and hurl him across the front yard.

Jimi was of average height, about 5-foot-9. Before her accident, Lana had stood barefoot just under 6 feet, an unheard of height for a female gymnast. But being the tallest competitor at every meet hadn't stopped her from winning several collegiate tournaments. Now, artificial limbs made her taller still, because the special shoes had built-up soles to cushion her springless step.

At first, Cade wondered if his skinny friend might not be hankering after more woman than he could handle; after all, isn't it best if proportions match down there? That was before he'd seen Jimi naked. Cade had called him "Babar" for a while after that.

Jimi's and Lana's personalities contrasted too, although less starkly than their bodies. Jimi had not begun his science career in marine biology; his lifelong fascination with the search for extraterrestrial intelligence had led him to earn a doctorate in astronomy and to spend a couple years with the SETI program at NASA. But in his late twenties, he fell into soul-searching after reading about the slaughter of endangered blue fin whales. "If we can't respect the rights of other intelligent—perhaps even sapient—species right here on Earth, why the hell are we trying to contact aliens, light years away?" He switched his research field to marine mammals and became one of the world's leading experts on whales and dolphins. His popular science book, *Water Brothers*, had been a N.Y. Times bestseller. Then his four-part TV documentary of the same name boosted him to celebrity status. The Washington Post called him "the Carl Sagan of cetaceans." Most folks in Cool Bay called him "the dolphin guy."

Lana, by contrast, had dropped out of college after the auto wreck and led a relatively private life, running Cool Bay Inn. She had once loved to read and travel, and in particular, had devoured romances. But after the loss of her legs, followed by her fiancée's betrayal, she'd given up such tales as too hopeful, and had cloistered herself at the inn. Not that she didn't still like people. But she preferred to meet them on home territory, where she felt safe.

Jimi MacGregor was a Jimi Hendrix freak. In fact, his real first name was James, but his teen-age friends had started calling him Jimi because of his uncanny impressions of Hendrix: playing Fender Stratocaster left-handed, plucking the strings with his teeth, playing the guitar behind his back and straddling the instrument while it burned with lighter fluid—all pantomimed on air-guitar, for MacGregor himself admitted he had barely enough musical talent to play the radio.

Lana loved music and had a fine contralto voice. As she cooked one of her fabulous meals, guests at the inn were likely to overhear from the kitchen a spontaneous aria, or some funky rhythm and blues, or a jazzy improv, for Lana enjoyed every kind of music. She liked Jimi Hendrix and owned a boxed-set of Hendrix CDs, which thrilled Jimi MacGregor. He was less thrilled when she put on a Dolly Parton CD or a world music collection that included Mongolian nasal-flute music.

They both had in common their deep love and respect for dolphins—and unless Cade did not read his sister as well as he believed he could—a love and respect for each other. Trouble was, Lana had been badly hurt in the accident, and while she was still on the rebound from that loss, a lover she had trusted had dumped her. She never managed to dig her way out of that cave-in. Now she had Haven. She had Cade. She had Tripod and her pets, and her beloved Cool Bay Inn. She could do without the risk of intimacy.

"Daddy, you like your pancakes?" Haven said, with her mouth full. Her chin was shiny with maple syrup.

"Mmmm. Delicious."

"You usually wolf down two or three by the time I finish my first."

"I was thinking."

"'bout what?"

"About how nosy you can be."

She wrinkled up her face and stuck out her tongue.

Jimi got up from the table. "I'm gonna go put on 'Music To Eat Pancakes By.'" He took a step toward the kitchen doorway and his expression froze. Cade turned part way in his chair to see Gen enter. She wore one of Lana's sleeveless blouses, a couple sizes too large, and some shorts, bunched around her waist with a cotton belt. Her unencumbered breasts swayed slightly as she walked to the table and sat down.

For a moment, everyone stared. Beautiful body, monstrous face; it was hard not to gawk. Then Lana flashed a warm smile. "Good morning, Gen. Have some pancakes." With a spatula, she flopped two golden-brown cakes from a skillet onto Gen's plate.

"Thank you," Gen said.

Jimi left the room and in a moment the ardent voice and guitar of Jimi Hendrix sang through two speakers mounted above the kitchen cabinets: *Well she's walking through the clouds, with a circus mind that's running wild...*

Gen closed her eyes and tilted up her face to the speakers like a thirsty orchid drinking rain. Jimi returned and Cade nodded toward Gen. "A fellow Hendrix fan."

Gen opened her eyes with a look of astonishment. "What kind of music is that?"

"Jimi Hendrix," Jimi said. "Never heard him?"

She shook her head. "I've never heard anything like it."

"'Little Wing,'" Jimi said, "it's my favorite Hendrix tune."

161

Gen held her breath, listening; moved by the music. When the heavy-amped guitar solo began, Lana leaned back against the stove, rubbing her temples with her fingertips.

"Hey, I'm sorry," Jimi said. "Headache? I'll go turn it off."

Lana nodded. "I hate to spoil the Hendrix party..."

Jimi dashed out of the kitchen and Hendrix's guitar cut off in the middle of a cry of passion.

"It's not a headache," Lana said. "Feels more like a bug. I was a bit feverish last night, and now I've got this humming in my ears, like when you stand near an electric transformer? That sound."

Jimi returned to the table.

"Hope you don't have a cold, Aunt Lana," Haven said. "Summer colds really suck."

Lana shot her a look.

"What?"

"Watch your mouth, please."

"What'd I say?"

"Oh, you're so innocent."

"Everybody says 'suck.'"

"*Everybody* says it? The Queen of England?"

Gen spoke up in a perfect upper-class Eton accent: "Jeeves, have we no other edibles in the manor? These crumpets really *suck*."

The others looked at her for a second, then burst out laughing.

Gen gave a shy smile, and Cade suppressed a shudder at her overwide mouth and big teeth. Her bare shoulders displayed flawless skin of a deep, caramel coloring; muscles sculpted her slender arms; feminine curves swelled her chest and hips.

Cade could not erase his first vision of her, standing nude on the deck of his boat. She had been like two poles of a powerful magnet, attracting and repelling him at once. Gen was both the loveliest and ugliest woman he'd ever seen, depending on whether his eyes took in her body below the neck or above.

Again, he felt terribly sorry for her and wondered if it would have been easier to have been born altogether deformed, rather than to live as a war of opposites. He resolved again not to pity her, but to be her friend. Over time, he would grow used to her appearance.

Haven reached out and gave Gen's hand a squeeze. "Try my aunt's pancakes, they're awesome."

But Gen stopped still, and the look of joyous wonder returned to her face. She had spotted a macaw in a birdcage on a screened porch off the kitchen. She leaped up from the table, nearly knocking over her chair in her haste to get to the parrot.

Haven looked at Cade and he shrugged. "Guess she really likes birds. And Hendrix."

"Careful," Haven called after her. "His name is Snapper, and he bites. Hard."

The green-yellow-and-blue parrot flapped one wing; its other wing missing. Snapper's original owner had found the bird pinned on the carpet by his tomcat and had brought the mess of blood and feathers to Lana to nurse back to health. Cade had carved a lower beak out of a piece of cow horn and glued the prosthesis to the broken stub. The owner no longer wanted the damaged parrot, so Lana kept Snapper, and the bird had thrived.

Cade watched Gen stick her fingers through the bars to stroke the bird's feathers. "Look out!" he said, jumping up. Gen shut her eyes in apparent pleasure.

"Uh-oh," Haven said.

Snapper cocked his head back and made a diving attack on her hand, crunching down with the same force he used to crack Brazil nuts. Cade was at her side a few

163

seconds too late. Gen opened her eyes and refocused on the outer world.

"I'm so sorry," he said. "Here, let me see your hand."

Snapper had bitten Cade twice in the past, and both times, the beak had broken his skin and drawn blood. He expected to see the familiar "V" mark from the parrot's sharp beak on Gen's flesh. But when he tenderly lifted her hand to examine the wound, her skin flashed with a shimmer of color—sunlight from the window?—and he found her hand perfectly unscathed, as if the fierce bite had been an illusion.

Cade frowned, dumbfounded. "I saw him nail you."

Gen only smiled her ghastly smile and shrugged.

The others joined them. "I'm so glad you're not hurt," Lana said. "He can be dangerous, but I don't have the heart to get rid of him."

"Wow," Haven said. "You should be a magician, Gen. That faked us out totally."

Jimi was staring at the parrot. "There's blood on his beak."

They turned to look. A crimson droplet of blood hung from the sharp tip of his upper beak.

"Where are you hurt?" Cade tried to lift Gen's hand again. She drew it back quickly.

"I'm not hurt. It's okay, really."

"You sure?"

She nodded, but her lavender eyes filled with worry; they shone on the verge of tears.

"Let's go back and finish breakfast," Haven said, and she took Gen's hand and led the way into the kitchen.

*   *   *

Back at the breakfast table with the others, Gen finished her pancakes. Lana had blended whole wheat,

164

buckwheat and white flour into her own special batter, and the pancakes with hot pear-applesauce and plain yogurt were incredibly tasty, but Gen still felt shaky inside from the close call with the parrot.

That had almost been her undoing. She'd spotted the beautiful bird, and before she knew what she was up to, she was halfway to its cage, wild to collect its DNA. She needed to be more careful if she wanted to keep her secret. She decided to make plans to move on as soon as possible, before she placed Cade and his wonderful family in Eberhard's path.

She suddenly realized Lana was talking to her. "...about your past? Where you're from? Anyone we should call?"

"Oh. No. Thank you for your concern, but I don't have anyone."

"You don't have anyone, or you don't remember?" Cade said.

"I don't remember clearly," she added quickly, "but it seems to me I was alone. I have a vague recollection of being by myself, taking care of myself. I don't think I had living parents, and I think that's been true most of my life. My best guess is, I must be an orphan."

"That must be so sad for you," Lana said. "Our parents died when Cade was just a boy. I hope you'll stay with us as long as you want. We'd love to have you."

Gen shook her head. "I really don't want to impose on your hospitality. I was thinking it would be best if I leave."

"Who said you're imposing? I could use help here at the inn. It's dead around here now, but we're usually full from September through May. I was thinking about placing a help wanted ad in the paper, wasn't I, Cade?"

He caught her look and nodded.

"You can earn your keep. You need money, right? How can you go anywhere without money? Please don't think about leaving. We haven't had a chance to become friends." She smiled at Gen.

It was as if Lana held Gen's heart strings in her hand and gave them a gentle tug. "Thank you," Gen said, her voice choked with emotion. "I'd like that."

17

After doing the breakfast dishes, Cade walked along the beach toward the northern arm of the bay and the ritzy community called The Palms.

Sailing and motor yachts glowed in primary colors at their moorings at the yacht club. A cluster of architect-designed vacation homes, all glass and pastel-colored stucco, straddled the dunes on stilts as if daring the reach of winter storm tides. A quarter-mile inland from the stilt homes, rose a twelve-story, pink-stucco condominium, named The Grove. To build The Grove, twenty years ago, Weston Fairchild's construction crew had leveled an entire grove of coconut palms. His grandfather's mind operated that way.

Weston owned The Grove and more than half of Coolahatchee Bay Island. His forebears had made their fortune running a sea island cotton and turpentine plantation worked by slaves. After the Civil War, Weston's great-grandfather continued to operate the plantation with low-wage black laborers. By his grandfather's day, Fairchild Plantation had become a dying enterprise, and the senior Fairchild began selling land to wealthy Yankees looking to build summer vacation homes. At the turn of the century, Vanderbilt, Carnegie, Rockefeller, Hunt, Getty, and a handful of lesser-known tycoons all had homes on the island. Five of those early mansions still existed, but all of them, like Cool Bay Inn, had been converted to bed & breakfast businesses.

Nowadays, what was left of the Fairchild real estate holdings still covered more than half the island and was worth a huge fortune—probably close to a billion dollars, Cade figured. For years, Weston had been selling the land in small, expensive parcels to stay liquid. But his latest project was anything but small. With the backing of Japanese and German investors, Weston was building a world-class golf and tennis resort that would sprawl across all the land he still owned.

In practical terms, it meant the undeveloped portions of the island were slated for development; pine forests would be bulldozed, osprey nests destroyed, and a dozen creeks fouled in order to build pricey condos and neighborhoods with names like The Pine Forest, Osprey View and Clearwater Creek.

Cade felt a knot of worry bouncing in his gut as he walked along the beautiful shore. For two years, Weston had been pressuring Cade and Lana to sell their land, but the two had never even considered it, even as his offers skyrocketed. *Some things are more precious than money. A lot of things, come to think of it. What good does it do you to gain the world and lose your soul, and all that. Cool Bay Inn was home. Okay, my home is not my soul, but my soul has strong ties to it.*

Yesterday evening on the phone, Weston had told him, "This is *not* about a new offer for your land." *So what the freak was it about, then?* Weston had disowned his only child, Elaine—Cade and Lana's mother—for the crime of loving a man of the forbidden skin color. *The cold-hearted old fart had not summoned Cade to his penthouse to kick back a few beers and share some belly laughs, that's for sure.* He'd said he had some very important information. *Like what?* Cade had no clue. But he especially had not liked the sound of, "I could have my lawyer deliver a letter…"

The mid-morning sun had not yet turned the air into a steam bath. A steady on-shore breeze flattened the in-rolling swells and flung white, lacy foam down the breakers when they hit the sandbar. Just beyond the shallow bar, a sudden froth of splashes and panicked mullet showed that something was feeding on the school. Probably dolphins. Cade watched for dorsal fins and was rewarded with a dolphin's high leap, twisting in the air with a mullet in its mouth and smacking down—just for fun, it seemed.

The sight made his thoughts return to Gen. All morning, she and Weston had taken turns occupying his mind.

Cade couldn't figure Gen. What was Haven's comment, yesterday? "She's mysterious." Girl, no joke. Truly mysterious, and truly a bullshitter. That amnesia stuff was pure crap. Gen knew who she was. She was hiding something, but he couldn't guess what it might be.

How does anyone—even given that she's in great physical shape—survive in the open water without a life preserver? He knew a guy, Tommy Brant, who'd managed to stay afloat without a life vest for forty-one hours, by tying off his pant cuffs and inflating the legs. But Gen had been as naked as the dolphins that surrounded her.

And, yeah, that was mighty strange, too, the way the dolphins had escorted her like a squadron of patrol boats. Wild dolphins. Not Sea World; Coolahatchee Bay. Atlantic spotted dolphins. They're beautiful animals; he'd tried to swim with them himself, many times—hell, so had every kid who grew up on the bay. Typically, wild dolphins won't let you any closer than a hundred feet.

And another thing: Gen had shown no signs of exposure to sun and saltwater: no hypothermia, no sunburn, no dehydration or cracked skin. Tommy had looked like a waterlogged, blistered corpse when they'd found him. But with Gen, it was as if she had suddenly dropped into the open sea out of nowhere, simply to take a quick dip to cool off.

And what about her hand? Man, that was straight out of Twilight Zone. He'd watched the parrot chomp down on her flesh. The bird had blood on its beak as proof he'd done

169

damage, but her skin looked untouched. So where had the drops of blood come from? Cue up theme music, Rod: *Dee-dee-dee-dee, dee-dee-dee-dee*.

Come to think of it, Gen's skin was altogether flawless. His sister had beautiful skin like their mother, Elaine. Guests often commented on it, especially women who wanted to know how Lana managed to look twenty-something when she was actually forty. But even Lana's smooth skin had a tiny mole here, a freckle there. Gen's nude body had burned into Cade's mind the vision of immaculate skin, as liquidy smooth as if poured from a jar of maple syrup. Even her face, malformed as it was, bore not a single freckle or blemish.

Haven had said she liked mysteries, so no wonder she liked Gen. Lana liked her, too, but that had been a given. Jimi seemed reserved, as though he hadn't yet made up his mind about the newcomer.

Cade had to admit he felt something for Gen, though he couldn't say exactly what. She seemed to be in trouble and to need help, and that brought out his instincts to protect the underdog. But she was lying about having amnesia, and that bothered him.

What was the truth about her? What was she hiding? Was she running from her past? If so, why? Everything about the woman seemed an enigma.

Something else bothered him. At breakfast, when he sat next to her, he could smell the fragrance of her body and hair and it had aroused him sexually with an intensity that caught him by surprise. As he got up from the table, his bare leg had brushed against hers and she had jumped in her seat, as if she, too, was overly sensitive to their contact.

That erotic charge between them disturbed him most of all. It felt as if his body betrayed him, making him a liar. For how could he respond to her so strongly, while at the same time, think she was grotesque? It seemed unfair to

170

Gen. As if his body was saying to her, "I want you," while his mind was on the verge of cringing every time he looked at her face.

His warring parts caused him to remember a stupid joke he'd heard in the locker room as a teen-ager: What's a two-bagger? A girl so ugly you put *two* bags over her head when you screw her, in case the first bag rips.

He frowned in disgust. He didn't like that kind of humor. It was rude and cruel. But if he gave in to animal desire, he knew Gen's alluring body could reel him in and make him ignore her face.

Does that mean I have the morals of a teen-age jerk?

Whatever the case, Gen had gotten to him. Breakfast was a couple hours ago, and here he was still dwelling on her. He couldn't remember the last time that had happened with a woman. This morning alone, he'd spent more time thinking about Gen than he'd thought all month about the latest romance in his life.

At the start of summer, the art director for the French edition of *Vogue*, during a photo shoot aboard a sailing yacht at The Palms, dropped a ten-grand Rolex Oyster into the bay. Cade free-dived the shallow anchorage, and for a five-hundred dollar salvage fee, retrieved the wristwatch off the sandy bottom. Then the art director, a former model herself, strolled into the yacht's master bedroom while Cade was changing out of his bathing suit. She helped him peel off his clingy wet Speedo briefs. She did not help him put his T-shirt and khaki shorts back on.

Her name was Layla. She was 36, Italian, with burnished copper hair cut in a European style that swished across her face. She wore scarlet lipstick, scarlet nail polish, a scarlet mini-dress, and below that, scarlet lingerie. She was the first woman Cade had known who polished her toenails. Scarlet.

She had tried hard to persuade Cade to enter the modeling profession. "I'll be your agent," she kept telling him, "I absolutely guarantee you'll become a star." No thanks, he'd said. Not his way of life, not his kind of work.

At the end of the week, Layla flew back to Paris, and now she kept phoning him—from London, from Venice, from the Spanish Riviera—begging him to join her at her expense. Sex with Layla had been great sport while it lasted, hot and raunchy and mindless. And meaningless. Cade felt no need to turn their fling into an international quest. He had dolphins to tag. He was happy here on the bay. He was home. He'd told Layla she was welcome to visit again anytime she needed recreation.

Now, he didn't want her to come back. Not with Gen here.

Why? Because Gen might think I'm just a player? Why should I care what Gen thinks?

Man, this was strange. Layla was gorgeous to the point of exaggeration, an erotic ornament; and she had been a sexual virtuoso, an athlete in bed. Yet this morning it was Gen, not Layla, who haunted his heart.

What the hell was going on?

Gen was un-gorgeous. Her *defects* were exaggerated. But Gen was fresh, unspoiled. Innocent. And she seemed so alive. He remembered when he was a boy, how his mother had looked so pretty to him, flushed with health, abounding with life. Or like a ripe peach that packages the sun and rain in its sweet flesh. Beautiful. That was Gen. Ugly Gen, so beautiful. It made him want to touch her all over.

"Jeez, Cade. Forget it," he told himself. "Really. Just forget it."

Today he planned to keep his distance from Gen, so he wouldn't have to deal with his sexual attraction to her. But what about tomorrow? And the next day?

172

He hoped she would get a little money in her pocket soon and move on.

Damn.

His life had been uncomplicated before he'd met the mermaid with the face of a monster...

Her eyes.

He would never see eyes like hers again.

That thought made him sadder than it was reasonable to feel about a stranger with no last name.

18

In the lobby of The Grove, a huge man in a gray silk suit approached Cade, and without shaking hands, announced, "I'm Eddie Helco, Mr. Fairchild's personal assistant. Follow me."

Eddie was built like a defensive lineman, and in his extra-large, double-breasted suit, he looked like an expensively dressed mattress. Eddie escorted Cade to a private elevator that he unlocked with an electronic key. They rose twelve floors and stopped at a marble-tiled foyer. Eddie crossed the foyer, swung open French doors, and ushered Cade inside the living room of Weston Fairchild's spacious penthouse. Then Eddie turned around and departed, ducking slightly to pass under the doorframe.

On the far side of the largest Persian carpet Cade had ever seen, Weston hovered over a bright yellow golf ball, concentrating on a 6-yard putt. He did not look up as Cade entered.

Weston's tall, broad-shouldered build, high cheekbones, and pure white hair gave him the look of a well-preserved elderly statesman. Below a masterful facelift, sagging skin at his neckline betrayed his years; still it was almost impossible to believe the man was eighty-one. Designer clothing adorned his impressive figure: a collarless shirt of royal purple silk, untucked, over cream-colored linen slacks and tan goatskin loafers. Cade figured his grandfather's platinum wristwatch alone cost more than Cade's dive boat.

Weston tapped the ball. It rolled across the plush carpet, past an ancient-looking hammered-bronze chest, and clinked into an etched-crystal wine flute tipped on its side. Weston reached into his pocket and plunked down another ball, still ignoring his guest.

Cade felt nervous, but he wasn't going to lose his cool. Two can play this game. He parked himself next to a glass wall overlooking the bay, his back to his host. Eventually the old man would acknowledge his presence. It took only thirty years for him to phone him, right?

Below the penthouse spread a panorama of the crescent beach of Coolahatchee Bay. Looking west, boardwalks crossed sugar-white dunes leading to the blue-green waters opening onto the Gulf of Mexico. To the Northeast, a pine forest bordered a saltmarsh flecked with yellow swamp buttercups and marsh bluebells, Indian tobacco and wild rye. Cade could see where recent bulldozing had uprooted trees nearly to the banks of the marsh. The raw earth, streaked with red clay, looked painful.

He heard Weston step up beside him. "Quite a view."

Cade nodded, turning his gaze southward. Beach-ball-sized inflated eyes hung from the top of the window to scare off seabirds from smashing into the glass. "I can see the tin roof of Kay's Kitchen on the far side of Taylor's." He pointed. "Six trawlers. All but two of the boats are in."

"Know what I see?" Weston swept the putter across the vista. "I see the future. I see paved streets with street lights, neighborhoods-by-design, an area by the shore with fine shops and restaurants."

Cade did not look away from the view. "Have you heard what the people of Marina and Taylor's think about your plans for their future? They don't want your blessings."

"Because it's so noble to be poor? Is that it? That's why they resist a better life?"

"No, it hurts like hell to be poor. But the folks I talk with want to find a way to make a decent living on the bay without spoiling the place." His eyes roamed the tree-lined shore. "You build your golf resort and pricey condos, throw in the gift shops, the cobblestone streets, all the other

175

touristy crap that goes along. Maybe you got another Palm Springs, maybe it's Key West, but it's no longer Cool Bay. This place won't be recognizable."

"That's your opinion. Think about the others, the kids. You know there's not enough work to go around. They grow up and leave because they can't find jobs here."

"But it's still home, even for them." Cade spun to face Weston. "They take memories with them that they wouldn't trade for the world. They come back to visit, bring their own kids. Some of them, soon as they make enough to put a down payment on a fishing boat or start a little business, they're back in a heartbeat, to stay."

Weston waved away the comment like smoke. "I'm not here to ruin the place for them. I'm spending a fortune to improve it, for chrissake. A country club is not a dump. A resort hotel is not a shack."

"*And* an air strip, *and* a new yacht club, *and* a tennis club, *and* riding stables—"

"So what? What's it going to hurt? All you've got now are pinewoods, marshes, mosquitoes, and gators. Taylor's Wharf is virtually a shanty town. Marina...well, one could be generous and call it a working class neighborhood." He snorted. "We're talking prize-winning architecture, ornamental gardens, fountains—the place would look like paradise." Weston turned and walked over to an architectural scale model inside a glass display case. On the wall above hung a framed copy of *Golf Digest*'s cover story on the new resort. "Come over here, look at this."

Cade stayed put at the window. "What you call a shanty town, my dad called...well, not paradise, but home." He sighed. "You're going to take away the low-income housing and put up condos the locals will never be able to afford. So then what? They'll be forced to leave the island, and commute here from some damn place, to serve the

176

winter and summer vacation crowds as waiters and maids. That your idea of a 'better life'?"

"There's nothing ignoble about those of lower social class serving those of higher status. One might learn something about what it takes to succeed in life," he said. "Besides, history informs us that's how the world has always operated."

"Your world. Not mine. I don't go around measuring people by how fat their wallets are. As if money is enough to make you special. We're all equal under the sun."

"Oh, please. You're sounding like a Marxist: Let he who is taller than his comrades chop off his feet so that we're all reduced to the same height," he said. "Down with those who excel. Enforce equality above merit."

Cade held up a hand. "Let's skip all this and get to why I'm here." He turned back to the window. "There's no point in us beating our chops. Lana and I aren't selling our land. Period."

"That's not why I asked you here."

Cade shook his head. "Build your resort, Weston. I can't stop you. Just keep it on the north and south ends of the bay. You can't have Stanton Hill. My sister is never going to fall out of love with the inn. We're not selling."

"That little inn of yours is sitting on the ninth hole of my golf course."

"Not my problem." Cade turned around to face him. "Call back the architects and get them to redesign it."

"Actually, it is very much your problem," Weston said. "Nothing is going to stand in my way."

"Look, I'm going to do you a favor," Cade said. "I'm going to walk out of here, before you make some kind of threat that pisses me off." He spun and headed toward the elevator. "Nice to meet you at long last."

"You don't understand," Weston called after him. "I didn't invite you here to *ask* you to sell the land."

"Build a goddam Putt-Putt amusement park for all I care," Cade said, pausing halfway through the French doors. "Just keep it off our property."

"It's *not* your property. That's exactly what I'm trying to tell you. The land already belongs to me."

Cade's stomach tightened around what felt like a jagged block of ice. He stepped slowly back into the room. "What the hell you talking about?"

Weston's lips turned up slightly in a smile. He crossed the opulent living room to a large, framed oil painting of water lilies by Monet. "I have a document you need to examine." He carefully took down the painting, revealing a wall safe behind it. He propped the painting against a leather chair. "When the old widow bequeathed Stanton House to your sister, I'm afraid there must have been some confusion about the ownership of the property it rests upon."

Cade's mouth went dry. Twenty-one years ago, Lady Francis had bequeathed her mansion to his sister. Just months later, the car crash killed their mother, Elaine, and crippled Lana. His sister had been nineteen, Cade, nine, when the ownership of the mansion transferred to them.

"What are you saying? A lawyer handled the transfer of title for her, Franklin Hauser."

"Ah, yes. Franklin." Weston spun a combination lock on the wall safe, swung open the thick steel door. "He was in my employ at the time, but I had to dismiss him. Incompetent on the one hand, dishonest on the other." He took out a parchment tied with a gold ribbon. "Didn't he become your sister's fiancé later?"

Cade breathed raggedly. Hell, he didn't remember even *seeing* any paperwork; and if Lana had signed anything, he doubted she had read it first. She had been recuperating in a hospital bed on the surgical ward, with bandaged stumps below her knees.

178

Weston untied the ribbon, unrolled the document. "It's a land lease agreement," he said, handing the paper to Cade. "For the price of one gold dollar, my father, Whitmore Fairchild, leased sixty acres to his best friend, George Stanton, so that Stanton could build his summer home."

Cade read the document, trying to stop the trembling he felt inside from showing in his hands. His gut knotted tighter around the icy stone at its core. The property that Lana and he had believed was theirs actually belonged to Weston Fairchild. It had belonged to the Fairchilds all along.

"It's a one-hundred year lease," Weston said, "the same period that China leased Hong Kong to the British Crown. I think old man Stanton relished that; he was quite the Anglophile."

Cade read the dates. The parties had signed the lease agreement July 31, 1901. It was due to expire at the end of the month. "I don't get it." His voice sounded thin. "If this isn't some goddam forgery, if you've owned Stanton Hill all along, why did you go through the motions of trying to buy the land from us?"

"I only discovered this document a week ago, myself, and I assure you, it's legitimate. My father never mentioned the lease. I had always assumed, as apparently you and Lana did, that the property belonged with the mansion. It came as quite a surprise to learn that it's Fairchild real estate."

Cade's face flushed hot and his voice quavered with held-in fury. "I don't believe you. I think you're lying."

"Think what you may. The issue of my veracity is irrelevant. The point is, I own the land Stanton House is built upon, and I'm eager to get started on the next phase of my property development." He stepped over to a work desk near the glass display case. "You have thirty days to relocate the building, or vacate it." He picked up a manila envelope from the desk, returned to Cade with the envelope held out. "Here is an eviction summons to that effect."

Cade refused to take it.

"As you wish," Weston said, withdrawing the envelope. "I'll have the notice posted on your front door. That will fulfill my obligation, according to Florida law."

Cade snatched the envelope from Weston's fingers. "Look, we can't afford to move the building; it would cost a fortune. Even if we could pay for it…thirty days…that's insane."

"What was the phrase you used earlier? 'Not my problem.'"

"But…be reasonable, here." Cade's mind raced, seeking a way out of the trap. "Take most of the property, but sell us enough land for the inn, a small lawn. The mansion is an historic landmark."

Weston shook his head. "I'm afraid a tall hill with a bed-and-breakfast on top would make an exceedingly poor ninth hole. I'm planning to level Stanton Hill."

Cade felt like the man had kicked him in the stomach. He dreaded how the terrible news would hit Lana; she'd be devastated. "Weston, please. Lana is very attached to the inn, emotionally. It's her home…her refuge."

Weston strolled to the far side of the carpet and stood over a canary yellow golf ball.

"She's your granddaughter, for chrissake."

Weston concentrated on the putt. "No. I disowned your mother. Legally, that means you two and I are not related."

"Not on paper," Cade said. "But by blood. Chrissakes, it's a biological fact."

Weston looked up, mouth twisted in distaste, as if he'd bit into a cherry and discovered a worm. "Your mother's ancestors ran a cotton and turpentine plantation on this island; they were the masters. Your father's ancestors

180

worked that plantation; they were the slaves. My forebears did not consider it proper to mix the bloodlines of masters and slaves. I agree with that wisdom."

Cade was speechless.

Weston glanced over at the architectural model of his resort. "Thirty days," he said. "On the morning of August first, I'm sending an army of bulldozers up Stanton Hill and right up the porch and through your front door."

Weston bent his head and refocused on the putt. The meeting was over.

Cade clenched his jaw, feeling furious, feeling powerless. From a rosewood pedestal atop the bronze chest, a pink jade statue of Kannon, goddess of mercy, subtly smiled at him; a Buddhist Mona Lisa. He felt the urge to snap her head off with his teeth.

He spun and strode out the French doors and closed them quietly behind him, for fear that if he slammed them with all the rage he felt inside, he would tear them off their hinges.

19

Col. Eberhard wondered how many people had heard a rabbit scream. How many even knew the animal was capable of it? Who would guess that a two-pound, fluffy rodent—Thumper and his pals—when injured, lets rip an ear-splitting shriek? Eberhard heard rabbits scream in the scrub pines around Fort Bragg where he bow-hunted as a boy. Now he heard the squealing at Redstone Military Laboratories where he performed his experiments.

The lab rabbit inside the isolation cage screeched louder than the bone saw when the steel teeth tore through its backbone. Blood sprayed the glass walls. Eberhard waited for the red liquid to drain down, like a curtain opening in reverse, so he could see to work. This was his second experiment on Prometheus, the rabbit he'd injected with Gen's nanobots. He'd named the rabbit after the Titan of Greek myth, whom Zeus condemned to eternal torture for stealing fire from Olympus in order to give the divine power to man. Zeus chained Prometheus to a boulder, and every day an eagle tore out the hero's liver from his twitching flesh. Each night, the organ regenerated, and the next morning, the eagle began again his all-day feast.

Prometheus struck Eberhard as a fitting name for a rabbit whose tissues hosted nanobots. Eberhard himself was Zeus, and he also played the role of the voracious eagle.

Funny thing happens when you saw a rabbit in two. If it's a common lab rabbit, $50-per-dozen from Pharm-Farm Lab Supply, the animal screams and instantly dies. The legs in the severed halves thrash for up to a minute, but that's just residual electrochemical energy firing neurons in the muscle tissue. Obviously, no ordinary organism can survive such ruin.

But enter Prometheus, Rabbit of the Gods—the infinitesimal gods that thrive in its cells. In last night's experiment, Eberhard had sawed Prometheus in half. The severed parts jerked and kicked and guts spilled out like pink sausages. Within seconds a silvery fog spewed from the bloody mess, like microscopic hornets swarming from a disturbed nest. The fog flowed over rabbit flesh, shimmering with rainbows of refracted light.

Then, the unbelievable had occurred. The severed halves sent forth wet, silvery tendrils, searching by touch for the missing part. The tendrils met in the middle and wrapped around each other like copulating snakes, then began shrinking and tugging, drawing the halves back together. The fog busied itself with fusing the rabbit into a whole, repairing and rebuilding its structures cell by cell.

In less than three minutes, the fog had been reabsorbed through the rabbit's skin. Prometheus, unscathed, retreated to a corner, where he huddled, trembling; flicking his whiskers and watching Eberhard with red eyes that bulged with terror.

For this morning's experiment, the colonel had devised a glass wall that he now dropped between the severed halves to keep the two parts separated.

"This should be interesting," he told himself.

He watched, fascinated, as the shiny fog spewed forth and flowed over the severed parts. Then the silvery tendrils stretched outward like vines groping for kindred flesh. They ran against smooth glass and fanned out in every direction, exploring the barrier. After a moment, the tendrils withdrew into each bloody half.

"Now what?" Eberhard stared with intense curiosity.

The fog rippled over the surface of each lump of rabbit flesh. The fog grew denser, busier. The familiar irregular rainbows shimmered over the flesh, but now the fog brightened to a glow. The swarmed-over mounds gave off tiny flashes, like sparkles in a disco ball.

The front half of the rabbit grew hindquarters. The living tissue filled in at about the rate a skilled artist might sketch the subject. In a moment, the front half had become a whole rabbit. It quickly hopped away to the far side of its cage.

Eberhard stared at the other mound of flesh and held his breath, licking dry lips. In a sudden eruption, the rear half sprouted front legs and began forming a new head.

Eberhard gasped. "No way," he whispered. "No fucking way."

The glass partition through the center of the cage may as well have been a mirror. Two albino rabbits scrunched in opposite corners—perfectly identical and equally terrified.

20

Cade headed back along the shore toward the Inn, clenching his fists and reeling from the terrible news Weston had clubbed him with. The Stanton Hill land was not theirs. They were going to lose Cool Bay Inn. How in the hell was Lana going to handle it?

He stomped down the long pier at Willingham's Marina and boarded his dive boat, *Dolphin's Smile*. He needed to do something; keep active so he could think, sort out this mess. He looked around the deck for busy work; still squeezing his fists into knots.

He maintained the deck in tiptop shape, and just last month he'd donned scuba gear and scraped barnacles off the hull, so he opened the hatch on the engine compartment and stepped down inside. The cramped engine space smelled like saltwater and diesel oil.

Carburetor. He could clean the carburetor. He went back topside to fetch his toolbox under the captain's bench. A moment later he had removed the carburetor from the Volvo Marine diesel and carried it up on deck.

Cade's mind replayed a fantasy of driving his fists into Weston's mouth and nose. Set him back a few facelifts. But, goddamit, there was really nothing he could do.

He spread a small tarp on the white fiberglass deck. Filled an empty coffee can with kerosene and dropped the carburetor into it—*ploip!*—fetched a clean rag for wiping down parts, fished out the carburetor, and began dismantling it.

Franklin Hauser, that son-of-a-bitch. He'd handled the paperwork that transferred the Stanton property into Lana's name. Had he been following orders from Weston to make sure Lana never learned about the lease? Hell, the bastard cheated on her later, after he became her fiancé—it wasn't hard to believe that he'd betrayed her from the beginning, hiding from her the fact that the Inn sits on Fairchild real estate.

Lana had signed the papers from a hospital bed, her brain floating in morphine. But Franklin could have made certain she understood about the land lease; if not at the time of the signing, he could have explained it later. Instead, he'd kept it secret.

The whole thing stank of conspiracy: Weston must have ordered Franklin to keep the lease a secret. But what was the point? So that Weston could have the pleasure of watching Lana build her dream, her sanctuary, knowing he would someday destroy it? That made no sense. Weston didn't hate their side of the family *that* much. Did he?

In any case, his sister's world was about to come to an end. Again.

He dipped a toothbrush-sized steel brush into the kerosene and began scrubbing the inside of the carburetor barrel. Very little gunk had built up on the walls.

The lease ran out at the end of July. Cade wondered vaguely if he and his sister could get a court order that would give them time to have the Inn moved. Yeah, right. Even with an injunction that granted them a year's reprieve, no way could they afford it. He ground his teeth. By the end of the month, he and Lana and Haven would have to abandon their home.

He bore down on the brush, scrubbing harder. "Abandon the Inn." *Scrub, scrub.* "To the bulldozers." *Scrub, scrub.* "To make room." *Scrub, scrub.* "For a golf course." The plastic handle snapped in his grip. "Fuck it!" He hurled the broken pieces into the water.

The sense of his own helplessness made him to want to burn down the sky, boil the sea, smash the earth. He chewed his lower lip raw as he put the carburetor back together. Maybe when he finished he would don scuba gear

186

and dive down to check the boat's rudder and screw. Whatever. Just stay away from Lana, so he wouldn't have to look into her big chocolate eyes while trying to hide his worry. He needed time to figure out how to break the news.

Suddenly, sadness overtook his anger in one heavy surge and Cade felt himself holding back a ridiculous need to cry. His heart weighted his chest like a leaden dive boot.

They were all meant to stay together. Cade, Lana, Haven and Jimi, too. Where would they go? Would Jimi stay with Lana and Haven? Should Cade find a place of his own?

And what about Gen? What would happen to her now?

He looked up from his work, squinting at sunlight glinting off the bay. The tide was ebbing and the rise and fall of swells seemed like rhythmic breathing. His concern for Gen surprised him. She was not his kin, nor 'almost family,' like Jimi. But the truth was, he really cared for her.

C'mon, man. After knowing her for, what…a whole day?

Yes, after knowing her for a single day. Amazing how deep his emotions ran.

When was he going to stop being suprised by his feelings for Gen and admit that she had plunged like an arrow, straight into his soul?

21

Cade looked up from reassembling the carburetor lying on the tarp between his legs. Why had Haven picked *this* moment to come aboard and drive him crazy?

"She really wants to go to the zoo, Daddy. She's like nuts about it." The late morning sun behind her hair made it glow a ruddy gold.

"Who are you?" he said. "Her spokesperson or something?"

"She's really shy. She doesn't even know I'm asking you."

Streaks of kerosene and grease coated his hands. "I've got a lot of important stuff on my mind right now, hon." With a Phillips screwdriver he wound the last screw tight. "What about your aunt?"

"Already asked her. Says she isn't feeling well. Besides, you know how she hates to drive, especially to Tallahassee."

"Jimi?"

"Guess."

"He's concerned about Lana."

She nodded. "He told her he'd be around if she needed anything."

Cade looked down the length of the wooden dock and up the steep hill to Cool Bay Inn. "Where is she now?"

"Lying in bed upstairs. I think she's asleep."

"I meant Gen, where's Gen?"

"She's getting ready to hitchhike. She was looking at a roadmap when I came down here."

"Dammit!" He tossed down a kerosene-soaked cleaning rag and it slapped the deck with a wet smack. "What's with her, anyway? She's too bashful to ask me to take her, but she's not too bashful to hitchhike?" He rubbed his nose with his forearm. "This is just not a good day to go. I've really got a lot on my mind. I'm in a bad mood."

"No kidding."

"Tell her I'll take you both this weekend. Maybe Lana will be feeling better. We can all go."

"She's going to go today by herself if we don't take her. I can see it in her eyes. She's all fired up about it. She'll hitchhike, do something crazy."

"What's up with her? She's driving *me* crazy."

Haven shrugged. "She's a big fan of zoos?"

"She's a spoiled brat, is what she is. Where the hell did she come from? Who are her parents? They must've let her get away with this shit, given her everything she ever wanted. Why won't she tell us anything about herself?"

"Aunt Lana said please don't curse in front of me."

He twisted his mouth. "She's right. Sorry."

"So, will you take us?"

"Scratch my nose, you little bug."

Haven giggled and scratched the bridge of his nose where a bead of sweat itched. He stared at the carburetor. He still needed time to think. And he wanted to avoid Lana's deep gaze that read him like a book. Maybe he could work out the dilemma while driving, instead of fixing engine parts that ain't broke.

He frowned and breathed out a big sigh. "Okay, all right. Give me a minute to stow this gear and get cleaned up." He held up oily hands. "Think she'll give me long enough to take a quick shower? Or should I drive us there like this?"

Haven laughed. "Thanks, Daddy. I'll go tell her." She turned and ran along the wooden planks of the dock.

"Slow down!"

She didn't. She started up the long hill, muscular brown legs still pumping. Cade grinned. God, she was a beautiful girl.

He cupped his hands around his mouth and called after her, "We'll go in the Land Rover."

Great. Now he had motor oil smeared on his face.

22

Gen watched a ragged squadron of rain clouds close in over the roadway and bombard the Land Rover. Fat drops snapped against the windshield and pummeled the top of the car, louder than a drum roll.

In less than five minutes, the rain shower was over. The car sped on, past cattlelands, magnolias, and pinewoods. She badly wanted to stop and get out and touch the beautiful things she saw. But her destination called to her. Maybe she could get Cade to stop on the way home.

They rolled past a pecan grove. Tall, dark trunks stood in long, straight rows like soldiers stiffly at attention. A murder of crows attacked their southern flank. The tree-soldiers held their line, unflinching.

Past the grove, a fenced pasture spread out along the highway, dotted with palms and palmettos and hundreds of head of roaming cattle. Near the fence, a black angus bull waded in a shallow pond that mirrored his massive body. The beast dipped his broad head and drank water from one end, while from the other he peed a splashing stream. Gen laughed, imagining Elton John singing "The Circle of Life."

She and Cade and Haven were on their way to the Tallahassee Museum of History and Natural Science. Gen had read about the museum and its small zoo in a pamphlet at the Inn. The National Zoo in Washington had loaned the institution a pair of rare Himalayan snow leopards. As soon as she saw the photo of the dappled white cats and read that the species was gravely endangered and on the brink of extinction, she knew in her cells she *must* touch them.

Just thinking now about the snow leopards brought forth an intense desire to reach out to them, to harvest their essence. The emotion swelled her heart, becoming an

191

almost erotic hunger, one that a single touch would deeply satisfy.

*   *   *

Cade had to admit he was enjoying strolling around the museum. It was set in its own natural jungle, and nearly all the animals were native to Florida—alligator, panther, black bear, fox, river otters—living in enclosures that replicated their natural habitats. The afternoon was hot and the humidity was thick as olive oil, but it was bearable under the shade of the heavy foliage.

And then there was Gen.

For Cade, a big part of the joy of being Haven's father was introducing her to the wonders of nature, to see the world afresh through her young eyes. Now, he was with Haven *and* Gen, and Gen was the world's oldest kid. She acted as excited as a five-year-old—if anything, more thrilled than Haven, which was saying a lot. What kind of upbringing had Gen endured? It was as if she'd been kept indoors all her life. She delighted in everything. Not just the exhibits. The most ordinary things—a squirrel scampering across tree branches, a robin hopping across a leafy forest floor—sent her into shivers of joy, clapping her hands, laughing with delight.

Trouble is, she wanted to touch everything. *Feel* the rough, dark bark on the live oak tree, *feel* the silky azalea petals, *feel* the slimy trail the snail left behind. Cade could only shake his head and watch her. She was beautiful to watch.

He caught himself. Beautiful? How could someone so malformed be beautiful?

He had to think about that for a moment. He looked at Gen's face. She couldn't stop smiling. Her mouth wrapped

192

around half her face. Conical teeth looked like they could rip flesh in two.

"Look, Haven!" Gen said. "A snake shed its skin. See?"

Beautiful. Because when he saw the world through Gen's eyes, the world was far more alive than when he saw it without her. She was more vital than anyone he'd ever met.

"Gen!" Haven said. "Quick! A walking stick!"

"Oh! Let me touch it!" Gen ran to Haven as if animated by an electric force. Haven put the walking stick in Gen's outstretched palm. Gen's eyes shone like twin purple suns.

"Look at it!" Gen said. "Isn't it great!"

Haven had picked up on Gen's excitement and was enjoying it as much as Cade. Her job was to find new things for Gen to touch. Then Gen would run over and beam the amethyst rays of her attention and love upon the treasure—a pine cone, a dead bee, a blue jay feather.

Cade found himself trailing behind the two kindred spirits, grinning all the while. He wished he had a video camera, but then again, some things just can't be captured on tape. Look at Gen's eyes. Look at the light that comes out of her face. He could watch her all day.

They entered a log-construction museum building used for natural science lectures. Gen was in heaven, because most of the exhibits were designed for handling. She closed her eyes when touching the objects with her fingertips, as if the sensations gave her a sensual thrill. Haven did her job, finding new toys for Gen to play with. First, a collection of skulls: raccoon, deer, armadillo, skunk, gopher tortoise, shrew, and many others. Next, examples of feathers from many native species of birds. A large collection of seashells behind glass brought out a look of sorrow and hunger on Gen's face that was almost comical. Not being able to

193

stroke the shells with her fingers was like telling a four-year-old she can't have birthday cake on her birthday.

Another building housed an exhibit of reconstructed dinosaurs and prehistoric mammals, many of them discovered in Florida. Extinct species of camels, llamas and horses found near the Manatee River; a saber-tooth tiger skull with an embedded spear point, found at Warm Mineral Springs; and a complete mastodon skeleton found at Wakulla Springs.

Gen stretched her hand past the railing and touched the tree-trunk-sized femur of the mastodon. A museum guard in a safari shirt and shorts snapped her fingers and said, "Miss, you're not allowed to touch the displays."

Nearby, the bones of the right foot of a Gigantosaurus, discovered in Argentina, were on display. Huge, scythe-like talons jutted from three toes in front and one toe in back. It looked like the foot of the raptor that gulped down Godzilla for an appetizer. According to an artist's illustration, the reptile the bones had belonged to had closely resembled a T-Rex, but so bulked up on growth hormones it made its ferocious cousin seem puny.

Standing next to Cade, a man with a gut that bulged as if he were pregnant with twins, said in a New York accent, "Now that's what you call a big lizard." He glanced at Cade to see if Cade had caught his wit. Cade half-expected the guy to tell him how they displayed big lizards up North, but the man waddled on to a different part of the room.

A full-sized diagram next to the exhibit showed the relative sizes of an average man and the Gigantosaurus. The man's head stopped well below the dinosaur's knee. In fact, the ceiling cut the dinosaur off at mid-chest and his entire upper body disappeared beyond the two-story building.

Cade thought of a macho friend of his in the SEALs, who had a Latin phrase tattooed on one bulging shoulder.

What was it? Something about being able to judge the whole from a part. He snapped his fingers when it came to him. "*Ex ungue draconis*."

"From the dragon's claw," Gen translated, and added, "we may judge of the dragon."

Cade couldn't believe it. "You know Latin?"

She nodded and smiled shyly. Cade turned to go when Gen quickly ducked under the railing and touched the skeletal foot of the Gigantosaurus.

"Hey. I told you, don't touch!" the guard shouted, and started toward her from the far side of the room.

"Gen, you're getting us into trouble," Haven said. She towed Gen by the hand to the exit and with the guard scowling at them, the trio escaped through the door into sunlight. "Did you see the dirty look the guard gave us?"

"I'm sorry," Gen said, but her eyes were violet flames.

"Come on, you two, I'll take you to the Reptile House," Cade said. "They let you *hold* snakes there."

Inside the Reptile House, a herpetologist offered a number of animals for handling during his lecture. Gen and Haven got to touch a six-foot indigo snake and half a dozen lizards, salamanders and small reptiles. Cade found watching Gen's face more interesting than watching the colorful creatures.

Next, the three of them followed a trail that led downhill past the animal exhibits to a boardwalk along a tributary of the St. Mark's River. At first, they couldn't find the black bears in their half-acre pen; then Haven spotted the male sleeping in a huge oak tree. A splash made them glance down. The she-bear was swimming in the river directly under the boardwalk below their feet.

Gen threw herself to her belly and tried to stretch her hand down to the bear to reach it under the planks of the boardwalk.

"Hey! Get up!" Cade grabbed her under her armpits and snatched her up. "That's dangerous. The bear could maul you."

Gen looked as if she might cry because she couldn't reach the bear.

"Look, black fur," Haven said, picking up a swatch wedged in a crack between planks. "Wind must've blown it."

Gen reached out and touched the fur, and her whole body relaxed with obvious satisfaction.

"You're the craziest woman I've ever met," Cade said. But the sensuality in Gen's expression, the soft curve of her smile, slight frown of her eyebrows as she concentrated on her pleasure made Cade unexpectedly aroused. He shoved a hand into the pocket of his jeans and adjusted himself.

"Come on!" Haven said. "The snow leopards are up ahead." She and Gen ran holding hands, like sisters. Gen was twice Haven's age in years, but the two shared the same degree of innocence and bliss. The world was their wonderland to explore.

Just ahead of the large penned area with the leopards, Gen stopped suddenly and knelt down to pick up an earthworm. A plain old stick-it-on-a-hook-and-let's-go-fishing earthworm. It squiggled in her palm. Gen wore the same look of stunned joy that models wear in jewelry ads as they accept the gift of a diamond necklace.

Earthworms are forever.

A moment later they stepped off the boardwalk and back onto the sandy path. Gen spied a tall anthill and veered toward it.

"No, they sting!" Haven and Cade both shouted at once. Too late. Gen grabbed a handful of fire ants. Cade caught up to her and seized her hand. A dozen fire ants had already twisted up their tiny bodies, sinking pincers into flesh.

Cade brushed off the red ants, getting several stings for his troubles. "You okay?" He held onto Gen's hand a moment. The fire ant stings had left no trace on her skin. On his hand, tiny blisters puffed up.

She pulled her hand back and stepped away. "Look how cute!" she said, and bent over again to pick up an acorn with a tiny mushroom sprouting from its top. A quartet of teen-aged boys came jostling down the path from the opposite direction and saw Gen bent at the waist in tight cotton shorts that hugged her feminine curves. The boys gawked with undisguised horniness. Then Gen straightened and they saw her face. The skinny kid in front gasped and lurched backward and his pals plowed into him. Then they hurried past, their eyes turned downward. As they started around a bend, Cade heard one say, "Holy shit, did you see her *face*?" They all started talking at once.

Cade's eyes caught Gen's. She immediately looked away, but not before he saw her eyes mist with tears.

"Come on, Gen," Haven said, and tugged her hand. "We're never going to get to the snow leopards if you keep stopping every three feet." The two rushed onward.

Cade heard the four boys laugh and whoop in the distance. He recalled his own reaction upon first seeing Gen close-up in the water. He hadn't averted his eyes, but he'd wanted to.

He looked at her now, hand-in-hand with Haven. Butterflies flitted around in his belly, finding no place to land.

23

Gen could not believe the beauty of the snow leopards. The female dozed beside a pool of water, her noble head resting on crossed front legs. The bigger male paced nearby, tail twitching, wary of the spectators beyond the fence of his kingdom. He sniffed the air and kept his great yellow eyes fixed on Gen.

To Gen, the pair were like creatures from mythology. Looking at Medusa could turn a person into stone; gazing at the snow leopards had turned Gen to warm butter. She ached from head to toe with a deep longing to touch them.

The fence around the pen stood a dozen feet tall and a deep trench lined the animal side of the enclosure. Even if she managed to get in, how would she get out?

Haven read aloud from a sign: The snow leopards had been bred from a pair trapped in Tibet in the 1960s. Few, if any snow leopards remained in the wild, and this pair was one of only a dozen kept in breeding programs at zoos.

Gen watched the male leopard pacing protectively near his mate while she slept, and her heart flooded with overwhelming love and sorrow.

Suddenly Gen felt the frantic drive of a mother trying to save her child in danger. I mustn't allow them to become extinct! The thought was utterly compelling.

How can I get over to them? I've got to touch them.

Before she knew what she was doing she had leapt up and pulled herself onto the low branch of a magnolia tree that overhung the leopard pen.

"No!" Cade shouted. "Gen, stop."

She knew she should stop. What she was doing was wrong. Posted signs warned, DON'T TOUCH FENCE, DON'T LEAN ON RAILING. Well, at least she wasn't going to touch the fence or lean on the railing.

She scooted along the thick branch until she was over the pen and beyond the pit. Cade was yelling behind her.

She jumped to the ground.

Almost as she hit, the male leopard leaped upon her, sending her flying backward. The leopard followed her to the ground, ripping at her throat with its fangs. She hit the sand with a thud that knocked the air from her lungs. Whites showed around the big cat's glaring yellow eyes. Its huffing breath smelled dark and meaty. It cocked its muscular forelegs and swiped three-inch claws across her chest, back and forth, like a boxer with a blurring fast combination punch, tearing her cotton T-shirt and the flesh beneath it to tatters. Blood sprayed and the leopard's snowy fur turned a soggy crimson.

Then the leopard straddled her torso and clamped its wide-open jaws down on her head. The upper fangs punched through the roof of her skull, the lower fangs caught hold through her eye sockets. The leopard picked Gen up in its mouth and dragged her, between its legs, back toward its concrete den.

People outside the pen screamed and shouted. But as the essence of the snow leopard passed into her bloodstream and into the genetic archives of the Abundance, Gen felt only the quenching of a dire thirst—and the gratification came as a gush of pure pleasure.

*   *   *

"No!" Cade shouted. "Gen, stop!" She had scampered up the magnolia tree so fast he hadn't had time to react. Now she was standing on a branch that extended over the leopard cage. My God, what's she going to do?

He grabbed the keys to the Land Rover from his pants pocket and knelt so that he came eye-to-eye with Haven. "Take these!" He stuffed the keys in her small hand.

199

"Daddy, I'm scared."

"Go get in the car in the parking lot. Wait for us there."

"I'm scared."

"Get to the car and wait. Hear me?"

She gulped and nodded.

"Good girl." Cade turned his back on her and shimmied up the magnolia tree after Gen.

She was already scooting crabwise along a thick branch that extended over the leopard pen. "Gen! Don't do it. You'll be killed."

People in the crowd below were shouting. A woman screamed. "Hey, you two!" a male voiced barked, "Get the hell down from there!"

The male leopard watched Gen approach on the branch above. He padded toward her, fur bristling, fangs bared, snarling. Cade hurried behind Gen.

"Gen, no!" he yelled.

She jumped down. Cade gasped. The leopard pounced and knocked her down and tore into her. Blood sprayed his white fur. Christ! Cade's gut coiled into a knot.

He scurried to the open space over the pen and jumped to the ground after her.

24

Cade landed in the leopard pen and pitched forward onto his hands. The male leopard was already dragging Gen away. The attack had lasted only seconds. Was she dead? Could anyone survive that mauling? He swore he'd heard fangs crunch down through her skull—an unimaginably sickening sound.

Cade bellowed from the bottom of his lungs and charged after the leopard. He hadn't the slightest idea what he was going to do when he reached the beast.

The leopard dropped Gen and jerked up its big head. It snarled and its bared fangs dripped blood. Cade circled away from Gen and the leopard tracked him, crouching low, muscles rippling beneath blood-soaked chest fur.

Cade stripped off his Hawaiian shirt and wrapped it around his forearm. Heartbeats boomed in his head like pounding kettle drums: *ba-boom ba-boom ba-boom*. In the SEALs, he'd excelled in hand-to-hand combat instruction, and he'd practiced a dozen ways to kill an enemy soldier without a weapon, but nothing in his military training had prepared him for this: man versus leopard.

His eyes shot over to Gen. *She's alive!* She had risen to her knees and now was standing up on wobbly legs. She looked at Cade and clasped a hand to her mouth, obviously afraid for his safety.

While his attention was distracted, the leopard sprang at his throat.

Cade whipped his arm in front of him, blocking the attack but catching a crushing bite through the wrapped cloth into the muscles of his forearm. The 175-pound cat would have slammed him down on his back, but Cade pivoted with the force of the blow and the leopard sailed by. The animal hit the ground and clawed and scrabbled and spun in a cloud of dust to lunge again. This time Cade thrust out his forearm, but spun his whole body at the last second before the leopard's teeth sank into flesh. With the cat directly under Cade's center of gravity, he dropped to one knee, driving his fist into the back of the cat's broad head where its skull and neck joined. The animal's dense muscles sent a shock wave up Cade's arm into his shoulder and his hand vibrated as if he had slammed a baseball bat against an iron post.

The cat crashed down in the dirt as limp as a sandbag. The blow would have snapped a man's neck, but Cade saw ribs heaving and knew the leopard wasn't dead. Or even defeated. He was relieved because he had only wanted to stop the animal, not kill it. But he didn't plan to wait around to see how long it stayed unconscious.

He kept his eyes glued on the female of the pair. She had backed against the fence on the far side of the cage, fur bristling, hissing like a monstrous alley cat.

"Nice kitty," Cade said. The aftershock of adrenaline zigzagged through his nerves, and he found himself giggling. "Nice pussycat."

Gen stood a few feet from him in a tattered T-shirt, breasts exposed, chest and throat slick with blood, yet seemingly unfazed.

"Get over here, behind me." He eyed the female leopard. "How bad are you hurt?"

"I...I'm not." She smiled weakly as she stepped over to him. "I'm okay."

"Let's get out of here." He grabbed her hand and tugged her over to the entrance of the concrete den. It was shaded inside and smelled strongly of cat piss. Cade scanned the cool darkness, just to make sure there wasn't a Siberian tiger inside as a bonus exhibit.

When he looked back to the female leopard, she had already crossed the compound and was crouched beside the

202

unconscious male, guarding him. Damn, she's quiet. She could have sneaked right up and attacked us from behind.

Suddenly the male lifted his head and looked straight at Cade. Dirt stuck to his bloody white fur in reddish-brown patches. Then he stood up, still a little wobbly.

Oh shit. Hope he's not in the mood for a revenge match. "Nice kitty-kitties," Cade whispered. This time he didn't giggle at his own joke.

He entered the leopard's den with Gen in tow. He wasn't going to let go of her hand until they were in the Land Rover heading home. A steel zookeeper's door stood at the far end.

Sawdust covered the concrete floor. The shadowed space reeked of animal musk that made Cade's nose itch. Sweat dripped off his chin. He licked dry lips and tried to catch his breath. "As soon as they open this door, run like hell to the Land Rover. We gotta go before we get busted."

Gen nodded. She wasn't even breathing hard.

"What the fuck got into you?" Cade said.

"I'm sorry." That tearful look again. "I couldn't help myself."

"Shit, that was stupid. Jesus. I thought you'd gotten yourself killed."

She looked down at her feet.

"How can you not be hurt?" He reached out and wiped at the blood on her throat with the shirt that still wrapped his forearm. The blood came off in a streaky smear. The skin beneath was unscathed. He wiped her chest, roughly jostling her breasts. His shirt sopped up sticky blood over skin as smooth and richly toned as coffee ice cream.

A key clacked and turned in the lock.

"Here goes," he said. "You stay behind me, like in football. I'm the running block, okay? The parking lot is the end zone."

The door swung open and a huge, red-bearded man in a khaki safari outfit stood at the other end along with two normal-sized human beings, a man and a woman. The smaller man carried a first-aid kit, the woman held a shotgun, and the big Viking held an electric cattle prod.

Cade knew the crew was here to mop up what was left of the stupid idiots who had jumped into the leopard pen, and he figured the police were on their way. The police would bring in the whole media circus on their heels, because newspaper and TV reporters monitored emergency radio bands for juicy stories. Like, deformed girls who jump down inside leopard cages and get slashed apart, and men who knock endangered species senseless. He didn't want to get arrested for Gen's obsession with touching every goddamn living thing she saw, and he especially didn't want to answer a lot of tricky questions.

He darted out of the den, cutting sideways past Erik the Red and the other two zookeepers, with Gen right behind him; the two bolted in a dead run toward the parking lot.

"Stop! Get back here!"

"I'm making a citizen's arrest!"

"Stupid bastards!"

In the parking lot, Haven had the Land Rover's motor running. She dove over the front seat into the back when she saw them coming. Bless her little criminal heart. She made a great getaway driver.

Gen ran like an antelope and reached the car fifty steps ahead of him. Cade hopped in behind the wheel, shifted, stomped the gas and the car roared out of the parking lot, spitting gravel. As they passed the Tallahassee airport, he slowed to a leisurely pace.

No point in getting arrested for speeding.

25

Lana had gone to bed thinking she had an unusual flu. She woke up feeling refreshed. She did not open her eyes but let the soft red glow diffuse through her lids.

This has to be the world's strangest virus, she thought. It produced a mild fever, but it was a fever of good feelings. Even her cells felt happy, like the first warm blush of falling in love.

She felt a steady hum of pleasure throughout her body. It had started that morning, low and indistinct, like background fizz on a worn audio tape. But the more relaxed she felt, the more melodic the noise seemed. Now, deeply rested and with eyes closed, she was actually enjoying the interior sounds as subtle music: the soft drone of a tamboura, overshot by the mellow trills of a bamboo flute. They should call this bug the Raga Flu.

As usual, Lana had been dreaming she had legs. Sometimes the dreams were about the simple freedom of walking or running. Other times she'd kick her dream-legs hard in a fast Australian crawl across the swimming hole, or pump a bicycle uphill, standing in the pedals, feeling the burn.

Most often, her dreams were about dancing; and lately, she dreamed about dancing with Jimi. In her dream just now, she and Jimi danced a flamenco-influenced ballet. Her beautiful long legs moved together with his to the hot and saucy music. Their dancing was as graceful as it was erotic.

At some point in the dream, her lower legs began to itch intensely; that's what had awakened her from the world's best nap. She occasionally suffered phantom limb sensations, like itching, but in her dream it was the worse attack she'd ever experienced. She still felt the itching now, although it had mostly subsided.

Weirdly enough, it sometimes helped to pretend to scratch the phantom itch. When she sat up to do so, she saw bulges under the covers where her feet should be.

What the hell? The artificial limbs, titanium-aluminum alloy and molded nylon, were stacked against the foot of the antique brass bed. She always removed the clunky things when she laid down to sleep.

Lana yanked off the sheets and let out a shriek. Her hands flew to her lower legs and squeezed. Quick, before the vision disappears! But the flesh felt warm and firm, resilient to her fingers. Very fine, soft hairs covered the rich, brown skin. The feet kicked, the toes wriggled. The legs worked.

She pulled off her summer dress and stared at her new legs. She couldn't catch her breath. When she finally forced air into her lungs, she let out another scream: "Jimi!"

When Lana had remodeled the mansion, she had removed all full-length mirrors. But now she leapt to her feet on top of the mattress to gawk at her reflection in the mirror of her dresser.

The soles of her feet touched the firm mattress, touched *ground*, touched *home*. It was the most welcoming sensation she had ever felt. She bounced up and down on the mattress until the slats broke.

*   *   *

Jimi sat at a desk in his cabin behind the Inn, entering notes in his dolphin research journal in a fluid scrawl that mixed printing and cursive. The way the dolphins had escorted Gen in the water fascinated him. He'd spent all morning online and he'd not found a single reference to such behavior. Several famous dolphins had guided ships through channels. Other dolphins reportedly had nudged shipwrecked sailors ashore or helped keep them afloat. But to witness an entire pod of dolphins encircling a human swimmer, apparently accepting the human as a member of their pod, was a unique and important observation. Jimi wanted to learn more about the behavior.

Who was Gen? The better question might be, *What* was she?

Was he the only one who noticed that her conical teeth were distinctly dolphinoid? Hell, her entire skull was dolphin-like. It became increasingly obvious to him the more he studied her features; the bones of her jaw, especially.

The arches of her maxilla and mandible were way too narrow and elongated. And the condyles of the mandible hinged at the temporal bone half a foot farther back than normal; meaning her temporal bones were not in the right place, or were themselves elongated, either of which would explain why her ears were set abnormally far back on her head.

In his waterproof notebook, Jimi drew a detailed profile of the bones of Gen's face and skull. Next to it, he sketched a dolphin's facial bones. He labeled the two anatomies with arrows pointing from a single list. The similarities were uncanny. Did no one else realize one could describe Gen's strange facial structure as a blend of dolphin and human features?

"Impossible," he told himself. Two disparate species can't reproduce, can't combine and blend their genes. It was one thing to breed horses and donkeys to get sterile mules; or breed lions and tigers to get sterile ligers. But *human* and *dolphin*?

Actually, there was no mechanical reason the two species could not mate. In fact, a few of the most eccentric dolphin nuts had reported having sex with the animals. Sexual intercourse, okay. Weird, but believable. But conceiving a human-dolphin embryo?

"No way."

Jimi set down his pen, lifted his glasses and rubbed his eyes. He wanted to interview Gen extensively, as soon as he figured out the best way to approach her. She seemed very shy and skittish about herself—

Lana screamed from upstairs in the mansion.

Jimi was on his feet and out the cabin door when she screamed his name. He raced through the Inn's backdoor and heard a noise above like wood splintering, followed by a loud *thud*. He flew up the stairs two at a time and flung open her bedroom door.

Lana was bouncing up and down on top of her broken bed, stark naked, laughing like a little girl on a trampoline, tears streaming down her face.

Jimi's eyes went to Lana's ample breasts, lifting and falling with each bounce. A delta of luxuriant black fur adorned the juncture of her thighs. The beauty of Lana's nude body so startled him it took a couple heartbeats to realize the whole miracle of what he was seeing.

Lana was bouncing on her own legs.

*　　　*　　　*

It wasn't possible. She was dreaming. It was a miracle.

The door flew open and Jimi stood in the doorway, his mouth hanging open.

She stopped bouncing. "Am I dreaming?" she managed to gasp out between laughs and sobs. "Is this real?"

Jimi crossed slowly to her, his arms outstretched like a sleepwalker. He touched her legs cautiously with his fingertips, as if he feared fresh paint might come off. Then he started crying, and clutched her legs so tightly in his arms that Lana lost her balance and fell back onto the mattress, dragging him down on top of her.

208

"How?" Jimi said.

Lana laughed, flinging tears. "You're asking me?" Then she started to sob, her chest and shoulders heaving. "Why...did...God...choose...me?"

Jimi just shook his head, dazed.

"Why me? There...are...others...more deserving." She squeezed her eyes shut and began to wail.

That made Jimi cry harder. "You deserve it," he whispered hoarsely. He almost sounded angry. He picked up a corner of the sheet and wiped at two clear streams that ran down from her nose. "You're an angel. You're the best. I love you, Lana. Goddamit, I love you so much."

Lana opened her eyes to see a boldness in Jimi's face she'd never seen before. As if all disguises had vanished and nothing but the truth could be told. His pale eyes shone like blue-hot stars.

Just then, Tripod bounded up the stairs and into the bedroom. Through a flood of tears, Lana gave a double-take to register what she was seeing. She gasped.

Jimi searched her face. "What?" Then he turned around to face the dog and saw the second miracle.

Tripod was barking and dancing in circles on all four legs.

Downstairs in the sun room the parrot began squawking in its cage.

Jimi burst out laughing. "Snapper, too?" He jumped up and started for the stairs. "Be right back." She heard his footsteps race down the stairwell like a drum roll.

Lana dashed over to her sewing table and grabbed a needle from a pin cushion. She bent forward and poked herself in the lower left calf. "Ouch! That really hurt!" But she pricked herself again in the right leg and grinned as if sticking a pin into your own flesh is great fun.

Tripod barked and barked, wagging his tail like a whip. Lana knelt and hugged his big neck and kissed his furry face. "We's got legs, good boy! We's got legs!"

Jimi came marching back up the stairs and carried Snapper, cage and all, into Lana's bedroom. The macaw flapped two bright green-and-blue wings. His prosthetic lower beak had fallen to the floor of the cage; a new, shiny black beak stood ready to bite careless fingers.

Lana stood up. "My God!" she said, and launched into another bout of laughing and crying. She reached through the bars of the bird cage and stroked the parrot's velvety feathers. Snapper allowed only Lana to do that with impunity. The macaw closed his eyes and snuggled his warm head against her hand.

"And Ray can *see*," Jimi said.

Lana blinked. "Ray, too?" Ray was a blind tomcat Lana had taken in a couple summers ago.

"He was darting around the living room pouncing on shadows. The fat cat can see." He laughed. "And look!" He held up his left hand, wiggled the little finger. "Been itching me bad all morning."

Yesterday the finger had curled upon itself, useless—the result of a whittling accident on Jimi's twelfth birthday when he'd finally received the folding Buck knife he'd begged for. Now the damaged finger functioned again.

He grinned. "I can really play air guitar now."

Lana laughed and shook her head. "This is too much." She couldn't wait to see Haven and Cade, to share this fabulous gift of joy. Jimi read her mind.

"Wait till Haven sees you! And Cade—he'll go ape-shit."

"But how do we tell them? It's overwhelming."

"*Tell* them? Would you believe it if I *told* you?"

She shook her head. "I can't believe it now."

210

"Don't put your dress back on. That'll do it. Just look at you. You're so beautiful." He knelt on the floor and kissed her legs below the knees.

The gesture was spontaneous, and Lana knew he hadn't meant it to be erotic, but she suddenly got wet between her thighs. She wanted to dance with Jimi, as in her dreams. She reached down and pulled him to his feet. He tilted up his chin and she kissed his mouth. His eyes smiled at hers and he did not conceal his appetite.

They fell onto the broken bed, hugging and crying on each other's shoulders for a timeless moment. Neither of them noticed the transition to making love. Neither of them planned when their joyful kisses would turn passionate and their caresses would begin to burn like sweet fire. The choreography just happened. Desire moved their bodies in an intimate progression until they were dancing as one.

Lana wrapped her slender, muscular legs around Jimi's back, and their hunger was not done with them for a long time.

26

Cade headed west on State Road 98, through loblolly pine woodlands broken by tiny fishing communities that hugged the shoreline. Each little town was modeled on the same civil engineering plan: one blinking red light, one gas station/grocery store, one oyster or shrimp packing plant, one seafood restaurant/lounge. The restaurants also adhered to a common vision: shack-like buildings with names like, "The Sea Hermit," with a rowboat or pram perched on the roof, and fishing nets and glass floats decorating the interior walls—theme: rustic Floridiana.

Cade slowed to pass through the metropolis of Carrabelle, population: 1,000. Offshore, fishing and utility boats in various stages of seaworthiness anchored over the sandflats. Always one or two boats rested on the shallow bottom with only the tops of their cabins showing above water at high tide. In another few hours, at ebb, the sunken boats would be exposed like barnacle-encrusted derelicts in a ghost fleet.

Cade drove with his window open. Sliding through the forest, the warm, humid air was fragrant with pinesap; along the shore, it smelled salty and fishy; near the seafood packing plants, it stank like a heaven for pelicans.

The three had driven in silence since they'd managed to flee the zoo. Just outside of Tallahassee, a green patrol truck from Florida Fish, Game & Wildlife cruised behind them for twenty miles. Cade had tensed, worrying that someone might have seen them tear out of the parking lot and reported their license number. But the four-wheel-drive truck turned off on a dirt trail into Apalachicola National Forest and disappeared in a cloud of dust. Less than a minute later, a Leon County Sheriff's car came zooming up in Cade's rearview mirror, its blue and white lights strobing. He had slowed to pull over, accepting defeat, when the sheriff car roared past, apparently after other evildoers.

The last hour had been uninterrupted greenery and late afternoon sunlight on still water. The tension in the car was still palpable, but Cade had calmed down enough to break the silence. Without yelling.

"Anybody hungry?" he said.

Gen shook her head.

"Haven?"

"No thanks."

Haven turning down food was like a kid at Halloween saying, Thanks just the same, but I'd rather not take the candy. Cade supposed she was feeling overwhelmed. She didn't know the details of what had happened, but of course she saw the bloody, tattered clothes and knew something very, *very* weird was going on. It was scary. Hell, he was in emotional shock himself.

Cade had unwrapped the Hawaiian shirt from his arm and given it to Gen to cover her breasts. The baggy shirt—which he'd bought for its kitsch appeal—featured dancing native girls in hula skirts in the foreground, with an erupting volcano behind. Now the volcano was belching dried blood for lava and the dancers wore skirts ripped by fang holes.

Carrabelle receded in Cade's sideview mirror as they headed into another stretch of pine forest. Ahead on the sun-dappled road, an armadillo had jousted with a car and lost; its armor lay shattered and its organs were printed on the blacktop like an anatomy chart. Cade wondered what degree of injury Gen could survive.

"Gen," he said. She didn't look his way. "It's time I asked you some questions."

She stared at the trees flashing by; they made a *whif-whif-whif-whif* sound as they passed her open window.

213

"Let's start at the beginning," Cade said. "What's your real name?"

She didn't answer.

"Gen?"

"You're calling me by it now."

"Gen who?"

"Just Gen."

"Even Madonna has a last name."

"They never gave me a last name."

"*They*? Who are 'they'?"

She shot a glance at him, then returned to tree watching. "Please don't ask these questions."

"Oh sure, just leave it alone," he said. "You jumped into a pen with two leopards. Why? Because you wanted to touch them." He forced a chuckle. "A little bit strange, no doubt, but, hey—I shouldn't pry."

She stared at the forest. The hem of Cade's shirt draped her knees.

"This isn't something I can just forget," he said. "The leopard sank his teeth into your throat. I saw it. Saw him rake you with his claws. I heard the fangs crunch down on your skull. Jeez, it sounded like a can opener punching into a can.

"So I jump down to pick up your pieces and I get a big cat hanging from my arm by his teeth. Then—*abracadabra*—half a minute later, you're perfectly fine. Not a scratch."

He was talking to the back of her head, and it made him angry. "I really think I've earned the right to ask you a few questions."

"I'll go away," she said in a shaky voice. "I'll leave the inn. Then you don't need to know about me."

That shut him up. He didn't want her to leave. He just wanted...what? To know who she was. *What* she was.

214

The Land Rover swept by a patch of woods where fire had scorched trees on both sides of the road. Ash like gray snow blanketed the forest floor and the air smelled like charcoal, but the tops of the pines were sparkling green, pushing forth new needles. Gen was like that; like the phoenix that rises anew from its own ruin.

"Look, I want you to stay," he said. "Okay? I... How can you be so magical? That's all. That's what I want to know."

She started crying. She made no noise, but her shoulders shook.

Oh hell. How can a woman who came out of a bloody mauling without a mark, seem so damn vulnerable? And how is it, after causing all the trouble, she could make him feel sorry for her?

He scratched absently at his forearm and realized the puncture wounds had not been hurting for some time. Fierce tingling had replaced pain. He rubbed off dried, flaky blood and caught a glimpse on his brown skin of the same shimmering glow he'd seen when the parrot nipped Gen.

The faint light faded. The thick, corded flesh of his forearm had healed perfectly. No holes. No scabs. No scars. As if the leopard had clamped his arm with fangs made of foam rubber.

"My arm!" Cade said. "How ...? Jesus. How did you do that?"

Gen snuffled, shook her head.

Haven piped up from the back seat in a solemn voice. "Are you an angel? I won't tell."

Gen laughed and sniffed. "I don't know what I am, honey. I'm not like anybody else."

"Lana says everyone is unique," Haven said. "One of a kind."

215

Gen turned in her seat to smile at the girl. "Guess I'm even more one-of-a-kind than most."

"No sisters or brothers?"

Gen shook her head.

"If you'll stay at the inn, I can be your little sister, and you can be my big sister."

Gen bit her lip, then her composure crumpled, and she turned away and buried her face in her folded arms on the window sill. Her shoulders trembled with quiet sobs. This time, Cade put his hand gently on her back to comfort her.

Her heart beat against his palm. That was all; just her warmth through the silly Hawaiian shirt, her heart thumping at the very core of her, while his fingers gently massaged her slender back and neck and shoulders. Somehow, it was one of the most intimate moments he'd ever felt with a woman.

He realized his perception had changed. His eyes took in the same images as before, but when he looked at Gen now, she no longer appeared ugly. She was fascinating and mysterious. Impulsive and driven. Childlike and vulnerable. Yet incredibly powerful, maybe even supernatural.

And most unexpected of all, Gen was beautiful.

His pulse quickened to match hers, two hearts meeting at his fingertips.

27

Cade shifted to low gear and the Land Rover crawled up Stanton Hill to the inn. Lana and Jimi were on the porch waiting for them as they pulled up. Cade shut off the engine and Lana burst into tears.

Now what? This had been a day for sobbing women.

Since finding that his wounds had perfectly healed, Cade had been thinking of his sister. On the ride back, he'd asked Gen if she could heal Lana, and Gen said she didn't know. This was a delicate situation. He didn't want to get Lana's hopes up, but he wanted Gen to try. He touched the undamaged surface of his forearm. With Gen, the impossible seemed possible.

He was halfway out of the vehicle as Lana flew down the porch stairs and threw her arms around his neck, laughing and crying.

"What?" Cade laughed. "I'm glad to see you, too."

Jimi was crying now, hurrying down the steps. Good grief. Was there some new kind of pollen in the air?

"What's going on around here?" Cade said. "You win the lotto?"

Lana shook her head, too overcome to speak. Then she scooped up Haven in her arms and spun around and around in circles. Haven squealed with delight. Cade's mind turned a somersault. Lana's cotton dress swirled up around her knees and his eyes beheld the miracle, but he already knew what had happened—you just don't twirl in circles on artificial legs.

His whole world blurred behind a sheet of tears. Okay, it was a day for letting it all out. He and Jimi sobbed openly with joy. Then Cade hoisted Jimi over his head and twirled in circles, too, until they both tumbled to the grass, laughing and whooping and tussling like wrestlers, slapping each other on the back.

Tripod charged down the porch steps and plowed into the two of them, barking and growling, wagging his tail furiously. Cade stared at the big dog. It jumped up and down, barking, turning in circles. It was a day for turning in circles.

"You too?" he said. "Sit, boy." He held out his hand. "Shake."

Tripod sat and extended his left paw, tail thumping the lawn.

"Not that paw, the new one." Cade tapped the dog's regenerated right leg. "Gimme this paw, buddy." The dog held out its right paw and Cade shook it. "We're gonna have to change your name, huh, fella?" He let go of the paw and the dog held it up again. "Newpod," Cade said, pumping the handshake.

Lana set Haven down. The girl's eyes shone with wonder greater than the thrill of every Christmas morning rolled into one.

"Hey, you guys—watch!" Lana said.

Everyone looked up at her. Lana took a running start on the lawn and launched into a roundhouse and two back handsprings. The fact that her routine ended with her on her butt, laughing, her summer dress tented over her head, would not have stopped Cade from giving her a 10, if he were the judge of gymnastic perfection.

"So much for the subtle approach," Jimi said, wiping his eyes. "We've been talking about how to break the news to you without blowing your minds."

Cade laughed. "Too late. I'll never be the same."

The golden retriever barked and held out his regenerated paw to shake again. Haven shook his paw and knelt down to hug his neck.

Gen had done all this, Cade thought. She had caused these miracles. He looked toward the Land Rover. "Gen?"

Lana got up from the grass, plucking a twig from her hair. She and Haven called out at the same time. "Gen?"

"Where is she?" Jimi said.

A shadow fell across Cade's tear-streaked face. "She's gone."

Gen ran, nearly blinded by tears. She reached the foot of Stanton Hill and hurried along the sandy path toward the boardwalk that led to the marina. She stumbled and fell, gashing her palm on a sharp oyster shell; the flesh healed before she leaped back to her feet.

Conflicting emotions tore through her soul like a gale shredding a mainsail. She felt joy for Lana's miracle; gladness for Lana and Jimi's blossoming love; moved that Haven had reached out to her like a sister. And even the deep yearning of the Abundance had not prepared her for the hunger she felt for Cade. The instant in the bay when she first took his hand she had collected his essence; otherwise, by now she might have broken down his bedroom door just to touch him.

Thinking about her friends swelled her heart with love. To be a lasting part of their lives would be satisfaction itself, but she knew she could never truly belong.

Yes, it had turned out the dread of mitobots infecting the world like a doomsday plague had been the opposite of the truth. The Abundance had proven to be benevolent; her body was like a bottle filled with microscopic djinn. Even so, Gen knew she would bring destruction into the lives of her new friends, for there was a real menace that followed her. Its name was Jack Eberhard.

Because one man hated her, the walls of Redstone Laboratories reached out from fifteen-hundred miles away, to imprison her still.

Eberhard was watching, she knew, biding his time, waiting for her to reveal her place of hiding. She could feel him, like a cold shadow always hovering before the sun. For all she knew, some zoo visitor had videotaped the crazy scene with the leopards. If so, the news media would spread it nationwide. Eberhard would hear about it, and he would certainly investigate. Maybe today's incident would be enough to lead him straight to her.

Eventually, something would betray her secret. Lana now had beautiful, strong legs. Such news would leak, it could not stay sealed. Something, somewhere, somehow, would reveal Gen's location to the one who hunted her. It was only a matter of time.

When he found her, he would kill her. And he would kill anyone who stood in his way. For the sake of her new friends, she must make sure Eberhard did not find her.

That feat turned out to be surprisingly easy. Eberhard did not know she could transform into other species. Even if he somehow guessed her new power, he would have to also guess that she had changed into dolphin form, and then be able to track her in the vaults of the deep blue sea.

She raced down the boardwalk, sandals slapping the planks. A sun-wrinkled man with a bucket of bait and a fishing rod stopped in his tracks and gawked as she ran past. Cade's boat bobbed at its mooring near the end of Willingham Marina's main dock.

Gen ran toward it. She couldn't let her pace slacken, because she so hated to leave. If she slowed to a walk, it would degrade to a shuffle, and then she would lose her will altogether and be unable to budge. She only wished her racing feet could carry her backward through time to where this episode began.

She should never have left the pod of dolphins that was her sea family. If she had not spied Cade standing on the deck of his boat like a bronze sun god, if she had not listened to his honeyed baritone voice and laughter—oh what's the use of second-guessing? She had chosen to emerge from the water and rejoin the human race. That's what hurt so much now.

She had to flee the ones she loved, to hide again in the sea. She had to swim far away where Cade could not find her, because…

He would come looking for her. A sob caught in her throat. It was true: Cade would come looking for her. It was the first time she had let herself believe that he cared, but she suddenly knew it with certainty: Cade did feel strongly for her.

The realization broke her heart, and sorrow poured out in hot tears as if from a burst dam.

29

The rabbit looked dead.

Eberhard couldn't believe it. Prometheus-A—one of the identical twin rabbits that had regenerated from the severed halves of Prometheus—sprawled in cedar chips at the bottom of its cage, smoldering like a burnt pot roast. Smoky haze drifted inside the glass.

Goddamned thing shouldn't be dead. It made Eberhard so furious he wanted to kill it again.

He had pinned down Prometheus-A with a manipulator hand and torched the rabbit's face with a half-minute burst from a blue-hot acetylene flame. Then he had punched the start button on his stopwatch.

"Destruction of the eyes," he'd spoken into his throat mike and recorder. "How long will it take the rabbit to grow new eyes and regain its vision?" A penlight taped to a finger of the waldo would test pupil dilation as soon as the eyeballs regenerated.

The stopwatch was still running. The rabbit's little face was a crispy mask of blackened meat and bone. Ten minutes had passed. No shimmering fog.

Eberhard jabbed the body with a stainless steel finger. A burnt patch of fur stuck to the metal. Not a twitch. No breathing, no signs of life. Eberhard stabbed the stop-button of his stopwatch. Stupid bunny was a lifeless carcass.

He withdrew his suited arms from the waldo sleeves. He gathered a syringe and Vacu-tube from a biomedical workstation near the animal cages. He inserted the gear into the cage through a miniature airlock, thrust his arms back inside the sleeves of the manipulator, and readied the bloodwork kit.

Eberhard gripped the dead rabbit in steel fingers and held it in the air. The body already was stiffening.

"What the hell's with you? Huh? Why'd you die on me?"

He withdrew blood from a fold of skin at the rabbit's neck, dropped the carcass, and sealed the test-tube with the blood specimen inside a second sterile container. He removed this container through the airlock. He had to repeat the steps in reverse to examine the animal's blood at a microscope workstation built inside Gen's former quarters.

Level Four Isolation Protocol was a real pain in the ass, and working an electron microscope by remote was a major part of that pain. Sweat ran down his brow into his eyes. He ground his teeth. After several false starts, cursing under his breath, he obtained a sharply focused image. Under high-powered magnification, he watched red and white blood cells float in a pool of clear plasma on the monitor screen. He saw fat globules. Platelets.

What he did not find were mitobots. The mitobots were gone.

His heart squeezed behind his breastbone. Why did they disappear? He pounded the Formica counter of the workstation. Why?

He hurried to the cage with Prometheus-B, passed a bloodwork kit through the airlock, and thrust his arms into a set of sleeves. The rabbit thumped frantically and crushed itself against the far glass wall of the cage. Then it tried to burrow down into its bedding, kicking up a blizzard of cedar chips.

"I'm just going to draw your blood, you little coward." Now that the rabbit was no longer invulnerable, Eberhard felt nothing but contempt for the beast. He withdrew a tube of blood and flung the rabbit aside.

Back at the electron microscope, he found the same results. No mitobots.

Eberhard jerked away from the video monitor. With sickening clarity, he understood exactly what had happened. He didn't even bother to check his watch. It had been more than twenty-four hours since he'd injected Gen's mitobots into the rabbits. The mitobots had reproduced a programmed number of times and died; then they had passed out of the rabbits in their urine.

Exactly as Ozzie had designed them to do.

Dark crimson rage drowned his vision. He clenched the steel hand of the waldo into a fist and hammered the microscope into junk. The image on the screen blinked once, then deteriorated to gray fizz.

"Gen." In the sound of her name he tasted defeat.

She was the one and only indestructible human. The mitobots thrived in her, but in her alone. The rabbits, Eberhard, everyone else, could only buy invulnerability for a short while, less than a day, until the mitobots had exhausted their lives.

Eberhard screamed in frustration. He shoved away from the workstation, knocking the metal chair to the floor. He felt as if the rabbits themselves had betrayed him, yanked his dreams from his grasp, and pissed on them. Hadn't they pissed out the mitobots?

He stomped back to the cage where Prometheus-B trembled, a white ball of fluff wedged in a corner. Eberhard shoved the blowtorch through the cage's airlock. Behind his faceplate, his lips curled into a sneer.

He ignited the three-inch-long blue flame.

*　　　　*　　　　*

Eberhard paced the roadway between the large concrete-and-steel laboratory building and his rustic bungalow. Several hours had passed since he'd disposed of

225

the animal remains in a high-temperature biowaste incinerator.

The night sky was bleaching to gray in the east. His shoes crunched the gravel of the quarter-mile circuit; his eyes looked ahead but focused on nothing.

He had accepted the fact that the mitobots thrived solely in Gen's body, remained and evolved only in her. In all others, they could live for only a short span—about twenty hours—until their functions shut down and they died.

Gen is the mitobots' reservoir, the mother ship. By injecting myself with her blood, I can become godlike myself, with the mitobots performing any necessary healing—but only for a day. *Less* than a goddam day.

Better than nothing, he admitted. How many ampoules of Gen's frozen blood did he have left? Five. No, four. Once thawed, the mitobots wouldn't survive inside the blood in the ampoules beyond the twenty-hour limit. He needed to harvest more of her blood before destroying her.

He truly hated her.

At first, he had envied her, wanting her power for himself. Invincibility—what could be a greater boon for a warrior? Now that he knew he could never attain her might, his envy congealed in his gut, solid as a cannon ball. All he wanted now was to eliminate her. But to do that, he first had to find her. Again, he went over every angle of the problem.

The morning shift guards arrived on four-wheel all-terrain cycles. They saluted as they drove past. Eberhard wiped perspiration from his brow and his handkerchief came up pink where sweat had mixed with red rock dust. The rising sun now overlooked Salinas Peak, and Eberhard had failed to come up with a better plan than the one already in operation.

Gen spoke scores of languages, and she could be anywhere in the world by now. But she couldn't hide forever. No matter where she went, her own strangeness would expose her. Even without witnessing her awesome powers of regeneration, people would notice she was extraordinary in body and mind. Eventually, news about Gen had to turn up; at least in local gossip, if not splashed all over the media.

Weeks ago, on the day the Navy crew found her transponder beeping from the bottom of the Gulf of Mexico, Eberhard had issued a bulletin to all military intelligence organizations of the United States and its allies: Keep your spy networks open for any talk of a young woman with mysterious abilities—key words: magical, miraculous, supernatural, witch, witchcraft, healer, saint, and purple or violet eyes. Report anything out of the ordinary to Col. Jack Eberhard, U.S. Army, via the Pentagon.

It wasn't much of a plan, but over time, it stood a good chance of success.

The hardest strain of all was the waiting.

30

Cade had never run so fast in his life. He'd run track in high school, and he'd jogged miles with his SEALs team with full field gear and a rifle. But that was easygoing compared to how he pushed his body now, arms and legs pumping, lungs burning. He couldn't let her leave. He had to make her understand how much he cared.

He knew where she was heading. Gen was a mermaid, or a sea-goddess, or whatever you're supposed to call a magical being who arises from the sea. He'd seen her dolphin-self turn into a woman; it had been no hallucination.

His mind was now a thousand times more open than it had been a couple days ago. His life no longer fit into the box he had built for it, and that was fine by him. The air inside the old box had been getting stale anyway. His life now included mermaids eating pancakes, and former amputees re-equipped with muscular legs, turning handsprings on the lawn.

Life included Gen. Wonderful and amazing. But now she was going back to sea. Maybe she needed to return to the ocean for awhile; maybe mermaids have to switch back and forth between their human and dolphin forms every few days. He didn't know anything about it. But if she was running away because he'd asked too many questions, he damn sure wanted to apologize. He had so much to thank her for.

At least let me get there in time to thank her. Please.

He forced his sprinting legs into higher gear.

*   *   *

Gen stepped down onto a runner off the main dock and hopped onto the deck of Cade's boat. Before swimming out into the bay to search for her dolphin pod, she needed to say good-bye to her human family. She opened a storage compartment under the middle seat where she'd seen Cade stow a white plastic slate and grease pen with his scuba gear.

Now she sat down and tried to shape her feelings into words. The pen hovered over the slate and her nose ran with hot tears. All the languages she knew could not express the simple principle of how much she cared for the people she must leave, how painful it was to go.

She had been born and grown up in an isolation lab, not even allowed to breathe the same air as ordinary people. She was radically different, not just 'unique,' as Haven had said, but bereft of kin; and the wounds her loneliness caused her every single day, even the mitobots could not heal. She had never dared to hope that she might someday have friends that she could live among—and touch.

Then came Toshi's sacrifice; giving his life to free her from prison. Next came Little Squirt and the dolphins, accepting her into their pod as an equal partner and soulmate—"Share this pod; share this heart."—as they say in their whistle language. And then came the hospitality of Haven and Lana and Jimi and Cade.

All of them were her true family. They had welcomed her, and she owed them more than they could know.

Tears of gratitude wet her cheeks, when at last, she wrote down her feelings as a simple formula:

Lana, you are my mother.
Haven, you are my sister.
Jimi, you are my brother.
Cade,

She hesitated, unable to name what Cade was to her. If she said "lover," it would be a fantasy; but other words for

229

Cade would be a disguise. The dolphins had taught her an ancient melody about the sea's longing for the moon; if she could, she would leave that song as her message to him.

She gazed out over the bay. The tide was flowing out and a foam cup floated among clumps of seaweed and tangled debris. She would swim out about five miles and begin calling her pod. Sound travels very efficiently underwater, they would hear and come. Little Squirt would dance over the waves with joy. She smiled, though the sky and sea shimmered wetly through her tears.

Time to go. She kicked off her sandals.

Gen knew that in the Tok Pisin language of Melanesia, people said, "Wansalawata" as greeting and farewell. "Wansalawata" meant "one saltwater," and acknowledged the truth that all life comes from and belongs to the same mother ocean.

She picked up the grease pen and jotted next to Cade's name: *You are I are one saltwater.* A fat teardrop splashed on the slate, as if to punctuate the emotion.

Beneath that line, she wrote, *Thank you all for being my friends.*

But she couldn't force her hand to write *Good-bye.*

*   *   *

Cade reached the dock and raced onward, footsteps thundering along the planks. Then he saw her at the bow of his boat. She quickly stripped nude and swept back her arms to dive into the water.

"Gen!" He flung himself ahead. "No! Don't leave!"

But already she was in mid-air, sailing over the gunwale. He heard the splash and his heart sank to the bottom of the bay.

"Gen! Wait!" he cried. "Please!"

He leaped down to the wooden runner and raced along its length. "Gen! Don't go!" When he reached the end of the runner, he saw her in the water, gazing up at him with amethyst eyes.

He dove in and swam to her.

He grabbed a steel cross strut between two pilings and held on while he pulled her to him in a tight embrace. Her breasts mashed against his broad chest through the wet cotton of his T-shirt. Tendrils of her wavy hair spread out around her in the water, intertwining with the dark snakes of his dreadlocks. The low sun bathed them in rosy light and the water surface gleamed gold and crimson, reflecting the sky.

"Don't go," he said. "Please. We want you...*I* want you to stay."

She closed her eyes and tilted up her face to him. He bent and kissed her strange, wide mouth and he kissed her homely nose and he wanted her to stay more than he had ever wanted anything in his life.

Abruptly, she broke off from his kisses and turned her head away. Iridescent flashes glowed on the water. Seconds later, she turned back to face him.

Cade drew back with a loud gasp.

Gen's face was stunning in its symmetry and beauty. He had never seen a woman so lovely. He stared, mesmerized, not completely sure she was the same person he'd been kissing.

"Gen?"

She smiled. "It's me."

Cade felt dizzy. Everything had become so magical, he halfway expected white-bearded Poseidon to poke his head out of the bay and shout, "Hey, you! What are your intentions with my daughter?"

Gen looked at his mouth and her lips parted slightly. His mouth met hers and he drank in her sweet breath. The fragrant warmth of her soft lips and the emotion that swelled his heart merged into pure sensation. He lost himself in a kiss that was all and everything for one time-lost moment.

Finally, he pulled back and stared at Gen wonderingly. "But *how*...?"

"I...it's because I'm next to you," she said. "This is my natural form." Her violet eyes searched his. "You see? You make me feel..." She blushed. "*You* changed me."

He didn't really see, but it sounded great. "You're amazing, that's all I know." He blew out a shaky breath. "Come on, let's get back to the others. Everyone wants you home. Lana said she was going to kick my butt if I didn't bring you back."

Gen smiled and fresh tears sparkled in her eyes. "For awhile. I'll go back with you for awhile." Sadness thickened her voice. "Today. Tomorrow...we'll see." She swallowed past the lump in her throat. "But I won't be able to stay."

His heart turned into a big lead sinker. "Why not?"

She sighed and her violet eyes clouded. "Oh, Cade, I really want to tell you, to explain everything."

"So tell me. You can trust me." He squeezed her shoulders. "You can trust all of us. If you're in trouble, we'll help."

"I know that." She bit her lip to hold back tears and gazed down at the water for a long moment. Finally, she looked up. "All right. Let's go back to the inn," she said. "I'll tell all of you who I am. Then you'll understand why I have to leave."

31

Night fell and the moon rose behind the inn; its light gilded the wrinkled satin sheet of the bay. Gen and the other adults sat on wicker chairs on the wide front porch. Haven had dragged herself to bed with utmost reluctance, but she had sensed the seriousness of the occasion and had not put up too much fuss.

Gen wore Lana's white terrycloth bathrobe; it enwrapped her like a collapsed tent and the plushy cloth held Lana's aroma, which she found comforting. Cade sat next to her, holding her hand. The heat from his hand traveled up her arm and down her belly. She wondered if he had any idea what his touch did to her.

She had told them everything. Her creation in the military lab. The Abundance. Eberhard's tests. Her escape with Toshi. His sacrifice. Swimming with dolphins.

Several times in Gen's story, Lana had wept. Cade had cursed under his breath. Jimi had stood and paced in tight circles behind his chair, until Lana and Cade both asked him to please sit down. The Abundance fascinated Jimi, and he asked a number of detailed questions. Gen tried her best to explain to him her compulsion to gather the essence of living things.

When she finished her tale, everyone sat for a while exchanging looks but not talking. Crickets chirped and tree frogs chimed and bullfrogs kept up a deep bass rhythm thrumming against her eardrums. Gen saw that her friends were stunned by what they'd learned; but the looks of concern and compassion on each face told her they had not rejected her, and gratitude replaced her earlier anxiety.

"Where is Eberhard now?" Cade said.

"I don't know."

"I definitely want to ask you a zillion questions about your time with the dolphins," Jimi said. "You know more about dolphins than I'll ever learn in a lifetime of study."

Gen saw that Jimi was at once thrilled and saddened by the realization that her weeks of direct experience had far outdistanced his years of research. "I'll be glad to let you interview me," she said, "a little each day, maybe? For as long as I can stay here."

"That's what gets my blood boiling." Cade said. "You're telling us you can't stay because of this sadist, this Col. Eberhard. He's going to track you down and kill you. Well, I say, to hell with that. Over my dead body."

Fear pierced Gen's heart. "No, please, that's exactly what I can't have happen. I don't want to put you in danger. Not any of you."

Lana got up and laid a hand on Gen's shoulder. "Nobody's going to hurt you," she said in a husky voice. "We'll make sure of that."

"You don't understand," Gen said, and her voice quavered. "When Eberhard shows up, he'll show up with an army. He's afraid of me, all the scientists are. They're not going to let me roam around loose. They won't stop until they've destroyed me."

"We'll take this all the way to the president if we have to," Lana said.

Gen shook her head. "Toshi told me the president herself authorized the H-bomb. It's the only thing Eberhard knows for certain can destroy me."

"Bunch of bastards," Cade said. "This is America, land of the free. No one just storms into our home and commits murder in the name of the friggin' state. Not while I'm alive, they don't." The voice didn't sound like Cade's, it sounded like the deep growl of a grizzly. "I'll defend you to my dying breath."

"No!" Gen yelled. "I forbid it." She looked around at their startled faces. "Look, I told myself it wouldn't really hurt if I came back for a time, if you learned the truth. Because when Eberhard arrives, I'll run back to the dolphins. He'll never find me."

The muscles in Cade's jaw stood out, he clenched his fists.

"But I would never have come back to you—I'll go away tonight, I swear—if I think you're going to get yourselves hurt trying to protect me. You *can't* protect me."

Cade shook his head. "Lousy bastards."

"Cade?" She took his square chin in her hands. "You won't be able to protect me. You have to let me go when the time comes. Then we'll all be safe. Understand?"

His eyes teared and he jerked to his feet and stalked off the porch.

Gen looked to Lana. "It's all right," Lana said. "He'll wander around a couple hours, punch a palm tree or two, maybe go for a five-mile swim. But he understands. That's why he's so angry, he hates feeling helpless." She sighed. "So do I. Isn't there anything we can do? We've got to think this through."

"You've welcomed me, made your home mine," Gen said. "You can't do more than that, and you don't need to. I can't put into words how happy you've already made me."

"Oh, honey, I'm so glad you came back to us." Lana knelt by Gen's chair and the two of them embraced.

Jimi snapped his fingers. "Wow, that's it. That's gotta be it."

They both looked up at him and Lana chuckled. "See that arch in his eyebrows?" she said. "That's his brainstorm look."

"You bet it is," he said. "I just realized what the mitobots—the Abundance—I just realized what they are. It explains everything."

235

"That I'd like to know, myself," Gen said.

His eyes sparkled. "First I need to check some of my books, get online. I'll see you two in the morning." He kissed Lana and hurried into the house to get to his cabin in the back yard.

Lana smiled. "He gets like this."

"I hope he can tell me what the Abundance is building toward. I feel their power growing in me, but I don't know what they're going to do. It scares me."

Lana squeezed her hand. "Jimi is brilliant. Maybe he can find the answers you need."

*   *   *

Gen's bed could not have been more comfortable, yet she couldn't sleep.

A treefrog had managed to get into the bedroom somewhere and it chirped non-stop like a featherless green bird. But that was not the problem.

An army of bullfrogs surrounded the inn, sounding like a convention of double-bass violinists, bowing their two deepest notes, ad infinitum, while a chorus of crickets provided a two-note counterpoint several octaves higher. But the noise didn't disturb her.

Moonlight through the tall window cast shapes on the walls, including an ostrich with a cowboy hat on its head, and one remarkably well-formed Noh mask that moved its mouth and eyes. The argent light was bright enough to read a book, but it was not keeping her awake.

The hum of the Abundance droned on inside her tissues like the crickets and frogs outdoors. Lying still, she felt so full of buzzing energy she wondered if she could light up a small town. But even that was not preventing her from sleeping.

The problem was Cade. His voluptuous lips, and the way he had kissed her in the water. His broad chest, and the sensation of her bare breasts pressing against slabs of muscle. His sculpted limbs, and the sheltering she had felt when the fortress of his arms wrapped her body. His dark green eyes, and the passion that lit them afire when their lips touched. Back to his voluptuous lips. Thinking in circles. Cade was the problem.

She sighed and got out of bed, naked. The full moon over the bay bathed her in silvery light and turned her breasts into twin moonlets. She could faintly smell her own sex and the fragrance was as alluring as any tropical flower. Should she open her bedroom door and wait for the honeybee to come buzzing to her on a trail of perfume?

She couldn't stop thinking about him, upstairs asleep in his bed. Or was he awake, too, thinking of her? Was he feeling the same need, to be in the same room, the same bed—close, closer, closest.

Oh boy. That really turned her on. She was making herself fiendishly horny.

She should march straight up the stairs to his bedroom, bang on his door. Where was it written that she had to wait for him to make the first move? On the other hand, desire was nearly overwhelming her now, leaving her heart defenseless and exposed.

To add to her uncertainty, she was both a virgin and not a virgin, innocent and experienced.

As a dolphin, she had made love a dozen times a day. That's what dolphins do: catch fish and play and have sex. She'd had several dolphin lovers; one of them a magnificent creature, speckled blue-gray and black, with shiny obsidian eyes and a name that meant "He-Who-Races-the-Waves."

But in her human form as Gen, she was indeed a virgin and had only been kissed, today, for the first time. What

237

sexual skills she had learned did not exactly befit the current situation. She and Cade could swim out into the bay, lock bodies, and spin in circles. Or maybe she should wait until this lusty fever cooled and she could think and act more rationally.

She stared out over the water at the huntress moon, lovesick and a bit drunk with the buzz of the life-force teeming inside her. Susurrations of waves lapping the distant shore mixed with her sighs.

Footsteps. She jumped back from the window. Barefeet padding in the hall, someone tall and heavy approaching her door.

She suppressed a squeal and hopped into bed, her heart drumming like a conga. Hormones flooded her bloodstream and mixed together excitement, joy, love, desire, fear, and lunacy. Goose bumps prickled her breasts and she shivered from the hot flush of blood to her skin. She threw the covers over her head and hid, blushing and giggling like a fool.

Good grief, am I behaving like a silly schoolgirl, or what?

The knock on her door was restrained, the baritone voice a whisper. "Gen, you asleep?"

Panting was probably not the most subtle way to answer. She slowed her breathing, reined in her runaway heart. "I'm awake." She pulled her head out from under the covers. "I'm awake."

"May I come in?"

"The door is unlocked." Non-committal response. Deep breaths. Show a little dignity, you witless wench.

The door swung open with the tiniest squeak. Cade entered quietly and stood by the foot of the bed. He wore a pair of cut-off jeans. Nothing else. In the moonlight, his masculine silhouette looked Herculean.

Okay. Breathing more smoothly, giggles under control. Good. Now just proceed slowly, with grace and nobility of manner. Keep the bedsheets pulled coyly to your chin and engage him in hushed conversation while he sits at the foot of the bed. Progress from the talking-stage to eventually holding hands, then move inexorably toward the second kiss of your life.

She tossed back the covers and moonlight illuminated her nude body. Cade's pupils grew huge. He climbed into bed beside her.

Oh boy.

*   *   *

The antique brass bed became their island, complete unto itself; beyond its rumpled shorelines, nothing existed. Each mouth was a sweet mountain stream to the other's thirsty lips. Loving hands carefully and unhurriedly explored moonlit landscapes.

Cade began a slow expedition down her body, covering its contours with kisses as he went. Gen gasped, astonished at the pleasure of his hot lips on her skin. His kisses were slaying her; she felt like she was about to come unglued. His kisses painted her belly and kept moving down to arrive like electricity between her thighs. Oh that did it. That was the end of holding on. She cried out at the brink of orgasm, but the sudden feeling of melting overwhelmed the blissful sensations.

Cells liquefied at the core of her body; she really *was* coming unglued. Oh, God, no. Not now.

"Cade, wait! Please, stop! I...I'm losing control."

"It's okay." His voice was soft, his eyes heavy-lidded. "Just let go. Go with the feeling."

She shook her head. He didn't understand: She was losing grasp of her human form. She was *morphing*. All joy forgotten, her chest tightened with fear.

This same loss of control had occurred weeks ago, the day she fell from Toshi's jet and awoke in sand dunes on the far side of the island. The beauty of the living world had seduced her into a kind of delighted trance; but then the Abundance had come on strong, changing her—into who knows what. She had managed to halt the transformation. But now it was happening again, and she still had no idea what she would become if she let the metamorphosis go on.

The internal melting spread toward the surface. She sat up in bed and shoved Cade away.

"Go! You've got to go now. Please, hurry."

"Huh?" He looked dismayed. "I…I'm sorry. Did I offend you?"

She beat at his shoulders "No time, get out—*get out*!"

He stared, eyes smoky with hurt and anger. Then he stood and looked around for his cut-off jeans.

She realized he was moving too slowly. The changes were about to erupt. She shoved past him into the bathroom and locked the door, her heartbeat thundering in her ears.

The room spun and she stumbled to the tiled floor. She was already part-dolphin when she hit, her legs and feet fused into a fluke. Then she grew lithe and feline, covered in leopard's white fur, and while still in the shape of a snow leopard, her fur turned into green-and-yellow feathers, then scales. She became a tarpon, then a king snake, no, both at once—many forms at once. Her gelatinous flesh cycled through dozens of creatures, giving off so much heat the paint on the bathroom wall blistered and peeled and the plastic shower curtain sagged like taffy.

She slid and crawled, slithered and groped her way into the tub and turned on the shower full blast. The water sizzled and steamed as magnolia blossoms burst forth from her shaggy black fur, long blue wings flapped spastically.

"Gen! What's happening in there?" Cade called.

She didn't answer. She had a beak instead of lips.

"Gen, you okay? Can I help? Let me in."

Just stay away. God, don't let him see me like this.

Gen felt terrified. Yet apart from her panic, the transformations did not cause her pain, but intense sensual pleasure. The changes were not even uncontrolled, they simply were not under *her* control. In spite of the apparent chaos of the metamorphosis, she knew the Abundance was moving in a definite direction, creating something new and wonderful—a life-form born once in a billion years.

But that was the most frightening part of the experience—the way the Abundance seduced her with physical pleasure to surrender to the changes and allow them to continue to their climax.

No! She just could not let it happen. She had her own life. It wasn't fair for the Abundance to ruin it for her. What about her relationship with Cade? Didn't she have the right to choose to remain human? Or was she only a slave to the mysterious power?

Please, stop! she screamed silently. I refuse to let go.

How had she halted the process the first time, on the beach? She remembered she had focused on her human form.

The water boiled furiously from the heat pouring off her body. The changes were slowing now. She was part speckled dolphin again, part golden retriever, part Persian cat. The mutations slowed further. Part blue heron, part snow leopard.

Part human. Her hair grew out in wavy strands. The strands turned into snakes, sea kelp, sawgrass. Wavy hair again. Then the tendrils turned into green vines with red berries. Wavy hair.

She closed her eyes. Concentrate. Remember the joy of being with Cade. Muscles bulged in her shoulders and chest and a heavy penis sprouted between her legs as she momentarily took on the size and shape of Cade.

Gen. Gen. Gen. I'm *Gen*. She pictured herself in the bedroom, thinking about Cade before he arrived, recalled her sexual longing, her feminine emotions. Gradually, she stabilized as Gen. She opened her eyes. Patches of iridescence shimmered and fizzed across her skin and were re-absorbed. The water stopped boiling.

The shower curtain had melted into glop. The bathroom reeked of scorched paint and vinyl. She slowly stood, stepped out of the tub in a thick cloud of steam.

Towering in the white fog like a lighthouse stood Cade, gaping at her. She had been too distracted to hear him break through the bathroom door. A blanket wrapped his body to shield it from the blast furnace of heat she had generated.

The look on his face told her he'd been standing there awhile. Her heart plummeted. He was no longer simply amazed or intrigued or fascinated by her. Fear chilled the same green eyes that moments earlier had been aflame with desire.

She reached out her hand. He drew back.

She turned from him and walked out of the bathroom, put on Lana's bathrobe and kept walking, outside the inn onto the front lawn.

Frogs. Crickets. The drinking gourd spilling dew onto the grass. Cade's mouth had been a drinking gourd to quench her thirst. The full moon set slowly over the bay. Her breasts had been daughter moons. For one sweet moment, she had belonged to the Earth. She had belonged. For a moment.

She understood now that deep pleasure triggered the Abundance to start the metamorphosis. It had first

242

happened on the beach; the natural beauty had intoxicated her and she'd lost control of her human form. Cade had spurred the reaction tonight when his kisses drove her to the verge of orgasm.

That meant she had to avoid powerful pleasures. Which meant she had to avoid making love with Cade. That shouldn't be hard, given the revulsion on his face just now in the bathroom. He didn't want to touch her hand.

A barred owl hooted from a nearby sweetgum tree. The Abundance compelled her to go collect their essences. She refused.

no harm my ass, she thought. You guys just broke my heart.

32

Gen sat at the wrought iron breakfast table on the porch with Jimi and Lana. She had not slept after her fiasco with Cade. Lana had come downstairs at six-thirty, and found Gen pacing on the porch, crazy to find out what Jimi had learned from his Internet research. So Lana went out to the cabin and returned with a bedraggled Jimi in tow, still in paisley cotton pajama bottoms.

He studied Gen across the table, adjusted his eyeglasses on his sunburned nose. Thick lenses magnified pale blue, bloodshot eyes and individual arterioles, like red threads in paper dollars. Auburn hair spilled loosely over thin, freckled shoulders.

Jimi shifted the eyeglasses up and down his nose, and then held them out at different arm lengths, peering through the lenses. "Damn. My prescription isn't working."

Lana grabbed the eyeglasses from his hand and flung them to the far side of the porch. They skipped once and flipped through the railing into an azalea bush.

"What the…?"

She laughed. "I've been wanting to do that to those butt-ugly glasses for five summers," she said. "You've got pretty blue eyes, Jimi MacGregor. That is, when you haven't been staring at a computer screen all night."

He blinked and gawked at his hands; surveyed the porch, the pond, the palm trees. His face stretched into a huge grin. "Hey, I can see! Everything's crystal clear."

Lana smiled. "Hallelujah."

Jimi swiveled his head, examining objects near and far, rediscovering his world in sharp focus. "My gosh, Lana, you've got African heritage—and all this time I thought you were a platinum blonde." He laughed. "No truthfully, you're even prettier than I thought. I really mean it. You too, Gen. The whole world is."

Gen's anxiety made her impatient. "Last night, you said you realized what the Abundance is. I need to know."

He nodded, took a deep breath. "I'm afraid what I have to say is going to sound very far-fetched….and it may come as quite a shock."

"Try me."

"Well…hmmm." He shoveled a mounded teaspoon of sugar into his creamy coffee, stirred. "How about if I start with my conclusion, and then work backward to show you how I arrived at it?"

"Fine."

He took a sip, watching her over the rim of the coffee mug. "Okay, Gen, here goes: I'm convinced that you are a very sophisticated probe. Or at least the mitobots inside you are. They're probes." He cleared his throat. "From another world, I mean."

"Jimi, good God," Lana said. "Aliens?"

Gen felt her heart beating faster. Jimi searched her face. "You're not laughing," he said. "You have a hunch I may not be totally full of it."

"I'm ready to believe anything, other than that I'm normal," Gen said. "If you were to tell me I'm just an ordinary woman who happens to have mitobots living in my tissues, then I'd laugh in your face."

He nodded. Lana reached over and took Gen's hand. "The mitobots are extraterrestrial probes," Jimi said. "Bio-engineered explorers that blur the line between machinery and biology. Their purpose is to voyage to new worlds, gather genetic data, transmit the data back to their home-world and also replicate themselves to travel onward to new planets." He sipped his coffee, studying her reaction. "Ever heard of John von Neumann?"

She shook her head.

245

"He was a mathematician who—"

The kitchen door banged shut. Cade stepped through onto the porch and slumped into a chair at the table. He didn't say a word or meet anyone's eyes.

"Well, good morning to you, too," Lana said.

He shrugged, gave a grunt under his breath.

"Gosh, you're in a cheery mood," she said.

He looked up, straight at Gen. "Trouble sleeping. Had a nightmare."

Lana watched the couple. "Don't take it out on the rest of us."

He glanced at his sister and forced a smile. "Sorry. Good morning."

"Care for some coffee?"

"Please."

Lana poured steaming coffee from a big pot into an extra mug. Cade swigged the coffee black and grimaced from its heat.

"Jimi was telling us that I'm a probe from outer space—another planet," Gen said to Cade. "Sound farfetched to you?"

"I'm ready to believe anything about you," he said. "Well, except one. You're not a woman."

"Cade!" Lana shot him a reproachful look.

His words cut deeply, but Gen tried to hide the hurt. "See? What did I tell you, Jimi?"

"What on earth is going on between you two?" Lana said.

Cade shrugged, stared down at his hands wrapping the coffee mug.

"Go ahead, Cade, tell them," Gen said. "That's what we're here to discuss. My alien-ness."

He sighed and shook his head.

"Go ahead," Gen said.

"We're going to have to repaint her bathroom," he said quietly, not lifting his eyes. "The walls nearly caught fire."

"*What*?" Jimi and Lana said together.

"She puts off a lot of heat when she..." he looked up. "When she goes through her changes."

"What are you talking about?" Jimi said.

He pointed to Gen with his chin. "She can become any animal, any plant. She can even be half a dozen of them at the same time. Wings, paws, flippers—all different species at once." He shuddered.

"Not *any* animal or plant," Gen corrected, "only the ones I've touched."

"Ohmigod! That's what I'm getting at!" Jimi slapped his palm on the table and coffee sloshed from his mug. "You're some kind of von Neumann probe."

"Am I?" Gen said. Her heart raced in her bosom, while she carefully managed not to jump up from the table and run away, screaming.

"The mitobots, I mean. Inside you. They're probes."

Gen made herself ask, "What's a von Neumann probe?"

"Back in the '50s, he proposed that an advanced civilization should be able to construct self-reproducing machines that could be sent as explorers to other worlds. Each probe would transmit data back to its home world, and also build copies of itself and the copies would travel on to new worlds, planet-hopping across space."

She nodded, feeling a queasy stirring in her gut.

"He calculated that by sending out only one probe, that built just two copies of itself to keep spreading forth—you know, two probes make four copies; the four make eight; eight make sixteen, and so on—the probes could flood our galaxy in a matter of centuries. In fact, in a few billion years the probes would be able to saturate every available planet in the universe."

247

She knitted her brows. "But how does that apply to me?"

"Yeah," Cade said, "I don't follow you."

"Well, von Neumann did the math. But others have developed his idea. What if the probes carried the needed information to construct virtually anything from raw materials? They could even build organic beings. Manufacture plants and animals from scratch. Do you see?"

Gen swallowed, afraid that she did see.

"You could send a machine with stored DNA patterns to a likely planet," he said, "and it could colonize that new world with these 'starter kits' of species from your home world. Each probe would be a kind of Noah's ark, but traveling only with genetic codes—"

"The *essence* of creatures," Gen said.

"The essence, that's right. So you wouldn't have to send organic tissue, like frozen fertilized eggs, on a space journey of a hundred thousand years or whatever." Jimi was tapping his foot excitedly until Lana touched his knee and he stopped.

"But I didn't come from another planet," Gen said. "I know that much. I was born in a military lab in New Mexico."

"Mitochondria," Jimi said. "Your mitobots were developed from mitochondria."

She furrowed her brow. "So?"

"I'm working backwards, here, stick with me. First, I need to explain something called 'panspermia'."

"'Seeds everywhere.'"

"You've heard of it?"

She shook her head. "I know Greek."

"Huh. Well, the term goes back a hundred years to a Swedish scientist named Svante Arrhenius; guy won the Nobel Prize in physics. He proposed that microorganisms wafting in from outer space, pushed along by stellar winds,

248

seeded life on earth. Others have suggested the spores didn't just drift here, but were 'mailed' here, in spaceships or however, by alien ancestors. Francis Crick—heard of him?"

"Nobel Prize in Physiology, 1962, with James Watson and Maurice Wilkins, for discovering the structure of DNA."

Jimi smiled. "Wish I had students like you. Professors, for that matter."

"I had lots of time to read in my isolation unit."

"Yeah, but your memory...You said you know Greek. Meaning what? Can you speak it?"

She nodded.

"Fluently?"

"Yes."

"And how many other languages?"

She hesitated. Her caramel skin faintly betrayed a blush. "Fluently? Two hundred sixty-three."

He whistled low.

"Human languages," she added softly.

His face brightened. "Do dolphins speak a true language?"

"Dolphins have two languages," she said. "Whistle, which is actual speech, and a picture language, where we...where they broadcast shaped sound images through the water."

"My god, you mean iconographic language, like hieroglyphics?"

"Well, it's usually representational—say, a realistic picture of a tiger shark; but yes, it can also be symbolic. A serrated tooth icon means 'predator warning.'"

"Wow," Cade said. "I didn't know dolphins could do that."

Jimi nodded slowly, eyes shining with tears of awe. "Neither did I."

"I'm sure there's a lot Gen could teach us," Lana said, and put a hand on Cade's shoulder, "about a great deal of things. If we keep our minds open."

Cade eyed his coffee, took a sip.

"I'm dying to ask you a ton of questions about dolphins," Jimi said. "I've compiled a list."

"Yes, but later, please," Gen said. "You were starting to say something about Francis Crick."

"Right. Panspermia. Crick calls the notion that Earth was intentionally seeded, '*directed* panspermia.' He wrote a very convincing book on the subject, I re-read parts of it last night," he said. "He argues against the orthodox view of the origin of life—that it arose by the chance collision of molecules in the organic soup of the primeval oceans."

Out of habit, he reached to slide his eyeglasses back up his thin nose, and smiled when he remembered he no longer needed them. "For one thing, the Earth itself was only a half-billion years old when the first cells appeared—and for the biggest part of that time the planet had been radioactive and hotter than molten iron. That leaves only a few million years of hospitable conditions before life developed. Crick says that's not enough time for a series of 'lucky accidents' to create a self-replicating molecule as complex and beautiful as DNA."

"Okay."

"He suspects life evolved during a very much longer epoch on another world—our ancestral home, if you will. Anciently, our progenitors sent abroad the molecular technology of life—DNA—to new worlds. The seeds have been spreading for eons."

"Fertilizing virgin planets," Lana said. "Sounds like male-scientist mythology."

Jimi chuckled. "Could be. But yesterday, Gen told us Project Second Nature genetically manipulated mitochondria, re-activating them in their aboriginal form as

250

free-swimming cells. That gave me a brainstorm." He brushed a long strand of auburn hair from his face. "I realized the mitochondria are perfect candidates for seeds from another world."

Gen tried to calm her breathing. Ugh. The uneasiness in her belly stirred around and around.

"We know mitochondria have their own, distinctive DNA, unlike any other on Earth, and that they became symbiotic with other primitive cells a couple billion years ago—"

"Hold on. You just said life began on this planet *four* billion years ago," Gen said. "If the mitochondria showed up ages later, the cells—the genes—that evolved into us were already here."

He nodded. "I've got a scenario for that," he said. "Maybe the first rain of seeds from outer space fell into the oceans four billion years ago and kick-started microbial life on Earth. Meanwhile, the probes kept reproducing and voyaging onward, right? The mitochondria were a *second* wave of spores." Jimi's long hair flopped in his face again. "The seeds are programmed to bolster life and never harm life that is underway. So when the second wave arrived, they *combined* with the cells already living."

He combed back his hair with both hands and tied it in a knot behind his head.

"Perhaps multiple waves of seeds arrived here," he said. "I'm thinking of dramatic accelerations of evolution, where new and more complex species suddenly burst forth in the fossil record—the Cambrian Explosion is a bold example, but far earlier, there was the leap from prokaryotes to eukaryotes, and then from single-celled to multi-celled organisms, and so forth. No one has accounted for a mechanism that would trigger these abrupt 'punctuations of equilibrium.' You with me?"

She nodded. "Please, go on." Her voice sounded tinny.

251

"If a progenitor race wanted to send out life-starter kits—seeds that serve a dual purpose as information-gathering probes—wouldn't they also want to cross-pollinate? Travel back and forth between worlds already teeming with life and swap the interesting news from all the distant cousins. See what I'm saying? Gene-traders. Not interested in conquering new worlds or in ordinary commerce, but crisscrossing the galaxy to trade *information*, biological information, recorded in the DNA. With a big enough swarm of mitobots—trillions—they could gather and deliver a whole planet's genetic code to a distant world."

Her head swam. She glanced at the faces around the table. Why did *she* have to be the alien? She'd much rather be the understanding human friend to someone else who was the alien.

Lana met her eyes and smiled warmly. Jimi studied her with barely controlled curiosity and excitement, like she was an...well, *exactly*. The two didn't seem frightened, but they hadn't peered through the steam last night while her oozing form turned into a polymorphous zoo. Cade, on the other hand, averted her gaze, but remained on guard in case she made a sudden move to suck out his eyeballs.

The rational part of her understood it was better to know the truth. Deal with the facts, Gen. If the scientists had unwittingly activated ancient alien probes inside her, then... Oh hell, who was she kidding? It made her skin crawl, scared her half to death.

She took in a ragged breath. "Okay, let's say the mitobots *are* alien probes, and they were triggered in me, switched on to carry out their original mission. So now they've been collecting genetic codes from everything I touch. What's next?" Gen's hand trembled and Lana gave it a squeeze. "I mean, to complete the mission they need to

252

transmit the information somewhere. How are they going to do that?"

Jimi rubbed his chin. "I don't know."

"You said with a big enough swarm—with trillions—they could carry a whole planet's genetic code to another world," Gen said. "But there's no need for such a swarm. I can taste... I *know* that every mitobot inside me contains the entire library of genetic codes I've gathered."

Jimi's eyebrows shot up. "Each *one* contains *all* the information?"

She nodded. "So there won't be a cloud of trillions traveling to just one new world," she said. "It will be trillions of DNA-laden probes heading to trillions of new worlds."

Jimi's mouth fell open.

"And I feel that they're ready now for that last stage of their mission." Her heart drubbed in her throat and she stood up from the table. "There's an irrestistable force growing in me, I can sense it building." She hugged herself and shivered. "Trillions. I can taste them aching to fulfill their duty. But *how* are they going to travel onward? *How*, Jimi?"

He glanced down, unable to meet the desperation in her eyes. "I'm sorry, Gen. I just don't know."

"It started to happen last night." She looked at Cade. "That's what I was going through, all the morphing, moving toward some final stage. It felt like I was...that if I let the changes keep going, accelerating, I was going to..." She waved her hands in frustration. She almost wanted to say "*climax*"—but how would they understand that she felt she had been heading toward an ultimate release beyond human imagining. "I thought I was going to ignite...*explode*, like a supernova."

Everyone was watching her fall apart.

253

"But if I blaze like a star…" Her voice broke with a sob. "…and the probes travel on, will there be anything left of me?"

She buried her face in her hands. "Who am *I*?"

Lana stood and wrapped strong arms around her. Gen pressed her face against the taller woman's neck and wept.

33

Cade and Jimi were still parked at the breakfast table an hour later, their coffee mugs long empty. Lana had taken Gen for a walk with the dog on a private jogging path through the woods of the estate. Neither of the men had spoken for a while.

Cade broke the silence. "Jimi, parts of this don't make sense to me."

"Just parts, huh?" Jimi gave a little laugh. "Hell, man, my mind is reeling like a drunkard."

"Yeah, okay. We're all in over our heads," Cade said. "For one thing, I can't understand how each teeny little organism—each mitobot—can contain all the genetic codes from all the species Gen has touched. How does one microscopic probe store that much information?"

"Good question, and I don't know the answer," Jimi said. "Remember, I thought it would take a swarm of trillions. But my hunch is, the DNA itself functions as a computer."

"Explain."

Jimi shook his head. "Can't. Don't know how it would work. But I'll say this much: Only about three percent of each DNA molecule contains the genes, the amino acid sequences that code for the manufacture of proteins. The remaining ninety-seven percent of the text doesn't code for anything that we understand. Geneticists call it 'junk DNA,' which of course simply means—"

"They don't know a damn thing about it."

"Exactly," Jimi said. "You and I each have 125 billion miles of DNA strands in our bodies, and nearly all of it has an unknown purpose."

"So let's just call it junk." Cade felt disgusted with the all-too-common smugness of human beings—himself included. Just days ago, his notion of the "real" world had been so much smaller than today that to return to it now would give him claustrophobia.

"Some math dude at MIT showed that, in principle, DNA might be turned into a four-digit computer that would be trillions of times faster than a supercomputer. Instead of using the standard binary code of zeros and ones, the nucleotide base pairs would function as digits."

Cade held up his thumb and forefinger as if measuring a sliver. "I'm getting about this much of what you're telling me."

"The nucleotides—the rungs of the DNA ladder," Jimi said. "They're constructed of four amino acids. That could give you a *four*-digit code to work with instead of a two-digit code like computers now use."

"Okay. I guess."

"DNA emits photons," Jimi said. "The light given off is extremely weak, but at microscopic distances the light is coherent, like a laser. Maybe it's a mechanism for reading and writing information onto the non-coding portions of DNA."

"Man, you're so far over my head I'm dog-paddling," Cade said. "But is that how Gen's so smart? So many languages?"

Jimi twisted his mouth. "Not sure. That might be how the mitobots are so smart. I think Gen uses her own brainpower; maybe she just uses a lot more of hers than we use of ours," he said, "or maybe her brain is a better design than ours." He shrugged. "Really, who can account for genius? In the 1800s, there was a Jesuit, a linguist...Rusk?...*Rask*—Rasmus Rask, a professor at the University of Copenhagen—he could speak two-hundred-and-thirty languages. That's close to Gen's number."

"Jesus."

"No, *Society* of Jesus."

256

Cade rolled his eyes.

"Look, Gen is not the mitobots, Cade. I mean, she is and she isn't, okay? Her mind is not their mind. That hurt her when you said she wasn't a woman."

Cade shook his head, squeezed the empty coffee mug in his big hands. "I'm real sorry I said that." He blew out a sigh with puffed cheeks. "Last night. We, uh…got intimate. But then, in the bathroom…she was this…the heat coming off her body singed my eyebrows!" He touched his thick, dark eyebrows; they had re-grown. "Well, they *were* singed," he mumbled. "She just kept changing and changing, becoming so many different animals. Plants, too. Scared the royal crap out of me." He wiped a hand over his whiskered mouth. "Man, I don't know *what* she is."

"Maybe not, but you know she's scared, too. And she needs us. Keep in mind what she did for Lana. My god, she's a miraculous healer—we know that much. We owe her our support."

Cade thought of the miracle of Lana's legs and felt ashamed of how he'd treated Gen. "But I don't know how to help her."

Jimi shook his head. "You don't know how to fix her problem. It's not the same thing, man. You *do* know how to help her—you can help her to not feel so alone."

Cade sat quietly for a moment, chewing his lower lip, musing; then he got up to leave. "I need to go tell her I'm sorry."

"Cade."

He met Jimi's eyes.

"You said you don't know what Gen is. Neither do I— she's a new form of life. But think about this: She contains within her own body the essence of thousands of species; it's as if she's pregnant with the life of the planet."

"It's true," Cade said. He knew that Jimi's eyes reflected his own amazement.

257

"In ancient times people had a definite name for what Gen is—a spiritual name."

Cade swallowed. "Goddess?"

Jimi smiled, nodding. "I was thinking, Great Earth Mother."

34

A thick carpet of pine needles softened the sun-mottled path through the woods. Gen strolled along, her hands moving about her touching, touching. She collected gene codes from a blackberry bush, a clump of poison ivy, a strangler fig, a rhinoceros beetle, a raven's feather, and the decomposing pelt of a fox. But while her compulsion to gather essences was as strong as ever, the physical pleasure the habit produced no longer felt gratifying.

She felt that the Abundance had betrayed her, or maybe her own body had become her enemy. Or both. Or were they now one and the same? Had her body and the sentient swarm within it always been identical? Whatever the case, she simply did not know who she was.

It was an irony: Now that she had found a human family that cared for her, she had lost touch with herself, which made her feel more alone than ever. She pictured the glass walls of the isolation chamber trapping her still, like a butterfly in a killing jar.

Lana walked beside her, meeting her eyes at times, but not talking. Gen wanted to say something, anything, to pry the weight off her chest, but her feelings had sunk to a depth where words had trouble surfacing. She could only let the sanctuary of the woods speak for her sadness, and hope that Lana understood.

Newpod turned to look back toward the inn and gave a happy bark. The panting dog actually seemed to be smiling. Cade was jogging easily to catch up with them.

Gen glanced around as if to find a place to hide. I can't deal with him, now. He hates me. Lana took her hand and gently squeezed. "It's okay," she said in a quiet voice. "I know Cade like a book, and it's a good read, I promise you.

It'll be all right. My guess is, he's coming to apologize to you."

Gen swallowed. Her heart ached, and she didn't want to launch into another crying jag. She had a lot to hold in. Now she was glad the invisible sandbags on her breastbone were so heavy, crushing her feelings inside her, keeping the sea dammed up.

Cade arrived and tussled the retriever's shaggy ears. "Good dog!" Newpod's tail thumped the ground.

Cade looked up at Gen. "Hi." He smiled sheepishly. "I came to find you. Is it okay if we talk a bit? There are some things I need to say."

"I'm going to let you two have some privacy," Lana said, and started back toward the house.

Wait, don't leave me with him! He's dangerous. He can tear my heart in two.

"Come on, boy, I can run now!" Lana said. "Let's race!" She tore off in a sprint. Her dark legs stretched out in long strides speeding up the grassy hill toward the inn. Gen and Cade watched the golden-blonde and chestnut brown racers, one barking, the other laughing, both of them delighting in their new limbs of power.

Cade swallowed. "Gen, I can't tell you..." his voice caught with emotion. "How grateful I am for what you've done."

"Don't thank me. I wasn't in control of any of it. I'm not in control."

Cade tried to meet her eyes, but she turned to the chaotic pattern the pine needles made at her feet.

"Look, I've been a jerk," Cade said. "I want you to know I'm sorry for the way I've acted toward you."

She shook her head hard at the pine needles. "It's not your fault. It's totally understandable. You don't have to..." Now the pine needles were swimming in a clear, salty broth. "It was terrifying, the changes...it was...*I'm*

260

terrifying. I'm a monster. I scare you." The first teardrops spattered the pine needles.

"No—I mean, yeah, I got scared. But you're not terrifying. You...you're wonderful. You're the most amazing person, the most amazing *event* that's ever happened in my life."

She wouldn't look up at him. The sandbags on her chest were starting to shift from the pressure of the floodtide pushing against them. She tightened her breathing to squeeze back the surge of emotion.

"Gen." His warm hand touched her bare shoulder. She shivered. "Gen." His fingers very gently lifted her chin until her eyes met his dark, serious gaze. "Let me tell you a story about when I was a boy." He took her hands in his.

"From the time I was seven, my father started taking me with him in the summers, out on the bay." His voice was husky with emotion. "I never loved anything so much as working alongside my dad, on the oyster beds, or scalloping, fishing, salvaging." He sighed. "Later, when he drowned, I didn't go out for weeks. I still loved the sea, but I couldn't seem to make myself go out in the boat and...then..."

He paused, earnest eyes drinking her in from an emerald depth. "Good God, you're lovely, Gen. You're like a painting in a children's book. I can't bear to see you sad and afraid. I would fight the armies of the world to keep you safe. You're family now. Do you hear? Family. I would die for you."

The levee of her heart burst and the sea gushed through and the sandbags flew away to the sky like doves. She flung herself into Cade's arms so hard she nearly bounced off his chest. She wept and nuzzled her face against the cotton of his T-shirt, against the sweet warmth of his lion's heart.

He laughed. "Hey, you're supposed to get all mushy *after* you hear the end of my story." He combed his fingers

261

through her wavy hair, kissed the top of her head. "Haven't you seen the way they do it in the movies? I never even got to the point."

She tilted back her head and looked in his eyes, tears streaming down her cheeks. "Tell me."

He laughed again. "Well...I finally had to admit I was scared of going out on the water. So Lana asked me, she said, 'Which is stronger, your love for the sea, or your fear of it?' That same day, I made myself get in my dad's boat and cruise out past the horizon, you know—face my fear, all that. But it worked. Sounds corny, but it worked.

"Anyway, I'd be a liar if I said you didn't shake me up last night. I know you're scared, too. But you're no monster. Hear me?" He squeezed her more tightly to him. Her breath poofed out; she would never have guessed getting crushed could feel so delicious. "You're like the sea, Gen—full of hidden power and bottomless beauty."

"Oh, Cade." She sniffled. You're a poet. And, oh, don't I know it.

"My love for you is stronger than my fear, that's the point. And I want you to know that I'm here—we *all* are here—to stand by you."

His body heat and fragrance, densely muscled contours...oh, it was starting to feel too good. Her heart pounded; she heard blood glub-glubbing in her ears, felt it pulsing between her thighs.

She pushed back from his chest. "I can't get too close to you." She gulped. "It's the pleasure. That's what triggered it last night. I start to feel good all over and then...I lose control."

He struggled to hide his own yearning. "We don't have to...you know. We can be friends." But his eyes betrayed his words, caressing her body with his gaze.

"Cade, I'm not sure I can even be around you. Just standing next to you…" She sighed. "You make me feel good all over."

"Thanks." He smiled tenderly. "I feel the same about you."

"Only you're not about to lose hold on your human form, turn into a zoo, catch the woods on fire."

He nodded, glanced around at the loblolly pines. "All right." He smiled bravely and took a deep breath. "We'll be like brother and sister." His smile didn't conceal his disappointment.

His eyes were too loving and hungry to gaze into. She looked down, remembering a Japanese saying that fit her own longing: *Yamai koko ni iru*—The disease lies in a part too innermost to remedy.

"It's gonna be all right," he said. "Let's get back to the Inn. Haven is dying to plait your hair into corn rows, I told her to ask you."

"I'd love that."

He reached for her hand. "Is it okay to hold hands?"

She snuffled. "Let's try."

Hand in hand, they headed up Stanton Hill to the Victorian mansion perched on its crest like a giant hope chest.

35

Eberhard sat beside a steel desk in a bull-pen office space at the Tallahassee Police Department. Detective Captain Charles Rybeck was briefing him about the strange incident at the zoo, but the report was frustratingly sketchy. What made it so maddening was that Eberhard had a strong hunch the incident involved Gen.

"It's the usual garbled shit you get from eyewitnesses," Rybeck said. "You know, one guy says they tore out of the parking lot in an Isuzu Trooper, another says a camper-truck or maybe it was a—" he glanced down at his notepad—"a Land Rover." He flicked the stubble under his chin with a cracked thumbnail. "Nobody got the license number. I got one witness who says the vehicle was green and brown; another guy says gray and brown, or—" he flipped a page—"gray and maroon, could be."

"What about the man with the video?"

"Well, now there's another thing. You can't get an ID, because the woman was wearing some kind of mask. One of those expensive Halloween jobs—you know, latex rubber, molds to your face, they look almost real. So my conclusion is: These two were just local college assholes out on a prank. Obviously, they already had it planned out, or she wouldn't have put on the mask."

"But the written report said she was wearing the mask when she entered the zoo. The cashier or whatever didn't think twice about that?"

Rybeck shrugged. "Cashier swears up and down it was no mask, that the woman was severely deformed. I seriously doubt it. You can see on the videotape she's got a great body—wish my wife was 'deformed' like that, you damn betcha. But there you have it. Your guess is a good as mine."

"Can I see the videotape now?"

"Sure." Rybeck called across the room. "Hey, Bill." An older man looked up from a burger and fries lying on a flattened, white paper bag on his desktop. Florescent lights glinted in his eyeglasses.

"Would you please take Col. Eberhard, here, to the conference room, and play him that videotape from the zoo?"

"Now?" Bill glanced down at his food.

"Now. This gentleman flew here all the way from..." He turned to Eberhard. "Where'd you say you came from, sir?"

"I didn't. But I am in a hurry. The information could prove critical in an investigation I'm conducting that relates to national security."

"No shit. Hear that, Bill? Show him the tape. You can warm up your chow in the microwave later."

In a conference room that smelled like stale cologne and new carpeting, Eberhard watched the tape on a color TV. The video image was grainy. Pudgy kid in Disney World T-shirt standing in petting zoo, feeding goat. Scene cut to same kid standing on the lower rim of a metal fence, leaning forward against a railing, near a sign in the corner of the frame: DON'T TOUCH FENCE. DON'T LEAN ON RAILING.

Zoom in to the pair of snow leopards in the distance, the kid blurred into a blob in the foreground. Suddenly the camera angle jerked and refocused on a woman dropping into the leopard pen from a tree. Eberhard sat forward. He saw the woman only from behind, but her gracefulness convinced him it was Gen. The leopard lunged and bowled her over.

Eberhard saw the woman's grotesque face. "For chrissake," he said aloud, and his mouth went dry. That's not Gen. No fucking way. The camera was jerking around

265

and the action was difficult to follow, but it looked like the leopard tore out the woman's throat. Then a man appeared in the frame, and the leopard lunged and clamped an arm. The man moved with strength and skill; he looked like he'd had martial arts training. The leopard attacked again and the man feinted and punched the animal in the back of its neck, knocking it out cold. A highly skilled move. Civilian martial arts, or military special forces?

The woman rose shakily to her feet. Blood darkened the front of her ripped T-shirt and painted her exposed breasts with slick crimson. But beneath the gore, she was obviously unhurt.

My God. What the hell happened to you, Gen? You're a goddam monster.

Eberhard rewound the video and watched the segment a dozen more times. Gen's bizarre deformity bewildered him, made him sick to his stomach.

She had been a young and beautiful teen-ager and then had morphed into a gorgeous woman. On his first viewing of the video, he had identified her body by its contours, the way she moved. He had recognized her breasts. It made him realize he had been sexually attracted to her for some time. Funny how it hadn't dawned on him until today; it seemed so obvious now.

He missed having her with him at the lab. He missed making her stand naked before him while he fired his weapons. It angered and depressed him that she was now hideously ugly. His stomach gurgled with nausea.

Christ, and to think he had been planning to inject himself with her blood. The mitobots had obviously mutated again. She was not in control of the changes. Why would she turn herself into *that*?

"Goddam you, Gen." He sighed, feeling despair, a heavy loss.

266

When the rabbits had died, he'd realized his prospect of becoming invincible for all time was hopeless. Now, he saw he couldn't even risk becoming a part-time god. He needed to toss out such pipe-dreams and get adjusted again to the fact of mortality.

To his surprise, some part of him also grieved over Gen. It was stupid to be feeling this way, he knew. But she had been so desirable, and the weapons tests had been a genuine thrill. Now she was repulsive.

Furthermore, it now appeared that Gen might be dangerous to life, after all. The mitobots were still evolving—who knew where that might lead?

He just might be saving the world when he caught up to her and destroyed her.

36

Jimi opened his eyes and yawned from a queen-sized brass bed. Lana was brushing her teeth at an antique washbasin that rested on a white marble and mahogany pedestal in a corner of the bedroom. On the wall in front of the washstand hung a round mirror with a porcelain art nouveau frame. Lana turned to him and smiled with a mouthful of blue-white toothpaste. "Time to get up if you're going to tag dolphins today."

"Mmm. Good morning." He stretched, sat up in bed. Haven had tied his hair in a hundred slender braids that hung down his back like red ropes. "I'm not going to tag dolphins; that's obsolete now. I've got a dolphin in human form to interview."

"Give her some space, Jimi. Don't push too hard."

"Not today. I'm going to spend the next couple weeks out on the bay with Cade, recording dolphin chatter. Then I'll get Gen to tell me what they're saying."

He got out of bed, nude. His elongated arms and legs and torso gave him the lanky look of a mantis. "She and I could create a human-dolphin dictionary on the computer, using a keyboard synthesizer and voice-recognition software. It'll be a translator program, see? I'll use underwater speakers to broadcast my speech, microphones to pick up theirs. We can have a dialogue, the dolphins and I."

"Great idea." She spit toothpaste into the basin. "They can tell you exactly what they think of the guy who's been stapling plastic tags on their fins and sticking them with needles for the past five years."

He came up behind her at the wash stand, wrapped his arms around her nude torso. It was like the sculpted marble of Winged Victory, only made of warm black flesh.

Their eyes met in the mirror. "That was hot sex last night," Jimi said.

She grinned. "I thought so."

"Beyond hot. Volcanic."

"*You* were the volcano. Think I slept in a lava pool all night."

He lifted the thick, soft coils of her hair to kiss the long neck of his black swan. "I thought good Baptist women don't scream in bed."

She laughed. "You kidding? You should hear us scream in church."

He continued kissing her smooth, fragrant neck. "Lana, you're a wonderful lover."

She pressed her palms together, bowed her head toward the mirror. "I am most honored, O Son of Heaven, that you take small pleasure in my homely self."

He chuckled. "Homely, yeah—like Nefertiti."

"I am most honored that you take delight in my *titis*." She turned to face him and cupped her hands under her generous breasts. He laughed and dutifully smothered the dark globes with happy kisses. "You make feel so good!"

She shivered with pleasure. "Keep on kissing me like that and I'll show you how good you make *me* feel."

"Shall we skip breakfast?"

She smiled vampishly. "Well, I wouldn't put it that way." She took his hand and led him back again to the big brass bed.

*   *   *

An hour later, two languid bodies—one dusky, the other pale—rested entwined in each others arms and legs.

Abruptly, Jimi said, "I think I may know what the progenitor race looks like."

"Hmm?" Lana was half-asleep.

269

"The ones who shipped out the life-starter kits. Our ET ancestors. I think I may know what they looked like."

Lana opened one eye. "You're too much," she said. "You just had, what? Two orgasms? Added to last night's. And your mind is still busy? You don't need sex, baby, you need a dose of elephant tranquilizer."

He laughed. "My mind had a nice rest, and then it came up with another brainstorm." He kissed her shoulder. "I promise you I wasn't pondering this while we were making love," he said. "But just now...I was lying here, smelling your hair and the skin of your neck and wondering about human pheromones and the possibility of manufacturing sexual attractants and what a genuine sex perfume would do to our society. And suddenly, out of the blue—*flash*—I realized what the progenitors may have looked like."

"How in the world could you know that?"

"Because I think I've seen their portraits."

Now Lana propped up her head on one hand, both eyes open.

"Kokopelli," Jimi said. "Ever heard of him?"

She shook her head.

"He's this little insectoid stick figure, kind of cute. You find his image carved on rocks from Mexico throughout the American Southwest."

"Kokopelli."

"He's associated with the culture of the Anasazi—you know, the ancient cliff-dwellers?—and their modern descendants, the Pueblo, Zuni and Hopi tribes. Get this; he's nearly always shown playing a flute." He touched her forehead. "Have you heard the flute sounds the mitobots make inside?"

She nodded. "Right before my healing... it's mostly gone now, but I liked it, it was soothing. Like a mellow bamboo flute or maybe several flutes being played from far, far away."

"Far, far *inside*. Within the cells." He shut his eyes. "I'm still hearing it."

"Okay, so this little guy plays the flute. So did Krishna. So does Hubert Laws."

"Yeah, but does Krishna go around toting a big bag of seeds on his back?"

"Really?"

He smiled. "Kokopelli carried seeds of living things and distributed them everywhere he went. That's how the plants and animals got here, according to the legend," he said. "The Anasazi taught that Kokopelli led human beings up from the underworld on a long, long ladder to emerge into this world. The modern Pueblo villages have sacred ceremonial buildings called *kivas*, where they perform this ritual of emergence. From down inside a pit in the floor, they climb up a ladder to exit on the kiva's roof."

"I think I once read something about that in a Western. A romance. The kivas are round? Made of adobe, no windows. The red-headed heroine and her Indian captor made love in the dark, on the ladder."

He rolled his eyes. "No European settler babes were around to get kidnapped. Anasazi means 'Ancient Ones' in the Navaho tongue—the cliff dwellers were already long gone when the Navaho first arrived in the Southwestern desert from Alaska."

She pouted, "Don't spoil a great work of literature."

"I do like the notion of making love on a ladder."

"I'll keep that in mind this spring." She winked. "When you help me wash windows."

"The underworld is a theme in so many creation myths," Jimi said, "and I've been thinking, maybe it stands

271

for the microscopic realm. The underworld is below our world, in the sense of being too tiny to be observed."

She nodded. "And we did emerge from below. We evolved upward from simpler, microbial life-forms."

He stared at her.

"What?"

"You really are a terrible Baptist," he said. "Why'd you ever bother going to church?"

"I love gospel music. They've got an awesome choir at Mount Olive, over at Taylor's, I used to sing in it." She smiled. "No, there's more to it than that. I haven't been to church since the accident. But I got something good out of it. Used to."

"You believed the stuff they preached?"

She shook her heard. "Not all of it, obviously. Not even when I was a girl. But the congregation gave us something else: acceptance. My parents were trying to provide Cade and me with a sense of community. The church folks didn't turn their backs on my mom and dad because of their marriage," she said, "or on Cade and me because of our mixed race."

"I guess when you're biracial, prejudice can hit you from both sides."

"Baby, you got that right," she said. "Blacks think you're too white, especially if you don't speak with a black dialect; and whites think you're too black."

"So the people at church accepted you and Cade as you were, and you accepted them the same way."

"That's it," she said. "And I do miss the choir."

"You've got a great voice. I love to hear you sing."

She gave him a kiss. "What were you telling me about? We got side-tracked."

He laughed and shrugged. "I love your soft lips."

"The ladder," she said.

272

"Oh. The idea of a long, long ladder leading up to our realm," he said. "See, DNA is built like a twisted ladder, with nucleotide pairs as rungs, plus the molecule is unbelievably long—just ten atoms wide and about a yard in length." He held out his hands three feet apart.

"Wow."

"Really. DNA fits inside the cell's nuclei only because it's so tightly coiled," he said. "So okay. You've got this humanoid alien, Kokopelli, playing his flute and leading human beings upward from the underworld, up a long, long ladder to this world, where he proceeds to scatter seeds across the planet from his seed bag: Johnny Life-Seed."

Lana stretched across him and grabbed a notepad and pen off the nightstand on his side. "Can you draw me a picture of Kokopelli?"

"Sure," he said, "it's kindergarten art. They just scratch a stick-figure image into a flat rock, like this." He drew a simple circle for a head with single lines for torso and arms and legs. Kokopelli's body bent forward from the weight of the seed-bag humped on his back; both his hands held a flute to his mouth; on the top of his round head were what appeared to be antennae.

"He's cute," Lana said. "What's with the two feelers on his head?"

"I don't know. He looks like an insect, but I think that's partly because he's a stick figure. Like me."

She laughed. "I love your skinny ass, Jimi. You make me laugh. You make me think. And you're great in bed, hotshot." She pretended to examine the top of his head. "But you don't have antennae. You really think this is a primitive image of our alien ancestors?" She put her hand to her mouth. "I can't believe I just asked that question— and I'm actually being serious."

"I don't know. I don't know how far you can take this." He retraced the pen lines on the page, rubbing his

273

chin with his free hand. "Now I'm starting to second guess myself, because I just remembered that Kokopelli is often drawn with a big penis hanging down, or a huge erection. Maybe he's just a fertility icon, pure and simple."

"Pure and simple? Playing flute, toting a bag filled with the seeds of all life. With antennae?"

"Or maybe it's a picture of the basic vertebrate body plan—you know: one head, two eyes, four limbs—"

"One big penis."

"Because I think a race of gene-traders would be shapeshifters."

"Uh, you lost me there, when you jumped into warp drive."

He sat up in bed. "Think about it: They trade genes. They seed new worlds and wait a couple billion years while their offspring evolve into an astounding variety of life-forms. Then they return to the worlds they've sown to record the new genetic codes to add to their vast collection of blueprints of life. It makes them capable of awesome shapeshifting."

"Like Gen changing shapes, into different species."

"Exactly. Shapeshifting would be the peak of evolution. It would mean near infinite adaptability, which means near perfect survivability."

"Whew. This stuff is so heady it leaves me breathless."

"It's only speculation. Everything I've said could be wrong." He shrugged. "It's just that Gen…"

"I know." Lana stretched her long legs. "She makes anything seem possible." She took the drawing from him and studied it. "Maybe you should tell her about Kokopelli. Maybe it would ease some of her fear. This tradition is ancient right?"

"At least a couple thousand years old."

274

"Just knowing there *was* a tradition, that others knew about this…knew something, maybe understood what she is."

He frowned. "Uh-oh." He flopped onto his back and stared up at the ceiling. "The Anasazi creation-myth says that Kokopelli led the humans up to the Third World. That's us, the Earth. Then, later, he would lead them on to the Fourth World." He pointed straight up. "The stars."

Her eyes followed his finger and she stared at the ceiling, too.

"The Anasazi vanished from their cliff dwellings about eight hundred years ago. Nobody knows what happened to them. It's one of the biggest mysteries of archaeology."

"I thought you said they had modern descendents: the Hopi and such."

"Yes, but some of those ancient sites were like huge apartment complexes; they held tens of thousands of people. Then came this mass exodus. One by one, their cities were abandoned. No one knows where the inhabitants went; it's as if they disappeared off the face of the earth. The modern tribes are descended from only a few hundred who were left behind, or perhaps chose to remain."

"What are you saying? What's that mean for Gen?"

"I don't know. But I don't think telling her any of this is going to ease her fears," he said. "Some radical change is stirring in her. Something extreme…consummate…is going to happen."

Lana felt a wave of sorrow break over her. "She's going to leave us, isn't she?"

He sighed and nodded. "Gen asked me how, and I don't know. But I think she really is going to journey on to the stars."

37

Lana relaxed at the breakfast table on the porch, watching two shrimp trawlers heading out through the mouth of the bay. The mid-morning sun poured hot, buttery light over the water. It glinted on the ripples beyond the harbor's smooth surface. The trailing boat was Toby Clark's *Cool Bay Baby*; the lead boat was harder to identify from a distance; it looked like Carlos Quentino's *Suzie Q*.

After twenty minutes in the kitchen, Jimi carried out a large tray loaded with food. He balanced the tray on one shoulder, with a folded dishtowel draped over one wrist, like a waiter. He served the brunch with a flourish, arranging on the glass tabletop the coffee, orange juice, grapefruit halves, buttered English muffins, bacon, and cheese omelets.

"Wow," Lana said. "I'm impressed. Thank you, sweetheart."

He smiled and pulled up a chair that matched the antique table's motif of interlocking oak leaves wrought in iron. Lana maneuvered a few plates so they could join hands across the table. They both looked up at the kitchen door opening.

Cade hesitated in the doorway. "Am I interrupting anything?"

"Have a seat, bro'." Jimi pulled out a chair next to him. "Have you had breakfast?"

"Yeah, thanks." Cade plopped down heavily.

"Want to go record some dolphin talk?"

"Boat's gassed up, ready to go."

"Where's Haven?" Lana said.

"Down at the swimming hole with Gen," Cade said. "Those two have bonded like epoxy."

"Gen can be just like a little girl," Lana said. "That's why they get along so well."

"Gen *is* a little girl," Jimi said. He looked over at Cade. "Well, in *some* ways. She's obviously a woman; but chronologically, she's been on the planet just five years."

Cade shook his head. "This whole thing…too much is happening at once. It's overwhelming."

"Is that why you're looking so glum?" Lana said.

He sighed. "Look, there's something really serious I need to tell you." He glanced up at Lana, but didn't hold her eyes. "I've known about it a few days, but I needed to double-check on it, and I guess… I hoped maybe I could do something about it. But I can't."

Lana set her fork down. "I'm listening."

He nodded. "I wanted to tell you both at breakfast, but you didn't come down." He chewed his lower lip.

"We're here now. So tell us."

"Well…you know how there's good news and there's bad news? It seemed too awful to tell you before, but with, you know, your legs—the *good* news—maybe now you can handle the bad news, and I sure can't keep it a secret any longer."

Lana banged her palm on the table. "Cade Seaborne, if you don't spit it out this instant, I'm going to jump over there and squeeze it out of you."

"We're going to lose the Inn." He stared at her, hunched slightly, waiting for her reaction.

The words hovered in her brain, not finding a place to land. "We're going to lose the Inn," she repeated. The statement did not register.

He nodded, swallowing. "Last Saturday, Weston called here, invited us to his penthouse for dinner. I tried to turn him down, but he insisted, so I went over there after breakfast Sunday. He's got a document. It's real. I checked it out yesterday at the courthouse at Apalachicola. Max

Fairchild *leased* this land to Stanton in 1901. This house"—Cade spread his arms—"Stanton built this house on Fairchild property."

Lana couldn't catch her breath. Jimi got up from his chair and came over to sit beside her, wrap an arm around her shoulders. "A lease?" she managed, finally. "This property was willed to me."

Cade shook his head. "Apparently, the Stanton House real estate never included the land. Just the inn."

"But...Franklin handled it. Why wouldn't he tell me that?"

"Several reasons," Cade said. "First, Franklin is completely inept, plus dishonest, as we both know. Second, Mom had just been killed and you were in the hospital, no legs. Hell, maybe he *did* tell you. How were you supposed to pay attention to all the legal shit? You just signed the papers next to the checkmarks, right?"

Her gut froze when she realized it was true. She had never read the transfer-of-title documents. "How long?"

"What?"

"How long do we have?"

Cade grimaced. "Till the end of the month."

"God, no."

"It's a one-hundred-year lease, runs out on July thirty-first. Then Weston is taking the land away from us."

"He can't." Lana burst into tears. "He can't do that."

Cade got up and went to his sister, hugged her from the other side. She felt the presence of the two men protecting her like bodyguards; but even the bastion of their love couldn't save her from grief. How could anyone take away the Inn—her home? She had raised Cade here, and Haven. Together, they had brought the old mansion back from the grave, and in return, it had been their fortress through hard times.

"I don't understand," Lana said. "Why'd he offer to buy the land from us, if it's already his?"

"Don't you get it?" Cade said. "He was tricking us. Keeping us in the dark until the last possible moment. Think it's just a coincidence he finds the lease now, with exactly thirty days to go? That happens to be the minimum notice required to evict someone from your property."

"Greedy bastard!" Jimi said, looking north toward The Palms. "I'd like to go shove a golf club up his ass. Sideways."

"You and me both," Cade said. "Don't think I haven't fantasized about making him eat that lease of his. But there's nothing we can do. He's sending bulldozers up the hill in four weeks to level this place."

She shook her head in disbelief. "Bulldozers." She glanced around the wide porch at the finely-detailed trim around the tall windows with cut-glass borders; she thought of the red oak flooring and the ceiling fans in every room; the lead-crystal chandelier suspended above the foyer like a private constellation; the hand-painted tiles, imported from Mexico, on the kitchen floor; the original gas stove that still worked great.

"But I need the Inn. It's…I'm safe here." She choked on a sob. "I can't go out there."

"You have your legs, now," Cade said. "You can do anything you need to."

"My legs." She held them out under the glass-topped table, kicked them up and down. "Don't you see? As soon as people see my miracle legs, they'll be crawling all over Gen like ants on sugar."

"She's right," Jimi said. "I've been worrying about that myself."

"No question," Cade said. "That's why we have to leave here, move to a place where no one knows us."

279

"Leave Cool Bay?" Lana said. "You could never do that. I couldn't either. It's one thing to be forced out of the Inn, but...off the island?"

"I've been thinking a lot about this," Cade said, "and I don't think we have a choice. It seems to me we were doomed to leave here in any case. Next month, we're open for business, again. What were you going to tell the Bryces? Old man Clayburn? Your other steady customers? You're running around on real legs, for chrissake. It's inevitable, Gen's miracles are going to be found out. And when people realize that Gen brings on miraculous healings, there'll be no stopping the mobs."

Jimi's face grew long. "He's absolutely right, of course."

"And it won't stop with Cool Bay," Cade said. "No way. The story will get out, it'll spread like flu. The media will go apeshit. People in friggin' Tibet will hear about it. Those who can afford it will swarm here from all over—they'll be chartering jets from Europe and Asia. Package tours. And if we try to turn them away, deny them access to Gen, they'll tear this inn to matchsticks."

Cade's words rang true. Cool Bay was in Lana's blood, a part of her. But Gen was part of her now, too. Gen had literally gotten inside her blood and given her the greatest gift—an impossible gift—her whole body, restored. For Gen's sake, she could leave Cool Bay Island. She would do anything for Gen.

"None of you need to leave Cool Bay," Gen said in quiet voice. "I'll go."

The three at the breakfast table turned as one to stare. Gen was standing with Haven on the porch. Both had towels wrapped around bare shoulders, wet hair dripping and puddles forming on the boards at their feet. Haven's eyes were huge; her mouth hung open.

"It's not fair that you should leave Cool Bay," Gen said, "and it's not even helpful, not in the long run. Wherever you go with me, people will find out about me sooner or later. That's inevitable. If we try to stick together, we'll all just be running from place to place, ahead of the mob. I can't allow that. That's not a life for Haven. Not for any of you."

Lana picked up a napkin and wiped her tears. Cade's hand trembled on her shoulder. She wanted to say something that would make things better, but she knew Gen was being realistic. Gen's eyes blazed like purple-blue sapphires. No, darling, your light is not a lamp we could hide beneath a bushel. Everyone will be drawn to your flame.

"I'm afraid things will turn deadly," Gen said. "The media will spotlight me, and Col. Eberhard will home in like a guided missile. I won't set you in his path."

Cade trembled harder, Lana gripped his hand. Don't stop her. She's making us face the truth.

Gen looked out across the bay and turned back with an expression of fierce tenderness. "It's time for me to go," she said. "I'm going to leave now, this morning."

"No!" Haven threw her arms around Gen's waist and clamped tight. "No, I won't let you!"

Gen hugged Haven and smiled down at her would-be little sister. A fat tear plopped onto Haven's damp forehead.

"I would like it very much if..." Gen choked on the words. "If you would all come down to the bay with me. To say good-bye."

38

Cade and Gen and the others strolled down Stanton Hill toward the dock. Newpod seemed to sense the weight of the downhearted procession. The dog stuck close to Gen, his brown eyes as sad as a doe's. They had waited until evening, when the setting sun turns the sky and bay into a symphony of colors. "We'll make it a ceremony," Gen had told Haven. "We'll dress up, it'll be beautiful."

Some ceremony, Cade thought. They couldn't give Gen a single gift or memento to take with her, for what can a dolphin carry? Jimi had suggested clipping a radio transmitter to her dorsal fin, so they could find her again, but she'd talked him out of it, explaining that Eberhard would also be able to track her down that way.

Haven had braided yellow and red hibiscus blossoms into Gen's long, dark hair. At Haven's insistence, Cade wore flowers in his hair, too; so did Lana and Jimi, even Newpod. Gen was nude beneath a white terrycloth bathrobe. Lana wore an ankle-length cotton dress to hide her miracle legs. Haven wore a pastel blue Easter dress and white straw bonnet with pink ribbons. Jimi wore a charcoal gray suit with a royal blue shirt and tie that matched his eyes; Cade wore yellow linen slacks and his best Hawaiian shirt with a necklace of white puka shells. Everyone except Lana went barefoot.

Cade held Gen's right hand, Haven held the other. Gen looked so pretty it hurt, so Cade kept his eyes fixed ahead, gazing out over the expanse of the bay.

Would he ever encounter her again, swimming and leaping with her dolphin pod? Should he just let her go and never even try to find her? He hated to think how much he was going to miss her. The pain was already gnawing the edges of his heart; he tried to steer his mind away from it, focus on the moment: holding her slender hand, graceful fingers entwined in his.

When Cade was ten his father had died; stolen away from him forever, just like that. The following year, his mother died; same rip-off, same grief and anger, but not just multiplied by two to account for the second loss—multiplied by infinity. So at nine, Cade began a rebellion against his damaged life and the snoring God who didn't give a fuck what the boy wanted or needed. If life was going to hurt him, he'd see what he could do to hurt it back.

Cade had fought at school. He had fought after school. He had fought on the beach, at the basketball court, on the football field, in the church yard. He had fought in his nightmares and in his daydreams. Finally, a county judge cut Cade a major break and allowed the seventeen-year-old to join the Navy instead of sticking him in juvenile detention for assault and battery (those two jerks should never have mocked his sister's awkward gait).

In the Navy, Cade trained as a SEAL commando, and went to the Persian Gulf in 1990 to fight an actual war. He had killed four Iraqi soldiers: one with a rifle bullet, from long range; two with a grenade, from shouting distance; and one with his bare hands, pressed up close, panting hard in the other's face, like lovers. He had watched a teen-aged Iraqi soldier die after a rocket attack, clutching his spilled intestines in his lap like slippery pink balloons. He had heard enemy soldiers burn to death inside their underground bunker, screams echoing around the walls like shrieks of bats in a cavern. And somewhere in the blast-oven heat of the Kuwaiti desert, with oil fields blazing like flares from Hell, Cade's anger had finally burned itself out.

There and then, he had made up his mind never to hate anyone or anything, especially not life itself, for he very much wanted to live, to redeem himself, make his life worthwhile.

Then, on the month-long voyage home from the Persian Gulf, he got shipmate Anna Rodriguez pregnant. Not the best start at being his new, responsible self. Anna had no use for a baby and wanted to abort the fetus. But Cade had talked her into having the baby and letting him raise the child alone, with absolutely no claims attached to her. Anna gave birth to a girl at the Pensacola Naval Hospital, handed over the newborn to Cade, and the following day took off to parts unknown with one of his SEAL buddies.

So at twenty years old, Cade had returned to Cool Bay Inn with an infant daughter and a humbled ego. He apologized from the bottom of his heart to Lana for being a terror during his younger years. She had welcomed him back with joyful arms, like the prodigal son, and had fallen in love with the baby at first sight. Cade took up running a dive boat in the winters and working some of his father's old salvage claims in the summers. In his spare time, he helped maintain the inn, and had learned to be a skilled handyman.

He loved his life on Cool Bay. He loved being Lana's brother and Haven's father. He loved helping with Jimi's dolphin research. He did not find himself falling in love with the women he fell into bed with over the years, but life was good. Lust was good.

Until Gen.

He looked out across the bay, squinting against the glare of the gold coin of sun. The orange clouds in the west spread their jibs in the offshore breeze and raced across the horizon.

In his sadness, Cade wondered if he could make love with a dolphin. Jimi had said that some humans had managed. Was that sick? Was that love? Hell, he'd *be* a dolphin if Gen could turn him into one. He'd do anything not to lose her.

But it was the same as with the loss of his parents. He was powerless again. His wishes and the workings of the universe did not jibe. He could thrash around like the angry boy who had smashed his fists into every jeering face, but another private war would not budge the stars, the meshing gears, the gods—whatever the hell it was that ran the show—one inch in his favor.

He felt trapped in a closed box. The box held the sun in daytime and the moon at night—a very big box, a *huge* box—but in the end, just a box. How do you get out of the box? How do you feel free? Death? Was that the only release from this box? You just had to grin and hunch inside it, embrace the limits, until the very end?

Dammit. He was feeling that old, familiar bitterness again, heavy and sickening in his veins, like poison. And, oh yes, here it came; he well-remembered the feeling that oozed through his heart now—that he was not valid, not good enough or important enough for his prayers to be heard, for his wishes to come true. That's how the eleven-year-old Cade had felt when he'd learned that his mother had died. His soul didn't count.

Oh, to hell with this self-indulgent horseshit. I'm not that hurt little boy any longer. Gen is leaving, and Lana and Haven are saying good-bye to her, too. We're losing the Inn. They need me to be strong, and I can be strong. Yes, I can. I can be a man.

In that instant, by willpower, his mind made a U-turn. With a deeper courage than he had used to parachute into the sea at night on commando raids, he took a breath and he smiled. Just that much. A full breath and a smile. No grandiose philosophy or answer to the riddle of it all. A few facial muscles curling his lips upward in the natural gesture of happiness. It was unreasonable to act happy at a time like this. But nobody claimed happiness was reasonable. It was a genuine smile, and he found to his relief that he felt real joy along with his sorrow. And yes, the box did have an outlet—the portal was his own heart. His smile broadened at the insight.

Haven's little shoulders shook with quiet sobs. Jimi looked miserable; the poor guy had never gotten the chance to ask Gen his questions about dolphin language and society.

But when Cade glanced at Lana, she was smiling, too, tears streaming down her face. Their eyes met and he suddenly realized that she had been worrying about *him*. In the midst of her own crisis, losing the inn, saying farewell to the person who had restored her legs, Lana had been concerned about how he was going to take it. Now she was smiling gratefully because she saw that he was going to make it through with his courage intact, and not retreat into hating the world. Seeing how much Lana loved him sent the tears flooding from his eyes, while his smile deepened.

The procession reached the end of the dock at Willingham's Marina. No one had spoken a word. Newpod, an incorrigible chaser of seagulls, did not bark at the gulls swooping and crying overhead. Gen embraced each person in turn, and knelt and hugged the golden retriever. Lana began to softly sing *We'll Meet Again* in her smoky contralto voice: *"We'll meet again. Don't know where, don't know when. But I know we'll meet again, some sunny day."*

Gen dropped the robe at her feet. She hesitated for an instant, then dived off the dock into the sun-gilded water with a crisp splash. She swam a few easy strokes toward the open sea. Haven's sobs deepened to noisy, sloppy wails.

"Gen!" Cade dove in after her, wearing his clothes. He caught up to her and wrapped her in one arm, drawing her into a long kiss. Then their eyes met and hers were wet, sparkling mirrors. Red and yellow hibiscus circled her dark crown like a halo.

"It's best this way," she whispered. "I don't know what my metamorphosis will bring, but I know I won't remain a dolphin for long. For all I know about the change that's coming, I could be dangerous to you. To the others. That would be much worse than this. I'm going away from true friends, to rejoin true friends—my pod." She forced a brave smile. "I love you, Hercules Cade Seaborne."

Cade's throat was too tight to speak, so he only nodded and touched her heart with his fingertips. Her beautiful face blurred behind his tears. He closed his eyes and let her go. When he opened his eyes again, a trail of hibiscus blossoms floated in her wake. A moment later, a dorsal fin in silhouette knifed above the darkening headwaters of the bay, heading swiftly out to sea.

Cade knew those violet eyes would haunt him all his life.

Even so, he smiled.

*   *   *

Walking along the sun-bleached pier back to shore, Cade carried Haven in his arms. His hair and clothes were dripping wet, but he could feel her warm tears on his neck. He wanted to say something to comfort her, but his own heart felt too full to talk. He made low, soothing hums—it was the best he could do. Lana and Jimi strolled ahead, holding hands.

Abruptly, Lana started walking in a jerky gait. Then Cade spotted Hank Townsend sitting in the shadowed cabin of his 1949 Chris-Craft cabin cruiser, *Crafty*. Oh, shit, how much had the old drunk seen?

The wiry old man with the yellow-white Santa Claus beard wore gray coveralls streaked with engine oil. He held a can of brass polish in one hand and a rag in the other. Wind, sun, and sand had gouged wrinkles into his narrow face; a Band-Aid hid a patch of skin cancer on one cheekbone; spider veins webbed his bulbous nose.

Hank stared with bloodshot eyes at Cade standing there sopping in his Hawaiian shirt and slacks. The old man's expression seemed unruffled by the oddity. An unlit cigar jutted from the corner of his mouth. Cade could smell alcohol on his breath from a dozen feet away, even with competition from the fishy water and the brass polish.

"Great sunset, eh?" Cade broke into a grin. "We made a little ceremony this evening out of watching it."

"Yep. I can see ya'll did." Hank set down the can and rag. "Tripod! Here, boy!" he called, and the dog scampered over and jumped down onto the deck of the pristine vintage boat. Hank squeezed the golden retriever's new leg, then looked up at Lana, his jaw hanging open.

"Yeah, he looks just like Tripod, doesn't he?" Lana said. "That's Newpod. Our new pet."

"Well, I'll be damned," Hank said. "Sure fooled me. Where's Tripod?"

The dog barked, merrily, as if to say, "Here I am! Right here!"

Oh, crap, Cade thought. Get with the act, boy. Help us get through this.

"We, uh, had to have him put down," Lana said, looking pained. "Got into somebody's garbage. Salmonella. He went into convulsions."

"Aw, Jesus. I'm awful sorry to hear that," Hank said. "I really loved that dog. He always had a tail wag and a howdy-do for me. Yessir. Shared my baloney with him one day, and he was my friend for life." He scratched behind the dog's floppy ears; its tail slapped the deck.

Lana nodded. "It was tough on all of us."

Haven had stopped crying; now she was holding her breath.

"But this *is* Tripod's collar, right?" He bent down, squinting. "Hell, this is his tag."

"We…uh, put it on Newpod for the time being," Lana said. "Tell you the truth, he hasn't had all his shots yet. The tag is just to make him look legit until he gets his own."

Hank pet the dog and stared at Lana. "Don't take no offense at it, Miss Lana, but I ain't never seen you walk so fine. Just now. Strollin' like a queen, you was."

She looked to Cade.

"Oh, she's been doing some new rehab exercises up at the inn," he said. "An artificial limb company's got a videotape out—'How To Walk Easier and Better With Prosthetics.'"

"Well, I'll be," Hank said. "Damn sure works!"

"Thank you," Lana said. "That's awful kind of you to say that." She looked back to Haven and Cade. "Well, we've got to get back to the inn. Haven's got chores before bedtime. Nice running into you, Mr. Townsend."

He nodded. "Same here." He tilted his chin at Jimi. "Hey, Doc. How's your dolphins?"

"Just fine, research is coming right along," Jimi said.

"What kinds of things they learnin' ya?"

Lana took Jimi's hand and tugged him along. "Sorry, but we really do have to get back." She smiled at the old man. "Bye-bye." She walked away in an odd compromise between graceful and stiff. Cade and Haven followed close behind.

Cade looked back over his shoulder and gave a whistle. "Newpod! C'mon boy!" Shit, he'd almost called the dog Tripod, out of habit. The retriever jumped onto the dock and caught up with the family group.

As if at a signal, when they stepped onto the powdery sand and started up the hill, everybody let out a collective sigh. They walked on, not looking back, Lana in her mixed-up gait.

Halfway up the hill, they heard Hank Townsend call out after them in his gruff whiskey voice. "Who was that pretty lil' gal ya'll come down here with?" he yelled. "I saw her dive into the bay. Where in hell'd she *go*?"

39

All cetaceans were once land mammals who long ago returned to their original ocean home; now Gen repeated that ancient path. With powerful kicks of her flukes, she swam beyond the mouth of Cool Bay, heading out into the deep waters of the gulf.

The pectoral flippers that steered her sleek dolphin body contained hand bones, complete with five fingers, akin to the human hand that had lately entwined with Cade's. Her dolphin heart ached with the same sadness as her once-human heart; her dolphin eyes wept the same tears of parting. *Wansalawata.* One saltwater.

For the sake of her human friends, she had put up a brave front when she'd said good-bye. She'd claimed she was returning to her pod. In fact, she was unsure if she'd be able to find them. Dolphin pods range over hundred-mile wide territories. The loudest sonar pings could travel only a mile or so and back. Already, her clicks had bounced off two different pods; she had approached them until their signature whistles told her neither pod was hers.

The full moon rose in the east like a glass fishing-net float. Gen headed farther offshore, pumping out clicks from the air sacs in her sinuses, amplifying the sound waves through the oil-filled bulb on her forehead and shaping them into narrow beams that carried farthest. She broadcast steady volleys of clicks as loudly as she could, searching the deep, wide waters for her friends.

Something large and dense to her left. She turned and bombarded the target with clicks. The echoing pings vibrated an acoustic bone in her lower jaw as she made out a detailed picture of a shipwreck the dolphins called "Ghost Whale." The ship had sunk long ago with a large air space trapped inside the hull so that it never plunged to the sea floor. It hung suspended underwater on its side, doomed to drift with the tides and currents until its hull rotted enough to let the air bubble escape and send the hulk to its sandy grave.

She swam on, whistling a two-note distress call and clicking in slow circles, repeatedly. A small pod swam close enough to whistle, "Lonely sister, come join us." It was not her pod, but a gang of adolescent male dolphins eagerly pinging her. She thanked them for the invitation and asked them to pass on her message: Eyes-of-Sunrise seeks the pod led by Races-the-Waves.

It was getting late. She was going to have to spend the night alone. That was dangerous, because schools of hammerheads and tigers plied the warm gulf waters at night, hunting. She felt tired and pinged more slowly. Her pings bounced off two shrimp trawlers working a grid to her southeast; the steady thrubbing of their diesel engines carried a long way underwater. The boats were no problem at a distance, but up close, their drag nets could be deadly.

Gen rested in dolphin-sleep. She glided below the surface languidly, in the same meditative state as a napping cat, shutting down one side of her brain at a time, but keeping one eye open and staying awake to scoot up to the air to breathe.

The breeze had died to a dead calm and the smooth plane of the water reflected the moon and stars like an obsidian mirror. Gen thrust her head high above the water and looked around. Aside from the red and green running lights of the distant trawlers, the gulf seemed as empty as the space between galaxies.

She missed Little Squirt. But if she couldn't locate her pod by tomorrow night, she might join the pod with the horny males; they were still a half-mile to her north, circling slowly in their nighttime rest period. Maybe if those big boys had sex with her, the pleasure they gave could trigger her metamorphosis.

That's what she wanted now. But she blinked with fear. It was a terrifying process, to completely lose control and transform into something unknown. What would she become? Would the new form retain anything of her present self? Or was she to be a sacrifice, annihilated in the transformation into a wholly new creation? If only she knew what to expect, then at least it would not have to be a blind leap into the abyss.

On the other hand—or flipper, whatever—nothing felt as oppressive to her as being alone. The military lab had forced upon her enough isolation to last a lifetime; she just couldn't endure any more. Her heart felt honeycombed with cracks, leaking sorrow with every beat. She'd rather vanish into a radically new form than have to suffer this loneliness.

She pinged and picked up chaos to the north-northwest; a group of hammerhead sharks slicing like whirling blades through a school of mullet. Gen panicked. Her heart boomed in her skull and drowned out the return-pings. Where did the sharks go?

She knew the Abundance could repair terrible physical damage, but surely that did not include being torn to strips of meat and gulped down by a school of sharks in a feeding frenzy.

She thrust her head above the water and twirled in a complete circle, crying out in whistle language, "Little Squirt! Races-the-Waves!" Red and green lights from the trawlers bobbed in a black void under the sparkling frost of the Milky Way. Her ears caught the faraway sounds of men's voices, laughter.

What am I doing? This is stupid. If I can't find my pod by whistling underwater, they sure won't hear me whistling in the air.

293

She calmed herself. The hammerheads were busy feeding; she was okay, for now.

I did the right thing. Leaving was the only way. Her friends on shore were safe from Eberhard, and that lent some comfort. But it hurt too much to dwell on them, especially Cade.

Cade.

Don't think about him now. You'll never see him again.

Her thoughts returned to finding a way to speed up her metamorphosis. Get this loneliness over with. But she doubted sex with the dolphins would work. Both times the transformation had occurred, it had been impelled by emotional, not merely physical, gratification. Heart fulfillment. True passion.

Oh, Cade! You sweet man.

—

40

On Gen's third night alone, the sun sank below the rim of the sea and darkness unfurled like a black velvet sail. Cancer the Crab skittered sideways up into the sky. To the east of the Crab, she saw the star Regulus, the Heart of the King, in the constellation Leo. The star made her think of Cade-the-Lion-Hearted. Everything else reminded her of Cade, too. Orion, the Hunter. The constellation Hercules.

The moon was no longer full, and Gen's spirit had waned, too, since she'd left Cade. Far from her human friends and unable to rejoin her dolphin family, she felt terribly lost.

She pinged a search pattern, but less regularly than before. She listened half-heartedly to the irrelevant noises and movements in the deep vault of her dark universe. A half-mile to the south, a school of hammerhead sharks swung back and forth, patrolling the blackness for schools of fish, or for loners, like herself. Fortunately, the sharks relied on their sense of smell and bio-electric fields, and could not see with long-range sonar. Otherwise, they would rush to tear her apart, like a wolf pack running down a straggler in a herd of caribou.

She swam northward, away from the sharks. After a time, she closed one eye and drifted in a resting phase; allowing one hemisphere of her brain to pass into sleep. In her tiredness and despair, she thought of Cade. Sea and distance had not quenched her emotions for him. Would time be able to make her longing fade?

Gen had stopped pinging and didn't notice the hammerheads circling, until they were almost upon her.

She awoke with a jolt of fear, whipped her flukes, and tried to race away from the closing trap. A burst of pings returned a vivid sound-picture of more than a dozen large sharks, charging toward the center in a fast attack. Several sharks swam above and below the shrinking ring, to head off escape. Her heart thundered. No way out.

I've got to be bigger, stronger, now!

Water boiled around her body and a disorienting feeling of melting overtook her senses. In seconds, she'd transformed.

The hammerheads had stopped their attack, backing off from the sphere of furiously bubbling water. When the bubbles cleared, the sharks could see that Gen was not a lone and vulnerable dolphin, but a mighty leviathan. They broke from their circling attack pattern and regrouped like a squadron of streamlined fighter jets, then moved swiftly off in the blackness to hunt less dangerous prey.

Gen realized she had become a whale. She kicked her flukes and drove through the water, feeling strong and unafraid; a living mountain. In a moment, her human mind understood she was a blue whale; the largest animal ever to live on Earth. She remembered gathering the essence of the creature from a jaw bone on display at the zoo.

Never underestimate what the Abundance can accomplish with its library of genes.

Her whale heart boomed slow, heavy beats, louder in her ears than a kettle drum. Each contraction pumped tubs of blood through her two-hundred-ton body, a hundred feet from baleen to flukes. The dolphin she had been could swim through the aorta of the whale she had become, like a kid slipping through a tube-slide.

In her whale-mind, she stored thousands of beautiful melodies, some stretching back to whale ancestors that swam in seas before man walked upright. She tried out her new voice and bellowed with delight as the ultra-deep notes resonated through her whole body as if she were a gigantic megaphone. She remembered that the low frequency notes of whale songs can travel hundreds of miles underwater, and that gave her an idea.

The huge tongue of the blue whale was incapable of dolphin speech. Gen willed the muscle to change to a dolphin-like anatomy. After several adaptations she found she could belt out a distress whistle to her pod, many times louder than her dolphin body had managed.

After an hour of trumpeting her message through the water with all the force of her whale lungs, Gen heard a distant reply.

"Who is hailing in the name of Eyes-of-Sunrise? We approach the rising moon to meet you."

Gen recognized the signature whistle of Races-the-Waves, leader of her pod. Her enormous whale heart filled like a bellows with emotion. "Yes! Eyes-of-Sunrise herself is hailing. I approach the sleeping sun."

Gen kicked her stupendous flukes and surged forward through the water, creating a turbulent wake. Within minutes, she sensed other dolphins led by Races-the-Waves pinging her. The tremendous size of the sound-picture echoing back from her body confused and frightened them.

"What Great Sister speaks our tongue? Who *are* you?"

She morphed into dolphin form and blasted her signature whistle again and again. "I am Eyes-of-Sunrise. I am Eyes-of-Sunrise. I am Eyes-of-Sunrise."

The dolphins closed the distance and Gen felt bursts of clicks ricocheting off her body from every dolphin in the pod.

Little Squirt darted ahead of the pack, corkscrewing through the dark water with rapid power strokes from his flukes, cackling with intense joy. They rushed each other and nearly rammed, sliding skin to skin as they zoomed past, banking hard to come around for a second pass, still laughing and squawking.

He drew alongside her and whistled the traditional greeting: "Eyes-of-Sunrise, share this pod; share this heart." Then he added, "Welcome home. I missed you so much!" Gen was amazed at how much Little Squirt had grown in the few weeks she'd been gone.

"The great sister whale," Little Squirt whistled, "I watched it change into you. And I saw you become a two-legged when you left us." Streams of bubbles shot out of his blowhole as he whistled underwater. "They say you are the legendary Mother-of-Forms. Is it true?"

"I am Eyes-of-Sunrise," she whistled, "your long-lost friend. That is all I want to be now."

In seconds, the other dolphins arrived, swirling around in a chaos of happiness, touching Gen's flippers, all chattering at once. She counted twenty-three dolphins—all her old family members, plus two new ones: a foreign male gathered from a pod of bachelors; and a baby girl, Sparkleface, born two weeks ago to Moon Catcher, in the harem of Races-the-Waves.

The baby nursed under its mother's protective flipper. In the dark, the baby pinged Gen, tracing the outline of her body with a feathery lightness. Gen laughed and with steady clicks, sculpted a mandala in the water between them. The baby darted out from its mother's flipper and knifed through the flower-like design, breaking the waveform of sounds into shattered stars. The baby giggled with delight, retreating to its mother.

Races-the-Waves swam forward in the dark and hovered face-to-face with Gen, nuzzling her beak with his. "Eyes-of-Sunrise, I am overjoyed you came back to us. To me."

It did feel like coming home. At least the dolphin part of her felt elated. She snuggled against the smooth barrel of the pod-leader's chest, sensing his masculine heart

298

thumping under the dense layer of blubber and thick musculature.

"Your new daughter whitens the sea with the milk of her beauty."

"Yes, she does. But I want to fill the sea with *our* offspring."

Typical alpha-male dolphin behavior. Erection and all. With his conical teeth he gently raked her back and rubbed a smooth flipper along her underside, nudging open her genital slit. Then he swam beneath her, pushed her to the surface and rotated his body under hers, belly to belly, to align their sex organs. She reminded herself it's what dolphins do. Eat and play and copulate.

It was comforting. She felt safe and well-loved.

The human part of her tried not to think of Cade.

41

Lana sat by stacks of books on the floor of the mansion's library, sorting keepers from those to donate to the county library. Cade sat nearby, carefully wrapping a stained-glass Tiffany lamp in strips of newspaper. Across the room, Haven taped a padding of thick cardboard over the glass of a framed photo of her maternal grandparents.

"You said Grandma Elaine was really nice," Haven said.

"She was. She was sweet, like you."

"I don't believe it."

"Why do you say that?"

"Because. How does a person who is so nice come from such a cruel family?"

"Good question," Cade said. He carefully packed the chrysanthemum-shaped lamp shade in a cardboard box filled with plastic peanuts. "How *did* Mom come from out of that clan? Or should I say, 'Klan,' with a capital K?"

"I don't know," Lana said. "To be honest, I've been wondering the very same thing these past few weeks. It's so admirable. I'd like to think it had to do with Dad. True love. She was a modern Juliet."

"Boy, that would make a romance novel, huh?"

She gave a wistful smile. "I won't be an innkeeper anymore. Maybe I'll try my hand at writing it."

"I hate Weston," Haven said. "I hate his guts. I really do."

Lana looked over at her niece. "How do you feel when you hate someone?"

"Like I want to wring his old neck."

"No, I mean, how do *you* feel, your body feel? Right now."

Haven sighed and thought a moment. "All hot inside. Like, kind of sick to my stomach. It makes me feel rotten."

"Exactly," Lana said. "See, when we hate people, even people who seem to deserve it, it makes *us* suffer. You're not hurting Weston right now by hating him. Not one bit. He's probably out playing golf with his buddies. While you feel rotten."

Haven's eyes brimmed with tears. "That's not fair. He's having fun, and he's hurting me."

"No, baby, you're the one who's hurting you. Your hate for Weston, it's disturbing your body. Can you feel what I mean?"

Haven nodded slowly.

"So you have to make a choice. We can feel angry at people who've wronged us. We should stand up for our rights. Always. But to hate...that does something ugly in our souls. It poisons our happiness." Lana smiled. "Let it go."

"Aunt Lana, I don't know how."

"Sure you do. Come over here and give me a hug. Love sweeps out hate every time." Lana rose to her knees and met Haven face to face as they embraced. "I've got you, and you've got me. Let's forget about Old Man Weston and do what we have to do."

"Yeah. Let's not bother ourselves over him," Haven smiled and wiped at a tear.

"Over who?" Lana said.

Haven laughed. "I can't remember."

"Deal," Lana said, and they shook on it. "Why don't you take a break from packing? Jimi's down at the boat. He told me you're a great helper. I'll bet he'll let you go out with him again to record dolphin talk." Haven was dashing out of the room before she finished the suggestion. "Get Jimi to call us from the cell phone," Lana yelled, "so we know what's up."

Cade stared at his sister. "Lana, you're amazing. You just explained to Haven what took me, oh, a dozen years to figure out on my own."

"Ha. I'm no sage." She smiled crookedly. "Reminds me of a story I read about Gandhi." She rubbed a kink in her neck. "A woman came to Gandhi with her son and asked the mahatma to tell the little boy to stop eating sugar. Gandhi told her to come back in a week. She did, and he told the boy to stop eating sugar. The mother asked Gandhi why he'd made her come back later. He said, 'Because a week ago, *I* was eating sugar.'"

"What are you saying?"

"I'm saying I was sitting over here stewing in my own juices, loathing Weston. But when I saw the pain in Haven's face, I realized we were making a bad time worse. So I threw away my hatred, too. Just now."

"Damn. Wish it was that easy for me," he said. "Weston. Eberhard. I'm so pissed off it's burning a hole through my gut." He knelt beside the cardboard carton and sealed it with packing tape. "Ouch," he said quietly, and glanced down at his hand.

"Paper cut?" Lana said.

"Teeth on the tape dispenser nicked me." He held up a fingertip with a fat drop of blood. "Now that Gen's gone, I don't heal fast."

Their eyes met. "You need a hug, too, big guy?" Lana opened her arms.

"Yes. I really do."

She stood and they embraced in the center of the room and held each other tight.

"God, I miss her," he said with a trembling voice. "You don't know how much."

"I do know, Cade. I do know how much."

*   *   *

By mid-day, Lana and Cade had nearly finished packing books and objets d'art from the library. The stuff from most of the inn's other rooms already filled boxes waiting for the moving van. Three rooms to go, she noted grimly. Cool Bay Inn had one week left to live. On the first day of August, Weston's demolition crews would flatten it and then level Stanton Hill.

Tall stacks of cardboard cartons sprawled through the mansion like building blocks leftover from the Great Wall. Most of the boxes and the furniture would go off-island to a storage facility in Apalachicola while she and Cade figured out the best way to sell the stuff—much of it valuable antiques. Plus there was still the little matter of choosing where they were all going to live.

It worried her that as soon as she left the inn, the local islanders were going to discover her miraculous legs, and her family was going to find itself at the bulls-eye of a terrible media blitz. Maybe it would be best to go into hiding for awhile. On the other hand, that would only postpone the inevitable crush of attention.

She was grateful Gen had gotten away to safety. Even if old Hank Townsend blurted everything he'd seen, not many would believe a drunk. Besides, although he saw Gen dive into the bay, he certainly didn't know she'd turned into a dolphin. He would probably guess she swam out to one of the sailing yachts anchored offshore at The Palms. A mile swim, but certainly not impossible.

Not a day went by that she didn't remember Gen with gratitude. She missed her. Haven was missing her, too. Cade was pining away; he'd lost weight.

Jimi seemed too busy to think about Gen. In a week he'd completed the prototype of an underwater audio system, built from a Kurzweil music synthesizer, laptop computer, guitar amp, digital recorder, and underwater speaker and microphone. He was determined to record the dolphin language, teach himself to understand it, and "speak" it through his keyboard. He spent his days out on the gulf digitally capturing dolphin chatter. He spent his nights writing software to analyze the phonemes and patterns of speech, and then programming the synthesizer to replicate the sounds.

Which had temporarily reduced the frequency of their lovemaking from Hot-and-Heavy Honeymoon to Happy Tenth Anniversary. But that's what you get when you fall in love with a genius.

She carefully wrapped a bronze art deco statue of the huntress, Artemis, and two greyhounds; the foot-tall nude figurine stood with a double-curved bow drawn back, arrow nocked in an invisible string. Jimi had told Lana she resembled the huntress, long and tall and elegant. She smiled. For an egghead, the guy could be very romantic. She placed the bubble-wrapped figurine inside a box of foam chips, taped the lid shut.

Something puzzled her, had been nagging at her for the last few weeks. Her grandfather had obviously waited until the last minute to deliver their eviction notice. But why? He could have told them a few months in advance; a year in advance. What difference did it make to him? It was his land. He had no need to worry about their knowing it.

Did he do it merely out of meanness? To hurt them as much as he could? Hard to believe. She'd only seen the man a couple dozen times in her life, and always from a distance; flashing by in his Maserati, out on a golf green, on the deck of his sailing yacht. They'd never exchanged a word. Their relationship was icy, not fiery with resentment.

So why the secrecy, the deception? Pretending for a couple years to want to buy the land, making a series of offers, knowing she and Cade would feel secure in their refusal to sell.

Weston was hiding something.

She stopped in the middle of stacking leather-bound books in a box. Suddenly, it seemed to stand out plainly, like a watermark when held up to a lamp. He *was* hiding something. Weston was guarding his ass, but from…what?

"Hey, Cade."

"Yeah?" His baritone voice resounded from inside a mahogany cabinet.

"What could we have done to stop Weston if we had known earlier that he owned the land?"

He pulled his head out of the cabinet and looked at her. A powdery smudge of dust angled across his forehead. "Still bugging you, huh? We've been over this half a dozen times."

"Humor me again."

He sighed. "We couldn't have done squat. I saw the lease registered at the courthouse. I read the Florida statutes that cover kicking tenants off your property. Legally, Weston's perfectly within his rights as landowner."

"But…could there be something, any little detail, that we're missing here, simply because we've got no time to look into it?"

He stared at the cardboard boxes and debris strewn around the Persian carpet like flotsam from a shipwreck. "He definitely didn't cut us any spare time. One week to go, and look at all this shit."

"Exactly. And why did he leave us with no time?"

"Because he's an asshole?"

She shook her head. "Not that. He's a manipulator, a chess master. He doesn't make a move without a strategy."

He regarded her from across the room. "What are you getting at?"

"Not sure," she said. "Let's think about what we could do if we had more time."

"Hmm. If we had more time…"

"We could do some research into the history of the land ownership."

He shook his head. "I told you, I saw a copy of the lease at the courthouse. Whitmore Fairchild leased this land to George Stanton for one hundred years." He drew a forearm across his sweaty brow. "And before Whitmore, a whole string of Fairchilds owned this island, going back to 1760."

"And before the Fairchilds?"

"Indians, I guess. Caloosas. Appalachees."

"Okay. The Civil War. They built a Confederate saltworks here. Turned out tons of salt daily from the sea. Then Yankee Marines, raiding from a warship attacked the saltworks. They burned down the saltworks, ran off the plantation bosses, liberated the slaves."

"Everybody knows this stuff, Lana. It's no secret. Hell, it's stamped in brass on the historic markers."

She spent a moment digesting the facts. "After the Yankee forces occupied the island, it would be incorrect to say it still belonged to the Fairchilds, right?"

"So? They got it back, right after the war ended. New Ireland Plantation started up again. Daddy's ancestors were sharecroppers—still slaves in all but name."

She frowned. "Hmm."

"Hmm, what?"

"I don't know what it is, but we're overlooking something. It's right under our noses. Weston knows about it and he doesn't want us to find out. So he's distracting us with all this frantic packing, getting ready to move."

"Crap, Lana. I thought you were on to something."

"I am."

"Right." He turned back to the mahogany display cabinet, clearing the shelves of glass and porcelain and ivory art objects, wrapping each item and packing it in a box. "Man, there's so much junk." He held up a blown

306

glass stallion that fit in his palm. "Maybe we should toss some of this stuff."

She laughed. "That little piece of 'junk' is a genuine Steuban, worth…oh, maybe five-thousand dollars."

He gave a low whistle. "Better let you wrap it." He humbly set the horse aside. "Did Mom ever tell you anything about this stuff?"

"The knick-knacks?"

"No, I'm still talking about the land. She was a Fairchild. Wonder what she knew?"

Lana shook her head. "Nothing, I'm sure. I remember she felt so proud of me when Lady Francis left me Stanton House. Never said a word about a land lease. And then the accident…that came, what?—just a couple weeks later? Before we'd even seen the paper work."

Cade nodded glumly and turned back to the display cabinet. The two of them worked in silence for a while, then Lana said, "You know, after Dad died, Mom was caught up in her own world. She was a different person; kind of obsessed."

"With what?" Cade said, his back to her.

"Well, it was weird. Dad died, and suddenly she was on a mission. She was all upset about the over-fishing of grouper."

"Really? I never heard this."

"Yeah. She was gung-ho on pushing for legislation against long-liners." Lana remembered the pamphlets arguing against boats trawling with two-mile-long fishing lines, covered with thousands of baited hooks. The long-liners were catching so many grouper that not enough breeding stock remained in the sea to reproduce in healthy numbers. "That's why we were driving to Tallahassee the day of the accident, she was going to do some more library research at the state archives, about commercial fishing. She had charts up all over her bedroom wall."

"Charts?"

"Navigational charts: coastlines, depths, reefs, currents."

Cade turned around to face her. "But that's…Lana, that makes no sense. There aren't any long-liners that operate out of Cool Bay. Never have been. Those boats come out of Tampa Bay, St. Pete, mostly," he said. "And what would she do with navigational charts?"

"They were Dad's charts. The ones he used for finding and registering his salvage claims."

"Those charts are all local," he said. "Long-liners fish halfway to Mexico and back, deep waters, they don't hug the coastline. Besides, she wouldn't need to study sea charts just to talk to people about banning long-liners."

They exchanged excited looks. "She had something else going on, Lana."

She stood up fast, toppling a stack of books. "This is it. The thing under our noses."

He maneuvered past an assortment of cartons to stand next to her. "Her involvement was a cover. But for what?"

"It gave her an excuse to go to Tallahassee often, for one thing," she said. "To snoop through the state archives."

"So what was she hunting?"

Lana rubbed the back of her neck. "Another question is, why was Mom hiding her real motives? Oh, Cade, this is giving me the creeps. I've got goosebumps."

He frowned, nodding. "She was afraid of somebody finding out."

Lana's mind sorted through the information. "Oh, my God!" A chill passed through her heart like an icy knife blade. "Oh, No!"

Cade reached out and grasped her shoulders. "What?"

"Dad used to go there, to the state archives, to hunt through Civil War naval records. He was searching for clues to the location of the wreck of the Yankee ship that had raided the saltworks here."

Cade pulled her into his arms. "You're trembling like a leaf."

She shivered against his warmth. "Dad and Mike died. An accident. A year later, Mom died. Another accident. Dad and Mom were both searching for the same thing, and Mom was scared to let anyone know she was looking for it."

"Aw, Jesus," Cade said. "Don't even think that way." Mike Garcia had been their father's crewmate and dive-handler since he graduated high school, and in his twenties, he became Lana's boyfriend. The two had seemed headed for marriage.

"Maybe they found something important enough to get themselves killed over it."

"Oh, come on," Cade said. "Stop it. That's too freaky."

"If he found the Yankee ship, what would be inside it?"

"He didn't find it."

"How do you know?"

"It was the *Emancipator*, an ironclad steamship. He never found it."

"You're sure of that?"

He twisted his mouth. "Well…he never told me he found it. We talked about the *San Pedro*, other wrecks. He never mentioned the *Emancipator*. He was always looking for it."

"I remember, Mom told me that Dad was going to change history, set things straight. That was right before he died."

"What's that supposed to mean? 'Change history'?"

Lana shook her head.

Cade glanced around the disarrayed room. "To hell with packing!" he said with sudden fury, and kicked at a half-filled box. "I'll leave a message for Jimi and Haven. We're going to the state archives."

42

The Florida State Library occupied the top floors of the R.A. Gray Building, a modern concrete-and-steel shoebox on Bronough Street, a block west from the capitol rotunda in downtown Tallahassee.

Lana and Cade had spent over an hour researching the history of Coolahatchee Bay, finding nothing but the familiar narratives etched on brass historic markers on the island. She was skimming through the master index of the *Florida Historical Quarterly* when a white-haired librarian approached her, introduced himself as Edward Thames and offered to help with her research. Lana introduced herself and Cade, thanked him for his offer, but explained that they weren't sure what they were looking for.

"We're interested in any information about the Yankee ironclad, *Emancipator*," she said. "In 1864, it raided the Confederate saltworks on the New Ireland Plantation at Coolahatchee Bay."

The librarian nodded, then dropped a bombshell: "Years ago, I had a young woman in here several times, hunting through the same material," he said. "I don't recall her first name, but her last name was Seaborne. Could that have been your mother?"

Lana's jaw dropped. "How did you know?"

He smiled. "Two things. She was a striking woman, hard to forget, really; and you both strongly resemble her. Secondly, she seemed absolutely on fire to find something in our Civil War naval records. That stood out. Not many people get passionate about this dusty old stuff." He glanced around the roomful of books, journals and archives, almost affectionately. "I don't know if your mother discovered everything she was looking for," Thames said, "but I do recall, she got very excited when she listened to an oral history of one of the former slaves from the island's plantation."

"You've got that?" Lana said. "The oral history?"

"Of course. Trouble is, I've got several of them. I'm not sure I'll be able to pinpoint the one she was listening to when she shouted 'Bingo!'" He chuckled. "I could here it from inside my office."

Cade eyes lit up. "We'll listen to them all if we have to."

"Well, I'm afraid there are several dozen recordings, but come on, follow me and we'll see if maybe something jogs my memory."

He led them to a large wooden cabinet and opened a file drawer under the heading *C-Coo*. Inside, plastic cassette cases were stacked like index cards. He ran a bony finger over the titles related to Coolahatchee Bay, reading them at high speed. "Mammy Bess," he said. "That's it. Mammy Bess. You're in luck, I remember the name." He lifted out a box and opened it. "Here, there are three of them, recorded on different dates." He snapped the case shut and handed it to Lana. "I don't know which of the three it is, but the name rang a bell—I'm sure it was one of these."

"Thank you. Your memory is amazing."

He smiled and shifted the glasses on his nose. "You really do look like your mother." He opened a plastic cassette case and read from a printed form inside. "These oral histories were recorded as part of a doctoral dissertation by Randall Kemper, a student at the University of Florida." He waved toward a small listening room. "You can get started in there."

The room held four tape decks with earphones. Cade took the second tape in the series and Lana began listening to the first. The cassette was labeled: "Mammy Bess, former slave, born May 19, 1855. Interviewed at her home on Coolahatchee Bay, August 2, 1962, at age 107."

The old woman's gravelly voice was surprisingly robust for someone born before the Civil War. The woman talked about her childhood, her parents and siblings, and a corn husk doll that was the most precious thing she owned. She answered questions and told ribald stories. At one point, she sang "Swing Low, Sweet Chariot" in a whiskey alto that sent shivers up Lana's spine. But none of her tales were relevant to Lana's search; she never mentioned the Civil War or the Yankee ship *Emancipator*.

Cade tapped her shoulder. "She's talking about the war. About the saltworks."

Lana stopped her machine and pressed her right ear against his left earphone. "...the Yankee ship come into the bay, black smoke curlin' up from two stacks, and they's got Marines with 'em. Lots of boats landing soldiers. Done run all the white folk off the island. Mm-hmm. Then the soldiers blowed up the saltworks with dynamite. Made a huge, mighty noise. And we all be celebratin' like the Fourth of July. That was spring of 1864, I'd just turned nine. I can see it clear as I see you sittin' there."

The interviewer asked a question that Lana couldn't make out. "Lawd. Jus' call me Mammy, sugar. Nobody call me 'ma'am.' Thas right. Just us colored folk was left on the island. Mm-hmm. We had it all to our ownselves. Several of the young men, Odie Seaborne and Beau Blakeman and...oh, I can't remember all them boys...but they up and joined the Yankees right then and there. They give Beau a Yankee sailor uniform and you ain't never seen no rooster strut around like that man did after that. They tried to give Odie a uniform, but it wouldn't fit. He was a big, big man. I had a crush on him don't you know, but he was already married, had a son. Anyway, Odie just wore a belt with a buckle says "U.S. Navy" over his work clothes, you know.

313

Mm-hmm. But those boys—five or six of 'em—steamed away with the ship and fought with them Yankees up the coast in some battles. They destroyed another saltwork and they attacked some rebel fort up northwest of here, done overrun it, too."

"What fort, ma'am? I mean, Mammy. Do you recall the name of the fort?"

"Naw. If I ever knew, I don't recall it now. But I remember this: Odie Seaborne killed a Confederate soldier with his bare hands and saved the captain's life. The captain's name was Robert Hargrave. You can look it up. A grayshirt was about to run him through with a bayonet, skewer him right through the back. Odie tackled that soldier and then tugged back on his head till it done broke his neck. Crr-aaack! Thas the story I heard from Darius. Oh, thas right—Darius Jackson, he was one of them boys who joined the Yankee Navy. Darius. He was there at the fort, fightin' along with 'em. And Zeke. Ezekial Jackson, that was Darius's brother. Hell, keep me talkin' long enough, I'm gonna remember 'em all."

"Did those black sailors survive the war?"

"Yessuh. All but Beau. He got hisself killed at that fort. Mm-hmm."

"And what happened after the war? When the men came home?"

"You mean the black men or the whites?"

"Those black sailors. When they came home."

"Now ya'll talkin' about something that sticks in my craw like a knife set edgewise. It never did get put right. No, suh."

"Tell me about it."

"Right before the end of the war, the captain, Captain Hargrave, he signed a military order that give all this here land, this whole island, to Odie Seaborne. It was official, fancy writing and all. After the war, Odie come home and

314

divided up the island into tracts of land that he give to all the slave families that had worked the plantation. But a few weeks later, the Fairchilds come back. You know, they just took it away again, by force. Lynched a dozen folks, got everybody else to tow the line.

"But Odie escaped. He don't know how to write to this Captain Hargrave, tell him what happened. So he travels all the way to Washington looking for the man. And he found him, too. Mm-hmm. When the captain hears that the Fairchilds has taken back the island, he sends a letter saying he is coming hisself to enforce the order. Coming back with his ship, the *Emancipator*."

"Capt. Hargrave returned with his ship?"

"Yessuh. He was bringin' back Odie with a whole shipful of Marines and he was carrying a brand new order that said the land belongs to Odie Seaborne. Old man Fairchild had burnt up them first papers, you know, so Capt. Hargrave had this order etched onto a brass plate. Mm-hmm."

"How did you hear about this?"

"Some of the servants up to the plantation house could read. They was like spies, you see."

"So, what happened when the captain got here?"

"He didn't never get here. Nothing never come of it, 'cause the ship never made it."

"What do you mean?"

"A big ol' gale blowed up. Just a sneeze shy of a hurricane. December, 1865. The ship run aground on Devil's Backbone, the reef that sits out there past the mouth of the bay. Fairchild's pilot boat could have gone out and guided the ship past the reef into the harbor, but nobody budged a finger to help. The ship sank. The captain, everybody drowned."

Cade cut off the tape, laid down the earphones.

Lana stared at him, her heart beating fast. "Odysseus Seaborne. The island was his."

"That's why Dad kept hunting for the *Emancipator*. He wanted to retrieve that brass plate, prove the Seabornes hold legal claim to the land."

Lana felt sick to her stomach. "I think he found the ship. I think Weston knew it. And I don't believe his death, Mike's death, were accidents."

"But they were diving on the *San Pedro* when they drowned."

"Devil's Backbone. The *San Pedro* went down on the same reef."

His pupils dilated. "Oh, my God."

She nodded. "Dad found the ship."

"Well, now I know where to find it, too." He set his jaw. "Let's go home."

He picked up the storage box to replace the cassettes. A page of folded paper fell out of the plastic box onto the table. He picked it up and unfolded it, a faded photocopy with handwriting in the wide margin.

Lana gasped. The writing began, "Dear Elaine..."

The photocopy was of Special Field Order Fifteen, issued on January 16, 1865, and signed by Gen. William Tecumseh Sherman, ceding most of the Sea Islands off the coast of Georgia and South Carolina to the "Negro populace of freed slaves of the former plantations." The order stipulated that "No whites apart from military officers and others in service capacities shall be permitted to reside on these island properties."

The writer had noted that, according to his research, President Andrew Johnson had allowed plantation owners to return to the Sea Islands after the war, but many former slaves had managed to retain small holdings of land. He believed Sherman's field order may have served as a model for the document U.S. Navy Capt. Robert Hargrave drafted

316

on March, 10, 1865, ceding Coolahatchee Bay Island to the freed slave, Odysseus James Seaborne. He believed that the document, if locatable, would still be legally binding on the descendants of the Seabornes and the Fairchilds.

It was signed, Randall Kemper, FSU Professor of Florida History. They both whispered what their mother had shouted a couple decades earlier: "Bingo."

Cade glanced at his dive watch. "This guy lives here. Let's call him, talk to him before we head home."

They made a photocopy of Kemper's note to their mother, emphatically thanked the librarian, and left. In the hallway, Lana used her cell phone to find the number of the history department at FSU. She dialed and got through to a receptionist.

"May I speak with Dr. Randall Kemper, please?"

"Say it's very important," Cade whispered.

"With who, ma'am?"

"Professor Kemper."

"Tell him you just want five minutes of his time," Cade whispered. "It's about Florida history." Lana shushed him with a wave of her hand.

"There's nobody in this department by that name."

"I see. Would you happen to know where he teaches now?"

"I'm sorry, I don't. I'm a new student here. Would you like to speak with the department chairwoman, Dr. Carlson?"

"Yes, please."

While the line was being transferred, Lana told Cade, "He's no longer at FSU."

"Damn."

A voice came on the line. "Hello, this is Lisa Carlson. How may I help you?"

"Yes. Hi. My name is Lana Seaborne. I understand Randall Kemper is no longer with your department. Could you tell me where he's teaching now, or how I might contact him? I'm interested in aspects of his doctoral research."

The voice at the other end hesitated. "I'm afraid Dr. Kemper would be very hard to contact, unless you happen to be a spirit-medium. He's deceased."

"Oh, I...I'm sorry."

"No, no, pardon my flippancy. It just that he died quite a while—let's see, I believe it was... hadn't I just joined the department? —twenty-one years ago. You caught me off guard when you said you wanted to contact him."

Lana's lungs froze in her chest.

"Hello?" the woman said.

Cade whispered in Lana's ear, "Ask her how he died."
She forced herself to breathe. "Dr. Carlson? If it's not too impertinent of me to ask, could you tell me how he died?"

"Car wreck. Fell asleep at the wheel, apparently. Hit a tree."

"Uh, thank you. That's uh...that's helpful to know."

Lana hung up and sagged against her brother.

43

Gen instinctively knew the basics of dolphin life, but had to be taught dolphin culture as if she were a year-old calf; and like a youngster, she had to practice her lessons often to learn them well.

With dolphins only half her size, she practiced hunting techniques, such as herding mullet into shallow coves, then circling the school and closing ranks like a drawstring purse to trap the fish at the center.

She mastered defensive and high-speed formation swimming; how to watch for the shift in the dark and light markings of the lead dolphin's fins that signal which way he will turn or dive.

She learned that Little Squirt—who was no longer called Little, but just Squirt—would be old enough at summer's end to go on a vision quest to discover his True Name. He would then return to announce to the pod his self-given name, before swimming away to join a far-ranging group of bachelors, seeking new bloodlines to mate with.

She discovered a subtle and complex body-language of postures and gestures. Some were used in everyday life; others only in sacred dances. The pod's story-keepers danced and sang of dolphin history tracing back to the age when sea mammals stood upright and roamed the primeval shores. One legend told of a pure white sea tern named Mother-of-Forms who could change into a dolphin or any other animal. The bird flew from the glacial north to the frozen south, collecting a tiny breath from every living thing until it had gathered enough wind to carry it up beyond the blue sky, to reach the stars.

The changing tides flowed on. The moon had been full when Gen left her human life; now the moon was full again.

A part of her still longed for Cade; that was a wound the Abundance could not heal. But she chose not to dwell on her sorrow, for time was running out. The Abundance teeming inside her created irregular and nearly uncontrollable energy surges, pushing from within toward the final change.

Races-the-Waves swam near her in the clear water, gesturing protection and pride. He drew closer and let his flukes caress Gen's bulging belly. In her womb, growing quickly day by day, was their baby. Gen had accelerated the growth-rate of the fetus, because she could not leave the baby dolphin inside her body when she entered her ultimate metamorphosis.

Moon Catcher, mother of Sparkleface, had promised to adopt and nurse the newborn. Gen's farewell gift to Races-the-Waves and her pod would be to birth her baby dolphin before she left the ocean and the planet forever. For she now tasted and knew, beyond doubt, the Abundance was bound for the stars.

44

Cade kept his foot heavy on the gas pedal, ignoring the speed limit on the two-lane from Tallahassee to Apalachicola. A late afternoon downpour slowed to a drizzle and steam wafted from the crushed-shell roadway. He and Lana talked in low voices about the ghastly implications of their discovery.

"It shocks me to the bottom of my soul," she said shakily. "Could Weston really have gone that far? Could he have ordered four people murdered?"

"Five," Cade said. "When he ordered Mom killed, he didn't care who was in the van with her. He couldn't have known you were going to survive the wreck. That's five people."

Lana shook her head. "I knew he was cold and greedy, but I never realized just how ruthless. God help us, Cade. Are we sure about this?"

"Look, Mom was afraid of what he might do, or she wouldn't have tried to keep her research a secret," Cade said. "Weston had everything to lose if she found hard proof the island belongs to the Seabornes. His entire fortune came from developing land that wasn't his. A man like him—"

"But his own daughter? He had his own daughter killed?"

"He despised her. He'd already disowned her. In his eyes she was dead."

"Our grandfather!" Lana looked at him, tears brimming. "Our grandfather killed our mother, our father. And Mike."

Cade gripped the wheel tighter. The truth was impossible to swallow, like trying to choke down a hot iron ball.

Lana gagged. "Stop the car, quick. I'm going to throw up."

He braked, downshifted, and pulled over. Lana unbuckled her seatbelt and lurched out the door, vomited in the palmettos.

Cade stared at a raindrop snaking down the windshield, wondering what they were going to do with their flimsy information. They couldn't go to the police. What real evidence did they have that Weston Fairchild was a murderer?

Lana climbed back into the Land Rover. She covered her face in her hands as Cade pulled back onto the roadway. "A part of me wishes we had never learned any of this," she said. "I don't know if I can handle it."

"Don't say that. We needed to know. We needed... *fuck*. But now we know. The truth is liberating."

"Liberating? What do we do now? I'm not even sure I can make it home without liberating the insides of my guts again."

"No, listen to me," he said. "I was angry as hell at Mike for being so careless. Any idiot knows not to run a gas-powered compressor in the same hold as the air tanks you're filling. Carbon monoxide. Duh. I used to think, 'You dumb fuck, if you're gonna be that stupid, why couldn't you have just filled your own tank, and not Dad's too?'"

Lana looked at him.

"I hated him. Took me years to forgive him. But now I see what really happened. The whole thing was rigged to make Mike look bad, so their drowning would seem an accident."

"That's why you knocked over his gravestone."

He hesitated. "You knew that was me?"

She nodded.

"And you didn't kick my butt out of the house?"

322

"You were just a kid; you were hurting bad," she said. "And in my worst moments, I was really pissed at Mike, too." She wiped at a tear that started down. "God, Cade, he was only twenty-two. I thought he'd gotten sloppy."

"Everybody thought so. The perfect set-up." He slapped the steering wheel with his palms. "We fell for it."

They drove along in tense silence. The Apalachicola National Forest rushed by on both sides, a shade greener from the fresh rain. A trio of deer darted across the road a quarter-mile ahead.

"So what do we do?" he said at last. "Weston plays golf with big shots, including the governor and attorney-general and half the Florida legislature. Do we go to the cops? We have no proof."

"Maybe we should talk to a lawyer, get some advice."

He shook his head. "The more I think about it, the more our position sucks," he said. "This time next week, they smash the Inn. There's only one thing to do: I'm going to have to find the ironclad. We know it sank on Devil's Backbone. Dad must have the wreck site marked on one of his salvage charts. I need to find it, dive it, and bring up the hard, legal proof that the land is ours—the brass plaque."

"Omigod, Cade. What if Weston finds out?"

He nodded. "You and Haven should leave the island tonight. Jimi will stay and help me dive."

"But—"

"It's the only way, Lana."

"No. Let him have the inn. I don't want anyone else hurt or killed."

"I can't just fucking let this go, and you know it," he said. "Look here, look at me." He waited until she met his eyes. "I can't let this go. So I'm going to bring up the plaque. Okay?"

She nodded slowly, chewing her lip.

Cade glanced at his dive watch. "Shit and goddam, I gotta step on it if we're going to make the early ferry."

"Cade?"

"What?"

"Please don't curse."

45

The National Security Agency computer room in the sub-sub-basement of the Pentagon was so cold, Eberhard almost expected his breath to form little puffs of vapor. Cray supercomputers, taller than refrigerators, circled the room like shiny black monoliths from an ultra-high-tech Stonehenge. The idiot-savant brains hummed day and night, encrypting and decoding military radio traffic worldwide over a network of communications satellites.

Despite the room's chill, half-moons of sweat dampened the armpits of Eberhard's Army dress shirt. The search for Gen had dragged on more than two weeks since the positive ID on the video footage from the zoo in Tallahassee. He was beginning to think this roomful of techies couldn't find their assholes with both hands and a GPS unit.

No further leads had come to light from interviewing the witnesses involved in the zoo episode. Everyone had been hung-up on Gen's purple eyes and freakish face. Many of them pointed out that the guy she was with was strikingly handsome. Eberhard heard lines like, "Beauty and the Beast, but in reverse," so often they became cliché. The eyewitnesses contradicted each other, as usual, but most thought the guy looked biracial. Several witnesses mentioned a little girl, also with biracial features, possibly the man's daughter.

By chance, one witness near the parking lot, an elderly lady, had managed to read a bumper sticker on the getaway vehicle. She could not identify the make or model or color of the vehicle and had not even bothered to check the license number, but she was sure about the bumper sticker. Go figure. It read: "Dimming shore lights helps sea turtles."

So maybe the vehicle's owner lived in one of the scores of oceanfront communities on Florida's gulf coast. Or was it the east coast? Sea turtles laid eggs along both; it's one long, long shoreline. For that matter, the guy could as well live anywhere and just happen to have a thing for sea turtles.

Eberhard had watched the video dozens of times, studying the way the man had handled himself against the attacking leopard. It was plain the man had martial arts training. That could mean a civilian martial arts school, but Eberhard didn't think so. His gut feeling shouted military training. Two Army Ranger instructors from Ft. Bragg had watched the tape and agreed the man had likely spent time as a commando.

Last night, technicians had digitally manipulated the man's profile from the footage inside the snow leopard pen. Special software had converted his profile into a frontal view of the whole face. Then, after carefully measuring anatomical landmarks—eye sockets, nose bridge, cheekbones, jaw line—the software converted the man's features into a numerical model. Normally the model included a numerical value for eye-color, skin-color, hair-texture, height, and body type. But the color imagery on the videotape was unreliable, and so were the eyewitnesses. That forced the techies to try to identify the guy based on his facial features alone.

A Cray computer was comparing his numbers to similar data-models that represented men who had served in the CIA, FBI, NSA, Secret Service, and Armed Forces. The computer had been mumbling to itself and blinking-thinking all day. So far, no matches.

Two near-hits, one Army Ranger, and one CIA, had turned out to be Caucasians with noses partly flattened by bone breakage. For lack of a better lead, they had no choice but to continue fishing through the data pools until they snagged the man's identity, or reached a dead-end. Given that the computers were now crunching their next-to-last database—U.S. Navy SEALs personnel, 1970 to 2002—it was beginning to seem hopeless to Eberhard.

He hovered over a young Tech-Sergeant parked in front of a terminal. Amber lights flitted across her eyeglasses in the room's dimness and her pageboy haircut gleamed like molded black vinyl.

"How far along are we?" he said.

She tapped a readout at the border of her screen. "We're, ah, eighty-four percent through the database, sir. Oh, eighty-five, now."

Eberhard glanced at his watch. "Shit." A waste of a whole morning. But he couldn't think of how to proceed from here. "Guess I'll just have to go back to the zoo, interview the fuckin' leopards." He turned to leave the room.

An image froze on the screen and the computer chimed. "Hang on, sir. Another hit."

Eberhard spun back to stare at the screen. The sergeant tapped a few keys and the screen split vertically, the enhanced image from the zoo video on the left and a photo from the SEALS personnel database on the right.

"Bingo. I think we've got him," the sergeant said. She fiddled with an electronic pen, tracing facial landmarks on the two images, but Eberhard didn't need to wait for the computer's confirmation. The photo on the right showed a younger, military buzz-cut version of the rastaman on the left.

"Christ, that's him. That's him."

He stared at the man on the screen. Hercules Cade Seaborne. Nearing his thirtieth birthday. Six-foot-two, 230 pounds. Six years of Navy service, all of them spent as a member of the elite Sea-Air-Land special forces. Persian Gulf veteran. Distinguished service medal. Navy Cross for heroism in combat. Resides at Cool Bay Inn, Stanton Hill Lane, Coolahatchee Bay, Florida.

A second techie had already pulled up a map of Florida on an adjoining computer screen. Coolahatchee Bay was an island off the west coast, near Apalachicola.

The computer chimed again. "Image comparison completed," the voice program said. "Positive match identified. Probability of error, one-hundredth of one percent."

Eberhard smiled. You're dead meat, hero. "Have we got a recon-sat we can send over the island?"

"I'll have that information for you in a moment, sir." The technician had already pulled up a moving map on her computer monitor that showed the real-time orbits of scores of military reconnaissance satellites. A tangle of multi-colored circles and ellipses crisscrossed the screen. She entered the latitude and longitude of Coolahatchee Bay and executed a search for the closest recon satellite. "Sir, we're in luck. Got a Keyhole satellite—multi-spectral digital imaging, plus radar—and it's definitely close enough. In fact..." she typed in more keystrokes. "Can nudge it over for a fly-by in, ah, forty-three minutes."

"Excellent. Do it."

He snatched up a blue phone from its cradle. He did not have to dial the Special Forces Operational Detachment, at Fort Bragg, North Carolina. "We've found her. A little island called Coolahatchee Bay, gulf coast of Florida." He spelled the name. "That's right. Assemble the team. We're going in. The staff here will transmit to you satellite photos, everything. We're going to hit them tonight."

"We'll need boats, sir. An island. They can escape by water."

"No shit, captain."

"What I mean, sir...we'll need more time."

"Fuck that. I'm hopping on a jet down to you as soon as my driver can get me to the airport. When I land in Fort Bragg, I *only* want to hear that Delta Force is good to go. No excuses. I want the field quarantine units ready. The biocontainment capsule with the liquid nitrogen. The choppers. The boats. And I want every one of your commandos to have a hard-on. Got that?"

"Uh, yes sir."

Eberhard hung up and took one last look at the screen, at the face that launched a thousand ships.

Then he rushed out of the room.

46

Cade and Jimi stared at the navigational chart spread over half the kitchen table. To the northwest of the mouth of Cool Bay, the coquina reef called Devil's Backbone stretched along the sandy seafloor like a knobby dragon's spine. Samson Seaborne had pinpointed the wreck site of the *San Pedro* and several other salvage jobs on the chart, but nothing indicated the Civil War ironclad, *Emancipator*.

Cade carefully traced his finger over the reef a third time. "Okay. Where the hell is it?"

"It's a long reef, man," Jimi said.

"But supposedly they were diving here, on the *San Pedro* when they drowned." He tapped the wreck site of the Mexican freighter. "My dad owned exclusive salvage rights. I figure they were using it as a cover operation, while they explored the ironclad—so I expected the ironclad to be very close. But it isn't marked. It's nowhere on the chart."

Jimi peered at the drawings and notes on the map paper. Arrows ran from the names of sunken ships to the reef. Next to most names, Samson had listed coordinates of latitude, longitude, and sea depth at high and low tides, and the date and time of discovery. He'd labeled several sites "unidentified" and next to one, he'd written "possible Spanish galleon."

"Spanish galleon?"

Cade grinned. "I checked it out. Turned out to be an oyster skiff. Most of the wrecks on the reef are pretty worthless. Nickel and dime stuff. The *San Pedro* was a major exception; he really made some money on that cargo."

"What's this wreck, here?" Jimi pointed to the outline of a hull penciled in next to the *San Pedro*.

Cade read his father's neat handwriting. "*Eleutherios.* Greek freighter, I think. We've got a couple of them. There's also a German sailing yacht and a Korean trawler down there. This reef sinks ships from all over the world."

"Hmm…I wonder. Did your dad know any Greek?"

"Well, yeah, some. My granddad, Moses—he was an educated minister—taught my dad a bit of New Testament Greek."

Jimi looked up at him. "Eleutherios. The word means 'liberator.'"

"Liberator?" Then Cade's eyes lit up. "Emancipator." And for the second time that day, he said, "Bingo." He stretched out a hand to Jimi. "You still with me on this, 'bro?"

Jimi shook his hand. "Like a weld."

"Good, because we're going to head out to the reef right now."

"Now? It'll be dark in a few hours."

"I've got a big tree of dive lights, brighter than a rock n' roll show." Cade refolded the chart. "Lana and Haven are packing. They're going to catch the last ferry, then drive a while and find a motel, maybe up in Georgia."

"Let's go tell them good-bye."

"Right. Then we're off to change history."

331

47

Weston Fairchild hung up a phone on the bamboo desk in his penthouse den, and heaved a sigh.

"Problem, boss?" Eddie Helco said.

He nodded. "That was the man I hired to tail Cade and his sister. They've been to Tallahassee, to the state historic archives. We've got to assume they know about the land, the ship, everything."

"Oops," Eddie said, "they just screwed the pooch." A partial smile crept to his lips. "What do you want me to do?"

Weston twisted his mouth in thought. Then he stood and crossed the thick carpet to a floor-to-ceiling bookshelf. He pulled out a slim volume. "Ever read this?" He held out the cover to his bodyguard. "Sun Tzu's *The Art of War*."

Eddie said nothing, but his eyes glazed over at the threat of reading a book.

"No, I don't suppose you ever have." He cracked the book open. "Sun Tzu's first principle is, "Know your enemy."

"Can't argue there."

"I know Cade. I know his weakness."

The man-mattress shrugged, bunching the large suit at his impossibly broad shoulders. He had a big head, but on his oversized frame, it looked smallish.

"The hero mentality," Weston went on. "He's stuck with it. When you want to hurt a hero, you don't attack him straight on. The utmost you can do then is kill him, and he'll go down fighting in a blaze of glory."

"I thought that's the idea, boss. Take him out."

"Yes, but this…hero has gotten stuck in my throat like a fishbone. I despise him, a Negro with my blood in his veins. He called me grandfather! Sickening. My traitorous daughter deprived me of true heirs," he said. "Now those mongrels want to steal my land, which my forefathers wrought from this island when it was nothing but mosquito-infested wilderness. And all because some Yankee captain gave away our plantation to a slave." His nostrils flared. "A slave! He gave New Ireland to a slave."

Weston pressed his lips into a thin line. "The Fairchild family, tracing back to Irish nobility from Carrick-on-Shannon, will be buried with me." He stared into space for such a long moment Eddie began to fidget. "No, I don't just want to kill Cade Seaborne," he said at last. "I want to hurt him. To accomplish that, one must hurt the people he feels he was born to defend."

Eddie looked confused.

"I want you to kill his little girl, Haven. And Lana. Before you kill him."

"Whatever you say."

"And the dog. Kill the dog."

"How 'bout I waste everything that moves in that inn? I do Cade last. Then I burn it all to the ground."

"Yes, yes, I believe that would do nicely." Weston replaced the book on the shelf.

Eddie drew a .25-caliber Beretta Tomcat semi-automatic handgun from a pocket holster in the pants of his linen suit. The toy-sized gun fit easily into his pocket and was ideal for close-up hits. A screw-on suppressor stifled some of the flash and noise, and pressing the barrel hard against the victim's temple smothered the rest—reducing the muzzle blast to a sharp spitting sound. He retracted the slide partway and checked the chamber was loaded; dropped the magazine into his palm, counted eight hollow-point rounds, and snapped it back inside the grip. He checked another eight-round clip in his other pocket. Then he turned to go.

"Eddie."

"Yeah, boss?"

"Don't underestimate Cade Seaborne. He was a Navy SEAL, and he's one tough bastard."

Eddie laughed. "Like you said, Mr. Fairchild. A real hero."

"That makes you laugh?"

"It's just that I was an Army Ranger for eight years, see. Lot of guys used to argue—Who's tougher, a Ranger or a SEAL? 'Course, all my Ranger buddies claimed Rangers are toughest. But I always said, 'Ranger, SEAL, Russian, or Chinese, it don't make a damn bit of difference how tough they are."

"Why is that?"

He cracked the quarter-sized knuckles on one meaty fist. "'Cause ain't no sonofabitch alive is tougher than me."

48

Hank Townsend had gathered quite a crowd. The group had spilled out of Kinky's Bar & Grill and onto the crushed shell parking lot, and people were still coming. Must've been fifty people or better gave him their rapt attention.

"Well, some of ya'll know about the cancer was on my face." He pointed to his left cheekbone. "Right here, it was. Looked kind of like a splotchy, dark red-and-brown mole. I also had it in my lungs, real bad. Doctors over at Tallahassee give me three months or less to live. Hell, I never even bothered to quit smoking. Been hanging out on my boat, mostly just waiting to die. I wasn't planning on ending up in no hospital. Had me a gun. Figured I'd use it when things got real painful and all."

"Get to the point, Hank. Tell 'em about the dog."

"Well, Lana and Cade had them a dog, up at the inn. Tripod. Three legs. Most of ya'll seen it," he said. "Folks, that dog now has four legs. He grew hisself a new leg."

The crowd tittered and someone said, "What you been drinking, Hank? Lighter fluid?"

Hank grinned. "All right, ya'll know I did drink. Modestly." That brought a good laugh. "But you can see my skin cancer is gone." He tapped his cheek. "Two weeks ago, I drove back over to Tallahassee; docs say there ain't no more cancer in me at all. My lungs is as clear now as if I never smoked my first Camel."

The crowd murmured. "C'mon. Get real."

"It's true. How many ya'll seen the top half my thumb was missin'? Whacked it off years ago shucking an oyster. Danny, you seen the stump. Billy, you seen it, too." He held up his right hand. The thumb was intact.

"Christ almighty," Billy said. "How'd you do that?"

335

"I don't know," Hank said. "It was the dog. I caught something from being around the dog. A virus, like. Makes you kind of buzz and tingle. But a good virus. It healed me up, total." Hank laughed. "But, man, you ain't seen nothing." His eyes swept the familiar faces. "Lana Seaborne has grown new legs!"

The crowd murmured loudly. Someone called out, "Bullshit."

"Now that I'd like to see up close," Randy Freers said, and his wife punched his arm hard.

"You folks aren't taking me seriously," Hank said, "and I don't blame you one little bit. We're talking about a miracle, and that you got to see for your ownself."

"Show 'em, Hank," Tammy Lopez said. "Show 'em what you showed me, how your cuts can heal and all."

He shook his head. "I can't, Tammy. The virus ain't working no more inside me. I need to get me a new dose."

"Yeah, sure," someone said. "Old fart." A few turned to walk away.

"You caught a dose, all right." That drew another laugh.

"Hang on," Billy said, "I want to hear what you're talking about, Tammy."

"Hank, show 'em," she said.

Hank took out a Buck folding knife from his pants pocket and opened the larger blade. "Look, a few weeks ago, even *I* couldn't believe what was happening to me. So to prove to myself I wasn't going crazy, I jabbed this blade right into my thigh."

"I saw him do it," Tammy said. "I screamed. The blood squirted like a fountain."

"And yeah, that sumbitch hurt like hell," Hank said, "but real quick, the pain faded away and it stopped bleeding. Tingled, itched like crazy, same as when my finger grew back. I just kept staring at my leg, real close."

336

"I saw the whole thing," Tammy said, leaving the crowd to stand beside Hank. "The wound just closed up. You know, like a film run in reverse. When Hank wiped off the blood, there wasn't even a scar."

Kinky Taylor, the gray-haired black woman who owned the bar said, "Tammy, you're the only person I know drinks as much as Hank. Pardon my French, but you expect us to believe two drunks?"

"When was the last time either of us was here, in your bar?"

Kinky shrugged. "Two, three weeks ago?"

"And did you see either of us take a drink tonight?" Tammy said.

"Hmm." Kinky frowned. "Can't say that I did."

Tammy smiled, showing two gold teeth. "Well, I can't show y'all a finger that grew back, or no cancer that cleared up, but I swear on a stack of bibles, I ain't had a drink in nearly three weeks. I'm not an alkie no more. The virus healed me, too."

The crowd erupted into chatter. From its edges, more people joined the group, pressing in to see what the fuss was about.

Hank recounted his miracle healing until twilight had turned the white sand mauve. "I'm walking on over to Cool Bay Inn now," he said. "Ya'll come with me and ya'll will see Llana's new legs, and ya'll will see what I been talking about."

Everyone cheered. "Let's go."

The crowd moved off along the shore like a single creature, with Hank Townsend as its head and more than a hundred legs providing thrust.

337

49

Two midwife dolphins hovered near Gen. She spun lengthwise, uterine muscles contracting in powerful spasms. With each contraction, milk from her teats squirted into the water in white puffs, like cumulous clouds appearing in clear sky. Then the baby dolphin slid out tail first, in a billow of blood, and the umbilical cord snapped.

A boy. A beautiful boy, with a black and gray body, sprinkled with silver and blue spots. Gen nudged his sleek little form to the surface and watched him take his first breath. He was adorable. She was in love. He floated alongside her at the surface and took another breath. Then he called to her, whistling the sweetest tune: Four notes, syncopated, covering an octave; starting and ending on the same note. By tradition, his original call to his mother would remain his signature whistle, his birth name, by which he could always be identified in the pod. She and the midwives whistled his name back, and he whistled his name again and again. It was the happiest music Gen had ever heard.

Then he shoved his beak under her pectoral fin and suckled. The strength of his suckling amazed her. The milk flowed from swollen mammary glands, but it felt to her like it gushed straight out of her soul and into his. After a few minutes, he switched to her other teat and gulped milk until his belly bulged. What a hungry little calf. Satisfied at last, he swam around to face his mother and drank love from her eyes.

Races-the-Waves and the other pod members gathered near to see the new baby. The father nuzzled his son's smooth body with his face and caressed Gen with his tail. The baby whistled his signature and each dolphin in the pod whistled it back to him several times.

Gen couldn't take her eyes off her baby. It saddened her that she must leave him, very soon, but she knew absolutely that she was right to have birthed him. He would not be left an orphan. He had his loving father, and the nursemaid, Moon Catcher, would make a good mother. Plus, he could always rely on the extended family of his pod.

Gen sensed only a day or two remained before her final metamorphosis. It was becoming harder to identify herself as human or dolphin, or to know herself as separate from the Abundance within her body. Gen was merging with the Abundance, and with all the life forms she had touched and recorded at the core of her being. She rode an unstoppable wave toward an ultimate transformation, when she would become the radical, new form that was her destiny.

Even now, despite the joy of her new baby, it was easy to lose focus on the finite world of the pod and the sea. She sensed the planet itself floating in a pod of many living worlds, alive in a shoreless sea of stars.

"Eyes-of-Sunrise, what name do you choose for our son?" Races-the-Waves whistled, breaking Gen's reverie. By custom, the mother bestows a formal name on her newborn, added to his signature whistle.

She looked at her son and his bright eyes held her gaze; eyes as dazzlingly purple as her own. In the whistle language of dolphins, the word for *purple* also meant *kelp* and *bitter-tasting*. That wouldn't do; and there was no word for sapphire or amethyst. Then she thought of an adjective for the color that appears when the ruby rays of sunset saturate clear, blue water.

"Deep-Sky-Water," she whistled. "Our son's name is Deep-Sky-Water."

50

"You go on to the car, Haven, I'll be right back," Lana said. "I forgot the cell phone."

Lana dashed back into the inn and hurried into the kitchen to retrieve the phone from the kitchen counter. She checked the wall clock. Yikes. The last ferry to the mainland was leaving the dock in twenty minutes. They would barely make it.

When she came out again a huge man was walking toward the car. Her senses slammed into full alert. She'd seen the man before, riding in Weston Fairchild's Maserati.

Weston's bodyguard. Lord have mercy, this can't be happening. The man was here to hurt them. She had to get him away from Haven.

"We're closed for the month of July," she called out, trying to control the quaver in her voice. He spun and stared at her. She climbed down the porch steps slowly, clutching the railing, faking the awkward gait of artificial legs. "May I help you?"

"Pardon me, ma'am, I've got a little emergency. May I please use your telephone?"

Her mind sped through the possibilities, trying to devise an escape, a way to protect herself and Haven. She had to get to the car. Then they could make it to the ferry, where there'd be witnesses and the man would be unable to attack them unobserved. But he walked toward her now, a mountain of flesh, blocking her path the Land Rover.

She forced a friendly smile and exaggerated her lurching, off-balance steps. She hunched her shoulders and drooped her head a bit, trying to look weak, when all her life people had admired her for being so strong. Her only weapons were her muscular legs hiding beneath loose-fitting slacks, and the element of surprise. Everything

340

depended on his lack of guard, and a ferocious burst of power from her. Adrenaline shot through her veins, her heart drubbed like an industrial pump.

As soon as he got close, he made a quick move to grab her, but she was ready for it. She dodged left, and in a blur of speed, cocked her right knee high and snap-kicked, nailing the heel of her foot into his groin. She felt and heard his pubic bone crunch. He folded inward and went down in a heavy heap, bellowing like a castrated bull.

Lana sprinted to the Land Rover, her heart in her mouth.

Haven was not inside the car.

She spun in a circle, eyes darting, searching everywhere. Her mind screamed for help. For Cade. For Jimi. For a way out of this nightmare.

51

A broad patch of blue-white light from Cade's lighting tree glared on the barnacle-encrusted hull of the *San Pedro*. The freighter sat upright on the reef in twenty-two feet of water; in another few hours, at low tide, the depth would shrink to a dozen feet. He and Jimi swam back to the bow of the ship and swam due east again in a zigzag search pattern. Cade pushed before him a lighting tree built from an aluminum frame rigged with six powerful dive lights, two 24-volt marine batteries and one air tank and buoyancy compensator to make the contraption maneuverable underwater.

It was almost dusk above the water, but they could see details of the pinkish-gray coquina reef in the blaze of lamplight. They should be seeing the *Emancipator*, directly below where they swam now, but the ship was not there.

Jimi tapped Cade's shoulder and signaled that his tank had reached the one-quarter-full mark. Cade checked his own pressure gauge; he still had half a tank. Jimi was breathing harder than Cade, typical of a less-experienced diver. Oh, well. What the hell. No point in wasting more time. They had crisscrossed the wreck site marked on his father's chart four times, and even swung out to cover a wider search pattern. The ironclad had vanished.

His dad's salvage chart had shown the outline of the hull of the *Eleutherios* only sixty feet from the *San Pedro*. If *Eleutherios* was not a code name for *Emancipator*, then it must be the actual name of some Greek ship that sank on the reef. So where did it go? It should absolutely be down there, right now, stark in his lights, resting on the bottom.

Nothing. Just two scuba divers and a school of barracuda hovering over a jagged mountain of coquina.

Cade felt a heavy pressure squeezing his chest that had nothing to do with the depth. He had felt such hope that he would find the plaque, bring it home, and not only save the inn and bring Weston to justice, but somehow redeem his loving memory of his parents. Change history, set things straight. That's what his dad and mom had tried to do. Now Cade had also failed.

He put his face mask close to Jimi's and pointed to the surface. They held onto the anchor line and followed their slowest bubbles up to the boat.

As soon as their heads broke above the sea, Jimi pulled out his mouthpiece and said, "Where the hell's the ship? We were right there."

"You got me, man. Makes no sense. We covered the site thoroughly."

They swam to the ladder that hung from the dive platform at the boat's stern. Jimi tugged off his flippers and climbed up to the water-level platform. Cade clambered up after and together they hauled in the lighting tree and slid it flat onto the deck above. Then they both climbed aboard. Standing on deck, they helped each other remove air tanks and vests. Jimi lifted the heavy set of twin tanks off Cade's shoulders, but Cade felt the weight of defeat still pressing down on him.

"So now what?" Jimi said. "What do we do?"

"Now we head home. Or should I say, back to shore? Home is not going to be there much longer."

I've failed. I have to tell Lana again that she's going to lose the inn.

Venus blazed in the twilight sky above the island like a signal fire. A soft curtain of darkness descended on Stanton Hill and Cool Bay Inn. Cade unzipped the neck of his wetsuit and warm vapor escaped like steam. In spite of the warmth, a deep chill of uneasiness snaked up his spine.

He turned to Jimi. "Lana is going to call you once she finds a motel, right?"

"That's the plan. Why?"

"She's got her phone on?"

He nodded. "Something wrong?"

"I don't know. Just got a really bad feeling."

"I'll call her now." Jimi picked up his cell phone and dialed Lana's number. His face took on a worried look. "Keeps ringing," he said, "but she's not answering."

The two men stared at each other for a heartbeat. "Stow the dive platform," Cade said. "I'll get the anchor." He ran to the bow and hauled the anchor aboard. Then he rushed back to the helm, cranked the engine, and shoved the throttle ahead full.

The *Dolphin's Smile* kicked up a white rooster tail as the inboard diesel hurled the boat toward Coolahatchee Bay.

52

"Haven!" Lana shouted. "Haven! Where are you?"

She shot back a glance to the man on the ground. He was groaning, curled up on the gravel walkway.

"Haven! I need to you at the car this instant. Run!" No answer.

The big man rolled over on his belly and pushed himself up, swaying, onto his hands and knees.

Lana jumped in the car, jabbed the key in the ignition. The engine started on the first crank. She threw the car in reverse, backed over her flower garden, and slammed it into first gear, tires spitting out black soil and roses as the Land Rover shot forward. She steered straight toward the man, who now scrabbled to his feet. He yanked a gun out of his pants pocket. Lana ducked her head low behind the steering wheel and kept coming.

The cell phone in her pocket rang. Not the best moment for one-handed driving. "Jimi! Cade!" she screamed at the unanswered phone. "Help!"

The man fired the pistol with a two-hand grip and three bullets smacked through the windshield just before the Land Rover rammed him. The impact knocked him up and onto the hood, and threw Lana forward against the windshield. For one weird instant, the two were pressed face to face on opposite sides of the glass. Blood from his nose smeared the pane. He struggled to raise his gun.

Lana stamped the gas pedal. The tires spun and the vehicle flew ahead. She stomped the brake, and the man sailed off the hood to land a dozen feet in front of the bumper. Then she hit the gas again to run him over, but he rolled out of the way at the last second. The tires caught one ankle and thumped over it twice. Even from inside the

345

car, she could hear the crunch and snap of bones. Again, he bellowed like an enraged bull.

Lana yanked the gear shift into reverse, and ripped through a three-point turn that took out half her vegetable garden. She aimed the car toward the gun man. She was going to keep driving over him until there was nothing left but compost.

Then she saw Haven, charging up the hill from the direction of the pond, eyes bulging with fright. Lana braked and blared the horn. "No! Turn around! Run away!" Haven stopped in her tracks. Lana cranked down the window. "Run, baby, get out of here!"

The girl turned to flee. From a prone position on the ground, the man aimed his gun and fired.

Haven pitched forward in the grass and lay still.

53

Lana's universe contracted to a single, diamond-hard focus: her niece's life. She leapt from the car and ran to where she'd watched Haven sprawl headlong into the grass. Lana's soul had stopped dead in suspense. She ran ahead as an empty body, waiting to learn the truth. If Haven was alive, the world might go on; if Haven was dead, the world was already lost.

She found the girl crawling through the tall grass. Haven looked up at her like Lana was crazy. "Get down, Aunt Lana. Like they do in the movies. He's shooting at us."

Lana's soul started up again. She became aware of her heart hammering in her chest. She flung herself down on all fours over top of Haven, shielding the girl with her body while they scurried downhill toward the pond.

A plume of grass and dirt erupted into the air in front of them.

"Hold it right there," the man yelled down from the hilltop. "I can shoot you both from here. Or you can get back up here and we can talk."

Another geyser of debris exploded only a couple feet from their heads.

"I'm not fooling around. Get back up here. Now."

Lana could see the whites around Haven's terrified eyes, and she fought down her own panic for the child's sake. Another bullet tore into the grass, a foot away. The dirt stung her face.

"We better do what he says," Lana said, making her voice seem calm. "I'll find a way out of this." She willed her hands to stop shaking. Then she took Haven's hand and led her back, keeping the girl partly behind her.

When they reached the hilltop, the big man limped toward them, dragging his fractured right foot. Blood streaked his boxy face beneath his broken nose.

"Been faking people out all these years about your legs, huh?" Pain thickened his voice. "What'd you do, rip off an insurance company, get a ton of money? I'd love to hear how you pulled off that scam. Jeez, must've been some brain-dead people on that case."

Lana said nothing, studying everything about the guy. He was in pain. He was tired. He was embarrassed and furious that she'd almost beat him. Where was the chink in his armor?

"Into the house," he said, and nodded with his head, instead of pointing with his gun. So he was not stupid. His heavily muscled build was turning to fat, but he'd moved incredibly fast when he rolled out of the way of the car.

"Who are you?" she said.

"The Grim Reaper, lady, that's all you need to know. Now get inside. Move it." He winced as he followed them up the porch steps, pulling himself up with his left hand on the railing. His right foot flopped and he sucked in his breath several times and groaned.

Before he entered the front door, he scoped the foyer out quickly, like a trained policeman or soldier, then moved inside right behind them. He made the same surveillance of the living room, then ordered the two of them to shove the cartons onto the floor and sit on the sofa.

Lana still held Haven's hand. She glanced around for a weapon, a shield, a rabbit hole to duck down—anything. Stacked boxes formed towers and canyons, spilling into the hall. The Steuban glass stallion that Cade had left unpacked stood on a lamp table beside her.

Cade had placed Snapper's birdcage in the living room while they boxed up items in the screened porch off the kitchen. Now the macaw was beating his wings frenziedly and squawking his green-and-yellow head off.

"Fucking bird," the man said. "That's why I hate parrots, never shut up."

He kept an eye on Lana and Haven while he shuffled painfully to the birdcage. He glared through the bars. "Shut the fuck up." Snapper kept up an ear-shattering racket. "I once saw a guy at a carnival bite a pigeon's head clean off. You want me bite your head off?"

Snapper had learned to bark by imitating Newpod, and now his cacophony ranged between squawking, screeching and barking.

"How 'bout I just wring your friggin' neck?" The man tried to unlatch the cage door with his free hand, but couldn't manage.

It takes two hands, Lana thought. Two hands. Put the gun down.

The man stuffed the gun in his pocket and pried the stiff door until it popped open.

Get him, Snapper. Nail him.

Snapper rocketed into the man's face, slashing with his talons, pecking and crushing with his beak. The man staggered back, clawing at the feathered blur of fury that shredded his face. He banged into a stack of boxes, lost his balance, sprawled backward and thudded into the wall, slid sideways into the doorway, still trying to fling the parrot away. Snapper gouged at his eyes and hung on.

Lana yanked Haven off the couch, ready to flee, but the man's body blocked the exit to the hallway. He dug into his pocket for his gun.

At that moment, Newpod came charging through the kitchen door with a fierce snarl, fangs bared. The golden retriever leapt over a row of boxes like Rin Tin-Tin and tore into the man's legs. The man kicked Newpod hard with his left foot, knocking the dog away. Newpod yelped, but lunged right back into the battle, sinking his fangs into the man's ankle, which had swollen like a water balloon. The man howled in agony and tried to force the dog's jaws apart, but Newpod clamped tighter and whipped his head back and forth like he was going nuts with a chew toy.

Lana grabbed the heavy glass stallion and charged the man like a banshee, smashing the artwork down on his head once, twice, again, again, until it shattered and the man quit thrashing and lay still.

Snapper flapped up to the ceiling, circled in a panic, then flew out into the hallway. One of the man's eyeballs lay halfway out on his cheek, like a torn turtle egg, leaking eggwhite.

"Newpod," Lana said. "Heel." But the snarling dog wouldn't obey. He ripped at the fractured ankle, splayed open to the white bone. Lana grabbed the dog by the collar and dragged him back. "It's okay, boy. It's okay. You did good. You're a good boy. Good boy. Now let go. Let go, Newpod. Good boy."

The dog finally calmed down enough to let go. Lana dropped to her knees and hugged his blood-soaked fur and bawled. "Good boy. Good boy." Newpod whimpered and yawned with fear. Haven stepped past them and Lana grabbed the girl's arm. "What are you doing? Stay back."

"I'm getting his gun. In his pocket."

"No you're not. We're going right out the front door. Come on." She took Haven's hand. "Run."

They raced out of the house and down the porch steps, then stopped abruptly on the path leading to the marina.

In the gathering darkness the crowd surging up the hill from the beach looked like a column of army ants.

54

"There they are," someone yelled. "Lana and the girl."

"Where's the dog?"

"Miss Lana," yelled a gravelly voice from the head of the crowd, "it's me, Hank Townsend. I brought some friends to ask you about the miracles and all."

A few people in the crowd started walking faster, passing Hank at the lead. One broke into a jog, which triggered two or three more to start sprinting. In a few seconds, everyone who was able began running up the hill toward where Lana and Haven stood.

"Oh no," Lana whispered. "What have you done, old man?" She backed up a couple steps and swept Haven behind her.

"Lana! It's Mary Castro," a woman in bulging pink sweats called out, huffing, and hurrying up the path. "Is it true? Do you really have legs?"

Lana shot a glance over her shoulder at the front door of the inn. Would the man inside still be unconscious? She looked toward the Land Rover. No way to get past this mob in the car; they blocked the driveway. Down below, a second pack of people swarmed up from the beach, trailing Hank Townsend's group. She patted the cell phone in her pocket, but she was out of time. Jimi and Cade were too far away to save them.

She whispered to Haven. "Walk to the car, do not run. Hear me? Do *not* run. Get inside and lock the doors. Keep low, stay out of sight until I come for you." She gave Haven a quick hug and her niece strolled toward the Land Rover.

The crowd arrived in twos and threes, but soon Lana found herself herded into the center of a hundred or more people. Faces crowded close. The smell of sweat, cigarettes

351

and beer breath. Elbows and knees jostling. She heard the Land Rover's door close and she prayed that Haven would be safe.

"Is it true?" Mary Castro asked. "Do you have new legs?"

Lana tried to think of what to say, how to defuse the situation. The gathering darkness triggered an automatic porch light to switch on. Abruptly, yellow light bathed the crowd, casting eerie shadows.

Mary Castro pressed closer, her sweaty face contorted with emotion and physical strain. "You know about Ricky, my crippled boy. Is it true what happened to you? A miracle?"

Lana worked her mouth, but couldn't invent the right response.

"Tell me," Mary said.

Lana nodded. "Okay...but...uh, let's just all try to be rational."

A man in an Evinrude cap and overalls dove to his knees beside Lana and grabbed her lower legs in his hands. He jerked back in shock. "Jesus Christ Almighty! They're real."

The shouts of the crowd exploded like thunderclaps.

Lana turned to dash into the house but clutching hands dragged her to the grass. People elbowed each other, jamming in tighter, to paw at her lower legs. Someone grabbed her slacks and yanked them down around her shoes. Then the shoes came off and the socks, and she was lying on the lawn in her underwear, smothering under the weight of hands, groping and prodding her everywhere now.

"How do we get the virus?" "Can you heal my Ricky?" Some woman was sobbing, another talking in tongues. "Help us!" "Show us how to catch the virus." "Praise Jesus, praise Jesus, praise Jesus."

The crush of people shoving, pressing inward toward her, caused many to stumble and fall, piling onto her in a heap of bodies. Lana couldn't move, struggled to breathe.

"Let us have some virus." "Hey, let me in there." "Get off me." "How do you catch it?" "Get up, it's our turn." "It's in her blood." "Out of my way." "Let us touch her, too." "She's got blood on her hand." "Let me touch her blood." "Hey, don't shove." "Lick the blood."

The mass of flesh pinned Lana to the grass on her back; too heavy to expand her chest to inhale. People twisted and turned her hands while tongues lapped at the blood from Newpod's fur. Her vision turned gray. She knew she was losing consciousness, but she couldn't budge.

"Hey, look," someone shouted. "On the porch. It's the dog with the new leg."

"That's how Hank caught the virus."

"It comes from the dog."

"Touch the dog!"

Like a tree trunk being hoisted off her torso, the crushing weight peeled away as people unwound themselves from the pile. Lana gasped and sucked air deep into her lungs. Her bruised ribs ached as she drank in more deep breaths. Several limp bodies sprawled on the ground. Mary Castro lay sideways across Hank Townsend, both of them facedown and unmoving.

Lana rose onto wobbly knees. The mob chased Newpod around the yard.

"Don't let it get away." "Circle round it." "It's got the virus." "Drink its blood!"

The frightened dog sprinted with its tail tucked between its legs, trying to find an opening through the chaos of people running after it. One man lunged and grabbed the dog around its hind legs, but Newpod twisted and nipped his face and he let go. The ring of people

353

widened across the lawn, cutting off escape. Newpod dashed in tighter circles as the crowd closed in.

The light came on inside the Land Rover as Haven threw open a rear passenger door. "Newpod!" she called. "Here fella. Hurry!"

Oh, no, no, no. Lana stood up, reaching out. "Stop! Haven! Don't!"

But the dog reversed course and dodged two captors to leap into the back seat with Haven. Lana saw Haven lock the door and duck down with Newpod before the light went out.

The crowd paused for an instant, as if to fill its lungs. Then, with a collective voice, it roared in outrage and stormed the car.

55

The mob pounded on the Land Rover's windows. Lana screamed at them, but it was like screaming to stop stampeding elephants.

"Give us the dog!" people shouted "We want the virus."

The gun. Lana remembered the gun in the man's pocket inside. She could fire a warning shot into the air, and if that didn't work, she would shoot as many people as it took to protect Haven.

She turned and darted up the porch steps, grunting from the pain of sprained ribs. A low, rumbling thunder echoed in the distance, quickly growing louder, nearer. She looked over her shoulder at the mob rocking the Land Rover, tipping it up onto two wheels, about to flip it onto its side. The thundering became so loud it shook the lawn. The crowd gaped upward and backed away from the car, frightened. Some sank to their knees in prayer.

Then a swarm of black helicopters burst into view, passing low over the inn's roof. The forward ships banked and fanned out as more choppers followed. In a moment, the sky was filled with hovering aircraft. Hyacinth and azalea bushes gyrated wildly in the rotor wash, a palm frond cartwheeled across the lawn. Screaming jet engines and thumping rotors turned the air into a shuddering gel of noise; searchlights plunged the people on the lawn in glaring pools, like escapees in a prison yard.

Lana quickly found her trampled slacks and pulled them on. She raced to the Land Rover and called inside for Haven to let her in.

The girl unlocked the door. "Aunt Lana, I'm so scared."

Lana hopped in and locked the door behind her. "I'm here with you now, baby."

Helicopters landed on the lawn, deploying teams of soldiers in dark helmets and combat gear. The soldiers spread out at a run to assume defensive positions surrounding Cool Bay Inn. They trained automatic rifles, machine guns, and shoulder-held rocket launchers on the mansion.

Giant, heavy-lift helicopters now passed over the inn, hauling under their tall frames mobile-home-sized metal buildings with red crosses painted on their sides. They alighted on the beach at the foot of the hill like monstrous, droning dragonflies. Three more black helicopters landed on the lawn. The latest arrivals disgorged troops wearing what looked like orange spacesuits. They fanned out through Lana's vegetable garden, trampling summer squash and tomatoes, eggplant, pole beans and okra.

Lana looked on from inside the car. The past hour sure had been hell on gardens.

*   *   *

Cade had taken part in enough helicopter assault missions, both in war games and actual combat, to instantly recognize the faint, distant droning over the roar of the boat's engine.

"Helicopters," he said. "Incoming." He turned his head, listening. "A shitload of them."

"Where?" Jimi glanced around the night sky.

"From the east." Cade slowed to half speed to enter the harbor's mouth.

"Oh christ, you're right, I hear them now."

Cade killed the boat's running lights just as a wave of helicopters zoomed into view over Stanton Hill and

356

scattered over the beach. Powerful searchlights crisscrossed the ground like spotlights at a circus.

"It's Eberhard," Jimi said. "Coming for Gen."

In the glare of searchlights and landing lights, Cade could make out Blackhawk troop ships and gigantic Sikorsky Skycranes hauling field hospitals tucked under their bellies. The Blackhawks set down on the hill and the giant ships landed on the beach.

Cade shook his head, worry eating at his gut. "I keep getting the bad feeling that Lana and Haven never left the island. They're right in the middle of that."

Jimi grabbed his cell phone and jabbed the buttons for Lana's phone number.

*   *   *

In the crush of sound vibrating the windows of the Land Rover, Lana almost failed to notice the cell phone chirping in her pants pocket.

She stabbed the talk button and yelled, "Jimi?"

"Oh christ, you *are* still there," he said. "Sounds like a war zone around you."

"Oh, Jimi, you don't know what we've been through. A killer tried to gun us down."

"*What*? A soldier?"

"No, no, before all this. Weston's bodyguard. He's in the house."

"Now? He's in the house with you now?"

"We're outside, in the car. We ran out of the house and got mobbed by people wanting to touch my legs."

"Oh, shit."

"But then the helicopters showed up, broke up the mob."

"What about the killer?"

357

"Out cold, last I looked. Now we're surrounded by soldiers. I don't think he'll try anything."

"Good god. You and Haven all right?"

"Physically, yeah, I think. But I'd sure like to share the adventure. Where are you guys?"

"Entering the bay," he said. "Here, talk to Cade."

Cade's voice boomed over the phone. "What are the soldiers doing?"

"I don't know. Running around, mostly. I see hospitals, or something, down on the beach. And some of the soldiers are wearing, ah, like spacesuits—inflated, orange spacesuits."

"What is your exact location?"

"Sitting behind the wheel of the Land Rover at the top of the driveway. Haven's here with me, Newpod, too."

"Okay. Good. That's good. Here's what I want you to do. Start the engine, but don't turn on the headlights. See if you can drive slowly down the hill and right on out of there."

"I'm going to just drive us out of here?"

"You have no idea how much confusion happens in a mission like that. Go on, try it. See how far you get."

"Yeah, okay." She started the engine. "Here goes."

A soldier stepped directly in front of the Land Rover and held up one hand to order her to stop.

"Got about ten feet, Cade," Lana said. "Now a soldier is pointing his weapon at me."

"Damn. You guys hang on. We'll be there soon."

She jabbed the END button and stuffed the phone back into her pocket.

The soldier gestured for her to kill the engine. She complied. He rounded the hood and opened her door like a valet, except that he had an automatic rifle leveled at her chest. He motioned for Lana and Haven to exit the car.

358

Lana got out, and Haven scooted out the driver's side. A hurricane of rotor wash whipped their hair like the leaves of the magnolias and oaks. The burnt kerosene odor of jet engine exhaust filled the air. Newpod barked and jumped over the back seat and out the door. Lana grabbed his collar.

The soldier nodded toward the throng of civilians. "Go stand with the others."

Lana shook her head. They weren't going to join those who had moments earlier mobbed them. She stood by the front of the car, clutching Newpod's collar and gripping Haven's hand.

One of the orange-spacesuit soldiers raised a bullhorn to his faceplate. "Your attention. I am Col. Jack Eberhard of the United States Army Chemical and Biological Weapons Response Team." His voice echoed off the inn's broad front porch. "The Governor of Florida has declared this island under martial law, under control of the United States Army."

Murmurs of alarm rippled through the crowd.

"Each of you has been exposed to a biological warfare agent. Repeat: You have been exposed to a biowarfare agent. You must proceed to one of the quarantine facilities we've set up at the foot of the hill." Thirty or so men in orange biohazard suits formed a line in front of the civilians. "You are ordered to cooperate with the evacuation team, who will escort you to the quarantine units."

Grumbles of anger and moans of fear rose from the crowd.

"The vector of this exposure is a young woman named Gen," Eberhard said. "It is imperative that we locate her. Gen has been seen with Cade Seaborne and may be staying at this inn. Her head and face are extremely deformed, and she has unusual eye color, described as purple or violet.

Does anyone have information regarding this woman's whereabouts?"

Instead of answering, people shouted their own questions: "What kind of disease? What's it do to you? Is it deadly? Yeah, tell us that. How do we—"

"Anyone with information about Gen should report it to the team member who escorts you to the quarantine units."

Lana put an arm around Haven's shoulder and squeezed. Thanks for your impeccable timing, Col. Eberhard. You just saved Haven's life. And no, you can't have Gen. She's already long gone.

56

A mile from shore, Cade backed the throttle down until the unlighted boat slid through the darkness in a wakeless crawl. "Jimi, take the helm." Cade sat on a storage bench and tugged on his flippers.

"What the hell are you up to?" Jimi said.

"I'm going to try to get Lana and Haven out."

"Are you nuts? Just how do you think you're going to accomplish that?"

"I don't know. Get creative." Cade fitted his regulator on top of a fresh air tank. "You take the boat over to Taylor's. Better yet, take it to The Palms. It's closer. We'll meet you at the yacht club."

"No, you listen, Cade. Gen's safe. Eberhard's never going to find her. And what's he going to do to us? See those field hospitals? It's a quarantine operation. Big deal. Don't do something stupid that's going to get you or anybody else shot."

Cade stopped and stared at him. "We don't know what Eberhard is capable of. The man's a sadist. And all he's got to do is spout the magic words—'national security emergency'—and there's no telling what he can get away with. He's going to try to force Lana and Haven to tell him everything they know, and he's got high rank and military secrecy to cover up anything he does to them."

"But there are witnesses."

"Not for long. Eberhard is treating this as a biowarfare contamination site, with soldiers in full biohazard gear. He'll quarantine anybody he finds anywhere near the inn. Get them out of the way, so he can capture Gen." He spit into his dive mask and smeared the puddle around the faceplate, to prevent fogging. "Only thing is, Gen isn't there. So he'll be angry, and desperate to find out where she is. An angry, desperate sadist with too much power—that's a very bad combo."

Jimi swallowed. "Damn...I see your point."

Cade clamped the air tank to the back of his BC vest, shrugged on the vest like a backpack, buckled and tightened the straps. Then he pulled on his mask and snorkel with a snap and stepped backward to the side of the boat, sat on the gunwale.

"Jesus, Cade."

"I'm Hercules Cade."

"Just...you be careful."

Cade grinned. "Nothing can hurt me...well, except kryptonite."

"Then watch out for the kryptonite, super-bro'. I'll be waiting for you at the yacht club."

"If we're not there in an hour or so, it means we're in quarantine, getting interrogated by Colonel Asshole."

Jimi nodded. "I'll keep my cell phone on."

Cade worked his lips around the rubber mouthpiece of the air hose, pressed his mask onto his face and slipped over the side of the boat without a splash.

He snorkeled toward the docks at Willingham's Marina in a smooth, fast Australian crawl. A quarter mile from the docks, he submerged and swam the rest of the distance underwater. When the wooden planks appeared over his head, he quietly breached the water's surface only yards from the beach. A dead pompano drifted by on a platter of seagrapes, but all Cade could smell was the oily reek of jet engine fumes.

A dozen mobile field hospitals parked in the sand, slung under huge Skycrane helicopters. Soldiers in inflated orange spacesuits waited near the hospitals for the first evacuees to arrive for quarantine.

One Skycrane straddled a stainless steel capsule that Cade didn't recognize. Refrigerator-sized metal cylinders and a clutter of pipes bulged from the curved sides of the unit. Then it dawned on him: the container for transporting Gen. He clenched his jaw and surveyed the nearest soldiers.

One of the orange-clad warriors had wandered to the edge of the dock and was looking out over the bay. The guy probably had nothing to do until the first quarantine patients arrived. What if he could disable the guy, take his spacesuit? Hell, yes. Perfect disguise.

Cade floated forward in the darkness, silently removing his flippers and mask. He reached over the stern of Hank Townsend's vintage cabin cruiser and laid the items softly on the wooden deck. Then he shirked out of his vest, and noiselessly placed the vest and air tank beside the other gear. The whine of idling jet turbines covered any sounds he might make, short of setting off a string of firecrackers, but he followed his stealth training by habit.

Cade glided toward the spacesuited man at the foot of the dock until his feet stood on the sandy bottom and the slush of small waves surged around him, buffeting him slightly. The soles of the man's boots were now directly above Cade's head, showing through the chinks between the planks.

Come on, buddy. Turn around. Face the hill again. There, that's it. Now just stand there a few more seconds…

Cade moved out from beneath the dock, crouched so low his nostrils were barely above water, legs coiled under him like a spring. But the guy started talking to someone over his helmet mike. Cade couldn't make out words, just radio static and babble. At least he's preoccupied, not looking down at me.

Cade glided back under the dock. That was stupid. He couldn't believe his oversight: He hadn't considered helmet mikes, the latest in battlefield communications. Now it was a whole new game show. The trick would be to get the man

363

incapacitated before he had time to yelp to his buddies over his helmet mike.

Cade peered up between the planks, running the problem through his mind. After rejecting a dozen strike zones because they were too deadly, he decided to grab the guy from behind in a choke-hold. The suit was inflated, but it was made of soft plastic. A tight enough squeeze should keep the guy quiet until he lost consciousness.

Again, he slipped out from under the dock, glided to the shoreline, and tensed his lower body to spring up behind the soldier. But the soldier turned around once more to stare across the bay.

Don't look down here, buddy. Don't look down. Nothing down here but seaweed and dead fish.

After a seemingly endless moment, the soldier turned to face north toward The Palms, his back to Cade.

Now! Cade lunged up from the darkness, raced two steps, hooked his arm around the man's throat and dragged him backward off the dock into the water. Cade shoved the back of the man's head forward, compressing his throat in the crook of Cade's elbow, which squeezed like plier jaws, pinching off the windpipe and carotid circulation. The man bucked and thrashed, but floating on his back in the water he had no footing or power. After a minute of resistance, he went limp.

Cade towed the spacesuited body like a swimming pool float back to Hank Townsend's cabin cruiser. He scrambled aboard first, clinging to one orange sleeve, then bent low over the stern to haul the limp weight up onto the deck. Now Cade could see the man's face clearly through the suit's faceplate. The bluish lips were quickly turning pink.

Cade popped an airtight seal and, with a half-turn, unscrewed the helmet and lifted it off. He reached inside to the neck ring console and switched off the fan. The man's eyes fluttered and started to open. Cade clipped him hard on the jaw with an uppercut that sent him back to dreamland.

He unzipped the spacesuit's outer nylon zipper and an inner, steel one, splitting the suit down the center of the torso. The heavy rubber gloves attached directly to the sleeves with rubber gaskets; it made tugging the man's hands free like prying meat out of a crab claw. Finally, Cade yanked the sleeves off the man's arms, rolled the body over and dragged the pants off by the attached boots. The man now lay facedown on the deck in a long-sleeved surgical scrubsuit and hood.

Cade opened the cabin door of the Chris-Craft Custom Sedan and dragged the unconscious soldier inside. He rummaged through a stowage bin and found a roll of duct tape, which he used to bind the soldier's wrists and ankles to the steel post of the captain's swivel chair, bolted to the deck. Lastly, he covered the man's mouth with a rectangle of tape, held in place by a long strip that wrapped the back of the head.

By now, Cade's body was slick with sweat. He peeled off his wetsuit, which left him wearing Speedo racing briefs. He walked outside and the sea breeze cooled his damp skin. Then he stepped into the spacesuit, pushed his arms through the sleeves and squeezed his hands into the tight gloves.

He felt an instant of panic when he couldn't shove his feet down into the boots; he wore size fourteen, and the boots were at least two sizes smaller. He used his dive knife to cut out flaps for his toes, and he managed to jam his feet in.

Next, he pulled on the helmet and twisted it to the right until it clicked. The airtight seal muffled the loud whine of the jet engines. Then he zipped up the inner and outer zippers and flipped on the fan, which gave him his second jolt of panic. The suit would not inflate because air rushed out the gash in his boots.

Think, next time.

Oh, well, the suit is so bulky, from a distance who can tell whether the damned thing is inflated or not?

And so what that there's so little air getting to my lungs? At least my toes can breathe.

He gripped his knife, and, careful not to do something *really* stupid—like stab himself in the throat—he used the point of the blade to punch breathing slots along the bottom of the plastic faceplate. Ah, oxygen.

Good to go.

Cade stepped onto the dock and walked to the beach; headed across the sand to the foot of the hill and started to climb.

Lana and Haven were sitting at the top in the Land Rover. He hoped. He would figure out what to do once he got there. He hoped.

His strategy, meantime, was to act like he was part of the evacuation team and knew exactly what he was doing. But it was hard to seem like a competent team member while shuffling uphill in an uninflated spacesuit with toes spilling out of the boots.

57

Eberhard spoke a clipped order into his chin mike of his Racal biohazard suit and a squad of soldiers in orange spacesuits identical to his entered the inn to begin a sweep of all the rooms.

The hard-plastic of his faceplate had fogged. A fan circulated filtered air through the inflated, rubber-lined suit, but as he sweated, the interior climate felt more and more like the tropics in monsoon season.

His eyes roamed from face to face in the crowd of over a hundred people. Gen was not among them. No report yet from Alpha team sweeping through the inn. The stink of rubber and sweat did not make the wait more bearable. Gen, please be here; don't make me look bad again.

People in the crowd were still shouting questions. "What happens when you get sick? Is there a cure?"

"I cannot answer your questions at this time," he said. "The quarantine lasts twenty-four hours. You will be informed in due course of any other information you may need to know." Then, into his chin mike: "Baker Team, move them out."

A squad of spacesuited men stepped forward.

A burly man in an Evinrude cap and overalls shot Eberhard the middle finger. "You and the governor can kiss my ass," he shouted above the noise. "I done my time in 'Nam, Green Beret, two tours, and I ain't taking orders from you, and I ain't going to no quarantine."

Eberhard nodded to a nearby soldier with his rifle already raised; the soldier fired a tranquilizer dart into the man's chest. A woman cried out. The man jerked backward, teetered a few seconds, then keeled over, knocking down three people next to him like bowling pins. Someone started sobbing.

"Non-cooperation of any kind will not be tolerated," Eberhard said. "You will proceed—"

A voice broke in over his headphones. "Sir, this is Alpha Team Leader. Sweep completed. The house is empty, except for one man. He, uh, appears to be infected, sir."

Eberhard's heart skipped a beat. "What do you mean, infected?"

"You'll see. We're coming out the front door now."

A woman shrieked and clapped a hand to her mouth, pointed at the inn's entrance. The crowd turned to stare at a big man who staggered out onto the porch, two soldiers in orange spacesuits following. Blood painted the man's face and shirt crimson. One ruined eyeball dangled from its socket. He dragged a mangled foot.

Eberhard felt a sickening jolt of adrenaline and his pulse began to race. Gen's mitobots did this? The flesh of the man's face looked like bloody ground beef. He was being taken apart, cell by cell.

"It's Eddie," someone shouted, "Fairchild's bodyguard. Look what the virus did to him."

Eddie lurched down the top stairs, stumbled, and pitched forward onto the gravel walkway. The crowd backed away in horror.

Eberhard raised the bullhorn to his helmet's faceplate. "Folks, do not panic." As if he'd given them their cue, people started screaming and fleeing down the hill. Baker Team hurried behind, guiding the rushing herd toward the quarantine units tucked under the heavy-lift helicopters waiting on the beach.

Eddie scrabbled onto his good leg, pushed himself up from the gravel, and hobbled forward. Pebbles stuck to the raw hamburger of his face. His wrecked mouth twisted in pain and rage.

368

Eberhard had never felt so grateful to be in a stuffy biohazard suit. The guy was a walking infection—a biowarfare weapon. He had to get him isolated from everyone else for at least twenty hours, until the mitobots in his tissues shut down.

"Sir, you must let these soldiers escort you to quarantine," Eberhard said through the bullhorn. Into his chin mike, he said, "Isolate this one, lock him in the BL-4 unit." The two soldiers trailing moved forward to grab the man by his arms. Eddie shouldered them away and lurched toward a Land Rover parked sidewise to the inn. Eberhard noticed a woman and girl standing at the front bumper, restraining a furiously snarling dog. They ducked behind the far side of the car, dragging the dog by its collar. The man kept on coming.

"Okay, give this asshole plenty of room," Eberhard said. "Get ready to trank him." Soldiers scattered well out of the line of fire, keeping their weapons trained on the man. Eberhard said through the bullhorn, "Sir, I order you to halt where you are, and cooperate with the evacuation team."

Eddie halted, wobbled on one leg.

"Good, now just—"

The dog yanked loose and charged around the car at the infected man. The girl leaped after the dog. The woman screamed and flew after the girl. The man raised a handgun and fired twice: *bam-bam*. A bullet struck the girl and spun her around.

"Gun! Take him out!" Eberhard shouted. A blizzard of bullets from automatic weapons tore Eddie open like a mattress stuffed with chopped meats. He thudded to the ground and bounced.

Eberhard walked over to inspect the scene. "Charlie Team," he said, "get this mess mopped up and into biocontainment bags. And mark the splatter area with paint.

If you're not wearing a Racal, do not come anywhere near this hot zone."

The woman knelt beside the girl. Eberhard could see a gaping hole in the girl's chest, below her right collar bone. The dog crouched in the grass nearby, whimpering.

He shouted at the woman through his clouded faceplate. "They can stabilize her in the quarantine center."

The woman looked up and shook her head vigorously. "Can't you see? She needs a hospital."

"No can do, lady. Quarantine first. Twenty-four hours. Nobody leaves the island."

The woman pressed her hand over the bullet hole and bright red blood seeped between her brown fingers. She sobbed and hugged the girl to her bosom. Eberhard noticed the woman's shoulder bleeding from a superficial wound.

"Colonel, this is Baker Team. You might want to hear this," came a voice over the headphones. "Old man over here says he saw Gen." A detachment from Baker Team was gathering up the half-dozen injured or unconscious people sprawled on the ground, placing them on stretchers. One of the soldiers waved a spacesuited arm.

Eberhard hurried across the lawn to find a grizzled man raising himself on his elbows from a stretcher. "I seen the gal, the one ya'll hunting for, 'cept she wasn't deformed—far from it. Virus must've healed her up."

Eberhard bent his face near the man. "Purple eyes?"

"Like morning glories."

"Where did you see her? When?"

The old man pointed. "At the marina down yonder. Maybe three weeks back. Cade and his people walked with her to the end of the dock. She dove into the water. Cade dove in, too. Then Cade and them walked back without her. Don't know where the hell she swum off to, but I never did see her after that."

"Her face was not deformed?"

370

The old man grinned. "She was as pretty as pretty gets. Had flowers in her hair. Swum away naked, and I caught me an eyeful. Like a poem in the flesh."

"Did she touch you?"

"Nope. But the dog did. That's how I got infected."

"What dog?"

"Lana Seaborne's dog." He jerked a thumb in the direction where Eberhard had just been. "Cade's sister. You was right to blow away that sumbitch shot her little girl. Wasn't her fault the virus did that to him."

Eberhard couldn't swivel the helmet of his suit, so he turned his whole torso. The civilians and the Land Rover were gone. Where the hell did they go? "Where are the gunshot victims?" he said over his chin mike.

"Sir, a soldier in a Racal suit loaded them and the dog into the car and drove them down the hill."

Eberhard turned and started downhill in a shuffling semblance of a run; the fastest he could manage in a puffy biohazard suit.

"The virus helped me," the old man called after him. "Didn't chew away *my* face. It heals some people. You know that?"

"All evacuation teams, listen up," Eberhard said. "The soldier who is escorting the gunshot victims, stop the car and report your position. I need to interrogate those two immediately. Over."

No answer.

"This is Col. Eberhard. Soldier who is escorting the gunshot victims, report in now."

Nothing came back to his headphones but a fizz of radio static.

371

58

As soon as the Land Rover reached the bottom of the hill, Cade shifted to four-wheel drive and left the roadway. They crossed a ridge of dunes onto the hard-packed sand at low tide. Newpod sat in the front passenger seat. Lana sat in the backseat with Haven lying across her lap, and kept her hands pressed to the sucking wound in Haven's chest. Cade drove slowly, without headlights, and gave a thumbs-up as he rolled by three soldiers in spacesuits like his own. Then he turned north and headed toward The Palms, forcing himself to creep along.

"Lana, call Jimi. Tell him we're on our way."

"I can't. I'm afraid to take my hand off the wound."

"Which pocket?"

"Left."

He watched in the rearview mirror until the soldiers disappeared behind them. Then he stopped the car and popped off his helmet, tossed it to the front floor. He unzipped the double layers of the suit, clamped his teeth on the fingertips of his right glove and tugged his hand out, then contorted his shoulder and worked his arm out of the sleeve. He leaned back between the bucket seats, dug into Lana's pants pocket and grabbed the phone. He stepped on the gas again, steering with his gloved left hand, shifting with his phone hand, pressing the number buttons with his right thumb.

Jimi answered the phone in the middle of the first ring. "Cade?"

"We're on our way."

"What the hell was all that gunfire?"

"Weston's man shot Haven. Chest wound. It's bad."

"Good lord, let's get her to a hospital."

"Quarantine—they're not letting anyone off the island. We've got to find Gen, or she's not going to make it."

"Gen? How can we find her? She could be anywhere."

"Your underwater speaker phones. We go out in the gulf and call for help."

Jimi said nothing.

"We try, goddamit," Cade said. "It's our only hope."

"Okay, I'm with you. But we need a faster boat, to cover more area."

"Frankie's boat moored near you?"

"Uh…yeah, I see it. Three slips over."

"Can you carry the broadcast equipment over by yourself?"

"I'm on it. I'll meet you at his boat, slip 14-A."

Cade tossed the phone onto the passenger's seat, not bothering to hang up. He glanced in the sideview mirror. The field hospitals had shrunk to specks in the distance. He flipped on the high-beam headlights and floored the gas pedal. The Land Rover raced up the northern arm of the crescent beach, toward the glittering lights of the yacht club.

*   *   *

Jimi staggered along the dock under the weight of an underwater speaker the size of a water cooler. He shuffled down three steps onto the wooden runner alongside Franklin Hauser's Donzi ZX speedboat, *Miss Behavin'*. Three V-8 stern drives made the long and narrow, sharp-prowed racer a water rocket. Many times Jimi had watched the all-black boat scream by at top speed. In the No Wake Zone.

Frankie stood in the forward cockpit of his boat with two blonde women who sported matching thong bikinis. The three had their backs to Jimi. Frankie propped his

373

elbows on top of the windshield, watching the military operation on Stanton Hill through binoculars. Jimi plunked the speaker down with a bang and Frankie and the women spun around.

"I need to borrow your boat," Jimi said. "It's a medical emergency."

One of the women giggled. Frankie sneered. "You need to *what*?"

"You heard me, borrow your boat." Jimi jumped down into the aft cockpit.

Frankie stepped toward him. "You're out of your fuckin' mind. Now get off my boat before I kick your ass overboard." More giggles.

"I've been exposed to a biowarfare agent." Jimi pointed with his chin. "Those helicopters and soldiers on the hill? They're looking for me. I'm infected. Everyone at the inn is infected." He twitched and made a show of scratching his right palm. "The soldiers are scared to death to touch us; they've got on biohazard suits. I doubt your golf shirt and shorts make a good biohazard suit." He moved forward. "What do you think, Frankie?"

Frankie eyes grew huge and he retreated until his back struck the windshield. The women huddled beside him, cringing.

Jimi formed the fingers and thumb of his right hand into the shape of a gun and reached out, pointing the barrel inches from Frankie's face. "I'm loaded with virus, a walking hot zone. Now toss me your key, or I'll shoot you full of what terrifies those soldiers."

"Okay, I...I'll toss it to you." Frankie fumbled through his pocket and lobbed the key to Jimi. "Now just let us go. Please."

"Sure. Soon as I wipe this itchy slime off my hand." Jimi dragged his palm down the front of Frankie's shirt and shorts. Frankie shuddered, and in the lamplight from the dock his pale face turned green. "You know, if I were you, Frankie, I'd yank off those contaminated clothes and jump in the water fast," Jimi said. "Then again, slime suits you."

The women glanced at each other, then hopped over the side with a double splash. It didn't take Frankie long to peel out of his shirt and shorts and underwear. He ran naked off the bow of the boat, smacked into the water with a bellyflop, and kept on swimming.

*   *   *

Cade drove the Land Rover right onto the concrete dock. A few people on their yachts shouted angrily as he sped by. He skidded to a halt at Slip 14-A and leaped out of the driver's seat, half his biohazard suit flopping. Newpod scrambled out of the car and hopped down into the speedboat.

Cade flung open the back door and tenderly lifted Haven from Lana's lap, carried his daughter on board.

"Aw, Jesus," Jimi said when he saw the girl. Jimi knelt next to Cade, helped him lower Haven's head to the deck. Newpod licked Haven's face, whimpering. Cade grabbed Jimi's arm. "Got the sound gear aboard?"

He nodded. "Already set up."

"Cade, do what you need to do," Lana said. "I'll stay with her."

Cade nodded and tugged off the remaining sleeve, yanked off the boots and stepped out of the spacesuit. "Jimi, help me hotwire the ignition."

"Got the key," Jimi said, dangling it.

Cade's eyebrows shot up. He snatched the key.

"I'll cast off the lines," Jimi said, jumping onto the dock runner.

Cade cranked the ignition and the three Bravo One V-8s kicked over with a roaring stampede of horsepower. He checked the fuel gauge—half-full tank.

"Lines clear," Jimi said, hopping down into the cockpit. Where Haven rested, fresh blood smeared the white fiberglass deck, shining darkly in the courtesy lights. Jimi ducked through a sliding door into the cabin to find blankets. "C'mon, Newpod. Get in here, boy." The dog followed him inside.

Cade nudged the 45-foot speedboat out of the slip and pointed its long, sharp nose toward the mouth of the bay. "Everybody hang on tight," he said, and shoved the triple throttle handles forward. *Miss Behavin'* blasted ahead with a deep-throated roar that echoed off the pink stucco walls of The Grove. The racer accelerated over the smooth water until it planed out on the last few feet of its stepped-hull. The three tachometers soared to 5,000 RPM and the speedometer hit 85 miles an hour.

In a couple minutes, the boat had raced beyond the bay into open water. Cade shot a glance over his shoulder. His daughter was wrapped in blankets, her feet propped high on a stack of cushions. Lana bent over her niece, talking close to her ear.

Cade felt as if his heart had been torn from his chest. Haven *was* his heart. If she didn't survive, his wound would remain as ragged as it felt now—forever. He resisted the impulse to collapse to his knees and blurt out prayers to an unknown god. "Be strong," he told himself. Be strong. Be strong. Be strong.

"Jimi," he called back, "how's she doing?"

Jimi squeezed Lana's arm and moved forward to join Cade at the helm. "She's not good," Jimi said. "Her lips are pale. She's bleeding internally." He knelt down and switched on his laptop computer and music synthesizer keyboard. "Oh, brother, I just hope this works."

376

"I'm thinking we'll park the boat in the area where we found Gen," Cade said. "Start there."

"How far?"

"Ten minutes."

Jimi shook his head. "Let's stop here. Dolphin pods range over a wide territory. They can swim seventy miles a day. This is as good a place as any."

Cade slowed the boat to a crawl, then shut down the engines.

"Okay, I've got to figure out what I'm doing, here," Jimi said. "Dolphins have got a two-part distress call. I've recorded it. Other dolphins in the pod hear it and they rush to an ailing dolphin, push it to the surface to breathe." He pressed a key on the synthesizer and two notes whistled loudly through the speaker lying on the deck. "I can broadcast this at top volume underwater." He nodded toward a Fender guitar amplifier. "That should make any nearby pods perk up and take notice. I think. But I don't know if they'll swim near, or if it'll just scare the hell out of them."

"We need a way to tell Gen that it's us; that Haven needs her help."

"That's the problem, exactly," Jimi said. "This keyboard can digitally reproduce the dolphin speech I've recorded." He pressed keys at random and whistles, clacks, squawks, and blats sang out of the speaker. "Trouble is, I don't speak dolphin."

"Got a microphone?"

"Right here." Jimi held up a headset mike.

"If Gen's mind is still part-human, couldn't we talk underwater, shout for help?"

Jimi shrugged. "That's a big *if.*"

"She came to us before," Cade said. "She'd been a dolphin, and she chose to become human. I've got to believe she still knows us."

Jimi nodded. "Let's try both ways—we'll call for help in Dolphin and English." He put on the microphone headset. "Lower the speaker into the water."

Cade carried the heavy speaker in its nylon harness to the side of the cockpit and lowered it underwater until it hung just below the hull. He tied off the harness cord on a cleat. Jimi immediately began sending the dolphin distress call at full volume. The two-note whistles rang through the hull of the boat repeatedly.

"Cade." Lana waved him toward her. "Haven is asking for you."

Cade hurried back to his daughter. It hurt him so badly to see her in pain, he had to force air into his lungs to talk to her. "What is it, baby?"

She whispered something he couldn't make out. He lowered his ear to her pale lips.

"Will...anything...happen...to Gen?" she wheezed.

"It's okay, sugar." He pretended not to understand, though he knew exactly what she meant. A battle of loyalties had waged in his heart since he saw Haven lying wounded on Stanton Hill. "You just hang on. Everything will be okay."

He combed sweaty hair off her forehead with his fingertips, but she gripped his wrist with sudden strength. "Don't let Gen get caught!" she blurted, and blood leaked out of her chest wound.

"Keep her still, Lana," he said, standing. "Don't let her talk!"

But the truth went without saying. That slick getaway from the inn wouldn't fool anyone for long. Eberhard probably had their location pinpointed by now. Easily done with an AWACS jet circling above, using Downlook Radar—standard battlefield intelligence.

Cade held up his hand. "Jimi, stop the calls for a moment." He listened. The trio of engines ticked as they

378

cooled. Swells lapped the hull. Then he heard it, the faint whisper of a jet riding high in the night.

He cursed under his breath.

They were all trading Gen's life for Haven's. If they did manage to contact Gen, as soon as she was on board, soldiers would swoop in from the sky and sea to capture her.

He looked at Lana, bent over his daughter. His sister's cheeks glistened with tears.

Gen was miraculous. Invincible.

Haven was just a little girl, dying.

Cade nodded to Jimi and he resumed sending the dolphin distress call. Every few minutes, Jimi lowered a microphone into the water to pick up dolphin sounds. Twice, he told Cade he heard a chorus of low-frequency warning whistles. He worried that the loud distress calls were frightening dolphin pods away. The two men switched to talking into the microphone, pleading for Gen to come to Haven's aid.

A half-hour passed. Cade started the speedboat and raced to a new position, ten miles west. He and Jimi resumed broadcasting their calls for help, and listening for dolphins. Cade shivered in his swim briefs and Jimi took off his long-sleeved denim shirt and draped it over Cade's shoulders.

Ten minutes, twenty minutes creeped by. Cade hurried back to check on Haven. She had lost consciousness and Cade felt terrified. "How's her pulse?"

Lana shook her head, too distraught to speak. Cade checked Haven's pulse and found it weak and fluttery. Time was running out.

They'd been on the water now for over an hour. Cade returned to Jimi's side. "We're losing her." Tears streamed down his cheeks. "What are we going to do?"

"The distress signal is working against us. Let's try something different." Jimi stuck a tape into his recording system and hit PLAY. The voice and guitar of Jimi Hendrix vibrated through the hull from underwater: *Well she's walking through the clouds, with a circus mind that's running wild. Butterflies and zebras, moonbeams and fairy tales, that's all she ever thinks about.*

Jimi hit PAUSE, and handed Cade the headset microphone. "They say music is the universal language. I don't know what else to try."

"We need you Gen," Cade said into the mike, and heard his own thick and trembling voice sounding into the depths. "Haven needs you now. Please come to us. Please hurry."

Jimi played more of the Hendrix tune: *When I'm sad, she comes to me, with a thousand smiles she gives to me, free. It's alright, she says, it's alright. Take anything you want from me—anything.*

Jimi stopped the song and put on headphones, listening for dolphins.

A minute passed, and Cade began to call for help again. Please, Gen. Please.

Jimi waved his hand. "Shush! I hear them." He stood up fast. "A pod is coming toward us from the northwest." He used both hands to press the headphones tighter. "Man, they're hauling ass. They aren't swimming, they're flying!"

"She's coming, Lana!" Cade shouted. "Gen is on her way!" He rushed back to Haven and cradled her clammy face, like holding his own precious heart in his hands. "Hang on, sweetie. You're going to be all right. Gen is on her way." Gen could do it. She could do anything.

Jimi punched PLAY, and the Hendrix crying guitar solo reverberated through the sea. He swayed on his feet, playing left-handed air guitar to the Hendrix riffs, picking and bending each note in synchrony with the music.

Fly on, Little Wing.

59

Col. Eberhard squirmed in the payload operator's cockpit of the CH-54B Skycrane, his butt going numb. He felt enormously frustrated. The heavy-lift helicopter perched on the beach, waiting to fly the liquid-nitrogen cooled holding capsule out to the target site. The AWACS "Sentry" jet crew, high above the gulf, kept a lock on the speedboat with Downlook radar and multi-spectral optical sensors. The capture teams stood ready in inflatable assault boats and Nighthawk helicopters.

Now it looked like there was not going to be a capture.

The AWACS crew had pinpointed Cade Seaborne zooming out of the bay in a fast boat, and Eberhard had held his teams back, watching and waiting to see where Cade would go. Was he trying to get the wounded girl to a hospital on the mainland, or was he heading straight to Gen?

Eberhard believed the group in the speedboat was racing toward Gen, in order for Gen to heal the wounded girl. Who could guess where Gen had holed up? Eberhard had hoped that he would soon find out.

But then the speedboat came to a stop. Not once, but twice. Engine trouble, apparently. It was so infuriating he could scream.

"Bird's Eye to Team Leader."

A call was coming through from the AWACS jet. "Team Leader, here," Eberhard said, "what have you got?"

"Sir, our sensors are reading a pod of dolphins heading toward the target."

"Dolphins?"

"Yes, sir. Moving toward the boat at thirty knots or better. They'll make contact in a couple minutes."

"What the hell do you think this channel is for, a nature show? I don't give a fuck about the dolphins. Is the boat going anywhere?"

"Uh, no sir. Boat is still dead in the water. IR shows the engines are not running."

Eberhard could hear his silent screams bouncing off the walls of his skull. All right, that's it. No more sitting around while my ass falls asleep. I can't wait for Cade to reach Gen. I need to find out what he and the people on his boat know.

"Attention, capture teams, this is Team Leader. All teams close in now. Repeat: All teams close in now."

The Skycrane's twin jet turbines revved to a high-pitched whine, generating ten-thousand horsepower. Six rotor blades, 72 feet in diameter, threw down a hurricane of thrust and the huge helicopter lifted off the beach, carrying below it a shiny steel capsule designed to hold Gen inside, frozen solid.

60

Cade felt Haven's pulse. It had grown weak and rapid, but Gen would be here soon to heal her.

"There!" Jimi said, pointing off to starboard. A couple dozen dolphins dashed toward the boat out of the dark sea, leaping and knifing across the glassy water. Cade's heart leapt up with them.

"Oh, Gen, hurry!" Lana shouted.

The pod reached the boat, chattering loudly. The sea boiled furiously around one dolphin who quickly took on the form of a naked woman. A baby dolphin darted close to the human Gen, brushing against her body, and Gen ran a hand across the baby's sleek face. Then a big dolphin burst out of the water, arcing high in the air and smacking back into the sea, and all the dolphins turned as one, and followed the big dolphin away at top speed into the night.

Jimi leaned over the side of the boat and hauled Gen up on deck with both hands. "It's Haven," he said. "She's dying."

Gen nodded slowly, seemingly dazed. She knelt next to Haven and pulled back the blankets. She put her hand on Lana's hand and pulled it away from the gunshot wound. Then she laid her hands on Haven's bare chest and closed her eyes. A fog spread from her hands, sparkling iridescently in the dim courtesy lighting of the cockpit. The fog grew thicker until Gen's hands and Haven's flesh seemed to merge, then disappear under an opaque, rainbow cloud.

Jimi stood nearby. Lana remained kneeling beside her niece, her hands lovingly caressing Gen's bare back.

In less than a minute, Haven opened her eyes. Cade sobbed and covered his daughter's face with kisses. Lana and Jimi were crying, too.

Haven stared at Gen with huge brown eyes. "Gen, you're here!" Then the girl's grateful expression twisted into a frown and she began to cry. "Go away, quick. Army men are looking for you. Go now."

Jimi wrapped a blanket around Gen and she stood. She leaned into him, seeming to be half-awake, moving in a dream.

"Haven's right," Jimi said. "It's dangerous for you. You'd better get back into the water now. Go back to your pod."

"I can't," she said.

"Why not?"

"My pod is gone. I told them to leave me," she said. "My final change is coming. I can't stay in the water, I need to be on land when it happens."

Cade heard rolling thunder, fast approaching. He gave Gen a fierce look. "Christ, Gen, go, go, go! Over the side. Get out of here. I hear them. They're coming for you."

She shook her head. "It's too late, Cade. You can't help me, and they can't hurt me. No one can stop what I'm becoming."

The helicopters hurtled toward the boat like giant black locusts. They flew so low over the water, white froth churned in their wakes. Cade stood quickly and pushed Gen to the deck. "Everybody stay down!" he yelled.

Three or four helicopters now stood off from the boat, the sound of jet turbines and whirling rotors deafening. An artificial gale rocked the sea and hurled stinging bullets of water through the air. Gen stood up and her blanket whipped away in the storm. She braced herself against the wind, naked in the bleaching glare of halogen spotlights.

Scuba divers in black wetsuits scrambled up both sides of the boat at once, using electric-winch grappling gear. Rifles bristled in every direction, with powerful spotlights affixed to the barrels. One diver slid open the cabin door and disappeared into the boat's interior. Ferocious snarling and barking arose, followed by a loud yelp, then silence.

The soldier stepped out of the cabin. "No personnel, sir. Just a dog. I hit it in the head with the butt of my rifle."

A tall soldier approached Gen. He unclipped a two-way radio from his belt and shouted into the handset. "Team Leader, this is Foxtrot Leader. I count five individuals on board; not four," he said. "Two adult males, two adult females, and one female child. And sir, one adult female has purple eyes. Affirmative, sir, purple eyes. She must have been on board the whole time, hidden in the cabin." He stepped closer to Gen, his diving fins hooked to his waist behind him, his rifle light glaring in her face. "Team Leader, I am now standing five feet away from the subject, and I guarantee you that her eyes are purple." He played the light across Gen's body, head to toe. "That is a negative, sir. She is presently naked, and she has no deformities. She looks very, ah, fit, sir. Healthy. Great…health."

The soldier listened to instructions then signaled the other soldiers, pointing up. A Skycrane helicopter slid into position, hovering only a hundred feet directly over the deck. Its rotor wash flattened the sea in concentric standing waves. A wire cage descended on a cable from the stainless steel capsule clamped under the fuselage of the Skycrane. At rifle point, the soldiers loaded Gen into the wire cage, and the cable hauled her up until she disappeared into a hatch in the bottom of the capsule. The hatch closed. Immediately, the helicopter banked and headed back toward the mainland.

"What are they going to do to her?" Cade asked the tall soldier.

"Mister, I don't have that information, and if I did I wouldn't be allowed to disclose it," he said. "You and your people got off very lucky. Team Leader was going to tear you guys apart to find her. Now we're pulling out. It's all over. We got what we came for. Boats are on their way to take you back to the island for twenty-four hour quarantine."

He signaled the other soldiers and they all slid over the side of the boat and swam to wire baskets waiting for them in the water, dangling from three Nighthawk helicopters. The combat divers rode back up the cables and swung into the open sides of the buzzing locusts.

A half-dozen inflatable boats appeared in the distance, zipping along the smooth water, approaching fast. Twin 50-caliber machine gun turrets poked from amidships of each boat.

Haven went into the cabin and returned with Newpod. "I wiped Gen's magic off on him. His head wound is okay, see?"

"Smart girl," Cade said. "Here, let me hold his collar."

The boats surrounded the Donzi speedboat on all sides, and lashed the hulls together. They began towing the speedboat to shore.

The four people and the dog huddled, holding each other.

Cade had one other thing to hold on to: Gen had said that he couldn't help her and they couldn't hurt her.

He had to believe with all his might that was true, or he couldn't take the anguish that caged his heart.

61

Col. Jack Eberhard sat at mission control inside an E-3 Sentry Airborne Warning and Control Systems aircraft. The four-engine jet circled high above the White Sands Missile Range, northwest of Alamogordo, New Mexico. Its fuselage bore the insignia of the Strategic Air Command: an armored fist clutching a zigzag thunderbolt as if it were God's own dagger.

Twenty-thousand feet below, a modified Humvee plodded along a utility road toward a concrete-walled vertical shaft sunk six stories deep in the sand at Omega Site: ground zero. At the base of the shaft, a steel-reinforced concrete vault held a thermonuclear bomb. The fusion device was designed to unleash, for a split-second, the identical force that powered the sun.

The Commander-in-Chief of the United States of America, and her senior intelligence, military and science advisors, had ordered today's mission to delete a dangerous glitch in a bioweapons research program. The dangerous glitch was a young woman named Gen. The delete key was the 50-megaton hydrogen bomb waiting for her in the vault under the desert.

The soldiers performing the mission referred to the woman as "the package." Right now, the package was hard-frozen in liquid nitrogen inside an isolation capsule fitted into the cargo bay of the modified Heavy Humvee.

At 0600 hours, the package was scheduled to arrive at the test site and immediately be transferred by freight elevator to the bottom of the shaft, Humvee and all. At 0640, the helicopter evacuation of all personnel from the blast area was to be completed and final checklists were to proceed toward detonation. At 0700, the concrete vault, the

Humvee, the package, and all proximate matter—mineral, vegetable, and animal—were scheduled to be vaporized.

If the package attempted a breakout during the trip to the bomb site, Eberhard would remote-detonate a W80 nuclear warhead—a 250-kiloton mistake-eraser—carried within the capsule inside the Humvee.

If the warhead failed to explode, a B-2 Stealth bomber, cruising in the stratosphere above Eberhard's aircraft, carried a W80-tipped cruise missile, radar-locked on the Humvee, ready to launch from its weapons bay.

And as final failsafe, a trailer-launched Pershing II guided missile with a 400-kiloton punch hunkered in the dunes at the base of Salinas Peak, also radar-locked on the slow-moving Humvee.

To carry out their delivery mission successfully, the two soldiers in the Humvee did not need to know any details about their frozen cargo. They did not need to know about the remote-controlled hydrogen bomb they straddled, or the guided nuclear missles that tracked their progress. Therefore, they did not know.

*   *   *

Airman Mick Colburn drove a lone Army Humvee toward Omega Test Site, in the god-forsaken middle of nowhere. Lieutenant Roger Henderson rode beside him in the cab. Both men wore camouflaged BWCS biowarfare combat suits, designed for dealing with Level Four hot germs in a battlefield environment.

A sliver of moon hung low in the west like the fallen petal of a night-blooming cactus. Clear, pink lacquer overlaid the brightening eastern sky. Free-tailed bats by the tens of thousands were flitting home to red sandstone caves in the Valley of Fires.

A paltry trace of dew already had evaporated from the stunted junipers and mesquite that dotted the scrubland. By midday, the sun would broil the white gypsum dunes until the oven-hot air bent light into mirages of rippling lakes.

Inside his rubber-lined airtight suit, Colburn sweated as if he were locked in a steambox. He shifted for the hundredth time, trying to find a more comfortable position, but the Humvee's seat was not contoured to fit a former Clemson All-Star tackle dressed in a bulky, inflated spacesuit. He felt like a manatee trying to gain an easeful perch on a bar stool.

Another minute of squirming only managed to give him a wedgie. Just great. Now cotton briefs strangled his manhood and he had no way—short of yanking off the biohazard gear—to relieve his misery.

With his chin, he clicked on the helmet mike. "Lieutenant, I'm splashing around in a puddle of sweat in here."

Lt. Henderson sat facing backward in the Humvee in order to keep watch through a heavy glass panel into the rear section of the truck. He never peeled his eyes from the cargo bay. "Check your cooling system again."

"I did, sir. Green lights. And I can hear the pump running."

"Coolant circulating?"

"Seems like it."

"Fan?"

Colburn squeezed his sleeve. "Suit's still puffed up."

"Sure that puddle is your sweat? Maybe—"

"—the coolant's leaking inside. I just thought of that, too. Damn."

"But then you should be getting a red light from the coolant pressure drop."

"Whatever," Colburn said. At least the leak was on the inside. The suit still protected him from bio-contamination.

He pictured himself lolling his tongue and panting like an overheated bloodhound. He twisted the temperature-control dial on his left wrist farther toward *COOL*. Didn't budge. It hadn't the last three tries, either.

Henderson checked a digital clock in the heads-up display in his helmet. "We're right on schedule. Can't stop till we've reached the test site. Another hour."

"Yes sir." Colburn blew out a loud sigh. "I'm just way too hot."

Henderson frowned. "You're not going to pass out on me, are you?"

"Oh, no suh, it jus' be a dog day down in the delta," Colburn said, exaggerating his Louisiana accent. "I can take it, if I have to. Sounds like I have to."

"Just give me some warning if you get light-headed or anything. Fuck, that's all we need."

"Will do."

"All right. One hour. Soon as we deliver the package, helicopter swoops down for evac, you peel off your suit. Fly back in your underwear."

"Ahhhh. Yes, sir. Can't wait. Gonna hang out in that breeze like a tickhound in a pickup."

"For now, hang in here, airman. Stay alert."

"Yes, sir."

Colburn drove and blinked back stinging sweat. It ran down in a steady trickle from his soggy crewcut into his eyes, and no amount of batting his eyelashes kept his vision from blurring. He wished to hell he'd worn a headband.

Every few minutes the lieutenant's rubber gloves squeaked on the glass panel as he brushed away a film of frost. A television screen mounted atop the truck's console enabled Colburn to keep his attention on the desert road and also monitor the cargo space behind him. The color screen displayed refrigeration equipment and stainless-steel tanks filled with liquid nitrogen, white with frost. In the cargo compartment's center rested a stainless steel capsule, and through a window in the capsule, he could see a clear box, built of six-inch-thick Lucite walls. Bolts the size of soup cans anchored the capsule to the floor.

"The package" inside the sealed box gave Colburn the creeps. Henderson seemed uptight, too. The lieutenant wore a military radio backpack with a whip antenna that ran outside the window. If the package so much as wiggled a little finger, he was supposed to report it ASAP by radio to Col. Eberhard, riding somewhere up in the blue.

Other than that, the two men were to do nothing. They didn't even carry weapons. They were not here as soldiers, but only delivery boys.

Colburn felt weird without his M-16A4 rifle. Naked. Like standing around at a frat party without a beer in your hand. His eyes watched the roadway and the view of the box.

He shuddered. Not because the package looked so threatening, but because it looked so harmless. To be going to so much trouble to kill—to *nuke*—a young woman really freaked him bad. Like his Creole grandmomma would say, "She mus' be da devil hisself!"

Frost clothed the woman's nude figure. In white patches it mottled her dusky skin, like pale lichens growing over smooth, dark rock. Frost and ice clung to her rippling locks, turning them into wavy icicles that sparkled like party glitter. Frozen eyelashes zipped her eyelids shut.

Spooky thing was, Popsicle Girl was a total babe. Off the chart on the Ten-Scale—like maybe a Perfect Twelve. But all she had to do was sneeze, or cough up some evil shit and it could wipe out everybody on the planet.

Damn sure couldn't be anthrax. Everybody had gotten a shot against that bug—one of those elective inoculation programs the brass insisted you "volunteer" for.

392

Had to be something gross and nasty. Like Ebola. No, worse. A *lot* worse. They were going to *nuke* her, for chrissake.

Probably some bioweapon hybrid where they mixed Ebola with AIDS with clap with friggin' Congo monkey-ass flu, or something crazy. One little exposure—say, just kissing a beautiful girl like her—and your belly bursts open like a piñata and your guts pop out like colored streamers.

Today's Army: vaporizing girls to save the world.

His superiors had told Colburn next to nothing during the mission briefing. She was highly infectious and blah, blah, they had said. An unstoppable plague.

But how much had they left out?

He stared at the restraints forged of tempered steel that locked down the girl's wrists and ankles, plus more steel restraints across her thighs and torso. What's up with that? She some kind of—what? *Super*girl?

Despite the muggy, Louisiana-bayou heat inside his suit, a chill slithered up Colburn's spine like an icy snake. He shuddered again.

You just keep frozen, babe. Just stay chilled out.

Outside the windshield, Colburn watched a pathetic little rain cloud trying to rain, but the raindrops evaporated before they hit the sand. The desert air wrung out the cloud like a threadbare rag and—*poof*—it was gone.

A half-hour later, Colburn had decided that after this duty he needed to find himself a more effective deodorant. The one he'd used that morning had lost its ability to mask the odor of his sweat. The atmosphere in his suit reeked like a locker room after the big game. Exactly—Lysol smell and all. Even a hint of urinals—that detail provided by the suit-contained plastic bag he'd just peed into.

Thanks to Eberhard's anal distress about mission safety, the Humvee was not to exceed thirty miles an hour. Hell, I've been in parades faster than this, Colburn thought.

He was a man of action, not the kind of guy who took well to sitting on his butt for long periods, delivering hard-frozen girls to nuclear bomb sites. He wished he could take off his sweltering gear, jump out of the truck, knock off his daily six-mile run, and then hop back in. He would sweat less jogging in the desert sun, than trapped in his own personal swamp while coolant drizzled down to pool in his boots.

He checked the package in the monitor again. The girl looked like a mannequin carved from frozen molasses. Supposedly, she was alive, but he did not know how that was possible. He hadn't seen her breathe once. The top left of the monitor screen gave an EEG readout, monitoring her brain function. Amber waves danced up and down rhythmically, so…yeah, somebody was home.

Colburn was supposed to keep one eye glued to the EEG, because if the package started spiking active brainwaves the lieutenant was immediately supposed to talk to the Man Upstairs. Not God, but Eberhard—though Colburn doubted the colonel bothered to draw a distinction between the two.

Above the roadway, the sky glinted silver-blue, like hot gunmetal. Sunlight flashing off shimmering white dunes pierced the windshield. Colburn squinted from a stabbing headache. He felt so overheated and nauseated he worried he was going to puke. Oh, that would be the end of it, barfing into his spacesuit. He'd go out of his friggin' mind. Tear off the suit and dive into the freezer with the plague queen.

A digital clock in the corner of the monitor showed twenty minutes remaining to get there.

Hurry up, you fuckin' clock!

A roadrunner dashed across the road, skinny legs a gray blur. Colburn grinned, and a rivulet of salty sweat ran into his mouth. He saw himself as Wily Coyote in an Acme biohazard suit, about to go splat. *Beep-beep!*

He tried to maintain his sanity by calling to mind the joys of a shower: all cold water, full blast. Lots of soap and shampoo. New (Improved!) b.o. spray. A chilly bedroom and a firm mattress with cool cotton sheets.

He thought of a frosty can of Budweiser, and suddenly felt woozy, like he'd already guzzled a six-pack.

He smirked. Some imagination. Maybe he should conjure up Popsicle Girl to go with those cool cotton sheets.

Dark sheets.

Black sheets with floating silvery stars.

His head wobbled.

Henderson yelled his name, grabbed the wheel.

The Humvee swerved off the shoulder, lurched and bumped, then steered back on the roadway. Colburn managed to brake, downshift, and stop. Then sky and earth traded places, and he passed out.

*   *   *

In the AWACS jet, flying a ten-mile-wide orbit, twenty-thousand feet above the Humvee, Col. Eberhard and a dozen communications and technical personnel manned stations at the mission control center.

Eberhard's thumb worried the button of a ballpoint pen, *clicket-clicket-clicket-clicket-clicket,* while his eyes stayed fixed on a digital map of the terrain and roadway below. A moving blip represented the Humvee's progress. A Global Positioning Satellite pinpointed the location of the vehicle to within a half-meter.

Suddenly Eberhard lurched forward, tapped the screen with the pen. "Shit, we've got a situation," he said. "They've stopped dead."

395

Eberhard radioed Lt. Henderson on the ground. "Doodle Bug, Doodle Bug, this is Sun Dog. Come in."

He waited a full minute without a reply. An electronics warfare specialist seated next to Eberhard shook his head slowly, chewing his lower lip.

Eberhard nodded to the EW specialist and removed a Permissive Action Link electronic key and a code card from a chain around his neck. The specialist unbuttoned his shirt collar and pulled out a chain with a similar key and red plastic card.

Eberhard nodded again. "Three, two, one. Go." They jointly inserted the PAL keys into independent locks on the separate panels before them. They turned the keys to the right, then punched in half a numeric code, and passed their code cards to each other to complete the sequence. A row of red lights on Eberhard's console turned green; the nuclear weapon was armed. He flipped up a yellow-and-black striped safety hatch that covered the weapon's trigger. His hand poised over the stainless steel toggle that would detonate the 250-kiloton warhead in the cargo bay of the Humvee.

"Sun Dog calling Doodle Bug," he said. "Sun Dog needs a status report, immediately. I repeat: immediately. Drop whatever you're doing and call in, *right now*."

Without waiting, he used a separate channel to contact the B-2 bomber above his flight loop. "Blackbird, this is Sun Dog, over."

"Blackbird reading you."

"Doodle Bug has stopped moving and is not reporting. Be advised I am proceeding with countdown to emergency response."

"Ah, roger, that, Sun Dog. Standing by."

"Countdown begins now," Eberhard said. "Ten...nine...eight..."

396

"Oh, Christ, here it comes," the EW specialist muttered and tightened his shoulder harnesses. Other crew members followed his lead.

"...five...four..."

Eberhard and the others yanked off their headphones to avoid the squeal from the electromagnetic pulse the nuclear explosion would generate.

Eberhard extended his trigger finger to flick the toggle. "...two...one..."

"Sun Dog, Sun Dog, this is Doodle Bug." The voice blurted over the radio speaker.

Eberhard jerked his finger off the toggle switch. It twitched in midair. He put on his headphones and slumped back in the chair. "Report, Doodle Bug. What is your situation?"

"The driver, Airman Colburn, passed out from heat exhaustion. The coolant is leaking inside his suit. Over."

"What is status of the package?"

"Sir, Colburn appears to be going into convulsions."

"Lieutenant, tell me the status of the *package*!"

"Unchanged," he said. "Sir, Colburn looks real bad. He's definitely convulsing now. I, uh...what do I do?"

"Push Colburn out of the truck and continue your mission, Lieutenant."

"*Sir?*"

"That is a direct order. You are to eject Colburn from the vehicle immediately and deliver the package on schedule to the test site. Understood?" A pause. "Acknowledge, lieutenant."

"But...his face is all red, he's not breathing right. He needs med-evac."

"I'll send a helicopter to get him." Eberhard rested his finger on the toggle to detonate the H-bomb. "Now, kick his ass out of the truck and *drive*!" he yelled.

"Roger, sir. Will comply."

397

In a moment, the blip on the screen began to move again. Col. Eberhard took his finger off the toggle and raked the trembling hand through his silver buzz-cut. Sweat plastered his cotton shirt against his skin. The EW specialist licked dry lips and put his headphones back on. In unison, he and Eberhard inserted their PAL keys and disarmed the warhead; the row of green lights winked red.

Fifteen minutes later, a Blackhawk helicopter had evacuated the stricken airman, zooming off toward Holloman Air Force Base. But Eberhard did not breathe easier until twenty-five minutes had passed and the Humvee was securely enclosed in the subterranean bomb vault.

A waiting Blackhawk evacuated Lt. Henderson and a handful of technicians from the site. At zero minus ten minutes, Eberhard authorized detonation and immediately proceeded with a checklist that ended with inserting PAL keys and arming the nuclear device.

He glued his eyes to the digital clock on the fire control panel before him. At zero minus one minute, he flipped up a red plastic safety cover, exposing a toggle trigger. At zero minus ten seconds, he began the countdown out loud. The other crewmembers in the aircraft counted along with him.

Right on schedule, at 0700 hours, the bomb detonated, generating the explosive intensity of 50 million tons of TNT. A superhot nuclear fireball vaporized the concrete vault and the Humvee. The surrounding sand fused into a lake of molten glass. An earthquake jolted the desert floor for miles around, bouncing rocks and lizards an inch off the sand.

After a moment, Eberhard imagined he could hear the deep-throated thunder rising from twenty-thousand feet below. Then he realized it wasn't his imagination. Pressure waves rattled the jet from nose to tail. Coffee sloshed from

398

his mug. He checked the seismograph recordings: 7.8 Richter shock at ground zero, followed by weaker aftershocks. In another moment, the temblors faded to stillness.

Goodbye, Gen. Even you can't survive an H-bomb blast.

Mission accomplished. Glitch deleted.

Eberhard's sweat-soaked body sagged with relief.

62

Along a lonely stretch of desert road in the military-restricted zone of the White Sands Missile Range, the Abundance had relived the biblical tale of Noah.

A flood of rain drowned Noah's world. But Noah had prepared by building an ark to save himself and the creatures of his land. He could not save each beast, so aboard his ark he took breeding pairs from every species: sheep and wolves, antelopes and lions—all. And when the deluge covered the flocks and packs and herds and prides of the old world, the ark ferried the rescued pairs to a new world, where the animals were fruitful and multiplied.

Inside a deep vault at ground zero, a flood of fire drowned the Abundance's world. But the Abundance had prepared by building an ark, to save itself and the essences of creatures it had absorbed. By the time the inferno erupted, the ark had already escaped.

The ark contained Gen's genetic code and a perfect recording of her mind—all her memories, her personality, intact and safe. The ark was a spore, a seed—able now to replicate Gen's mind and body along with myriad other lifeforms. And all this precious cargo, stored as pure information at the quantum level, fit neatly inside the several hundred-thousand molecules of the ark—smaller than a sugar grain.

A woven mesh of diamond threads formed the ark's tough hull. Thousands of whip-tailed flagella propelled it forward. The frigid environment slowed, but did not stop its journey. It swam through the icy slush of blood from the visual cortex at the back of Gen's brain, forward along the optic tract. It crossed the thalamus, passed the optic chiasma and traveled on to pierce the retina of her left eye; voyaged across the polar ocean of the vitreous humor to exit the pupil. There it paused, atop the curved world of the cornea.

Then the ark engulfed a tiny bead of liquid nitrogen, forming around the droplet a chamber with an open nozzle. The chamber generated a burst of heat by rapidly oxidizing glucose. The nitrogen exploded into gas, driving the ark like a microscopic rocket through the frosty air of the Lucite vault.

The ark reached a seam in the vault's walls, found a weakness in the seal and grew a cutting tool of a hundred diamond-toothed cilia to bore through the flaw, while chemical enzymes and dissemblers broke down the Lucite molecules.

Moments later, the ark broke out of the vault and jetted like a self-propelled pollen speck to the cargo door of the Humvee, escaping through the gaping chasm of the door seams.

Outside, the ark tumbled and bounced in the truck's slipstream, busily reconstructing itself. The ark grew much larger, its flagella morphed into wings that drove it upward through the air with a high-pitched whine. Now the size and shape of a mosquito, it buzzed toward a flitting river of screeching bats, seeking to hitch a ride with a temporary host.

By the time the nuclear fireball had turned Gen's abandoned body into hot plasma and scattered its atoms, the ark that carried her genes and a copy of her mind was safely far away from the funeral pyre. It flitted over white sands in the gut of a free-tailed bat.

Inside the creature, the ark disgorged its passengers. Go forth. Be fruitful and multiply. Mitobots spread through the bat's bloodstream. Replicating. Taking control of the animal's brain and muscles.

Now the ark had become a mammal with strong, leathery wings and it made good headway through the pink dawn sky. The ark broke away from the swarm of other bats, no longer drawn to return to the shelter of a cave.

The time had arrived at last for the Abundance to fulfill its mission. The bat flew on for many miles away from the bomb site. Then it alighted on the white gypsum sand and began the final change to reach the stars.

*   *   *

Gen experienced herself as more than human, or dolphin, or even any creature from Earth. She was an integral part of a vast web of life that carried within it the histories of countless worlds, all stored in the quantum computer mind of DNA.

Jimi MacGregor had touched on only part of the truth when he'd suggested that mitochondria were seeds sent out by an ancient, progenitor race to jump-start life on other planets. The reality was grander than that—and much, much tinier.

Bodies are mortal; genes are immortal. Long before the Earth was born, the progenitors had gained immortality by uploading their minds into quantum computers constructed as self-replicating, double-helical molecules: DNA. They had engineered mitochondria as their ships, becoming microscopic explorers, voyaging forever to new worlds, bearing life. Over the eons, they had seeded life on Earth and innumerable planets, combining and recombining the essence of creatures, gathered throughout the land and sea and sky of diverse evolving worlds.

The Abundance was not a probe in the ordinary sense; there was no home world to report to. The civilization that had sent the mitochondria, lived *within* the mitochondria. Now the time had come to launch another pollination mission from the rich zoo of Earth, to cross the galaxies trading genetic information, the news of life.

402

A dense, shimmering mist spread from the free-tailed Mexican bat, consuming matter from the surrounding desert. The assembler nanobots replicated exponentially, making trillions of copies of themselves. Soon, a crater formed and deepened as the assemblers converted tons of mass into the construction of a tall diamond tower. Roots plunged a thousand feet into the desert, and buttresses rose on all sides, anchoring and bracing the tower in position.

The Abundance communicated to Gen, and now she readily understood their chemical language. The beings offered her a choice: Her mind could travel onward to new worlds, as a member of an ageless civilization; or she could remain behind, resurrected in the form of the young woman she had been. But if she chose to stay on Earth, the powers of the mitobots would remain with her for less than a day. Then she would revert to being an ordinary human, all mitobots gone from her body.

The exterior of the tower formed first, and now a complex interior architecture took shape. The whole construction hummed with molecular activity.

Meanwhile, Gen discovered Toshi Yamato present with her, talking to her in the quantum stream of mind. She flashed intense flavors of surprise and love. Toshi was saying farewell. The Abundance could resurrect his body-mind from its recorded patterns, but he had chosen to travel to the stars. He already knew she had chosen to stay behind, to rejoin Cade. He could taste all her experiences with Cade and Lana and Haven and Jimi. Delicious. He felt happy for her. Toshi said he was with someone he wanted Gen to meet.

Suddenly Gen knew the soulful flavors of her own mother, Arista Monteverde. Gen had never known her mother, or heard her own last name. Her mother's DNA blueprint provided Gen an intimate knowledge of the woman. Her mother had been a gifted dancer and lover of music. Gen resembled her strongly, and recognized much of herself in her mother's genetic traits. Gen learned that her mother had not gone insane and killed herself, but Col. Eberhard had eliminated her, so that she could never reveal the secrets of Gen's birth. In a fraction of an instant, Gen and her mother savored each other's mind and tasted the sweetness of perfect understanding.

Strong-flavored_joy and sorrow mixed in Gen's awareness. She communicated the taste of saltwater; she and Toshi and her mother were *wansalawata*: one-saltwater. Good-bye, Toshi. Good-bye, Mother. I am part of you, you are part of me.

Another mind—a vast, collective consciousness—reached out to Gen with the flavors of kinship and benevolence. Images arose of insectlike beings, each with a thin, flutelike appendage for a mouth. The flute-mouth served many functions, including sex and egg-laying—and enabled the creatures to communicate with musical tones.

Gen realized with awe that she was seeing the bodily form of the ancient progenitors themselves, as they had physically existed before they became immortal beings, patterns of pure information. The hive-dwelling race, creators of the Abundance, called itself *K'o-K'o-Pelli*.

The diamond spire was now complete. Gen understood the giant, gleaming structure was a spore pod, a tower for launching seeds into space. In an underground reaction chamber, heat and pressure intensified as a coiling serpent of energy. The rising energy now felt undeniably pleasurable, even intensely erotic, and the powerful sensations kept building, flooding the length of the tower in fast-pulsing waves of bright light, and sounds like high-crying flutes or whale songs.

The rapture that Gen had resisted before, transported her now; but this time, she welcomed the blissful climax with all her being. Harmonics vibrated upward through the crystalline tower, growing steadily stronger until the whole diamond spire rang like a choir of a million glass harmonicas. Just when Gen felt that she would shatter from the ecstasy of the angelic chord, hydrogen atoms smashed together in the reaction chamber and fused into helium, unleashing thermonuclear fire.

The launch sequence began.

Microscopic starships, encased in diamond for their journey through interstellar space, were injected into the launch barrel and propelled through the bore with nuclear-powered electromagnetic pulses. A thousand-billion diamond spores shot out of the tower at one-tenth the speed of light, scorching the atmosphere, slicing lightning-bolt trails into deep space above the blue curve of Earth, streaming onward in a trillion different trajectories, like miraculous stardust.

*   *   *

Gen awoke, naked, standing in the sand. She swayed a moment, panting, sweating, wondering how she had not exploded into a supernova from the force of the orgasm.

She examined her hands carefully, turning them over before her eyes. Same hands. Same self. The Abundance had kept its promise, restoring her bodily as the young woman, Gen Monteverde.

The diamond spore pod before her towered as tall as a skyscraper. With its flying buttresses, it looked like a futuristic cathedral sculpted of cut crystal. As she watched, it collapsed inward upon itself, not shattering and tinkling like glass, but dissolving into clouds of glittering powder that made a deafening *whooomph* as it fell to form a mountain of bright snow.

Gen turned around once in the now-empty desert. The fusion fireworks had probably triggered alarms at most of

405

the strategic defense systems in North America. She needed to get out of here.

Her heart tugged her toward Cool Bay Inn. But first, she had a problem to fix, and only about twenty hours to do so with the help of the Abundance still active in her tissues. The irony was that now that the life span of the mitobots was running out, she had finally attained full communication with them—and total control.

Gen closed her eyes and sorted through her set of genetic codes. Birds. She needed a raptor, strong and fast, to fly to Redstone Labs. She chose an osprey, a large hawk, and simply willed her body to transform into the bird.

The Abundance went to work: Code readers gave osprey-building instructions to microscopic engineers that broke down and rearranged the human anatomy. Gen sighed as her skin softened like melting wax. Her body shrank rapidly, shedding excess mass as a heavy mound of gooey flesh that bubbled and steamed and charred the white sand.

The osprey's head was white; its body, dark brown above and white below. A dark line, like Cleopatra's mascara, ran through the osprey's eyes. The only abnormality in the hawk's appearance, Gen knew, was its purple eyes.

Gen leapt into the sky, pumping broad wings. She opened her beak wide and gave a piercingly shrill call: *k-yewk, k-yewk, k-yewk.*

Twenty hours. She was truly going to miss the alchemy of shape-shifting.

63

Gen spread her two-foot wingspan, circling high above the twenty-acre complex of Redstone Military Laboratories. A birdwatcher would have found it odd to spot an osprey, a fish hawk that belongs along coasts and inland waters, flying above the desert. But none of the soldiers and technicians below bothered to look up as they shuttled between the lab and the loading ramps of three Army trucks.

Gen's sharp vision roamed the compound. She saw Col. Eberhard exit a small adobe bungalow and stride toward the main lab building. So that's where he lives. Gen tucked her wings and dove toward the bungalow's rear window, smashing right through the glass and tumbling across the wooden floor. The impact broke the osprey's neck; it healed in seconds. Gen hopped on talons into the bathroom and found what she needed: a hairbrush, with silver hairs caught in the bristles. Gen touched a single hair from Jack Eberhard and read his genetic blueprint.

Mitobots disassembled and absorbed most of an antique cast-iron tub to gain two hundred pounds of mass needed to create Eberhard's clone. Seconds later, Gen stood naked in human male form: Eberhard's genetic double. In the bedroom, she put on the dress uniform of a U.S. Army colonel. Then she turned before a full-length mirror, working to make her copy more exact.

Eberhard looked older than the clone Gen had created. She aged the cells, silvering the hair and deepening the wrinkles; then added the pale scar that ran across his square jaw. Now she looked much more like Eberhard, except for the anomalous purple eyes.

But in spite of the fact that her very cell structure duplicated Eberhard's, her version of the colonel still didn't look convincing. Gen-Eberhard looked like she could be Eberhard's identical twin, but she didn't look completely like the man himself.

Then she realized her copy was missing the colonel's attitude. Gen-Eberhard tried on a demeanor of arrogance. Puff out the chest. More. Add a furrow of perpetual anger to the brows. Good. A subtle sneer. Better. Now tweak the expression with an overlay of stress. Wow. She shuddered to recognize her nemesis.

Gen-Eberhard grabbed a pair of dark sunglasses off the dresser to hide her purple eyes. Then she exited the bungalow and strode toward the lab with an air of personal power. Her plan was to enter the isolation suite and release dissemblers to destroy the lab and all records of Project Second Nature.

Two guards snapped to attention and saluted Gen-Eberhard as she entered the lab's main area. The colonel paused and gave the men a hard look-over. "Standard security procedures," Gen-Eberhard said, "A quiz: Who gets notified during a laboratory emergency?"

"You do, sir," one guard said. "Immediately."

"Yes, of course, but I mean a catastrophic accident," Gen-Eberhard said. "Suppose the entire laboratory is consumed in flames. Who gets notified then?"

"Hollomon Air Base, sir," the second guard said. "Capt. George Hughes, security chief for White Sands Missile Range."

The other guard nodded and licked dry lips. Gen-Eberhard glanced at a wall clock. "Contact Capt. Hughes now, and relay to him my orders to execute an emergency response to Redstone Labs at eleven-hundred hours."

"Which drill, sir? The fire scenario?"

"Tell him men are wandering in the desert, bewildered. They don't even remember what happened to them."

The guard frowned. "Sir…?"

"Just follow my orders."

"Yes sir. Right away, sir."

She turned and headed toward the Biohazard Level Four isolation suite. In front of her, a technician in a white lab coat walked through an aisle lined with aluminum pens, and the rabbits inside paid little attention. But as Gen-Eberhard passed the same rows, the sight of the colonel made the animals go berserk with fear, scrabbling into corners, trembling so hard their pens rattled.

Gen's heart cried out for the creatures. She remembered how she used to shiver with dread every time she heard Air Lock One hiss open. If it turned out not to be the colonel, her whole body would sigh with relief; but whenever she saw Eberhard striding toward her in his blue spacesuit, she, too, had felt like scrambling to the corner of her glass cage to hide.

The painful memories tapped an anger in her that lay buried beneath strata of fear and humiliation. She had never let herself feel the heat of her rage, because she had been helpless before to do anything about her imprisonment and Eberhard's experiments. But now she felt anger seething in her soul like magma bubbling deep inside a volcano.

How dare you! Eberhard, and all the rest of you!

She stopped at the eye scan unit in front of Air Lock Three, placed her chin in the chin rest, and removed her sunglasses. A camera read the unique pattern of cilia muscles in the clone's right iris, and a computer matched the configuration with Eberhard's. The red light winked green and she entered the air lock door.

Air Lock Three opened into the staging room. It startled her to see on a TV monitor that none of the workers in the isolation suite were wearing blue biohazard suits. Then she noticed dozens of deep-freeze biohazard containers lying on a worktable, and realized that all her tissue samples had been allowed to thaw, and the mitobots had deactivated. Technicians appeared to be dismantling equipment and packing everything for moving. Gen-Eberhard passed through air locks Two and One, into the isolation suite.

Then the odor hit her. The acrid stink of Envirochem liquid disinfectant. The trace of ozone from electron microscopes. She even smelled, or remembered, the oily reek of jellied gasoline mixed with smoldering flesh, and tasted blood in her mouth, like an iron nail. In dizzying flashbacks, she relived not just her own horrors, but the sufferings of the piteous rabbits Eberhard had brutalized right outside her chamber, while she buried her head under pillows, to drown out their shrieks. It had been an unending chain of atrocities.

Now she was here to put an end to it. This torture chamber was not going to be loaded on trucks and reestablished elsewhere.

She had planned only to disassemble the place; break everything down to molecules. But bad memories made her sweat profusely; she felt the volcano inside her about to explode. And at that moment, she came face to face with Col. Jack Eberhard himself.

Workers stopped what they were doing to gawk at the twins.

"Who…?" Eberhard said, and glanced at the name EBERHARD over the pocket of the uniform his double wore. "Who the fuck are *you*?"

Gen tossed the sunglasses to the floor.

Eberhard's eyes grew huge. He lurched backward, knocking a centrifuge off a table with a loud clatter. "Security!" he screamed at a video camera that monitored the area. "Weapons teams. *Now!*"

Others in the room moaned with panic. A technician backed into a large rack of test tubes; they crashed to the floor in a sparkling explosion.

410

"How?" Eberhard said. "How is it possible? I killed you, you bitch. I vaporized you."

The anger at the core of Gen detonated. The cloned Eberhard-body wasn't big enough to express her gigantic rage; she needed to be huge.

"*Ex ungue draconis!*" she yelled, and leaned against the thick plate glass of the isolation vault. Clouds of mitobots billowed from her flesh, fogging the room like a steam bath, consuming tons of matter to build her new form.

"From the dragon's claw," Gen croaked in a deep, guttural voice, "you will know the dragon!"

The metamorphosis took only seconds. The dinosaur's body erupted from the ripping uniform like a reptilian mountain. Where the colonel's double had stood, a gigantosaurus hunched low, ducking its massive-jawed head to fit under the room's twenty-foot ceiling. Gen filled her mighty lungs like huge bellows and roared. The air in the room quaked and the glass rattled. It felt so good. She gave the scurrying little humans another ear-splitting roar, and another.

Workers scrambled into far corners, trying to claw their way out of the sealed room. But there was only a single airlock exit, blocked by a bellowing dragon out of a medieval knight's worst nightmare.

Gen raked her scythe-like talons and whipped her heavy tail, splintering tables, crushing equipment, smashing holes in the walls, sending up showers of electric sparks as she ripped through wiring conduits.

Eberhard screamed and pissed his pants. A couple technicians raced to a ladder on the far wall that reached up to a maintenance hatch in the air filtration ducts. Eberhard saw their escape plan and dashed to the ladder, yanked one man away from its base by the back of his collar, then

411

scrabbled up over the back of a second man who had already started climbing.

Gen roared and kicked a microscope workstation, shearing off its floor bolts; she kicked it again and it went airborne like a half-ton soccer ball and embedded in the far wall, just above Eberhard's head. The impact jolted Eberhard and the other men off the ladder and they thudded on the floor in a squirming heap. Gen chomped on the ladder with ten-inch fangs, ripped it off the wall and flung it sideways, knocking down a dozen men like bowling pins.

The ceiling was too cramped for the rampaging gigantosaurus, so Gen lay down on her side and kicked with all her strength and fury. Her first kick caved in the wall by Air Lock One, and she kicked and kicked at the air lock itself until the unit tore loose from its concrete foundation. Then she punted the air lock like a tumbling automobile, through the heavy glass walls of her old isolation chamber. The thick glass pulverized with a white noise like a booming waterfall. Gen roared thunderously and a final, wobbling glass panel crashed to the floor in the blast of sound from her lungs.

Then the gigantosaurus scrabbled back to its clawed feet and stood, shoving with immense leg muscles to burst through the ceiling and bite and tear out some headroom, shredding aluminum air ducts like strips of tinsel. Now Gen stood at her full height, showered by cascades of electric sparks that spit and snapped from tangles of torn wiring. She could feel the triumph blazing in her purple eyes, and she trumpeted explosively.

Then she sent forth a swarm of trillions of dissemblers, and the scales of the multi-ton reptile smoked with fog and sizzled loudly, like water on a red hot skillet. The deconstruction mitobots spread everywhere as a self-propagating cloud.

412

Security forces leaped out of Air Lock Two and glanced around, thunderstruck, at the gaping hole where Air Lock Three had stood, and at the ruin that had been the isolation unit, and at the two-story tall monster that glared down at them.

Five soldiers crouched with automatic rifles and began blasting away at the dinosaur. Gen squealed like colliding trains—one man dropped his weapon and clapped hands over his ears from the deafening volume—the gigantosaur's version of laughter. Seconds later, the security team's rifles had dissolved, along with helmets and boots and combat clothing, leaving five naked men huddling in terror.

Then the room and all its inorganic objects shimmered and began to vanish. Concrete and steel walls puffed to the floor as ultra-fine, soft powder. Floors opened to the raw earth beneath. Ceilings gaped to the blue sky. Mitobots disassembled everything in their path. Furniture, lab equipment, computers and monitors, video cameras, telephones, and all records of Project Second Nature broke down to atomic smithereens.

No longer trapped by walls, the naked technicians and soldiers ran screaming from the avenging dragon and the rectangular dirt field where the laboratory buildings had stood. Rabbits escaped into the rugged hills in every direction.

A fog smothered the three cargo trucks packed with lab equipment for transportation to a new bioweapons lab site. The trucks collapsed to the ground like talcum powder. The fog spread through the compound with a speed that generated its own breeze, leaving dust piles puffing up in soft clouds behind it. When it had disassembled the outer, razor-wire capped fence, the fog settled to the bald ground like a blanket. Slowly, the blanket faded and grew tattered as the fog dissipated to nothing.

413

The men's memories of the last half-hour also paled to nothing, as mitobots erased the short-term neural traces. Naked men moaned and sobbed, then grew quiet—too dazed to remember what they had been sobbing about. They ran, walked or hobbled beyond the perimeter of the obliterated military compound and kept going.

Only Col. Eberhard remained behind, trapped inside a cage of glass that had crystallized around him in the bare dirt.

He cried out from the scorching heat as the gigantosaurus shed tons of extra mass and reverted to human Gen. The jelly-like mountain of excess matter deconstructed itself to dust.

Gen stepped toward Eberhard, dressed in a sparkling robe of woven diamond threads. Eberhard hunkered naked in the cage. She touched the glass and it poofed into glittering powder.

Eberhard ducked his head and whimpered. "Don't hurt me. Don't kill me."

"Not like you killed my mother."

"I...no...your mother was mad. She went crazy. She committed—"

"That's a lie. I met her. She's a wonderful, beautiful person. She's immortal now."

"Yes, she's in a better place, no more suffering. She's with God."

"Something like that." Gen took another step toward him.

He cringed, unable to look at her. "What are you going to do to me? I can't hurt you. You're invincible. I'm no threat to you."

"Maybe I'll share my mitobots with you. Then you'll be invincible, too, even if I tear off your head." She frowned. "At least I *think* so. You never tried that

414

experiment. Let's do it—fill you up with mitobots and rip off your head, see if it grows back."

He held up trembling hands, still staring at the ground. "No, please...please. Why are you tormenting me?"

"Is that what it's called? I thought it was military science."

"All the information is lost. I can never repeat the project. Why can't you just let me go?"

"I'm thinking about it."

He looked up at her for the first time. Tears of fright wet his cheeks.

"But first I've got to devise a way to keep the world safe from you," she said.

He licked his lips. "Listen, we can work that out, Gen." His eyes darted back and forth. "I...I promise to...resign. Okay? I'll retire. I won't design weapons anymore."

"You still would be a dangerous man. At least to defenseless creatures. You don't know how it feels to be little and powerless."

"I can learn. Okay? Give me a chance to learn."

She half-smiled. "That's not a bad idea." She reached out her hands and billows of shiny fog puffed from her palms and fingertips and streamed into his pores.

The whites of Eberhard's eyes bulged and he opened his mouth to scream. It came out a high-pitched squeal as he rapidly morphed, shedding extra matter in a steaming, wet blob.

In seconds, on the ground at Gen's feet, hunched a white rabbit with pink eyes.

Gen gazed out over tuffs of brushwood and sunburnt grass mottling the rugged hills. "Not exactly fluffy bunny territory. But the local jackrabbits can show you how to survive."

The rabbit stared up at her with shock and confusion in its beady eyes.

415

"I know you understand what I'm saying, Colonel. Your mind is in a new body now. You'll figure it out. So off with you. Scoot, little bunny. Or some devil might catch you and use you for lab experiments."

The rabbit backed up, then spun and dashed off, scampering as fast as its blurring legs would carry it, until it disappeared into a mesquite thicket.

Gen heard the warbling drone of helicopters approaching from the mountains. She transformed herself into a golden eagle, beat her dark brown wings and leaped into the sky.

She soared eastward, toward home.

64

A few miles beyond the vanished labs, the bald eagle landed in the desert. The Abundance would remain active for about fourteen more hours, and Gen had a distance of fifteen hundred miles to cover. The eagle couldn't make it back to Cool Bay in the time remaining.

She needed a faster vehicle.

At quantum computer speed, the Abundance scanned sets of genetic codes, and found dozens of blueprints for pterosaurs, including the 35-foot wingspan *Quetzalcoatlus northropi*. But it did not turn up any flying creature that could travel fifteen hundred miles within the shrinking frame of time.

The bald eagle ruffled its feathers. Come on. After escaping an H-bomb and putting an end to Redstone Labs, she was not going to let a transportation problem defeat her.

It occurred to her that the search she'd directed the Abundance to perform had been limited to the genetic codes of Earth creatures. It had ignored sets of genetic essences from innumerable other planets—a mind-boggling menagerie of living forms to choose from.

She closed her eyes. The Abundance now scanned the blueprints of flying and floating creatures of a gas giant world, in the heart of the Andromeda galaxy. She tasted the characteristics of many beings, thousands of species at a time, until she found the ultimate sky traveler. It took seconds to transform, leaving behind in the sand a red hot, glowing crater.

Gen had become a flying wing. Simple and elegant, made almost entirely of silica, like a crescent-shaped blade of blown glass. Electricity-generating organs streamed ions from nozzles along the trailing edge of the wing, propelling the bird at supersonic speeds. A number of spherical eyes floated inside its clear body, seeing in every direction, which took some getting used to.

The flying wing was big—bigger than the Jumbo Jet she sped past over New Orleans. When Gen saw the startled look on the pilots' faces, she strobed colored lights across her wingspan and blared a mating call that sounded like a thousand pipe organs hitting all the black keys at once. Then she banked sharply and zoomed away with a burst of acceleration that sliced the moist air into vapor trails.

An hour's flight from the desert, the Gulf of Mexico appeared. Then the west coast of Florida. In mid-air, Gen deconstructed the alien bird, creating a rainfall of powdered glass that bent the sunlight over the sea into a double rainbow. Now in the form of a Great Blue Heron, she flew onward with Coolahatchee Bay in view.

*   *   *

Cade stepped out of the portable quarantine building onto the dark beach. Lana and Haven, Jimi and Newpod, had been kept in separate quarantine units. Nighttime now, twenty-four hours had passed, and they were free to go. Hank Townsend and the people from Taylor's Wharf community had been released a few hours earlier, and had gone home.

The soldiers had catalogued the sound equipment confiscated from the speedboat: laptop computer, synthesizer, underwater speaker, and assorted cables. The gear was waiting in tagged cartons outside Jimi's quarantine unit when Jimi and Newpod stepped out. The golden retriever barked and ran to Cade. Jimi presented a receipt to a soldier and signed for his belongings, without even checking to be sure it all was there.

He joined Cade, and they waited a moment for Lana and Haven. Then Cade shouldered the heavy speaker, and the group trudged up the hill toward the inn.

Behind Cade, the twin turbines on the Skycranes began to whine. He and his family did not look back. The whine became a jet engine scream. The group never glanced up as the big helicopters lifted off the beach. They disappeared into the night, and the noise faded like rolling thunder.

Only after the invaders had gone, did the family turn around. Cade and Jimi set down their gear. They all held hands in silence on the foot path, gazing out over the flat, obsidian sheet of the bay. The lump in Cade's throat would have made speech difficult even if he could find words to express his sorrow. He figured the same was true of everyone else, because no one ventured a word.

They had done the right thing. Without Gen, Haven would have died. Gen herself had told Cade, "You can't help me, and they can't hurt me." While lying sleepless in quarantine, he had replayed those words, watched Gen's face saying them, a thousand times. "It's too late, Cade," she had said. "You can't help me, and they can't hurt me. No one can stop what I'm becoming."

What did she mean, they can't hurt her? They were going to strap her to an H-bomb and set it off. By now, they'd done it. His heart shriveled at the thought. How could she have survived that? What could Gen become that was mightier than a nuclear warhead?

She'd had the chance to leap into the water, return to her pod. Eberhard would never have found her. If Cade had known she wasn't going to try to escape, was going to let herself be captured... But what would he have done differently? He couldn't let Haven die. What kind of choice is that?

This is how grief drives people crazy, trying to make sense of the senseless, like trying to read Braille with your elbow.

The bay looked like a dark and glossy plain. Gen's dolphin pod was out there, somewhere, hidden beneath the black mirror of water. Gen had family; people and dolphins who loved her. But she had been alone in her final moments. Had she been afraid? Cade wished he could have taken her place at ground zero, or even just been there with her, holding her close while the clock ticked down.

A collective sigh seemed to be a cue for the group to move on. The two men stooped and picked up Jimi's sound gear, and everyone continued up the hill toward the inn. When they reached the porch steps, Newpod barked and dashed up to the front door, wagging his tail, thumping the planks.

Cade set down the speaker, stepped inside the door and smelled the mixed perfumes of fresh-cut flowers. Floral arrangements decorated the foyer and spread into the living room. The inn's vases had been packed away, so the flowers filled every pot and pitcher in the house. Not only camellias, roses, and hibiscus, which grew in gardens right outside, but tulips and lilacs, orchids and frangipani; flowers that were not in season, or did not grow in Florida. The others crowded in behind Cade, gawking.

"Flowers," Cade said.

"Flowers," Lana and Jimi and Haven echoed.

Newpod whined, and the force of his wagging tail twisted his hindquarters in a crazy dance. The flower girl appeared in the living room archway in a dress made from one of Lana's cotton blouses, cinched with a cloth belt. She wore a crown of violets and orange poppies; and she held garlands of exotic flowers, to welcome home each of her loved ones.

Gen smiled at Cade and his heart galloped away like a mustang stallion, free again, running wild.

*   *   *

After a mid-hallway collision of bodies, and plentiful hugs, whoops, laughter and tears, Cade thanked Gen repeatedly for saving Haven's life.

Everyone ended up in a huddle on the living room floor. The furniture had been shoved against the wall to make way for moving. They had to clear out and abandon the inn within five days; the moving van was arriving in two. Cade had seen a squadron of bulldozers parked to the north at the bottom of the hill.

"This whole nightmare has taught me what I truly value," Lana said. Haven leaned back in her aunt's lap, with eyes closed, while Lana stroked the girl's hair. "I cared too much about this old place." She looked at the faces around her. "Weston can have the land. Wherever we go, we'll be together as a family. How many people in this lonely world get that blessing?"

Gen told them about her escape from the H-bomb. She did her best to describe the awesome spore-pod and the unspeakable rush of joy when the seeds blasted off to the stars. She told them about Redstone Labs turning to dust, and the fate of Eberhard.

Cade clung to Gen. He filled her in on the details of their library research and their unsuccessful dive on the reef. He and Jimi had failed to find the *Emancipator* and its brass plaque, the legal proof that the Seaborne family owned the island.

Gen stared at him. "The ship—the *Emancipator*—it's not all iron, right? The hull is wooden. The deck and keel are wooden, too."

421

"That's right," Cade said. "It's an ironclad: armor plating on top of wooden sides."

"Except the iron tore off most of one side. That's why it rolled."

"What are you talking about?"

"Ghost Whale," she said. "The dolphins call the shipwreck Ghost Whale. Cade, you couldn't find the ship because it never sank—not all the way to the bottom. It floats around underwater, on its side. Trapped air keeps it from sinking deeper."

"You've seen it? You know where it is?"

"I've spotted it with echolocation, several times, but I don't know where it is now. It's always drifting."

"But the dolphins could find it, right?"

"I'm sure they could, but—"

"That's it. You can ask them to help us. Tell them we'll trade them tubs of mackerel."

"But Cade..." Gen reached her hand to her throat. "I no longer have the anatomy to speak the dolphin language."

Cade grinned at Jimi, who was already running toward the front porch. "Wait till you see what Boy Genius has invented."

Half a minute later, Jimi flew into the living room with a synthesizer keyboard and a laptop in his arms. He plugged in the keyboard, pressed the keys and an assortment of squawks, clucks and whistles came out of the tiny laptop speakers.

Gen laughed and clapped her hands. "That's fantastic."

"I've been recording dolphin chatter and assigning the digital samples to the keys," Jimi said. "It's just a beginning. Eventually, I want to create a translator machine, where the computer tells me what the dolphins are saying and translates what I say into their language." He scooted the keyboard across the floor toward her. "It plays

422

over two hundred sounds, but I only know what a few of them mean."

Gen tested the keys and quickly found a meaningful pattern. "This says, 'Over here, guys, lots of fish.' If you add this"—she tapped another key—"it means *mullet*, specifically." She played the short series together. "So this says, 'Over here, everybody, a school of mullet.'"

Jimi smiled. "It works."

Gen nodded. "I can figure it out. I'm sure I can send at least a simple message: 'Find Ghost-Whale. Lead us to Ghost-Whale.' The pods can talk to each other, relay our message. With several pods searching, they can probably find it within a few days."

"We've got exactly five." Cade said. "On the morning of the sixth day, a whole fleet of bulldozers is riding up the hill to make kindling out of this place."

"We can do it," Gen said, and her eyes blazed with an inner fire. "We'll find the plaque."

Cade wondered how he could have lived out his days and nights without those purple lamps to light up his world. "At dawn," he said, "we go treasure hunting; not for gold—for brass."

"Can I help, too, Daddy?"

Cade had thought Haven was asleep.

"Yeah, Boo-Boo. We go as a family."

*   *   *

An hour later, Gen found herself in Cade's upstairs bedroom. She found herself in bed with Cade, a vanilla scoop of moon in the window, softly lighting the hills and valleys of their bodies. She found herself rich in textures, aromas, and flavors, kissing the man she loved, kissing for hours, with no time that she had to stop or run away.

Cade touched her passionately, yet with unhurried, intelligent hands. The kissing and touching were full movements in the symphony of their pleasure, complete songs in themselves, but also building upon a theme that reached ever deeper into body and soul.

Cade's green tiger-eyes looked hungry. He looked like he was going to eat her all up. And he did. After a while, when he returned to kiss her mouth, she smelled and tasted the sea on his lips. *Wansalawata.*

Gen felt her pleasure take on an invisible shape, a rising energy-wave. The wave swelled in power and beauty, climbing higher and higher.

Cade hesitated in his lovemaking.

Gen panted, on the brink of rhapsody.

"You sure it's okay for you to have an orgasm?" he said.

"Yes, oh, god! Yes, please, yes."

Now he did not hold back. He stirred the sea like a storm, driving the wave to tremendous heights. And she carried him along on the ride, like the perfect wave finding its surfer at last. When the wave touched heaven, it came splashing down in an explosion of ecstasy, moans and grateful tears.

The orgasm was not the same as when she had been intimately linked to the consciousness of the spore pod. Her climax with Cade did not actually blast her right off the Earth toward distant planets.

It only felt that way.

Coolahatchee Bay Island
National Wildlife Refuge

Haven squealed with giggles. Cade tossed her over his shoulders and she splashed into the surf. Gen stood nearby in the water, laughing at their antics. A summer squall had built the shorebreak to a rare size—three to four-foot waves crashed on a sandbar just off the beach. People up and down the beach were body-surfing and riding boogie boards.

No jet-skis or speedboats were allowed, no golf courses, no land developments. The whole island was now a wildlife refuge, because of a Civil War-era plaque that proclaimed Cade and Lana's forefather the rightful owner of Coolahatchee Bay.

It had been a year since Gen's pod found Ghost Whale. Dozens of other pods had helped in the search, and they had located the ironclad in less than a day. Races-the-Waves retrieved the plaque before Cade and Jimi even arrived on site with scuba gear. Cade learned that his father had attached floats to keep track of the submerged hulk, but someone had cut the lines.

The descendants of a slave, Odysseus Seaborne, became the owners of Coolahatchee Bay Island. Turning the island into a national wildlife refuge had been Lana's idea.

She and Cade had retained the Stanton Hill sixty acres, and had granted to all the original Cool Bay families the properties they lived on. All latecomers, who had bought land illegally from Weston Fairchild, were reimbursed from Fairchild's bank accounts, and court-ordered to leave. Lana and Cade sold the remaining land, about half the island, to the United States government, under the provision that the area be designated a federally protected avian and marine park, patrolled by park rangers and marine wildlife officers. Now, scientists and nature lovers arrived from around the world to conduct research and to enjoy the pristine beauty of the seashore.

Weston Fairchild got his country club—a country club prison. Four homicide charges had been dropped for lack of evidence, but convictions on real estate fraud put him away for thirty years at a federal facility in Maryland for white-collar criminals.

Gen stepped on a razor-edged oyster shell. "Ouch!" She lifted her left foot and bright blood trickled down her big toe. The wound did not heal instantly, because Gen had no mitobots in her tissues. It reminded her that she had not seen Deep Sky Water, her dolphin son, for six weeks. Anyone he let touch him absorbed his mitobots, and within minutes, responded with amazing healings.

Gen sorely missed him. She longed to hug his sleek body, kiss his bottlenose. He usually swam into the shallow water every few days to visit with his family of two-leggeds, and especially, to play with Haven. Those two were more like brother and sister than two human siblings.

But Deep Sky Water had accelerated his growth rate to make himself older, and then had left the pod on a vision quest. There was no way to tell how long he would need to find himself, his true identity—and give himself his own True Name.

"Gen, look at me!" Haven shouted. She stood with her feet in Cade's hands and he sent her soaring up and over; she cleared his head by three feet and landed with a splash behind. Gen smiled at her gorgeous husband, feeling warm tingles in secret places. She liked the name Cade, but Hercules fit nicely, too.

True Names. Cade's great-great grandfather had been named Odysseus; his great-grandfather, Atlas; his grandfather, Moses; his father, Samson; and Cade was

426

named Hercules. But after his dad had died, Cade had felt too small and powerless to own such a heroic name, and had started using his middle name.

Gen looked at his brown body, like that of a champion athlete from classical Greece. Only she called him Hercules, when they were in bed and he sent her soaring up over the world, into the sea. With a splash. Those tingles were getting intense. When the three of them went home for lunch, she and Cade definitely needed to lie down for a "nap."

Jimi and Lana were up at the inn, supposedly making lunch. But Gen wouldn't be surprised if the newlyweds were making lunch upstairs in the bedroom. They, too, napped a lot. Lana was pregnant, at forty-one, and they both were thrilled. Jimi told Lana the pregnancy magnified her beauty; he said she could wear a sweat suit and still look as regal as a Nubian queen. That kind of talk led to more naps.

Jimi had created a year-round dolphin research station, headquartered at Cool Bay Inn—the Institute for Cetacean Language and Culture, better known as I-CLAC. Grad students and marine biologists from around the world were on waiting lists to study with Jimi on the island. With Gen's help, he had created an English-Dolphin speech translation system, and Gen was working on dolphin translation software for scores of other languages.

Last year, I-CLAC's television spots hit the networks. Dolphins themselves pleaded with humans to stop hunting whales and dolphins for food, stop drowning dolphins in tuna nets, stop polluting the seas. The effect worldwide was like a religious awakening—although 'awakening' was too weak a word—more like a conscience-bomb detonating, with consequences as far-sweeping as Jimi had ever imagined would occur after contact with an extraterrestrial intelligence.

427

Now Jimi, Cade and Gen were filming a documentary, "Planet Ocean," about the evolution of life on Earth, told from the point of view of dolphins. Races-the-Waves, Moon Catcher and Squirt—whose True Name was now Sun Leaper—were being interviewed for the project. It was going to shake up human society, even though the filmmakers had decided to omit, for now, the facts about panspermia, the seeding of the oceans with life. They would begin the dolphin history from the era when dolphins roamed the land on two legs.

Gen thought more about the dolphin concept of True Name.

Haven. Perfect name for her. Haven possessed her aunt's love for animals, and she helped Lana run the Cool Bay Wildlife Hospital, mending broken wings and torn beaks—and sometimes accomplishing miraculous healings, thanks to the spread of mitobots.

True Name: Gen Arista Toshi Monteverde. She smiled at the memory of her mother and friend. She was overjoyed that Arista and Toshi were together, light years from Earth, traveling on an immortal adventure, spreading life. She whispered a Shinto prayer of gratitude to her ancestors, K'o-k'o-pelli, the age-old progenitors.

Gen crouched in the shorebreak, diving under waves, laughing at Cade and Haven's roughhousing. She felt happy. But she watched for dolphin fins, for her pod, for her son. She wanted to embrace him, tell him how much she had missed him.

Cade and Haven stopped playing. They stood still together, staring past Gen. A small wave knocked Haven off her feet, but she hopped back up, never taking her eyes off the enrapturing vision.

Gen felt hairs tingle on the back of her neck.

"Mother, I have found my True Name."

428

Gen turned around to gaze upon her son. He stood in the shallow water, a beautiful naked boy, seven or eight years old, with cinnamon skin and amethyst eyes.

"My name is Sky Monteverde. I have come home to you, to be your human son."

Gen stumbled, splashing, to grab him and draw him into her arms.

"I will live ashore with you, part of the time, mother," he said, "and at sea with my pod, part of the time."

Gen wanted to say things about love and family and home and belonging, but all that spilled out were tearful blubberings. She pressed her son's head against her bosom; smelled his wet, black hair. It smelled of saltwater, of life.

Cade and Haven rushed to them and joined the embrace, and Gen's heart melted like a dolphin made of sugar swimming in the deep blue sea.

Made in the USA
Charleston, SC
03 June 2013